LOVE AND LIES

He was looking at her now, his deep, black eyes were silently asking her to do as he had bid her earlier. To come away with him. To make a stand on his side.

She was, at this moment—through her own deception, living a portion of her sister's life. The two men who had loved Colleen were standing here before her now, not knowing who she really was, and both of them were battling over her.

Calum's eyes narrowed. In the stony silence then, he turned, stepped into the stunned crowd, and slipped quickly out of sight.

But Barry remained, as she knew he would. Still, it was clear to her now, painfully so, that she was not the only one keeping secrets.

Books by Diane Haeger

Beyond the Glen
Pieces of April

Published by HarperPaperbacks

HarperChoice

DIANE HAEGER

BEYOND THE GLEN

HarperPaperbacks
A Division of HarperCollins*Publishers*

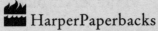 HarperPaperbacks
A Division of HarperCollins*Publishers*
10 East 53rd Street, New York, NY 10022-5299

This is a work of fiction. The characters, incidents, and dialogues are products of the author's imagination and are not to be construed as real. Any resemblance to actual events or persons, living or dead, is entirely coincidental.

ISBN 0-06-101329-3

HarperCollins®, ®, HarperPaperbacks™, and HarperChoice™ are trademarks of HarperCollins Publishers, Inc.

Cover illustration © 1998 by John Ennis, based on the photograph © 1998 by Nagele, E/FPG International

First printing: June 1998

Printed in the United States of America

Visit HarperPaperbacks on the World Wide Web at
http://www.harpercollins.com

❖ 10 9 8 7 6 5 4 3 2 1

For Lisa Nordquist Goodman,
If I had been blessed with a sister,
I would have liked her to have been you

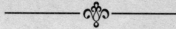

There is always one moment in childhood
when the door opens and lets the future in. . . .

—Graham Greene

BEYOND
THE
GLEN

May 12, 1990

Dear Mairi,

Where are you? Have you really forgotten me, after all? Today is just so special that I couldn't help writing to you one more time. It makes me feel closer to you somehow, even when your reply never comes. Today is my wedding day, Mairi. I can barely believe it. It was sudden enough, me deciding to go through with it. But I need to do something to break from Da. You, of all people, would understand that. It's more than time for it. And it's a good lad I've found. A little wild sometimes, I'll admit. But he's fair full of love for me. I have no doubt of that. And he's got such grand plans. A move to Glasgow in a couple of years. A future for me, Mairi. Something to hope for, at last. I doubt you'd remember him, it's been so long since you left. But I know the two of you would get on grandly. I still hope and pray one day the good Lord will give us all a chance at that. But what I wish, most of all today, is that I knew where you were and why you've given up on our promise.

Colleen

CHAPTER ONE

May 1983—Killin, Scotland

She ran, trying to keep up. But Colleen was faster, and Mairi was thickly set, a more awkward child, as their bare feet sank into the fertile, mossy ground leading into the glen. Heavy tree branches hung low in the shadowy distance—a bough of emeralds, it seemed, thick green ferns rising up to meet them. And in the center, the mossy, centuries-old Promise Stone. It was a mystical stone of great local lore to everyone in Killin, but one past which the girls dared not tread.

"We canno' go in there!" Mairi called to her sister, older and taller, slim and pretty, her long, thick hair billowing back behind her like a copper sail.

"Come along!" Colleen teased, turning back, beckoning her sister, with an outstretched hand through the pine-scented air. "'Tis an adventure we're after! 'Tis our secret adventure!"

Mairi felt her stomach squeeze with fear. Their father had warned them many times not to tread this far. Never into the glen. Never past the Promise Stone. Forbidden land, they had always thought of it. But what were the secrets through the glen and past that heavy clump of trees? Hidden. Beckoning . . . Irresistible to children intent on adventure.

"Come along, Mairi!"

Drawing in a breath and pressing past her trepidation, Mairi followed her older sister, finally feeling a giggle work its way up from deep in her own throat. *Free.* Here they were free. Not as they were at home. With Da. Not the way he raged at Ma. At Mairi too, for the unpardonable sin of not being the beauty her older sister was. Not the way he drank and yelled if supper wasn't just so. Or if Mairi forgot her proper pleases and thank yous the way he thought she ought.

A lapwing cried above them, and Mairi glanced up. The sky was clear and blue. Cloudless. She pushed her own chestnut hair, long and tangled, from her brown eyes and then ran faster.

Deeper. Faster. Into the glen. Toward the forbidden. The trees were an ever-thickening lacy lattice above them. Clumps of gorse beneath her feet steadily became an obstacle course that could trip her up if she was not careful.

Ahead, unfolding like an intricate fan, Mairi saw the spire of a ruined abbey, crumbling stone. Then another spire. Her heartbeat quickened. She had never had any idea there were ruins of any sort back here.

Nearer, she saw the wheat-colored thatch of a rooftop. Then a chimney, and a white plume of smoke spiraling up toward the heavens. There was a secret cottage hidden here as well. But whose? Was this why Da forbade them to go beyond the glen? Was this where the woman lived? The one everyone spoke about in hushed whispers. The mysterious woman no one but that strange orphaned lad, Barry Buchanan, seemed to know.

How curious indeed. And how wonderful.

Then very suddenly, softly, like magic through the trees, came a thin, haunting sound—music that sounded like something from a flute and yet more piercing. Mairi looked into the tall trees, straining to find the origin of the lovely sound.

Mairi took a step forward. Then she saw him. He was sitting alone on a mossy stone, holding something to his lips. Dark hair fell into his eyes. Eyes that were deep and bold, cut into a slim face full of angles. *Barry Buchanan.* The lad who had not stayed in school after the death of his parents. Who preferred to roam the hills and valleys. Restlessly. And alone. But for the woman—a fallen woman, they called her—who lived somewhere out here and had befriended him.

Colleen saw the same thing, heard the same lovely music, and ran forward. "Let's go listen awhile," she called out. "I'm sure he'll play a tune for us."

"Slow down!"

Colleen turned around again, weaving through the gorse. Laughing. Her teeth white and bright and perfectly straight. Beige freckles sparkling on her shiny cheeks. Tangles of her long coppery hair bristled before her fern-colored eyes.

And then, so suddenly that Mairi never saw it actually happen, Colleen collapsed onto the ground. Only the slightest groan escaped her lips as she lay in a heap, shrouded in ferns when she reached her sister, and knelt beside her. The sky, bright a few minutes before, began to darken. A threatening wind wailed through the trees just as suddenly, and Mairi shivered. It was Colleen's ankle, she could see by the swelling.

"Can ye walk on it?" Mairi asked.

"I'm no' certain."

"Ye've got to try. Da'll be furious at me when he sees the stains on your dress!"

Colleen glanced down at the green and brown mud and grass streaks, unmistakable evidence that they had gone where they ought not. She let Mairi help her up, brace an arm around her shoulder. "I'll be fine by the time we get home," Colleen did her best to assure her younger sister. "'Twill be our secret. Just like this place."

Mairi pulled back the rusted latch on the door, silently praying that their father had not yet come home from the woolen mill. He made large, bulky sweaters twelve hours a day for tourists down in Glasgow and Fort William, and he was rarely happy about it. Or about much of anything else, until he'd had a dram or three of Scotch.

The oak door creaked as she drew it carefully back. The thick, acrid smell of smoke from his pipe felt choking in the warm, firelit air. Mairi hated that. Pipe smoke. And a part of her—her wounded child's heart—hated *him* for not loving her as he did Colleen.

"I'm tellin' ye, Viv, if that lass has led Colleen where they ought no' go, 'twill be hell to pay in this house tonight!"

"They're only a few minutes past suppertime," she heard her mother defend them softly. "They're not really all that late."

"Ye're always makin' excuses for her, Viv." He was

getting more angry. "Because she's a miserably plain child does no' mean she canno' have a bit of the devil in her heart."

"And just because she isn't Janet's child, like Colleen, doesn't mean she does!"

"I tell ye, she's no' a good child!"

"What you mean is that she's not a *pretty* child, isn't it?"

Mairi stood stone still in the doorway, having heard each painful word her father had uttered, and the betrayal at that was deep and raw. Tears filled her eyes as Malcolm's head jerked toward the door just then, his face blazing with anger.

"All right, then. Where've ye been?"

Mairi felt her stomach vault into her throat. His question was directed pointedly at her. And he was such a big, sturdy brick of a man. That barrel chest. Corded arms. Suspenders bowed over a red woolen shirt. So much a presence to a young girl, with his fiery auburn hair and intense, dark eyes. His booming baritone.

"'Twas my idea, Da," Colleen bravely confessed, pushing past her younger sister. "We just started runnin' and I lost track of the time."

Malcolm bounded forward, hands shooting to his hips. "Ye've been into the glen, haven't ye now? Aye, I can see it in your eyes! 'Tis no use denyin' it."

Mairi saw, with a mounting panic, the way her sister's face had colored. "I'm the oldest," Colleen said, moving a step closer to him, limping slightly. Grimacing. "'Twas my fault, Da."

Then suddenly everything stopped. Mairi watched their father's angry expression melt away as he looked down at Colleen. "Saints above, child! Ye've been hurt!"

"'Tis only a turn of my ankle."

His head jerked on that thick stalk of a neck. "After ye help her get her leg up, Vivienne, fetch some ice straight away!" he commanded his French wife. "Now, sweet lass." His tone changed instantly as he looked at Colleen. "Go along there, before there's more swellin'!"

When her father spun around, his body was tensed again, arms bent in rigid Vs at his hips. And Mairi was alone in the room with him. "'Twas truly your idea, wasn't it, lass?" he growled. "Goin' into the glen like that. Your ma's child in every way, aren't ye now? Defiant! Wild! I canno' control either of ye!"

There seemed little point in arguing. Or in putting up a defense. Mairi had seen enough of her father's frightening rages to know that there would be no excuse she could give to alter what would come next.

The belt came swiftly from his waist. Worn, black leather. Soft. Supple. Deadly. It was not the first time she had felt its wrath.

"Ye'll no' be defyin' me, Mairi Gordon! I'll no' have it! That glen is forbidden! *Forbidden!* And that ye'll learn if I have to take a pound of your flesh to teach ye!"

She heard the crack and it seemed a moment suspended in time before she felt the searing pain of the first blow. Then another. And another. Her mind spun. Her bottom throbbed. Even the small of her back stung from the blows.

Suddenly, her mother was behind her. She could hear her struggling with her father, trying to tear the belt from his hand. And Vivienne was screaming at him in quick, sharp French, then moving to block Mairi with her own small body.

"That's enough, Malcolm!" she finally said in English, her accent thick, her voice high.

"Another blow will make the lesson that much harder to forget!"

"And any bit of affection either of us ever felt for you will go with it!" Something in that seemed to register with him, and there was silence.

With a nod from her mother that the punishment had been meted out, Mairi stubbornly lifted her chin and walked toward the first-floor room she shared with Colleen. She would not give Malcolm the satisfaction of seeing her run from him. Pride was the one thing of value she had gained from her father.

Mairi was never going to be like her mother with a man when she grew up. Weak. Possessed by love. It was awful to see. And even more awful to consider enduring when you weren't a child, and you didn't have to.

"Are ye all right? He did no' hurt ye too badly this time, did he?" Colleen asked her sister afterward, as they huddled together on the downy-soft quilt on top of Colleen's twin bed. Beyond the closed door, their parents were still arguing.

"Why d'ye suppose he's so fearsome like that about the glen?" Mairi asked after a moment, vanquishing the pain of her punishment by refusing to acknowledge it, refusing to cry.

"I think it has somethin' do with that woman everyone in town whispers about."

"Like what?"

"I don't know, you eejit," Colleen smiled devil-ishly. "Maybe she draws men out there to her cottage to read Robert Burns."

The girls looked at one another for a moment, then giggled, knowing, from the way everyone in town talked about the woman, how unlikely that scenario would be. "How's your foot?"

"Grand."

"No, really."

"Throbbin' like a bass drum, if ye must know. But how's your backside? Why don't ye take a bit of my ice here."

Drawn by childish curiosity, Mairi carefully peeled back the towel and the chunks of ice. "'Tis as purple as a plum," she sat back on her heels.

"Just lovely." Colleen rolled her eyes, then took two pieces of ice, wrapped them in a handkerchief from the bedside table and helped Mairi put them on her own wound.

"Think of all the attention ye'll get from Paddy McShane at school on Monday mornin'," Mairi said, as the horrible burning pain was replaced with cool relief.

"'Tis no' exactly the sort I'd fancy,"

"Who ye *do* fancy is that older lad we saw today. The one who sells clay pots by the roadside, called Barry Buchanan, is it?"

"I do no' suppose I'd mind if he'd give me a glance. And it's called pottery, what he sells." She lay back and looked at the ceiling. "But I do no' expect such a fantasy with him is there in the cards. Me not even bein' past the age o' consent."

"Ye're near to sixteen."

"He's near to twenty."

Thinking of the adolescent boy who spent most of his time alone or at that makeshift stand on the road leading out of town, who wore mostly black sweaters and denim jeans, Mairi wrinkled her nose. "He's just so intense. He never talks to anyone."

"I think he's mysterious."

"I think he's too much like Da."

There was a wonderful complicitous silence between them after that. Something rich and fine, like silk, wrapped around each of them, connecting them, as they sat together in the lamplight and shadows. "I do wish we had the same ma. Then we'd be *real* sisters."

"We *are* real sisters," Colleen insisted. "And ye're no' ever to forget that."

"I'm glad you believe so."

"'Tis only the truth. Vivienne's your ma, and she's been mine since I was a wee bairn. She's a good woman. Even if Da does no' realize it."

Mairi began to play with a stray thread that had come loose from her sister's comforter. "I never asked ye this."

There was a silence then. And she seemed not to know how to ask the question.

Colleen looked at her. "What is it then?"

"Do ye miss her sometimes, your real ma?"

"'Tis nothin' to miss, me not ever knowin' her." Colleen had answered quickly. Then, in the second silence that followed, she looked appraisingly at Mairi.

"Go on. Say it. There's somethin' more workin' itself around in that head of yours, isn't there?" Mairi urged her, seeing the hesitation in her pale green eyes and knowing a shorthand that had been etched deeply into each of them. *Sisterhood*.

"Well, I do wish Da and Vivienne did no' have to do battle so often."

Mairi lowered her eyes. "Ye may not miss your ma, Colleen. But Da surely does. I think he still loves her."

"Aye."

"And he despises me for no' bein' a part of the cherished past, the way you are."

Colleen sighed. "'Tis near impossible for Vivienne to compete with a memory."

"I've heard others say as much in town when they think children do no' hear things. There goes that poor runt with no true country, they say. Thick and plain. Half French. Half Scottish. A whole lot of nowhere. The poor lass, they call me."

"Ye're no' to be listen' to others, Mairi Gordon. 'Tis only what's in your own heart that matters atall."

Mairi waited a moment as she looked into her sister's eyes. So full of the confidence and wisdom that the two years' difference in their ages brought. "Do ye suppose we'll always be together like this?" Mairi asked.

"What d'ye mean?"

"All of us. As a family?"

Colleen tried to smile. But her face had a flicker of anxiety. "I'd like to hope."

Their parents were still arguing. The old house on the hill shook now with the sound of their bitter words. The accusations. Recriminations.

"I really do despise you!" Vivienne railed, lapsing back and forth between French and English, in a way she could not seem to help when she was angry.

"No more than I despise *you*, with your high and mighty city ways!"

"But what you really despise me for is the unpardonable sin of my *not* being your beloved Janet!"

His voice was hard and cold. "Do no' bring her into this, Vivienne."

"Well I can never be *her!* And *you* can never have her back!"

"I prayed God, from the day I married ye, that I could!"

More yelling followed. Her mother's came now in a flurry of Gallic expletives. Her father's, a wild angry bark. And then the sound of flesh upon flesh. A crack. And a wounded little cry. It was all like lightning. And both girls knew then that their mismatched parents had no hope of surviving together. But they didn't say it, because they could not bear to. It was easier for two girls whose heads were full of dreams to talk in possibilities than absolutes.

"And if Ma and I go away from here one day," Mairi started again. "Will we still be sisters then, do ye think?"

There was a tremor in her voice that Colleen pressed back as she tipped up her chin, green eyes glittering. "No matter where ye go or what ye do, Mairi Gordon,"—she pushed herself to smile brightly—"sisters we shall forever be."

"Are ye all right, Ma?"

Mairi was standing at her mother's side, watching her at her dressing table as she brushed her sleek, chestnut-colored hair, the very color she had given her daughter. The moon was full, and silver streaked into the large second-floor bedroom through the open windows as a breeze issued in through the muslin curtains. "You're not to worry about me, *chérie*. I will be fine. It's you who has suffered tonight. Let me have a look at—"

Mairi turned her backside away from her mother, refusing again to acknowledge outwardly what had been so cruelly done to her. "Why'd ye let him treat ye like that?" she wanted to know.

Vivienne stood a moment, watching Mairi's response and hurting far more for her than she did for herself. "It is complicated."

"He hurts ye. And he makes ye cry. 'Tisn't so complicated, is it?"

Vivienne took her daughter's hands. Her wide brown eyes were shining with sudden tears and a purple bruise puffed up the right side of her face. "It does seem simple when you say it that way."

"Ye should no' let him, Ma. 'Tis wrong, the way he is."

She kissed her daughter's cheeks, slowly, lovingly. Then drew her close. "Yes. It is wrong. But things will be better. You'll see."

They walked to school together a few days later, down the long dirt road that twisted along the shore of Loch Tay, through a lacy grove of moss-furred beech and oak trees. The sky above was cloudless, the color of glass, as a crisp spring breeze rustled the leaves. The sound was fairies whispering, Mairi always thought.

"I've a wee bit of money left from my birthday.

Enough to buy a blackberry tart at Quinn's Bake Shop," Colleen offered with a smile. "We could share it."

Mairi looked at her with surprise. Her own smile faded. The memory of her father's whipping and his continuous lack of approval was fresh in her mind. "Ye know well how Da does no' favor us bein' frivolous with money."

"'Tis nothin' better I fancy than a fresh Quinn's tart," Colleen giggled mischievously. "Who says 'twould be frivolous in light of that?"

When Mairi could think of no quick retort, Colleen reached out her hand and the two sisters broke into a run, their cotton skirts, one blue gingham, the other white muslin, flowing out behind them, like sails on a ship's mast.

Both had legs that were pale and lightly freckled. But while Colleen's legs were long and slim, her younger sister's were thick, and both knees were scabbed. The pair of white socks sagged at Mairi's ankles and met scuffed loafers. In spite of the marked differences between them, both girls had complexions that were ruddy and clean. The faces of innocence. The reflection of life lived in a small Scottish village.

The girls were still holding hands as they came into town, breathless and giggling. The small brass bell over the weathered white door at Quinn's Bake Shop tinkled as Colleen pulled back the handle. Morning sun streaked in through the large storefront window as the earthy aroma of warm bread, tea cakes, and scones surrounded them like a thick, heady perfume.

Jimmy Quinn, his thick hands covered in flour, wiped his hands on the white apron around his middle, then turned around at the same time as his wife, Catriona, in her tweed skirt and cardigan sweater, did.

The Quinns looked startlingly alike, Mairi had always thought. Stout and smiling, with the same small, bright blue eyes, like azure buttons, lost in their two plump, well-scrubbed, rosy faces.

The Quinns were a well-suited couple. They worked together side by side. Lived together. And had managed, after twelve years, to produce a cherubic, fat-cheeked little girl named Jennie, whom Catriona held in one arm as she served customers with the other.

"Top of the mornin' to ye girls," Catriona said as she picked up her child, and Jimmy Quinn pressed back the beige muslin curtain, disappearing into the magical inner sanctum from which all the delicious smells emanated.

"And to you, Mrs. Quinn," they both replied.

"'Tis a bonny sight to see the two of ye this fine mornin'."

"And you, ma'am." Their manners were as perfect and eager as their smiles.

A tall, strongly built young man they did not recognize came in behind them then, with a large sack of flour over his shoulder and a glum expression marring his surprisingly sculpted face. Mairi tipped her head, studying him for an instant. He could have been handsome, she thought, with his thick waves of dark hair and eyes that glittered like chips of onyx above a square jaw. If he didn't look like such a brooder.

He was certainly far older than they, she surmised. Probably long out of school, with a broad back like that and thick forearms coming out of rolled-up plaid

sleeves; arms that looked like tightly twisted cord. Like
their father, this boy was moody and restless, she could
see. It turned her cold, a boy like that. Handsome and
silent on the outside. A firestorm within. A shiver rippled up Mairi's spine. One thing was certain: It made
her want to keep her distance.

"'Tis my nephew from Glasgow," Catriona said
when she saw Mairi's wrinkled expression. "Calum, say
hello to the Gordon girls. That's Mairi there. And her
sister, Colleen." He did not bother turning fully
around and the sound of acknowledgment that
escaped his lips sounded something like a grunt. Until
he saw Colleen.

It was a recognition that had come from the corner of his eye. Suddenly, he put down the sack and
looked straight at her. Colleen was transfixed too.
Mairi could feel the charge between them.

"He's here for the summer," Catriona explained as
Calum and Colleen starred silently at one another.

Both girls smiled politely, suppressing adolescent
giggles. Catriona Quinn was a kind, pleasant woman
liked by everyone in town. At the moment, it was difficult for Mairi to imagine Calum and Catriona being
related by any amount of blood. It was even more difficult to conjure up how her sister could be the least bit
drawn to him.

"Well, then," Catriona said, her smile so radiant
and warm. "What'll ye have?"

They gazed longingly down into the glass display
case, forgetting quickly about her brooding nephew.
Quinn's baked goods were better than jewels, they
both thought. An illicit pleasure to girls raised by a
strict man who allowed them few enjoyments. "A

blackberry tart, if ye please," Colleen smiled brightly and drew forth a few coins from a side pocket in her dress. "We'll share."

Catriona looked at each of them. The child squirmed in her arms and grabbed the shiny gold crucifix at her mother's neck. She wouldn't mind a bit if her Jennie turned out like the Gordon girls. Endlessly sweet. And as perfectly polite as they came. That, of course, was Vivienne's doing, with her lofty French manners and her great show of dignity. She acted almost regal, Catriona thought, even when she was down on her hands and knees, up to her elbows in manure, digging endlessly in that garden of hers on the side of the house at MacLaren's Bend. To her credit, she shared her lovely flowers liberally. But she had cultivated few friends beyond Mrs. McShane, whose husband ran the hotel in town.

Few, it seemed, had ever quite fathomed the chemistry between Malcolm Gordon and his second wife. They were certainly worlds apart. Beyond sharing the upbringing of Colleen, and then the surprisingly plain daughter who had been born to the two of them, there seemed little else. Their loud battles were the stuff of great gossip all the way down to Mallaig Harbor.

There was a time, long ago, when Catriona had designs on the handsome Malcolm Gordon who lived in the house on the hill. But there was Jimmy to think of now. And it was a betrayal of her dear husband's great devotion to remember any of that ancient history. She kissed the top of their baby daughter's head, happy now with what life had brought her, happy that she wasn't like Vivienne, Malcolm's second choice, *after* his beloved Janet.

With thick, blunted fingers, Catriona drew a tart from the case. Then she reached for another, and handed them in slips of waxed paper across the counter top.

"But we can only afford the one, Mrs. Quinn," Mairi earnestly explained, her mahogany eyes full of innocence.

"'Tis a pleasure to see my bakery eaten by two such appreciative customers," Catriona smiled broadly, most keenly at the poor lass who had not been blessed with her sister's slim, undeniable beauty. "Besides, I fancy your bright smiles. Brings a ray of sunshine inside here. Now off with the two of ye. And enjoy them!"

"Thank ye indeed, Mrs. Quinn!" they both chimed as they took the tarts.

Outside, the wind blew their hair and skirts. Mairi ate her tart slowly, wanting to make it last. "What'd ye suppose Da would do if he saw us?" Colleen laughed mischievously as she took large, ravenous bites. Mairi loved the sound of her sister's laugh, the confidence in it.

"'Tis a question my backside canno' quite yet bear to consider." She returned the smile, then took her own dainty bite as they started to run back toward school, down the old road, crested on both sides with a grotto of color: blossoming rhododendron, feathery Queen Anne's lace, and clumps of pink and purple lupine.

Suddenly, Mairi felt his eyes. Felt them before she saw them.

She slowed, her glance drawn into a grove of beech trees with tops as tall as castle spires. Beyond them lay those heather-blanketed Highland peaks in the color her mother called magenta. Her eyes settled, not on any of that, but on the boy, a man now, really. Barry Buchanan standing there alone, watching them run.

It was curious, the way he looked at them. From a distance. Observing them, but with a strange sort of longing to be included. Her mother didn't like the Buchanan boy, as she called him. Because he was rootless. Because he had no ties with the town now. No people. Both of his parents were dead. And he had no siblings.

It wasn't even clear where he lived. *Beyond the glen,* was all Vivienne had told them. But once Mairi had heard her mother and Mrs. McShane whispering at tea about the woman who lived in shame and seclusion out there.

She'd sinned against God by her profession, they said, drawing decent men from their faith. And from their wives. But Mairi could never get her mother to explain precisely what that meant.

The woman inhabited an old crofter's cottage, past those shimmering beech trees, that stood like a barrier to the mysteries beyond. Its shock of butter yellow broom and thorny gorse, they were certain, was the pathway to some delicious mystery.

And then, when the woman was mentioned, they always heard with it the name Buchanan, Barry Buchanan. It certainly was not proper, Mrs. McShane had whispered.

As Mairi watched him looking at her, she wondered for the first time if he too was part of the reason their father was so against them going beyond the glen. But as soon as the thought came she dismissed it. Mairi knew the boy was kind. Mysterious, but kind. She knew because Colleen liked him.

Mairi held out a hand and waved to him, but he did not return the gesture. Rather, Barry turned and walked back through the yellow thick of broom and gorse and disappeared behind the trees. And she could not help but wonder where he was going now.

They were to have tea in town served properly by old Miss Barrie, the spinster who, with her widowed brother Jamie, owned the Dun Whinney. It was the little restaurant in the center of town. It had all been arranged by Vivienne, who thought her daughters, as she called them (even though Malcolm frowned when she included Colleen), should have a proper tea. She wanted them to join her at a respectable establishment now and then, since they were both of an age for it to do them good.

It was an old kind of place. Lots of mahogany, lace on the windows, and delicate yellow tea things that clattered on the trays as they were brought from the small kitchen. Miss Barrie served their tea while they waited for Vivienne. Mairi filled her cup with milk first, then added a few drops of tea from the pot.

"Ye're a brave one," Colleen grinned.

"Well, we've got to learn to do it out in public, don't we?" Mairi smile back. "Properly. That's why we're here. To prove to Ma we can be proper ladies."

Colleen's smile faded. "Where do ye suppose she is? Ma's never late."

Mairi rolled her eyes, but she was still smiling.

"No, she never has her hair done and gets to talkin' to Mrs. Mason about hair dye, or stops at O'Meira's to try on a new hat, if they've gotten some in."

Suddenly, that boy, Catriona's sullen nephew, passed by outside the Dun Whinney, and Colleen nearly broke her neck straining to watch him pass.

Mairi was incredulous. "Ye do no' actually fancy *him,* do ye now?"

Colleen demurred, pouring her tea first and then the milk to regain her status as elder sister beneath the coming affront. "Perhaps. He's no' a bit hard on the eyes."

"He's dull as a tree stump!"

"He's from Glasgow! His parents have means. Margaret, at school, told me so."

"What about Barry Buchanan?"

Colleen leaned back, fingered her teacup. "I'm no' sure. There's just so much of the world out there I've no' seen."

"And ye're more likely to see it with a lad from Glasgow?"

"Well, Barry does no' have the funds to take me away from Killin."

"What ye mean is away from Da."

Colleen was defensive suddenly, frightened by the thought. "If Vivienne leaves him one day, I'll be left alone here. 'Twould be a bleak existence, Mairi, him pinin' after my other ma. I'd *have* to do somethin'."

Miss Barrie brought tea cakes and a plate of small sandwiches then and inquired about their father. Both girls smiled at her politely and said he was fine indeed. Everyone asked about Malcolm. He had lived his whole life in Killin. He was a part of the place. "Polite" was what they did. Politely smiled. Politely replied. Made believe in a wonderful life in the house at the top of the hill. Their silence was a bond, like so many other things between them.

"Well, ye could sure have Mrs. Quinn's nephew if ye wanted him," Mairi said faithfully when Miss Barrie had gone back into the kitchen. "In fact, I'll bet ye could do just about anythin' ye wanted to, *if* ye were to set your mind to it."

"'Tis strange to hear that," Colleen smiled again and looked directly at her sister. "I always thought 'twould be you who'd one day take the world by storm!"

They waited for Vivienne through tea and several of the cakes and sandwiches. But she never came. They were both worried as they walked solemnly back to MacLaren's Bend.

"Do ye suppose they're at it again?" Mairi asked in a quiet voice.

"Vivienne would have been there if 'twas anythin' else."

They glanced at one another. The air was cold now. Especially for a spring evening. There was a frigid wind up off the water. Mairi wrapped her arms around herself and wished she had worn a sweater as they continued on up the dirt road that passed through town, past that small strip of alpine buildings, the few gray stone houses, the flower-filled town square, and the old bridge sitting astride a rushing stream.

MacLaren's Bend was a large pink-washed Georgian style house, a private home for two hundred years. It was Malcolm Gordon's great-grandfather who had added the architecturally unsuitable veranda so that he could watch the sunset on the shining waters of Loch Tay.

Vivienne's painstaking addition to a place that had never welcomed her was the garden around it. She had tended it lovingly, filling it with lilies, daffodils, and those temperamental violets no one else ever seemed to be able to grow.

It was through the grand bay front window, as they approached, that Mairi and Colleen first saw them. And saw what they always feared most.

A cold fist of dread knotted in Mairi's throat.

Their parents were facing one another in evening's silhouette. And once again they were arguing. Malcolm's fists were raised. His body was tense. Vivienne looked small and fragile before him. But her mother was not cowering. Even though his angry words could not be heard through the pink stone walls, her defiance was clear.

Suddenly, Colleen took Mairi's hand and squeezed it. "Come with me."

"Where?"

"Just come! Quickly!"

They ran together then, hands still linked, back down the hill away from the house and into a thick of trees that circled the loch. They didn't stop until they came to a large, mossy stone in the middle of a clearing. "The ancient stone?" Mairi asked.

"Ye know the legend."

"Touch it and the promise you make will one day be fulfilled," Mairi repeated the tale they had both grown up hearing about a stone that had been here for centuries.

The sisters looked at one another. "Do ye believe it?" Colleen asked.

"I'm no' certain."

"Well, I do. I believe it with all of my heart. Let's make a vow now, a promise, that if we are separated, we'll find a way to be together again one day."

"Ye think Ma is goin' to leave him, don't ye?"

"I canno' say I'd blame her."

Then Colleen took her sister's hand and drew it down with her own upon the cool, mossy surface of the stone. Looking up solemnly then at the heavens, Colleen said, "So it is promised. If fate should separate us, t'will also bring us back together one day."

Mairi felt tears prick her eyes at the suggestion of a parting she could not imagine. But, in the end, she pressed the stone firmly. "Aye. 'Tis promised."

With heavy hearts, they returned then to Mac-Laren's Bend and walked together slowly up the front steps, their hands linked, wind lifting the strands of hair that lay across their shoulders. "Whatever happens . . ." Colleen said softly. But her words fell away.

It was what she always said to Mairi at times like these.

They stood on the porch, stone-still both of them in the cold, gusting wind, watching for a moment. Things between their parents had escalated. Vivienne was shouting back now. And she was crying. Mairi could sense the danger in that room acutely. As she drew open the front door, their angry words came at the girls with full force.

"I'll not put up with the lies another day, you cold, heartless bullock!"

"Ye know she means nothin' to me. She and that

Buchanan lad need the money. 'Tis a business arrangement when I go out there."

"Oh, don't insult me, Malcolm."

"Maitland's a trollop."

"And what does that make *you*?"

"A man, Vivienne, with needs!"

"I deserve better than hearing that week after week, year after year, when ye go out into that glen!"

"Then ye should have married better! 'Tis what ye think anyway, isn't it?"

"Perhaps I should have!"

His voice was thick and booming. "'Tis no' too late!"

They watched Vivienne pivot away and Malcolm's massive hand go out like a vise to stop her. It clamped onto her wrist, a powerful manacle, and she angled back, her loose hair flying into her face. "Let me go, Malcolm!"

"Ye'll no' be goin' until I *say* ye'll go!"

"We're not suited. You know that! You've said it yourself a dozen times."

"But, suited or no', ye *are* my wife!"

"God save me from hearing that another time!"

The blow was swift and powerful and landed with a deafening crack. The girls watched in silent horror through the window as Vivienne fell to the floor. It became slow motion, each movement after that. Mairi could hear the breath in her own throat. She could hear her heart pumping. But for a very long moment—an eternity—there was nothing else.

"He's killed her!" Colleen finally cried from beneath her hand, and the sound was like razors on Mairi's skin.

Through the haze that wrapped itself around her

head, Mairi bolted forward, in through the front door, fear and anger propelling her trembling legs forward. Her father did not see her. His rage and the subsequent shock of seeing his wife lying lifeless before him had frozen him. He stood looking down at Vivienne, his hands still balled into fists at his sides, his great barrel chest still heaving.

The years of watching them battle, her mother always weaker. Always bruised. Apologetic. It came to Mairi's mind all at once like that. The anger. The helplessness. The fearsome need to protect her mother.

Mairi's heart was thundering in her ears now. That horrid pipe smoke, so sickeningly acrid, from a pipe he'd left nearby in an ashtray, was choking. She couldn't think. The first thing she saw beside him was that blue Sèvres vase of mother's. The one she'd said had come from Paris as a wedding gift. It was heavy, Mairi knew. And blindly, in that same whirling moment as she dashed at her father, Mairi grabbed the vase, and swung it up at the back of his head.

The impact vaulted through her as the glass connected, then shattered all around him, raining those brilliant, sparkling chips of priceless blue glass. In a silence that went on forever, her father spun around. His dark eyes were wide like emerald prisms, mirroring back the shock and pain.

Mairi thought of running once he saw her. Once their eyes met. Father. Daughter. *Enemies.* For a moment, everything was frighteningly still. But then the huge bulk of a man began to melt before her, like a balloon very slowly losing its air. Malcolm Gordon sank onto the carpet, blood streaming from the gash at the back of his head, and all she could do was watch.

Now they're both dead, Mairi thought. *There's only Colleen and me. All we have now is each other. . . .* But that thought did not frighten her so much as what they would do, alone in the world with no parents. And more than that, how she and Colleen could make people believe that she had killed her own father in her mother's defense.

For a moment, Mairi felt like the older sister. The one in control. The pride at that swelled within her. But it was a short-lived sensation as she glanced back at the lifeless bodies of both their parents. Then she looked over at Colleen, who stood back beside the door, hands over her gaping mouth, eyes as wide as saucers.

All right, a voice shouted inside Mairi's head. *Now what'll ye do?*

Suddenly, a moaning cry tore through the eerie stillness. It filled the room so unexpectedly that Colleen shrieked in terror. Mairi pivoted back, her own face the color of parchment. It was her mother. She was still alive. Da had not killed her, after all.

Mairi and Colleen both rushed to Vivienne as she struggled to sit up. She was holding her forehead. Her face was streaked with blood where she had hit the sharp corner of the tea table.

"Ye're all right, Maman," Mairi murmured, tears welling in her eyes as she used the French appellation she stubbornly avoided most of the time. "Oh, thank God in his heaven that ye're all right."

"Yes, I am." Vivienne's voice caught with emotion. Until she saw her husband. Then in that horrendous moment, her small painted mouth fell open and a small gasp escaped her lips. "Dear Lord, help us. What . . . what have you done, Mairi?"

But as soon as she saw the broken glass and her own daughter's expression she knew the answer. And Vivienne's beautiful face, so full of pride, with its perfect features and flawless apricot skin, crumbled then, into an expression of panic. She reached over to Malcolm and put her bloodied hand on his chest to check for a heartbeat. It left a gruesome imprint on his white undershirt.

Colleen was weeping. "Is he—?"

"No, darling," Vivienne said. "Your father is alive."

"Then I'll get help!" Mairi announced, shooting back to her feet, bound by a purpose.

"Help me up," Vivienne instructed, her voice shallow now, the words uneven as she moved onto her knees and then, with great effort, stood.

"But ye've been hurt, Ma!"

"*Chérie,* my dear girl." She tried to be calm but her voice was high and shrill. "There isn't time for that. We must leave here. And quickly."

"Leave?"

"Do as I say, Mairi. Go now." Vivienne's wide eyes narrowed. The gash in her forehead was still bleeding. She reached up and grimaced as she touched it. "Go and find someone with a car who can take us to the train station. There won't be time for us to walk. Colleen can stay here and tend to your father while I pack."

Mairi felt a high, throbbing ache in her throat, feeling as if, in those awful moments that had just passed, she had single-handedly changed the course of all their lives. Forever. "But Ma! Maybe if we just—"

"Go, I said! Quickly!"

❖   ❖   ❖

She was running blindly, and stumbling, moving up into the heather-covered hills behind MacLaren's Bend. The wind was strong. The great gusts fought against her, the unforgiving force violent against a young girl. The tears she cried dried like icy ribbons on her pale cheeks. Mairi was not certain where she was going or who could help her. She knew only that this was the shortest route into town.

"Help!" she cried out, not realizing any sound had escaped her mouth. "Oh, please somebody help!"

She was moving wildly. Not looking. Heading down the steep slope of the hill now that came down behind the main street. There would be someone there. Surely. She could do this. Find someone with a car. Her mother was counting on her. She felt fierce in that moment, protective. Strong.

Mairi wove in and out among the thorny gorse, the thick, brightly colored heather. The wind battered her. She tripped on a stone then and stumbled. But she righted herself quickly and kept going.

A few more steps, and she fell again. This time, Mairi felt the skin tear on her palms as she reached out to break her fall. And she felt gorse thorns, like needles, scrape her cheek. A little cry of pain moved up from her throat, but there wasn't time for that. With long tendrils of her loose hair whipping into her eyes, Mairi scrambled back to her feet yet again and ran. Ran and ran . . .

Until she slammed headlong into something big and still.

At first, it felt very like the trunk of a tree, hard and unmoving. But then she felt something else reach out and clamp onto her forearms. Her head shot up with wild eyes blazing, and she gave a low moan of sheer terror.

Barry Buchanan. Once again, it was that strange young man, as if he'd come right out of thin air. But now he was standing before her, holding her arms and starring down into the sheer panic in her eyes.

"What's happened?" he asked in a deep, calm voice that reached over the wind.

"I've no time! I've got to find a car! Got to get my ma and me away from here!"

He seemed to understand without asking her any questions, and took her hand firmly, leading her, not into town, but back up the hill. "I'll take ye," he said in a voice that was unexpectedly deep and steady. His tone calmed her. "I know where there's a car. Go back to your house and I'll pick ye up out front in five minutes."

Mairi looked for a moment into his eyes. Deeply into them. They seemed to swallow her up with their depth. It was a strange sensation, being drawn like that. Pulled toward another human being. And she thought, with her youthful mind, that it felt a little frightening.

It was the first time she had ever been this close to the young man no one knew well nor trusted. But there wasn't time to question him. Nor anything else. Only to believe that he could help and that she and her mother could get out of MacLaren's Bend before father woke up and realized what, and who, had hit him.

The mist drifted in around MacLaren's Bend as Barry Buchanan helped Vivienne onto the front seat of a dented blue Morris that seemed to have materialized out of nowhere, much as he had. Mairi stood beside her and then, very suddenly, looked back up onto the veranda of the house. It was a place she and Colleen had played and laughed for as long as she could remember.

Her sister stood there, an arm wrapped around one of the thick white columns. Tears stood in her eyes. She could see the shimmering green and the long gold lashes as their eyes met in the last of the pale afternoon sunlight.

Mairi touched the small gold Celtic cross around her neck, a cross Colleen had only just given her. Taken from her neck. Something that had once belonged to her own mother. A treasure.

Mairi knew well that it was the most valuable thing her sister had to give. Mairi's heart squeezed like a vise as she looked one last time at Colleen, at the long, wild copper hair, the slightly upturned lips struggling to convey a hopeful smile.

"I canno' take this," Mairi had gasped as her sister hooked the chain behind her neck moments before.

"Ye can if I'm givin' it to ye. Go on now. Keep it to remember me. And remember this place. Just in case they do no' manage to patch this one up."

There were tears standing in Mairi's eyes. "I surely do no' need a necklace for that."

Her sister smiled and spoke gently. "'Twill only help. As time goes by."

"They'll let us see each other, won't they?"

"'Tis a fair distance between here and France. One no' easily passed when anger stands between it."

Mairi climbed into the back seat of the old car,

never once breaking her gaze from Colleen, holding desperately onto the cross until the final moment. Her sister's last words, as they had stood together, were carved into her mind like initials into the trunk of a tree.

"Ye're the only one, Colleen. The only one in the world who's no' reminded me that I'm as plain as I feel."

"Ye're beautiful, Mairi Gordon. Beautiful in your heart," she said with the deepest conviction. "The rest'll come in time. I can only hope I'll be there to see it."

"I don't want to go," Mairi had wept, holding her older sister's slightly larger hands, squeezing them. She could still feel them. The warmth, the reassurance there.

"But ye *must*. 'Tisn't safe here for ye. Nor for Vivienne. No' with him so full of that rage all the time."

"I'll never forget ye, Colleen."

"Ye promised on the stone ye'd find a way to come back."

"Then it must come true."

Barry Buchanan turned the key and the car began to rumble. Mairi lay her head back against the torn seat and gulped back tears. But still she could see Colleen, that slim, lovely figure on the verge of womanhood, standing there with tears raining openly down her cheeks, and the cool breeze off Loch Tay picking up and tossing her hair. No matter where they went, Mairi would remember this moment.

This vision, always.

CHAPTER TWO

Outside, the day slipped by under a persistent drizzle. All it did in Paris was rain, Mairi thought. And it was so dreary here. Gray. Everything. The sky. The buildings. That metal monstrosity everyone here called *la Tour Eiffel*. Even the people; sour, city expressions were pasted onto their pale faces as they walked in their gray coats and hats down streets that were too wide and too fast to be imagined back home.

She sank against the window at the *Hôtel la Bourdonnais* and thought of the rain at home. Scotland. Yes, that was still home. It had only been a week, but she missed it already. She missed Colleen. The first couple of days, she kept expecting her father to come and get them, just as he always did when he and her mother had a row. Bring them home. Apologize for frightening them, for making her hit him with that vase as she had.

But this time Malcolm did not come.

Her mother assured her daily that none of this was her fault. That sometimes in a marriage things happen. People grow apart. It was for the best, her mother said. And this time the breech was permanent. Her father was not coming to get them. There would be no going back to MacLaren's Bend. Nor to Colleen.

They would make a new life here in Paris, the city in which her mother had been affluently raised. But it would be different now, difficult, Vivienne tenderly explained as she put her child to bed. They were in a third-floor room at the respectable hotel in an upper-class neighborhood just off the quai d'Orsay. Mother's aristocratic parents, who had not been amused by her choice in men, would contribute no financial help. *Faites ton lit,* they now said. Which was a rough equivalent, Mairi understood already, of making one's bed and needing to lie in it.

Vivienne pressed back the hair from her daughter's face. Still, they would make it, she assured Mairi. Their Gallic determination and the strength of will their heritage gave them had served them well so far.

Her mother always sounded so positive. But Mairi was worried as she looked into Vivienne's tired face. There were more lines there now than she remembered. More signs of worry. And the luster in her mother's striking chestnut hair was dulled here in this city with all of its noises and rushing people, its lack of sunshine and fresh summer breezes.

Vivienne had been out looking for work every day since they had arrived, and she was quite plainly exhausted.

"I don't like it here. 'Tis a city for rich folks. And I miss Colleen, Maman," she said to her mother as the mist turned to rain and beat like pebbles against the small windowpanes of their hotel room. A sudden gust of wind blew the draperies, rippling them at the place

where she kept the windows parted for fresh air.
"Perhaps we could just ring—"

But Vivienne cut her off with a hand firmly raised.
Her perfectly arched brows knitted swiftly into a
frown. "That part of our life is over now, *chérie*. There
will be no telephone calls."

And with that, Mairi said nothing else. Because
she was still only thirteen years old. And because she
knew, by the determined expression in her mother's
deep, brown eyes, that there would be no convincing
her otherwise. Mairi lay there in the silence after
Vivienne had left the room, counting moon shadows
on the ceiling. And missing her sister anyway.

They found a small apartment nearby, on the avenue
Bosquet, in the week that followed. It was a garret,
really, high up on the fourth floor. But it was in a chic
neighborhood spotted with expensive antique and art
dealers. The musty little shops were stuffed with
Pissarro paintings, old andirons, tapestries, and Victorian chairs and sat companionably beside butcher
shops, wine shops, and lovely, fragrant *boulangeries*.
The aroma of their freshly baking baguettes made the
air sweet. *But nothing so sweet,* Mairi thought longingly, *as the air around the glen.*

After another week, Vivienne had found a job as a
secretary for the Paris Office of the *International
Herald Tribune*. Her long hours there were compen-
sated for by the things she lavished on her daughter,
things she had not been able to give her in Scotland.
Vivienne bought her daughter the most lovely pink
party dress she had ever seen, with tiny pearl buttons

and white patent leather shoes. Then they both
dressed up and went to dinner at the restaurant over
the Café la Terrasse and sat looking down on the street
below, watching the people who scurried past them at
the cross of avenue de la Bourdonnais and la Motte-
Piquet.

"This is what your life should have been from the
start, *chérie*," Vivienne told her as she took Mairi's
hand and held it on top of the cloth-covered table
between them. "These people. These sounds. Hear
the beauty of your own language. Take it in. And you
will become a part of it, just as it is a part of *you*."

Mairi watched her mother's face shining full of
hope, and she tried her best to smile. She could see
how much Vivienne wanted this for her. For them. But
she felt nothing. Least of all, French. She was Scottish.
Mairi Gordon. From a long line of Gordons, who lived
in the lush and mystical countryside.

You can bring me here, she was thinking as she
kept trying to force that smile. *Change me. Mold me to
your wishes, since I am still a child. But my heart is
mine. There, and in my soul, I belong only to myself.
And I will return there. To my sister. Some day.*

I will!

Mairi walked with a crowd of fast-moving commuters,
feeling a little like she was a lamb being led to the
slaughter. Out on the boulevard des Invalides, she
dragged along, scuffing her shoe heels with each step.

School. *Lycée* in French. And that was what all of
life would be.

From now on. *A la Française.*

Her mother said she was up to the task and that it would take no time at all, with what bits and pieces of the language she had learned as a little girl. Madame la Directrice, a dour-looking woman with a face like a prune and dark, deeply set eyes, concurred.

"And, after all, *chérie,* you *are* French," her mother said again. But her smile was as insistent as it was firm. This was to be the mantra. The past was over.

It was autumn now. *La rentrée,* they called it in Paris. Back to school. And Mairi longed quite painfully now for Mrs. Keenan's very unruly classroom at the stone schoolhouse; the mighty Highland peaks dappled with heather outside the wide windows. And there were the fragrances, too, that filled her memory and her heart; when her life now was so jarringly full of cars, buses and exhaust fumes.

There were the blackberry tarts and fresh scones from Quinn's Bake Shop, which she could almost taste if she thought about it. The aroma of freshly burning peat from the cottages around town. And breezes off the marshy water that lapped at the edges of Loch Tay, just down the hill from MacLaren's Bend.

She longed for all of that.

And, most especially, she longed for Colleen.

As each day passed, Mairi still could not imagine that her mother really meant to keep them apart permanently. Or that their father would allow it. Surely when the anger died away, when her parents spoke, just like always, things would return to normal. It couldn't go on like this much longer.

The car at the intersection before her came to such a screeching halt just then that she cried out and jumped back with a start. The air was suddenly

thick with the scent of burned rubber from the skid-
ding, and her bag of books tumbled out like domi-
nos.

She had been so lost in thought that she had not
even seen it coming.

The driver shook his fist and hollered something
she did not understand before he sped away down the
wide, beech-lined boulevard.

Everything here was on such a grand scale, Mairi
thought again. Massive. Formal. Intimidating. The
streets were wide. The buildings, like this old one
beside her, were all several stories tall, wrought of ven-
erable old yellow stone and iron, with huge heavy
doors that seemed absolutely mammoth when a young
girl faced one that was closed.

As she drew steadily nearer her new school, Mairi
thought of Colleen again, sitting in the little stone
schoolhouse today. Colleen had Mr. McKonigle this
term, the lean old man with the moody brown eyes
and that awful nasal drone. A smile of recollection
turned up the corners of her mouth. It was the first
thought that had made her smile for weeks.

*If only I hadn't hit Da . . . If only he hadn't loved
his first wife so much more than Ma . . .*

She stopped cold when she reached the address.
Stubbornly, she pushed away the thought. That
wouldn't help her now. It was too late to wish for things
that might have been. But her memories of an only sister she could still safeguard, lock away; they were
something no one could take from her.

It was a formidable, massive limestone building
like all of the others Mairi faced now, its deep blue
street-front doors with the large brass rings, one in the

center of each, opened, revealing an arched entrance and a forbidding courtyard beyond.

Mairi's stomach churned.

But she drew in a brave breath and tipped up her chin against it. She remembered what she had told her mother, who had been in tears when the newspaper would not permit her to take the morning off for her daughter's first day at school.

"I'll be fine, Maman," she had said so reassuringly, in her sticky, imperfect French.

After all, Mairi had told herself all morning, *I'm thirteen. Nearly grown-up.* Inside the cold, forbidding classroom, she sank into one of the dark wooden chairs facing an empty student's desk and clasped her hands tightly together so it wouldn't be so obvious that they were trembling.

The man behind the teacher's desk at the front of the class leveled a gaze out at the children, all of whom took their chairs around her with frighteningly quiet reserve. There was a blackboard behind the man that said only *Monsieur Guillaume* in a perfect, elegant chalk-drawn tilt.

Mairi listened to the sea of French names during the roll call that sounded startlingly foreign to her. *Xavier LeBon. Clarisse Paul. Pierre Duchatel . . .*

"Marielle Girard."

The name came and went without response. The other students glanced around.

"Marielle Girard! *Répondez s'il vous plaît!*" Monsieur Guillaume's repetition of the name was quite indignant.

Mairi glanced around along with the other students. Until her eyes settled on Monsieur Guillaume.

His small, dark eyes glowered down at her from beneath bushy pewter-colored brows. "Mademoiselle?"

Her heart was pulsing high in her throat as she met his gaze. At this heart-pounding moment, she felt horribly ugly and out of place. She longed to be anywhere but here. Anywhere she might fit in. "Monsieur?" she struggled to say, but the accent was all wrong, and she could hear murmured giggles from those around her.

"Comment vous appelez-vous, mademoiselle?"

"Mairi. Mairi Gordon, monsieur."

"Your name, it is right here." He pointed to Mairi, speaking in what sounded very like a deep French bark. *"Nouvelle étudiante.* A girl from Scotland. Your mother was very specific with the *Directrice,* Madame Dupont. Marielle Girard. That is your name. Ma-ri-elle Girard."

That was her mother's maiden name, Girard. Mairi felt as if something inside of her heart was being snatched away. It was painful. And a little blinding.

The eyes of all the other students who sat so neatly and quietly, like little tin soldiers, at their wooden desks, hands clasped, bore into her like fire on paper in the sunlight. There was not the slightest sound of a whisper now. But the intensity of the moment was chilling.

Unwelcome tears welled in her eyes. But once again she tipped her chin up proudly against it and gave him a stubborn look. "My name is Mairi Gordon, monsieur," she said in French. "Mairi. It is the Scottish spelling and pronunciation of Mary."

"Your name in this classroom, mademoiselle, shall be *Marielle . . . Rien d'autre. C'est tout . . .* Ma-ri-elle."

She watched the blue vein pulse in his neck as his eyes locked with hers. It was a standoff with Monsieur Guillaume, the little toad of a man, with his beady, coal dark eyes. But position and age, definitely had the advantage.

"Oui, monsieur. J'ai compris." Mairi sank against the hardwood chair back of her school desk, wishing quite literally that the floor could swallow her up. Willing herself with a steeled determination not to cry.

So there was to be nothing about this existence that was to remain the same. Her mother had cut out all remnants of their life in Scotland. Even she was supposed to be someone else. She was Marielle now. That was how things were . . . .

Or at least they would be until she found a way to see her sister again.

Vivienne sat erect behind the reception desk at the *International Herald Tribune,* stylish in her crisp straw-colored linen suit that had cost a week's salary, and looked politely but firmly up into the face of the man standing before her. He was a handsome man, tall and well built, with sandy blond hair and startlingly blue eyes. The phone on her desk had rung for the third time and she had not picked it up.

"I told you, sir," she said in English because the man was American. "Monsieur Chabrol is presently in a meeting."

"He'll see me, doll. Just let him know Jaeger is back."

"Sir. What part of *no* did you not understand?"

"Really," he smiled affably. "If you would just buzz him—"

"I am paid to screen the visitors to Mr. Chabrol's office. Not flirt with them."

Unfazed, he leaned over the desk and, in a tone of such sincerity that it left her breathless, he said, "Now, tell me. Is that any way to talk to the man you're gonna be spending the rest of your life with?"

The air was instantly charged between them. Vivienne felt as if she could not breathe. He was handsome, confident. And very presumptuous. Although not in a way that was unattractive.

Suddenly, as both of them continued to gaze at one another, Hervé Chabrol, small and stout, with a dark wave of greasy hair, stomped out into the reception area, hands at his temples as he exhaled an irritated sigh.

"Vivienne, why did you not tell me at once that Jaeger was here waiting?" he snapped at her in rapid French. "He's definitely first tier. Always interrupt me for Jaeger."

She could feel herself flush at her boss's angry tone and the mistake that she had clearly made, and she despised that about herself. The skin that was like porcelain also could betray her with a ruby veneer at the drop of a hat. *"Excusez-moi,* Monsieur Chabrol. I didn't know."

"There's no problem, Hervé," the man with the devastatingly blue eyes said casually as he wrapped an arm around the squat, portly editor in chief with whom he obviously had a history. "I only just walked through the door this moment. There wasn't time for her to do more than she did, which was to welcome me quite properly."

He gave her a gallant look, after that. Then he followed the editor in chief back toward the door to his office. As if he had forgotten something, the man then motioned to Hervé Chabrol to go on. And he turned back around.

"Have dinner with me this evening," he said, his deep voice dripping with confidence and charm. Vivienne felt a shiver bolt up the length of her spine and a memory sear her mind like fire.

This was how it had begun with Malcolm, she thought, gazing up into his blazing crystal blue eyes that blotted out everything else. *Not again,* she decided with a faint determination that was melting by the heartbeat as he looked at her.

My heart is not nearly ready for that. Still she knew, in spite of her protest, that they were going to have something together. She could feel it, as sure as a summer storm approaching. Feel it, yes. But he *knew* it. She had seen that in his eyes from the first moment they settled on her. A total conviction of purpose.

As Vivienne looked at him now, as he looked at her, she knew her voice would shake. She struggled against it. She pulled in a deep breath and sat straighter still. "Thank you for the invitation," she said in a formal tone. "But I cannot."

"And why not, may I ask?"

"I have a child at home, Mr. Jaeger. I have dinner with *her.*"

He cocked an eyebrow. The smile was lethal. "Have you a husband, as well?"

"Not any longer, no."

"Good." The smile widened. His teeth were white and straight, his smile made it impossible for her to think. "Well, then, bring her along. We'll go out to the

Bois. There's a carnival there all week. Don't you think she would enjoy that?"

Vivienne was uncharacteristically flustered. "Well, I suppose any child—"

"Great. Then it's a date."

He seemed to take her stunned silence after that for tacit agreement. It was impossible not to like this man standing before her in his green and buff camouflage jacket and denim jeans, for the sheer audacity of him. "Since it's our first date, you'd probably prefer to meet me there. Neutral territory and all. Let's say seven o'clock?"

"But I don't even know your entire name," she sputtered out as he began again to turn away.

Her words brought him back, his blue eyes shining at her. "Ron Jaeger."

CHAPTER THREE

He brought goldenrod for the fever and would make a poultice of mugwort for the pain in her stomach, because his dear sainted mother had always said it worked best for what ailed women. And because he had no money to buy her proper medicines in town. Then Barry Buchanan walked softly into the cottage so he would be certain not to wake her.

He closed the door gently and went to the fire. It was dull orange now, and smoky. Nearly gone out. He had been away too long and it needed to be stoked. Without making a sound, he took the bellows from beside the hearth and pressed air into the embers until they glowed and the fire flared.

He placed another piece of wood on top of a few others then sank into the chair he had set at her bedside. He took up her hand. Regan's skin was still so cold. If only there was something more that he could do for her. Barry would have given her the moon if he could. This woman, after all, this scarlet woman of the glen, had given him back his life, a home, and a precious bit of security after he had buried his father.

No one understood Regan Maitland. But only *he* had tried.

It had been easier for everyone else to brand her a harlot for the mistakes she had made and be done with her. Barry watched her face now, its seams and imperfections in the place where once he had seen only flawless beauty. Eyes once vivid and shimmering now were more deeply set and rimmed with dark circles beneath.

But five years ago it had been different. Five years he had lived here in this cottage with her, beyond the glen. First as a lost and troubled boy whom no one else would have. A boy who had bitterly surrendered his only remaining parent to heaven. Then as her young lover—someone *she* had come to need as much as he needed her. The other men stopped coming for a while after that.

But now, once again, the pendulum had swung. And it was Barry who cared for her in that kind, nurturing and parental way with which she had once saved him from despair.

The romance had faded away a year ago. But the friendship had remained. The only thing of real permanence in either of their lives.

An indelible tie.

Gazing down at her now, Barry could still remember thinking how it was when he first saw her. He could still see her as beautiful. Nearly as beautiful as Colleen Gordon, that lovelier-than-heather lass at MacLaren's Bend who now lived alone with her father.

Barry didn't see Colleen much anymore, now that her stepmother and sister were gone from town. Now that Colleen was alone with that bitter old wretch, Malcolm Gordon, who had chased away a second family and made that poor remaining girl his entire life. That was a year ago now next month that Barry had caught her frightened, crying little sister, Mairi, up on the ridge behind town. When he had offered her a ride to the train depot in Regan's old car.

And it seemed to Barry, when he did see Colleen, that the light that once had shimmered so brightly in those pale green eyes of hers had already gone out. She had left school shortly after that and made Malcolm Gordon the center of her life. It was a sin, he thought, for someone so young with such beauty and promise to surrender her future as she had.

Barry turned his thoughts back to Regan, who lay so still before him, her chest rising and falling with the gentle rhythm of her breathing, her red-gold curls splayed out across the pillow. There was still reassurance for him there.

"Will ye leave me one day, do ye suppose?" she had asked him only last night, before the fever had taken hold. Her eyes were wide then and pleading against an answer she could not bear to hear.

"I don't plan to be goin' anywhere soon," Barry smiled back at her, brushing the hair from her face. Wanting to give her what she wanted. What she needed. And yet knowing that on both counts now it was impossible.

Regan knew that she was losing him. They both did. He wondered now, looking down at her, whether she knew in her heart that she had never really had him. Not in the way that mattered for eternity between a man and a woman.

When he thought of that—the sensation that squeezed a lad's heart in two and blinded him forever—the only girl he had ever seen clearly was the strangely proud little Mairi Gordon. A child, really. And not an attractive lass at all. But one with a fiery soul. She was someone he knew without doubt would one day surprise everyone by becoming great.

Neither Mairi nor her sister had ever judged him. Always waved, smiled. They treated him even from a distance as if he were like anyone else, not the cottage mate of the town whore.

Barry knew well what people in town thought of him. The way he lived his life. Out here with a fallen woman. A divorced woman who had been reduced to taking money for her body to pay her debts. A harlot. It was what they called her. *That Maitland harlot.* The way that sounded now, even in the safety of his own mind, made him cringe. That wasn't Regan. Brash or low. She certainly was not dangerous to anyone.

All she had ever been was a vulnerable woman who had lost the man she had loved. A man on whom she had hung the hopes and dreams of a lifetime. A husband who had taken her life savings to start over with a newer, younger girl.

Regan had slept for almost eighteen hours when she finally opened her eyes again the next morning. A weak smile instantly turned up the corners of her full mouth at the sight of him, slumped over in the chair beside her. "I did no' think ye'd be here," she said, her voice waking him.

Barry squeezed her hand for a moment, then lifted a cup of water from the bedside table to her lips. "I'm here," he said in a voice filled with reassurance. "Don't ye go worryin' about the rest."

She drank all that he gave her, then laid her head

back against the white pillows piled behind her. "You're too good to me, Barry Buchanan."

"Only so good as ye've always been to me." He touched her forehead where a thin patina of perspiration lingered. "I think your fever's broken."

"I'm sorry about this, ye know."

"No regrets. Remember?"

A smile moved across her face, then disappeared. It was what they had told one another from the start. That if their two unlikely souls could be there for one another, if they could be stronger as two than as one, then they must try. But there must be no regrets for the criticism that would surely come from the town.

Barry could hear the wind moving through the trees outside. "Could ye bear a bit of soup, do ye think?"

"That sounds nice."

"I've made black bean. 'Twill bring the color back to your cheeks fast enough."

"Only turnin' back the hands of time could do that now, love."

Love. It was what she called him. Once, when the world had seemed a dark and forbidding place, that word on Regan Maitland's lips had filled him with warmth and reassurance. Now, he felt imprisoned by it. By his long commitment to a woman old enough to have been his mother.

But he must not tell her that. Not let her see.

She deserved the world for her goodness. And he was the only one left on this earth, it seemed, to give it to her.

❖   ❖   ❖

He'd sold two large pots today on the roadside going into Killin.

Two couples from Surrey on holiday together had been thrilled for the souvenirs, and even paid what he'd asked without haggling. Barry smiled all the way up the hill, the same hill where he had once found Mairi Gordon, and then down again into the heavily wooded area that lay beyond the glen, where the sunlight came through the tall trees in a delicate mosaic pattern.

There was enough money for food for a month. And if they were careful, perhaps he could even buy Regan that white cable-knit sweater with the tiny pearl buttons she had seen in the storefront over in Fort William. Regan deserved nice things, he thought. And she'd had so few of them in her life.

He was weaving his way among the trees, the pines and beeches back up over the ridge, to that clearing where Regan's cottage lay.

Suddenly, he stopped. There was someone there. He moved behind a tree, catching a glimpse, then settling in to watch her. Colleen Gordon, with her hair long and flowing down her back, like copper-colored velvet, bent over in a dress of pale ivory and sea green, picking wild flowers. As he stood behind the solid trunk of an old beech, he could see that she was alone.

She drew up a wild dandelion and added it to a collection of long-stemmed flowers that lay like a sleeping baby in the crook of her arm. A breeze came up, whipping her hair and her skirt. And he was struck by how sad she looked, and how lost. The world was not the bright place of promise for her that it once had been.

Barry knew Colleen wasn't allowed to come this

far alone. She was defying her father, a man who entirely possessed her, and he found himself wondering if she might not need a friend—as he once had so desperately needed one. He smoothed back the hair from his face as he lingered behind a tree, watching her for a moment longer.

She stepped nearer and he looked squarely into her face. Flawless. A mix of cream and apricots in color, with a smattering of Scottish freckles, and great green eyes, yet all of it full of a complicated life already lived up at MacLaren's Bend.

"Hallo, Barry," she said. Her voice was lower than one might expect, out here where only he and the wind and the trees could hear.

"Colleen." He nodded.

They were awkward with one another after that. There was their history, life in the same small Scottish town, and yet adulthood was a different matter. He knew she knew now about Regan. About the life he had lived since leaving school. He watched her, still not judging him, still able to smile kindly at him.

"I have no' seen ye around much lately," Barry heard himself say.

"No. I'm kept fair busy these days at home."

In the echo of that, he could have clubbed himself. The words had escaped his mouth almost without his knowing. *Of course she has no' been around, you eejit! She's tenderhearted enough to have made herself a pawn of Malcolm Gordon's bitter loneliness!*

"Oh, right," Barry said, feeling sheepish and a little stupid around her. She had always seemed to him a bit above it all. Not haughty. Just naturally set apart from the other girls in Killin.

"I saw your sister once in this very spot," he said.

In the intense silence, Barry looked out, remembering. Hearing the wind. Seeing the great trees rustle. His mind made him see once again the sheer panic in Mairi Gordon's eyes that day. The belief there that she might actually have killed her own father. And yet he had seen something more, hadn't he? A kind of spirit behind the panic that said, if she had done it, if she had killed him, then he had deserved it.

A shame she didn't actually manage to do the deed properly, a small voice inside him said. But Barry did not listen to that. The sour old codger meant too much to the daughter who had been left behind.

For a moment, his mind caught and eddied again, like a stone in a shallow brook, on the image of Mairi Gordon, that awkward, slightly stout child with the chestnut hair and wide mahogany eyes, a child who had kindled only violence and anger in a man too tied to the past. And Barry hated him for that too—for wounding a bright and bold lass that would leave a scar on her soul, he knew, forever.

"Do ye hear much from her now?"

He found he really did want to know that.

Colleen's face changed quickly. She looked older, suddenly. Sad. "I'm afraid I do no' hear from her at all."

That surprised him, and he did not say anything else for what felt like an eternity, not wanting to offend her.

"I'm sorry."

"Thanks."

It was difficult to believe that no matter how badly things had ended for Malcolm and Vivienne Gordon, they had not managed to be civil. At least for the sake of their daughters—two girls who had been so inseparable.

But hope hung most heavily on Mairi. Barry had watched her, the way she had grown from a chubby, awkward toddler to an unsure adolescent, one who rarely smiled. Before she had left the glen, he'd seen the way circumstances at MacLaren's Bend had shaped her into a serious girl. And if inscrutable, dark eyes and determination were a fair indication, she would one day take the world by storm. And it surprised him when he found himself wishing he could have seen that.

"Oh, please, tell it again, Ron," Marielle pleaded as the three of them pealed with laughter. They sat in the shimmering sunset of the place de l'Opéra as the sun dipped beneath the gray, jutting Paris skyline.

They had been sitting at an outside table at the Café de la Paix for over an hour. Vivienne and her daughter had been enraptured by the tales of Ron Jaeger's exploits in his years as an investigative reporter. Tales of searches through Afghanistan. Beirut. And Tibet. Uncovering a smuggling ring coming into France from Bengal.

But this was a story of a different sort.

The image of Ron, biting back gulps of laughter, as the duke of Cumberland conducted a very proper speech on the dignity of royalty in the twentieth century, nose in the air and fly quite noticeably unfastened, had sent Marielle into a fit of giggles. The far more reserved Vivienne had even laughed in spite of herself.

"Now, now. A story is only so good as the telling, dear one," he said kindly, his bright eyes twinkling as an irrepressible little smirk crossed his face. "Anyway, now you know the way it turns out."

Marielle sipped Orangina from a straw in the bottle. Her mother, dressed gracefully in oyster-colored silk, fingered a small, elegant *kir*. He was a good man, Ron Jaeger, and Marielle was happy that her mother had found him. They had taken her nearly everywhere with them these past months, drawing her into their romance as if she were a part of it. And Marielle found that she liked being included. It felt warm and comforting to be around a man who did not look every day as if he might beat her senseless.

She thought of Malcolm then, and the little-girl longing welled up inside her. Just like always. A longing to please a father who was not to be pleased. A towering tree of resentment who despised her for not having been born to his beloved first wife.

Such is your life now. You must get on with it. It was what she tried so in vain to tell herself when the thoughts of the tiny Scottish village swelled to bursting in her mind, making her not Marielle, but Mairi again. *If only I had been a bit smarter. A bit prettier. A bit more like Colleen.*

She glanced out over the place de l'Opéra and the other Parisians all huddled at their tiny tables with *café au lait* or *un verre de vin*. And she watched the world go by as her mother and Ron began to move a little nearer to one another and to speak in the hushed whispers of two lovers. Marielle saw it from the corner of her eye as he took up her hand and kissed it. It was sweet to see them, and still a little foreign, their tenderness with one another. Her parents had never held hands. Never whispered like that.

"Our life in Scotland is gone, *chérie*," her mother always said when she asked to send a letter. "It is best to let it be."

"Best for who, Maman?" she always asked then— in French, because her mother now insisted. "Best for Colleen? . . . Best for me?"

It was spring again in the city of lights. Dazzling. Vital. Nearly a year to the day of being a part of this place, and yet it was still not home.

And *she* was still not really Marielle Girard.

Marielle stood in line at the *poste* after school, holding the letter in both hands. She knew she was going against her mother's wishes. But she must do this. Must try. Last night she had dreamed of home again. She had heard Colleen laughing. The sound had been so rich, so real. She had woven a path among the tall pines on the old dirt road, following the sound. And then suddenly up ahead, there she was. Just like always.

Come, Mairi! Faster! Come on!

Colleen was wearing that lovely white eyelet dress with the ruffle at the hem, which her father had bought her for Christmas when she was twelve. The same year he had gotten Mairi a blue bathrobe. It was also the same year that Mairi had first seen him hit her mother. *I thought you'd outgrown that dress long ago. Thrown it away*, Mairi had thought in the dream. But then the sunlight caught it and the colors shimmered.

The line inched forward, drawing her back to the moment.

Marielle squeezed her eyes. She was nearly fifteen now, they had a new life here in Paris, and yet still everything inside of her was telling her not to let go of the past. *I am not you, Maman. I am me. I am Mairi, Mairi Gordon, no matter what you will call me. And a part of me will always be there in Scotland—with Colleen. . . .*

"*Qu'est-ce-que vous voulez, mademoiselle?*" The gaunt-faced man glared down and asked her in French. The foul smell of the Gitanes that had stained his teeth was heavy and sour on his breath.

Marielle looked at the crisp white envelope she had taken from her mother's desk. It was addressed to *Miss Colleen Gordon. MacLaren's Bend. Killin, Scotland.* Threads of Mairi Gordon, the girl she used to be, wound themselves through her heart each time she thought of that place, a world away from Paris. Each time she closed her eyes tightly and smelled the mist off Loch Tay again. The trees. The heather. The brilliance of the colors. The absolute stillness of the night air, dazzling with silver stars. She was surprised at the keenness of the ache even now.

"How much to post this, monsieur?" She handed him the letter.

The man glanced at the address. The expression on his face was impassive. "Twenty *centimes,* mademoiselle."

Marielle felt something swell inside her, as if by hearing that she had taken the first step back to Killin. She understood how she was betraying her mother in this. But there was no choice. Marielle was driven in this above all else.

And, after all, she had promised.

The postal worker took the coins she had laid on the counter without looking back at her, then tossed the letter beneath the counter. Marielle turned away and walked back out onto the boulevard de Grenelle. The cool air hit her face, and she smiled.

Come back one day? . . . Colleen's words echoed in her mind through the steadily deepening shadow of time darkening like a coppery veil around the memories.

She reached up and clutched the Celtic cross at her neck. Colleen's cross. That was still vivid, concrete, something to hang onto. Once again she felt that swell of fierce determination, devotion to the one person in her life who had made her feel special. "I will," she murmured, walking quickly back into the crowd of people. "We promised on the stone."

The postal clerk, a cynical, middle-aged man named Jean-Luc, picked up the telephone receiver once he had served the last customer in the small postal annex. He glanced at the clerk sitting beside him as he dialed the number from the slip of paper that had sat crumpled in his breast pocket for several weeks. Then he smiled. The man knew what unexpected money would mean to his wife.

"She has come, Madame Girard," he said blandly once the beautiful neighborhood woman picked up the receiver on the other end. "*Oui*, I have her letter here. To Scotland, *oui*. Now, madame, I don't like being indelicate, but I must remind you that even with this phone call I am breaking the law. Putting myself at tremendous risk by tampering with the mail."

He smiled at the response on the other end. "That would seem like a fair inducement. *Merci beaucoup.* You have my home address? *Oui. Exactement.* Mail it there. And I shall take care of your daughter's letter. *Oui,* madame. Any time."

CHAPTER FOUR

Calum McInnes frowned as he starred down at the violet-sprigged Hammersley plate just set before him by the new butler, and neatly laid out with scrambled eggs, lightly buttered toast points, two graceful slivers of melon, and weak tea. He rolled his eyes, when all he really wanted was a good strong cup of coffee and maybe some kippers and toast from Poachers over on Ruthvan Lane. But then this wasn't about him. This was about Celina McInnes, his mother, and what *she* wanted. Like always.

She had dragged herself up from the mediocrity and obscurity of "that dreadful village," she always liked so dramatically to say, and no son of hers was going to backslide into a place like Killin permanently. No matter how intent he seemed on screwing up his life.

At the other end of the long, polished Hepplewhite table, Celina McInnes sat erect, dressed at eight o'clock in the morning, as if she were holding court. Crisp and tailored in a beige suit, the signature strand of pearls at her throat, she had short, neat hair, a lovely golden-brown nest of curls with little silver wings at her temples. Those she kept for the drama, she said.

Celina took a delicate sip of tea from the china cup, settled it back in the saucer and then glanced at the front page of *The Scotsman,* folded by the butler beside her plate as neatly as the linen napkin.

There were only the two of them home now that his father had filed for divorce, and Calum hated all of this pretense just for breakfast. He pushed the eggs around with one of his mother's gleaming Cartier forks and, waiting for her to begin, glanced at his reflection in the heavy baroque mirror behind her.

Calum McInnes had always been too handsome for his own good. Broad-shouldered, with thick, dark hair and deep, penetrating eyes, his looks had paved the way through a life that was all but arranged for him. His smile alone had seen him out of more scrapes and into more beds than he could even recall. To Calum, life, with the prescribed nature of how it all worked, already seemed tiresome. The only real joy he got anymore was in shaking it up a bit. In taking the alternate path anywhere he could.

A moment later, like clockwork, Celina glanced up from her newspaper. "What's the matter, darling, don't you like the eggs?"

"They're fine."

"Because it'll only take a moment for Margaret to cook you some fresh ones—*Margaret!*"

"Mother, they're fine, really. I'm just no' very hungry. I was up studyin' early this mornin' and I grabbed a biscuit and coffee already."

"So are you going to tell me what happened last night or not?"

"What?"

"Did you ask her?"

Calum took a sip of hot tea with milk, feeling once again like a caged lion. Wishing he could be far from here. Maybe back in that little village his mother so despised. With his Aunt Catriona and Uncle Jimmy. Helping out at their bake shop, as he'd done for so many summers. He had been sent there by his father to get him out of Glasgow quickly whenever he had been caught fighting or in some other situation that had embarrassed his mother.

"Did I ask who what?"

"Oh, really, Calum." Her neatly painted lips broadened into a pursed smile. "This is your mother to whom you are speaking. Now then. Did you ask Alana to marry you last night or not?"

Calum shifted in his seat. "No, I didn't ask her, Mother." *Here it comes. Batten down the hatches. Tighten up the mizzenmast. The first squall of the morning. One, two, three, four—*

"You didn't ask her?" Celina's thin, overly cultured Scottish lilt, long ago freed of its working-class Highland burr, echoed through the dining hall. "I thought we had it all planned, you'd ask her to marry you at the Morgans' ball."

"No, Mother, *you* had it all planned."

Actually, he did understand her surprise. Calum and Alana McEwan had gone about together since their earliest school days. He'd given her a ruby promise ring. And last spring she had finally given him her virginity.

Now that he was nearing the end of law school with the promise of a prosperous future ahead, marriage seemed the next logical step to everyone concerned.

Or so it seemed to everyone but Calum.

No matter what he did, how he tried to ignore it, Calum had realized, with an almost aching clarity, that something was missing in his relationship with Alana. That indefinable spark of something extra—the "something" he always felt when he looked at that beautifully aloof country girl, Colleen Gordon, every time he went back to Killin. And he hated himself a little for realizing it. Partially when he saw his mother looking at him now with such wide, hopeful eyes. But most especially when he realized that Colleen was not romantically interested in him.

"Calum Edward, for heaven's sake! I've asked you a question!"

"What?"

"What stopped you last night? You had the ring and everything."

A Cartier two-carat solitaire his mother had chosen for him sat in the little red box up on his dresser. *Let me choose it for you, son. I know the sort of thing a young girl like Alana would treasure. It'll be best that way. After all, she's going to be wearing it for the rest of her life . . . and the rest of yours.*

"I'm no' sure I'm ready for something so monumental as marriage."

"Not sure? What on earth do you mean, not sure? It was all planned. You and Alana have loved one another since you were children!"

And you have loved the connection of a McInnes to a McEwan for nearly as long.

Poor Mother, he thought. *So invested in ridding yourself of your own humble past. Of washing away the ordinary life you and your sister Catriona lived in*

the country. Always wanting more for me so that the
warm light of success can shine down on you as well.

"I *thought* this was what you both wanted."

"So did I." He shifted in his chair, a Stuart-period
tall oak chair with family crests embroidered in
needlepoint on the backs and stools, as the stiff, silver-
haired butler filled his china teacup.

"Did something else happen that I should know
about?" It was certainly not the first time she had
needed to see him out of an awkward situation.

"The point is, Mother," he equivocated, "marriage
is a big step."

"First the problems at university, and now this as
well?"

"I just need a bit more time," he lied.

Her thin face began to fold in on itself as she
frowned. He watched her stiffen, knowing how angry
she was. "I don't understand you, Calum. I have everything so meticulously arranged for you. You have simply to walk with a firm gait along the path your father
and I have laid for you, and you will have an incredible
life. Yet you seem absolutely determined to sabotage it
all!"

"So this isn't entirely about Alana, I take it."

"You know quite well that she is not the only key
avenue to your success that you are closing off with
those stunts of yours!"

Calum new what his mother meant, and for a
moment he was silenced by it.

It wasn't that he didn't ultimately want the things
she wanted. Celina just worried too much. Tried to
plan too much. And some things simply weren't meant
to be laid out so neatly as she believed.

It would all work out. He would get his marks up at university in plenty of time to find a good post with a law firm. He would be a wildly successful lawyer, in spite of how things looked at the moment. And he would even get his famous temper under control. What he would *not* do was marry the wrong girl to fulfill his mother's grand plan.

"And speaking of university—"

He arched a brow. "Were we?"

"Calum, if you don't get your marks up this term, I'm telling you, you are not going to be fit to counsel a derelict down at the Barras!"

He pushed a crumb off the tablecloth. "You worry too much."

"*You* make me worry."

His eventual success would silence her. Success was the key to a life of his own design. His own grand house in the city. A cottage in the country. Money. Power. Freedom. But Calum's design did not include being bound by the demands of another woman before he had entirely shorn himself of this one. Nor did it include doing things the way Celina McInnes, for all of her good intentions, had determined he should. He was not a conformist. Nor had he ever been.

Calum would find success, and a wife, that was assured.

But both he would do, his own way.

Marielle forced herself to ignore the nervous feeling in the pit of her stomach as she held the classified section of *Le Monde* in both hands to keep the newspaper from trembling. She stood outside the quaint little bistro with the red awning that was tucked on a charming alleyway called rue Amelie. The owner had run an advertisement for help, and Marielle now willed herself to find the courage to open the front door and go inside.

Yes, she was young. But the ad had been there in the same paper for nearly a month, so she was hoping that the owner of the little restaurant around the corner from their apartment would be easier to persuade to hire her. After all, she was nearly fifteen now. Not exactly old enough, by French law. But, like Colleen, she looked older than her age. And that, she hoped, was advantage enough.

Money was power in the world, Maman always said. And if she had money of her own, and when the time was right, she could get back to Killin for a visit, Vivienne's blessing or not. After all, Maman was so tied up with Ron these days that one day soon an occasion was bound to present itself.

And there must be a reason she had not heard from Colleen. Of course she knew in her heart, among those possible reasons, there could really only be one: If it was Malcolm forbidding Colleen to write back to her, then Marielle would face him directly. Their da certainly had no power to hurt her now.

Marielle finally drew back the door of the restaurant, with a deep intake of breath to steady herself. But still as she moved forward, her heart bumped up into her throat. A skinny man with dark, clipped hair and a pencil-thin mustache, dressed in black and white, moved toward her quickly, shoe heels clicking across the floor.

"We are not open now. Go away. Go away," he called out to her, shooing her as if she were some sort of insect.

Marielle drew in a second deep breath, knowing it was now or never. She needed money if she was going to see Colleen. And since her mother would be no help at all, she must somehow earn the money herself.

When she did not back away, the man eyed her sharply, his gaze narrowing. She knew that her cheeks were flushed with nervousness. But Marielle ignored that. There was too much riding on her convincing this man that he needed her.

"Qu'est-que vous voulez, mademoiselle?" he demanded, his voice clotted with irritation when she did not move.

"I wish to discuss the position here, monsieur."

He arched a brow. "The position?"

"The one you are advertising."

"You?"

Her lips curved up slightly in a tentative smile. "Me."

"But you are little more than a child!"

"I may be young, monsieur, but I work hard. You'll see."

"Not here, you won't. There are laws about that sort of thing in Paris! I could not hire you if I wanted to. Which I most certainly do *not.*"

"How can you know that until you have given me a moment?"

"You waste my time," he hissed at her, flicked his wrist. "Now go on. Get out of here!"

With her cheeks burning, and tears pressing at the backs of her eyes, Marielle nevertheless lifted her chin stubbornly and stared deeply at the man, willing herself to think of them as equals. Willing herself not to be undone by his rejection.

"Look, monsieur," mimicking her mother's hauteur so believably that she surprised herself. "I need a job and you have not been successful at finding someone to work. Let me help you, for free, for one week. If by then I have not convinced you that it is worthwhile to pay me, then I will go away quietly."

"What is your name?"

Scotland flashed through her mind just then, memories of another place, another name. But she pressed it back. That was never going to get any easier. And she was growing up, facing a harsh reality. "Marielle," she firmly said. "Marielle Girard."

There was a silence descending between them that became awkward. The man with the greasy hair and pocked skin was looking at her curiously, crossing the chasm of *politesse* that she had been taught to maintain with any stranger.

"All right," he said at last, his sour face mellowing slightly. "You may wash the dishes here. You will be in the back where no one will see. One week. *Seulement.* Six until midnight. We shall see the sort of constitution you possess with grease and half-eaten food." Then his face changed again as he studied her. "Tell me. Haven't you a mother and father who care where a young thing like you is in the dark of night?"

Marielle felt her spine stiffen at the question, and the way he had asked it. *Think of the money,* she told herself. *Think of the independence.* "That will not be a problem."

"*Bon.*"

"Shall I return tomorrow evening then, Monsieur Moulet?"

His smile was curious, grim in its bony upturn. "We shall begin then. Oh. And call me Pierre. That will be much more conducive."

Marielle had been too excited to ask what he meant before she walked alone back out onto the street. An autumn wind had begun to blow and the air was cold. Golden leaves flew over rooftops from the boulevard beyond and settled languorously onto the pavement around her. The sky was bright and cloudless. It was a beautiful, crisp Paris day. Almost . . . almost a Scottish country kind of day. But she saw little of it for the elation she felt.

She had done it. Marielle had found a job. All on her own. And she had done it in a city where it should have been impossible. She felt like flying. Or dancing. Pride swelled inside her heart like a bright red balloon.

Colleen would have been proud of her ingenuity. Especially in the face of that awful man who smelled like pastis and looked like death. But it didn't matter. *He* didn't matter.

She hugged herself around the waist and giggled. Once she had money of her own she would have independence. Two weeks before her fifteenth birthday, things were definitely looking up.

It would not be difficult to escape the apartment in the evenings. Not on these long, warm summer evenings. Marielle's absence could pass virtually unnoticed, since things with her mother and Ron Jaeger had gotten so intense. Vivienne dutifully ate an early supper with her daughter after work, then oversaw home-work. Later, she went to meet Ron for several hours, returning home only after her daughter had gone to bed.

In anticipation of the new order of things, Marielle stuffed a quilt and two pillows under her blankets and positioned her favorite stuffed brown bear beside the mound. Then, after studying it from the door and making a few minor adjustments, she switched off the lights, went down the narrow corridor, and checked herself in the hall mirror.

She had tied her hair back in a ribbon and dressed casually in jeans and a gray T-shirt. Certainly no *haute couture* would be needed in a tiny kitchen with a sink full of grimy dishes, she silently mused.

And still, jokes or not, her heart sank a little at the thought of what lay waiting for her. But it was a means to an end, she reminded herself yet again. That was what Monsieur Renard, the science teacher, said of homework. A means to an end. In this case, it was also a way to take some control. To get what she wanted: to see Colleen.

There were no customers yet as she opened the front door of La Petite Auberge and strode in white sneakers past the two neat rows of small tables covered in long white cloths and spotted with unlit candles covered over with glass globes. Beyond a red fabric partition, however, she could hear the clanging of pots and the clattering of dishes. The restaurant was warm and airless.

Marielle drew in a breath to still her heart. There would be no turning back now.

A moment later, Pierre Moulet, that spindly,

emaciated man, emerged and came forward with the
same bland expression on his face with which she had
left him yesterday. He stood before her in a black
tuxedo, white shirt, and black tie. All of it had a worn,
tired appearance, not unlike the man. "Ah, yes. So
then you are here."

"Where is your waiter, this evening? Your chef?"
she asked carefully.

His crow black hair shimmered in the evening
light. "The chef is ill, Marielle. Tonight, I shall attend
to everything myself."

Something strange rippled up the length of her
spine. She could feel it; something impending. Like an
oncoming storm. She glanced back. Still no customers
had arrived.

"Until I am ready for something more from you,
however," Pierre Moulet said. "You may occupy yourself with that."

Her gaze followed his hand past the open crimson
curtain and fixed on the old sink piled high with
crusted stock pots, saucepans, and china smeared with
dried gravy and stuck with bits of food. Her stomach
lurched at the sight. She had never seen such a pile of
filth. "The product of *le déjeuner*," he said, almost
proudly, as he watched her appraisingly.

What on earth are you doing? a voice inside her
desperately asked. Stubbornly, she ignored it. Marielle
did not intend to give Moulet the satisfaction of seeing
her hesitation. Nor would she honor the part of herself
that had so little faith. No. She had come this far. Now
she must make this a success. She took a soiled apron
from him that once, long ago, had been white and tied
it around her waist. Then she faced the vast well

before her as though it were an opponent to be vanquished.

An hour later, as a cloud of steam rose around her from the faucet, and she was awash in perspiration, she wondered what the proud Vivienne Girard, who had escaped the bourgeois life of a Scottish country town, would have thought of her only daughter now. But she wiped a hand across her glistening brow and forced herself to scrape another plate instead of answering the question. *I must do this,* she told herself again.

Lost in her absolute determination, she did not hear the footsteps behind her. Suddenly, Marielle felt two hands clamp onto her shoulders. A body, clearly a man's, pressing up behind her. Touching her neck with nicotine-stained fingertips. Pressing his mouth into her hair. Her stomach lurched when she realized it was Pierre.

Marielle pivoted back around, arching away from him over the sink of soapy water. "What do you think you are doing?"

"Surveying my new acquisition, *bien sur,*" he answered her haughtily.

"But the customers—"

"Foolish girl," he chuckled, in a thin, tactless way. "This is Monday. Did you not bother to read the sign posted outside? We are closed on Monday evenings."

Blood rushed into Marielle's head and her heart at the same time, making her whole body pound like a drum, flushing her pale cheeks crimson and hot, making it impossible to think. His eyes were small, startlingly black, sunken, like a bird's. She was breathing too quickly with his nearness, panicking, she could feel it.

He was so close she could smell him. Nicotine and Pernod. Foul breath. She tried to pull away, but he was stronger. And she was still young. Vulnerable. Alone. With one hand he held her tightly against the sink. With the other, he began to stroke her, to cup a hand over one of her small breasts. And he was kissing her throat. Marielle felt as if a part of her was dying inside.

Then, very suddenly, anger took hold of her, rising up from within her in a powerful way, so that she was able to summon all her strength and tear herself from his grasp. Pierre Moulet stood before her, shock brightening his miserably sour face.

Finally, with a wry arch of his brow, he said, "You wished to be tested. So I was testing you."

When she exhaled, it escaped in a dizzying rush. "I wanted a job, monsieur," Marielle snapped in her haughtiest voice. "Honestly and openly."

"There was nothing honest and open about our arrangement. You are under age. I went against the law. You knew that from the start. There is a price to be paid for the risk I took on your behalf."

"I needed money. You needed help."

"Ah, *ma petite mademoiselle*," he laughed wickedly. "Such is the way of the world. Only, one like you must be bold enough to play its games well."

"I despise games."

"Then consider it a gift, giving the tools of success to a plain *petite fille* who, alas, shall never get by in this world on her looks."

Marielle's wide eyes shimmered with tears. "You will be sorry you did this."

"I cannot imagine how."

"No," she quivered. And her voice shook. "I'm certain that is true. But I promise you, one day—"

"Ah, threats. And they are so charming when they come from one so young and naive," A dry laugh rattled up from his throat. Then his face darkened again. Swiftly. Frighteningly. "Now. Get out of my restaurant before I call the police and have you arrested for soliciting. And with my impeccable reputation, you can bet they'll believe me."

Shivering with cold, and dripping from a sudden rain shower, Marielle walked in a daze through the poorly lit tangle of cobblestone alleyways behind the avenue Bosquet. A half-starved alley cat came out from under the eaves and brushed up against her leg. But she kept her pace. Needing to walk. To move. To let the rain wash away how horribly dirty she felt.

She swallowed hard, the awful images from moments ago, still so fresh and raw, tumbling over and over inside her head, their harsh edges wounding her. It felt like a hammer. Scotland, the beauty and simplicity there, seemed very far away.

Marielle gulped back tears, failure weighing like a stone around her heart.

He had never meant to give her a chance. He had wanted only to seduce a child. Vile bastard! And yet who could she tell? Certainly not Maman. And she had made no real friends here in Paris, pushing away everyone who tried to get too close. *I won't be staying*, she had repeatedly told herself. *As soon as I find a way back, I'll be going.* But her world with Colleen seemed distant. Time was changing the images. The memories.

And the hopes. Tonight had irrevocably altered her, taken away the last few fragments of the trusting little girl left inside her. But from the remains, a new Marielle had emerged. Stronger. Wiser. But, yes, scarred.

Like her father, Pierre Moulet had taken advantage of her trust. He too had been violent. She despised that from the deepest part of her soul. And from that same place a promise came: No man like that would ever win her heart, tie her down, or betray her. As Malcolm Gordon had done to her mother. As Pierre Moulet had now done to her.

But Monsieur Moulet would pay a price.

And no man would ever get close enough to her to do it again.

Calum McInnes sat alone at the well-worn, rich wooden bar of the dark and suitably gritty Heraghty's Pub on Glasgow's south side. Dressed in a blue tartan shirt, denim jeans, and dark boots, he was hunched over a pint of Guinness, lost in his own thoughts, enveloped in a crescendo of laughter and noise and a thick ring of blue cigarette smoke.

He liked it here. It was so different from any place that his mother would have approved, one of only two pubs actually left in Glasgow without a ladies' toilet. Vulgar, she would have called it, actually sending ladies next door to the facilities there. But Calum liked that. Pushing the edge of propriety. He liked the mantle of upper-class renegade.

"Hey, McInnes!" a big, broad lad with a fleshy, freckled smile exclaimed as he slipped onto the empty stool next to Calum, smelling of tobacco and unwashed flesh. "Where ye been keepin' yourself?"

Another boy, lanky and unkempt, sank onto the stool on the other side of him. "Loan me a few quid, heh, Calum?"

A dour expression set itself onto Calum's square and ruggedly handsome face. These were not mates. They were trouble. And at the moment, Calum felt he had plenty of trouble all on his own.

"I'm fresh out of loans today, Johnny," he said, without looking at the boy who asked him the same thing nearly every time they met.

"Still spendin' it all to get a tickle out of the McEwan lass, are ye then?" the first boy cackled raucously. It was a coarse, grating sound that made Calum grimace.

"Now, he's doin' more than a wee bit of ticklin' for the kind of money a lass like that requires."

"Is she worth it, McInnes? I've heard around that she's *fair* worth it."

Calum felt the hair on the back of his neck spring up as if an electric current had just shot through him. "You're over the line, Robert Fraser," he said deeply, looking away for the first time from his pint and settling his eyes on the stout boy with the fat lips, ruddy cheeks, and small, cold eyes.

"Oh. That's right. I forgot. Ye're part of the hoi polloi from the west end who likes to do a bit of slummin' from time to time, aren't ye now? But when it comes to the lasses, ye fancy only the best. No harm, I suppose in gettin' prime cut. If ye can."

The fire inside Calum, the burn that had settled low and hard in his gut years ago, flared wildly just then.

It was his defense for having been the taunted "rich lad" from Green Square that had first hardened him.

Powered by history now, Calum reached up swiftly and, without warning, let his temper reign, slamming the big boy's face roughly against the bar. His broad, sloping back was pinned down by Calum's other powerfully coiled hand. He wasn't going to marry Alana McEwan. But neither was he going to sit here on this pub stool and listen to these louts bandy her about as if she were common.

"'Tisn't how ye talk about a lady."

"Who says she's a lady?" the boy grunted bitterly.

"You will if ye value your health, lad!"

Before there was any answer, Calum pulled him back by the scruff of the neck and struck him hard in the face with a closed fist. Blood streamed from a slash over his left eyebrow.

"I'm givin' up! Stop, McInnes, before ye turn my face to a bloody pulp! I've a date tonight!"

"Apologize."

"Aye. I do."

"Say it. Say, I'm sorry I defamed Alana McEwan."

"Aw, to the devil with ye, is what I say!"

Again Calum pummeled the boy hard with his fist. A group of drinkers gathered around and were shouting as the bartender was commanding him to take it outside. But Calum heard none of it. The heat, the violence, possessed him. As his dark eyes glinted in the light from the bulbs overhead, his roughly handsome face changed, became crazed.

But the anger came from deep inside of him. Not from this fleshy no-account who meant nothing to him. "Say it, Robert Fraser! Say it!"

A hand on the scruff of his neck pulling him up and away from the bar, a loud chanting around him, drew Calum finally from the blackness of his thoughts and back to the moment. A police officer had him and was drawing Calum's hands up and behind his back. Another had done the same with his fleshy opponent.

His mother would be furious, Calum thought a little wildly as he was shoved very unceremoniously out the front door of Heraghty's Pub. Good, he decided with a strange satisfaction. If she was going to harp at him, at least this time it would be for something really wicked.

She had not come to the station house to pay his bail. Celina McInnes had sent her butler for that objectionable business. Calum knew his mother would not have dared to be seen in a place like that in Glasgow. It was bad enough to have had to send a member of her household staff, a person who could gossip.

She had not come to the door but was waiting for him, still as a stone statue, on the red leather sofa in the library. This was not her favorite room, with all of her lovely Victorian antiques, hand-blocked wallpaper, and thick, chintz-covered furniture. This had been father's room. Mahogany, crimson leather, and brass.

The curtains had been drawn as though she were harboring a criminal, but little bands of light bled through, throwing shadows over the oak side tables and heavy, gold-framed portraits of ancient Scots. He could see, by the tight expression on her face, the pinched mouth, that she was still enormously angry with him. Calum came into a room that was grand by any standard—his mother's favorite room in which to fire servants or to handle business.

It had never been used in dealings with family. Until now.

When he leaned over, as always, to kiss her cheek, Celina did not move. Her rich, ebony eyes, the same as his, were focused straight ahead, rooted on a television that was on but with no sound.

"Have you been hurt?" she said in a tone that said the answer, under the circumstances, was unimportant.

"I'm fine," he said blandly.

"Good. Then I trust you will be ready to accompany me out of Glasgow in the morning?"

With that she had surprised him. His mouth dropped. "I can't go anywhere, Mother. You know perfectly well that I am in the middle of exams."

"Yes. That will set you back a term now, won't it? But then perhaps you should have thought of that before you landed yourself in jail like a common street hoodlum."

There it was. Finally. A hint of the anger that lay just beneath the surface. He could deal with that far better than the stony silence she liked so much to inflict as punishment. "I am sorry about that, Mother. But truly, the lad did ask for it."

"I was told by the officers that you were the only one to throw a punch."

"'Tis true enough. But—"

"Then there's no excuse for how you insist on embarrassing me with those low friends of yours. I do not deserve it. And I will not tolerate it. Now. We will go away for a few weeks until my friends forget they have any sort of gossip to torture me about."

Cool and imperious, that was Celina McInnes. He loved his mother. He just did not like her very much. Calum rolled his eyes. "Couldn't you just send me to Aunt Cat's, in the country, until it all dies down a bit?"

"You've something in you bound to defy convention, don't you, Calum McInnes?"

"What I have in me, Mother, is to sample a bit of life before I'm forced to settle down with a house of my own and a wife."

"From what I have seen, you have *sampled* quite enough already." Celina McInnes drew in an exasperated breath. "And that is precisely why I am taking you to Paris!"

It was a week later, a Saturday afternoon, and the autumn sky was very dark. As Vivienne took a bath, Marielle sat on the sofa with Ron, playing gin rummy. She loved this special time alone with him, when her mother attended to her "toilette," as she liked to say in that overly dignified way she had that Ron Jaeger found strangely endearing. But it didn't matter what they did, because then she had their wonderful man all to herself.

But as it had been for a week, her mind was a million miles away. No matter what she was doing, Marielle was able to think of little else but that horrible Pierre Moulet and how, by toying with her, he had ruined her chance of getting back to Colleen.

"Don't you feel like beating me at gin rummy this

evening, sweetheart?" Ron asked with a smile. "You always win, you know."

It took a moment for that to register with her. When it did, she looked up from her cards. "I'm sorry. Was it my turn?"

"For some time now, actually," he chuckled. "Ah, but I see there is something else weighing on your mind. Can I help?"

"I need money."

Ron lay down his cards. "May I ask what for?"

"For independence, mostly."

He looked at her appraisingly for a moment, his gentle kindness washing over like a soothing balm. Healing the harshness of Pierre Moulet. Of her own father's memory. "You have secrets with Maman, right?" she asked.

"I suppose."

It took her a moment, a heartbeat, to ask the next question. "And could the two of us . . . do you think we could have our secrets too?"

"You trust me, do you?"

"I'd like to."

"It wasn't easy with your father, was it, my sweet girl?" he asked her with a gentle kind of crooning that required no response. And none was given. He drew her against his chest and stroked her hair. Marielle felt safe. Peaceful. As if Ron Jaeger could protect her from everything, all of the difficult things the world had in store for her. And always would, because she was not beautiful nor rich.

"How I wish I had had a daughter like you, dear Marielle," he said with a sincerity in his voice that made her want to weep. "You may tell me anything you like and your secret will be safe with me."

Marielle believed him. Because she wanted so very much for it to be true. "It is sort of a question rather than a secret."

"All right."

"So, how does someone my age earn their own money?"

His eyes, the color of a summer sky, settled on her and he lay down his cards. "You're not in some sort of trouble."

"No. Nothing like that." She could see after a moment that her sincerity had assured him. The small lines between his brows softened. His frown gently faded.

"What, then?"

"I want to see Colleen."

Surprise registered on his face, lighting it. "Your half sister?"

"My *only* sister."

"And have you written to one another?"

"Colleen hasn't answered my letter yet. But she will. I *know* she will. We made a special promise."

He pulled her to himself again in response. "Oh, my dear, dear girl. I had no idea you were anything but glad to be away from Scotland. Your mother has always told me—"

"My mother told you only what she wanted you to know. Just as she does me."

"You have asked her to buy you a ticket to see Colleen?"

"Only a million times since we left."

"And?"

"And each time the same answer. 'That part of our life is over, Marielle.' She refuses to pay for me even to telephone her." Marielle repeated the words that had become like a mantra to her. "She took me from my sister. Took my name. Forced me to speak another language. . . . She made me into something here that was her own creation. But inside I'm still the same girl. I still miss the hills, the glen. . . . I still miss Colleen." She looked up with tear-brightened eyes. "So, if I could just earn some money somehow I wouldn't have to trouble Maman about it, make her angry for the way I cannot help feeling. I would be able to find my way back all on my own." She drew in a breath, as those secret thoughts of hers tumbled over her words. "Perhaps one weekend that you might take Maman on holiday, I could just slip away?"

He brought her hands together, then lifted them. Kissed the knuckles. Marielle raised her face. It was a unique face, still possessed of the purity of youth. "You won't tell Maman what I have in mind, will you? She would be so angry with me for wanting—"

"Shh," he told her gently. "Your secret is safe with me."

In the silence, they heard her mother singing a French tune beyond the closed bathroom door. The rain beat against the window glass. There was a fire crackling in the hearth beside them, making the room almost too warm.

"So do you think you could loan me the money for a train ticket until I find a way to earn some of my own?"

"I'm sorry, sweetheart." Ron still held her hands. "Your mother would be furious with me for going against her wishes. And I really would feel as if I were betraying her."

Marielle's hopeful smile fell. She loved that about him, that he was a man of his convictions. But right now the gloom welled inside of her again. Ron Jaeger had been her last chance. She looked away into the fire. Watched the flames lick the hearth. Listened to the damp wood snap. "That is why I wanted my own money. I despise needing to depend on anyone for things."

"Have you learned to type?"

She looked at him again. "I'm taking a course in typing just now."

"How good are you?"

Her smile was twisted. "I'm not awful, if that's what you mean."

"Well, as it happens, I have a little secret of my own I can let you in on."

"Oh, tell me."

"For the past few months, I've been working on a book. Stories of my travels around the world, that sort of thing. I haven't told your mother about it yet because I wanted to wait until it's finished before I show it to her."

Marielle's eyes flashed with excitement. "A book! Oh, Ron. How exciting."

"The point is, I've been jotting it all down in notebooks for ages and it's in pretty awful shape. I need to have it typed out."

"I could do it!"

"Now, it wouldn't be easy, I have to warn you. They tell me my penmanship is atrocious. So I'd certainly have to pay the going rate for anyone brave enough to take the job on. And that wouldn't be a loan. It would be wrong if I *didn't* pay you. What you did with the money you earned would really be none of my business."

"I can do it, Ron! Oh, honestly, I can. Just give me a chance."

Ron Jaeger stroked her hair back away from her face, his own alight and happy. His eyes were shining again. "You know, you really are the most extraordinary girl, Marielle. Full of so much spirit and determination. On the cusp of something quite grand, I would say. You actually remind me a bit of myself. When I was much younger, of course."

There was something between them. A bond. Special. Pure. Something usually between a parent and child. Yet they had that. Marielle trusted him. And she loved him. As she had wanted so much to love her own father. But that did not matter anymore. Because now, like a great gift, there was Ron. And he would be there always. He would not go away. And unlike her father, and the rest of the world, it seemed, he would not disappoint her.

CHAPTER FIVE

Her sixteenth birthday. Marielle was certain her mother had forgotten. Vivienne had said nothing at all about it in the preceding days. There were no packages hidden in closets. No cards tucked into drawers. She knew, because she had looked.

She walked slowly up the curved stone stairs inside the apartment building. Her mind was so wrapped in thought that at first, she did not see Madame Brisson, the building's concierge, kneeling on the second-floor landing ahead of her, scooping something into a dustpan.

"Bonsoir, madame," she said, now with a perfectly toned accent. The old woman, thick and gray-haired, with a broad face and a wide, flattened nose, did not hear her as she muttered something vague about rats, and so little anyone could do about them in winter. "May I help you with something, madame?" Marielle asked politely.

When the old woman looked up, Marielle could see the dead gray rat she had scooped into the dustpan, its long pink tail still hanging over onto the white marble floor.

She pressed a finger to her lips. "Oh, dear."

"The place is infested with them, I'm afraid. But all of Paris is when it turns cold. Our chic city's dirty little secret," she grumbled in a French that was deep and throaty. "I've set as many traps as I dare, even put out cheese with arsenic, but still a few escape and die like this, and these highbrow tenants blame me for the objectionable sight when it happens. What is a poor concierge to do?"

"May I take that down to the trash bin for you, madame?" Marielle asked sweetly. "It is so cold and dark down there this time of night."

The old woman smiled at her for what Marielle thought was the first time. "You're a good girl, Marielle Girard," she said, as if it were a pronouncement. Then she patted Marielle on the shoulder with a gnarled hand and, with the other, handed her the dustpan. "I shall have to tell your mother of your kindness."

"*Merci,* madame. But Father Guissolt reminded us all at Sunday mass that God should be the only judge of our deeds."

The old woman squinted, looking more closely at Marielle through pointed glass frames that were old and years out of date. It seemed for a moment as if she were trying to study her. "Extraordinary," she grumbled finally. "Just when an old woman loses faith in the youth of today . . ." she muttered, shaking her head and walking back down the stairs. *"C'est incroyable, ça. . . . Simplement incroyable."*

"Not really so unbelievable," Marielle said to herself as she went on alone, not down to the refuse cans, but up to the fourth floor to her apartment, thinking that she must remember to return the dustpan later.

❖   ❖   ❖

Marielle moped alone for over an hour after her
mother was due to be home from work. It wasn't like
her to be late. Especially today. Since they had been in
Paris, they had always spent her birthday together, and
with Ron. Usually out at the Bois de Bologne or in a
cinema on the Champs Elysees.

In so many ways, they had become a family.
Doing family things. Sharing all of their special times
and holidays together. She wondered privately now
so often why her mother and Ron had never married. And she wondered if Vivienne and her father
were actually divorced. What Marielle had discovered very early on was that any discussion of
Scotland, or her mother's private affairs, were strictly
forbidden.

Finally, at half past seven, she heard her mother's
key in the lock. She picked up a copy of *Paris Match*,
the magazine her mother had left lying on the antique
flea-market coffee table, and began to scan the colored
pages.

"*Salut!*" she said, managing a tight smile through
her disappointment as her mother and Ron came into
the apartment together.

"Well," Vivienne said reservedly. "Is that the best
you can do?"

Marielle put down the magazine and stood.
"Sorry, Maman. How was your day?"

"Very hectic, as a matter of fact. Ron and I had to
go all the way over to the rue de Rivoli after work this
evening, and the traffic both ways was positively horrendous."

She looked at each of their faces. "Why were you way over there?"

"Well. It is your birthday, as you know. And this is a special year."

"Sixteen," Ron said with that beaming, gallant smile of his.

"So Ron and I would like to honor that."

"We are taking *you* to dinner, sweetheart. Somewhere special. To celebrate."

They hadn't forgotten at all. They were treating her like an adult. No theme parks or children's movies anymore. She was to be treated now as a young woman. An equal. "Thank you," she beamed. "But you still haven't told me why you were all the way over on the other side of town."

Ron and Vivienne exchanged a glance. He was smiling. "Well, your mother and I have a little something for you that we thought you might like to wear this evening with your dress."

Ron drew a small blue velvet box from the pocket in his favorite herringbone blazer and handed it to Marielle. "Happy birthday, sweetheart," he said as he took off his jacket, then laid it on the back of the wing chair.

Marielle sank onto the sofa clutching the small, beautiful box, wrapped with gold braid, as if that alone were the gift. Her mouth had gone very dry. She was trembling. She could not recall ever feeling happier in her life, or more surprised. Ron sat down facing her in the wing chair, and Vivienne sank onto the arm beside him, resting her hand casually on his shoulder. Marielle glimpsed the movement. Subtle. Yet so full of meaning. When she watched her mother's eyes, eyes that had seemed flat for so long, now they smiled with what she knew was love for this wonderful man.

"Well, open it, *chérie,*" Vivienne instructed her daughter with a little nod.

Marielle felt as if her heart might actually burst. No gift could be better than what she felt right now. Still, she unwound the gold braid and carefully drew back the lid of the box. Inside on another piece of velvet lay a thin gold chain and, hanging from it, a diamond chip mounted inside the bud of a rose. As she gasped, her lips parted.

"It's so beautiful."

Marielle felt tears sting the backs of her eyes as she gently touched the most lovely thing she had ever seen. "A fitting gift for a beautiful young woman, I'd say," Ron said in that smooth, kind-hearted voice of his.

"So now you can take off that old thing you always wear and replace it."

Marielle felt the blood in her body go absolutely cold as her mother's words settled with a great thud on top of her heart, snatching away the joy from the moment before.

She took the Celtic cross between two fingers and pulled it away from her neck far enough to look down at it. There was no single possession in all the world that meant more to her. *Come back one day, will ye? . . .*

Colleen's face swam in her mind; her request was still so vivid.

She felt a sob gathering in her throat. "I can't do that, Maman."

"Now don't be ridiculous, Marielle. That pendant from Ron and me cost a small fortune. We had it made especially for you. You're a young woman now. It is time to cast away childish things."

"Please don't ask that of me. It is the only thing in all the world I have of hers."

Vivienne sank into the chair arm and rolled her eyes. "Oh, for heaven's sake."

Ron was silent for a beat or two as he surveyed the scene. The deep throb of loss in her child's voice had muddied the air. "Can you not keep them both, sweetheart?" he asked Marielle carefully through the tension. "I don't see any reason—"

"Of course you don't!" Vivienne snapped at him, her eyes suddenly blazing as she sprang from the chair and pivoted to face him. "And this really does not concern you."

Marielle watched the jolt of recognition physically course through him as he realized why her mother had been so insistent that it be a pendant, and nothing else. It was still about Scotland, and her obsession with cutting all ties there—not purely the generous surprise for an only daughter on the doorstep of womanhood— that had motivated her stand.

Ron shot to his feet with that reality between them, his honey blond brows merging into a deeply troubled frown. "Vivienne. You really can be the most cruel woman when you want to be."

"You have no idea what I went through."

"I don't suppose I do. And that is only because you insist on keeping me so at arm's length about it all."

"And what you do not know you cannot judge."

"I can when it comes to Marielle."

"She's *my* daughter, Ron. Mine alone. Never forget that."

Vivienne was a lioness suddenly. Her brown eyes flashed full of fire. Marielle sat stunned as she watched them quarrel for the first time. Old memories, dark images of angry times, reared up quite suddenly and startled her. It felt like Scotland again. Her parents. Their hostility. And the horrible uncertainty of her childhood years.

A furious light flashed in Ron's eyes. "And that's the way you mean to keep it, isn't it, Vivienne?"

"I cannot change what is."

"Maybe not where I am concerned. But you *can* give your daughter her sister back. That would have been a birthday gift with *real* meaning for her."

The charged silence was deafening. Marielle saw the high, angry color cross her mother's flawless ivory face. "*That* is a subject not open for discussion."

With that, Vivienne pivoted and stormed into the small open kitchen at the other end of the room. Ron lunged to his feet and followed her with the same quick, angry steps.

Then he was standing behind her, both of their backs to Marielle but even with their tones low the apartment was small and she could still hear what they were saying.

"I will not send her back into harm's way! I won't do it, Ron! Believe me, whatever fantasy Marielle has of what might occur if she did return would be overshadowed tenfold by Malcolm's bitterness and cruelty! Remember, I lived it with that man for over fourteen years!"

"Shouldn't you let her be the judge of that now, though, when she wants so badly to see Colleen?"

"Marielle is a child! She doesn't know what she wants!"

Ron's tone was incredulous. "Then let them at least write to one another, for Lord's sake, until she does!"

"Malcolm doesn't want her back in his life or Colleen's! He made that abundantly clear in his last letter. Don't you see? You can read it for yourself if you don't believe me. 'Your girl is nothing to me, Vivienne,' he said. And those were his exact words. *Your girl*. Nothing but a mistake. Just like our marriage."

A wave of anguish washed over Marielle, and she felt for a moment as if she were drowning in it. All of that hatred was too much like the past. Not this beautiful new future full of healing that they were all building together.

Now, here, on her sixteenth birthday, she had heard what she had suspected for so long: that her own father cared nothing for her. That in his eyes she was a mistake. A sour taste worked its way into Marielle's throat and she felt as if she might be sick. It was one thing to suspect it; it was something altogether different to hear it as fact. Marielle watched, stupefied, as Ron turned around and saw her still sitting on the couch, looking up with those wide brown eyes. Seeing everything. Hearing everything.

Ron's tone was sharp, angry, as he turned back to Vivienne, lifted his arms and crossed them over his chest. "Then let me send a letter to Colleen for her. I can be an intermediary. There will be protection for her in that."

"No."

"You know, Vivienne, I am beginning to think this is more about you and Malcolm than it is about

Marielle. Your own wounded pride at a failed marriage. Maybe you should think about *that* instead of hiding behind an innocent child!"

Her mother's hand was a fearsome weapon as she reached up and struck Ron hard across the cheek. For a moment, he only looked at her, the anger sizzling between them. Marielle gulped back tears as she helplessly watched the bitter scene play out.

"Get out," Vivienne said flatly as tears shined in her eyes.

"All right. If that's what you want."

Marielle sprung from the sofa. "No!"

Everything in that moment next seemed to fade into slow motion, her heart thumping in her ear like a loud, low drumbeat, as it had been on that final afternoon between her mother and father. She remembered all of that now with a disturbing clarity. The anger. The accusations. And the bitter, bitter final words. With the same feeling of complete helplessness as a bystander, Marielle then watched Ron Jaeger pick up his herringbone jacket and walk very purposefully out of their apartment.

Marielle dashed into the kitchen, her eyes wild, her head spinning.

"Well, thank you so much, Maman, for making this a birthday I will *never* forget!" Marielle cried bitterly at Vivienne who had turned back toward the kitchen sink and had begun, unbelievably to her daughter, to wash dishes as though nothing at all out of the ordinary had just occurred. Marielle shook her head in disgust and then ran out the door after Ron, hoping against hope that there was something she could do to make him come back.

❖   ❖   ❖

He was at the end of the block by the time she caught up with him. Ron was walking in moon shadows very quickly toward the métro stop, just past the corner of avenue la Motte-Picquet. Marielle broke into a run to catch up with him. The air was chilled and the night sky was clear. People were strolling, walking dogs, all around her. But Marielle saw none of them. She knew only that she must follow Ron. That he must not get away, or something told her he might never come back.

He walked quickly down into the métro station, and Marielle followed him. She was still running, her heart pounding in her ears. He drew a small, yellow *billet* from his pocket and pressed it into the slit beside the metal turnstile, then went through. Marielle reached into her pocket a few steps behind him and felt a jolt of panic when she realized she had no ticket and no money. She hadn't thought to bring a jacket or purse when she had dashed out of the apartment.

"Merde!" she growled, slamming a palm against the metal spoke of the turnstile. Then, in a move of desperation, she jumped up and leapt over the top and dashed on into the echo-filled tube, lined with movie posters of Simone Signoret and Alain Delon.

For a moment, her mind was not on Ron but on Malcolm. Memories bubbled up, images of what she had endured, the taunts, the indifference. Hoping for her father's love. Craving it. Always with a little girl's heart. Wounded. Desperate.

As desperate as she felt now.

"Wait! You can't go!" she called out, running as fast

as she could after him. "Don't leave. Ron, please. It's my birthday!"

He stopped cold where empty train tracks lay to his left and a wall of empty benches sat to his right. He turned around slowly. The underground hollow métro tunnel, covered in a mosaic of tiny white tiles, echoed her plea. One woman sitting alone on a bench looked up and watched them.

"Come back."

"I can't, sweetheart."

Marielle's heart was in her throat. "Ever?"

The question was so pointed, her tone so painfully vulnerable, that Ron went to her and swept Marielle in his arms. "I'll be back," he smiled. "Just not tonight."

After a moment's silence they walked together to a second bench and sat down.

He wrapped his arm around her again. And as they sat very still like that, she thought how snugly she fit with him like this. How wonderful it felt. The great sense of security. Under his arm, her head just beneath his chin. She tried to recall if there was ever a time when she had sat this way with her father. But there was nothing that came even close.

"I do dearly love your mother, you know," Ron said as if to reassure her as he took her hand and gave it a little squeeze. "But sometimes I do believe she is the most maddening creature on this earth."

They watched a train come into the station and the woman get on. For a moment, they were alone. "Can I ask you something, Ron?"

"Fire away."

"You fight like husbands and wives. So why haven't you married Maman by now?"

"Direct, as always," he smiled. But she could see by his face that he was still deeply troubled. "Honestly, sweetheart. She won't have me. I've asked her at least a dozen times to marry me and the truth is she says marriage isn't right for her anymore."

"Can't you make her change her mind?"

"I don't know." A few people filtered into the hollow station and sat on the benches around them. Others stood up near the tracks waiting for the next subway. "I *do* know that your father hurt her deeply, and changed her view of a lot of things."

"I wish *you* could be my father, Ron."

"That would be aces with me, sweetheart." His smile was radiant, the confidence in it warming her. "But it's not as important, I don't think anymore, as staying with my favorite two women in the world." He kissed the top of her head then paused for a moment. "I'm sorry the way tonight turned out. I really had such a different evening in mind for the three of us."

Marielle felt a weak smile touch the corners of her lips. "It doesn't matter, Ron. As long as you're not going away for good."

"You won't be able to get rid of me *that* easily."

He drew her to him again and, for a moment, Marielle felt as if she could just exist in this sensation, beneath his big, strong arms, drowning in the protective warmth of him. The earthy smell of musk and the old wool of his slightly shabby herringbone jacket, which she so loved.

"I tried, about Colleen," he said. "Sorry about that too."

Marielle played with a leather-covered button on his jacket. "It's not your fault," she told him.

And suddenly it didn't matter anyway. What she knew now, unequivocally, was that she did not want to be responsible for pushing this wonderful man out of their lives. Seeing Colleen again was *her* challenge. No one else's. Besides, when she had finished his project for him, typing his book, Ron would pay her. And she would finally have money of her own. Money to do with what she wished. And, as always, there was only one thing in the world that Marielle wished. Something she herself was going to have to make come true.

A man of his word, Ron did come back.

The next afternoon, as rain showered down around Paris and rattled the tall window in their tiny apartment, a bouquet of white roses arrived for Vivienne. There was a small card attached that had made her mother weep and which she tucked away quickly somewhere inside that mysterious, inaccessible room she called her boudoir. But it was almost another week before he was admitted back to the apartment. Before things seemed even close to normal again.

As Ron sat with his arm around Vivienne on the coffee-colored sofa with its smooth camel back, the next Saturday evening, Marielle watched them together and felt for the first time in days that she was actually breathing normally again. She watched the way Ron looked at her mother as she spoke, the pure adoration at her smile. And the light had come back to Vivienne's eyes too. This was how it was meant to be, she thought. Forever, she hoped. With all of her heart.

"Well, sweetheart," Ron said as Marielle sat in the

chair facing them with the small antique coffee table from the *marché aux puces* between. "It seems that your mother and I owe you a birthday dinner."

"Have you any idea where you would like to go, *chérie?*"

Marielle considered the question silently by biting her lower lip. But there was only one choice. "How about La Petite Auberge?" she said with a smile so innocent that there was no evidence of the iron will behind it. She was her mother's daughter in that. And it was every bit Vivienne's determined smile.

CHAPTER SIX

He had been in Paris for three weeks with his mother, and now Calum McInnes thought he might actually go mad. She had taken him to every museum and art gallery in the city. The Louvre. L'Orangerie. Even out to the Chateau de Versailles, which was actually painful to him, since a lifetime of private schooling still had not taught him to value that sort of excess.

When they walked into the small *auberge* where Celina McInnes had seen to reservations for dinner on their final evening, there was only one other table occupied.

A man and a strikingly attractive woman with chestnut-colored hair, sat together with an adolescent girl whose face he could not see, since it was hidden behind a large crimson menu. He hadn't seen anyone even close to his age for days. Part of the punishment, he knew.

Calum rolled his eyes at the music being piped inside the small restaurant with the crisp white table linen and the glittering candles on each table. Maurice Chevalier. It was all too French, he thought, longing for the comfortable familiarity of Scotland, a pint of Guinness, and a plate of salmon and chips.

Celina did not speak to her son as she waited for the waiter, a tall, gaunt man with crow black hair, to bring her a glass of champagne. So Calum watched the family at the table ahead of him. The woman seemed oddly familiar. As if he had seen her before. But of course that was not possible. In the silence, he tried to think of who in Scotland she might remind him of. No names came to mind as his mother was served her drink and they both ordered veal croquettes.

A few moments later, he centered in on the laughter at the next table. The man with an American accent was leaning forward, telling a story. The woman and the girl leaned forward with him. They were all enjoying themselves. It seemed like forever to Calum since he had really enjoyed much of anything.

Calum and Celina ate in relative silence, exchanging an occasional word about their meals, the ambiance, and what time the flight left the next morning. As they ate, the restaurant began to fill with other patrons. The one waiter, working alone it seemed, but for the small, gray-haired woman who waited at the door to show customers to their table, had become harried. His face glistened with perspiration as he dashed in and out of the kitchen with plates, bottles of wine, and trays full of food.

Still Calum focused on the next table. The joyous laughter. The clinking of glasses. The girl whose back was to him had the most extraordinary hair, he realized as the candlelight and shadows settled on it. Long to the middle of her back, it was the color of fresh chestnuts. From the occasional glimpse he caught of her face when she turned, he guessed her to be in her midteens. Plain but unique-looking, with smooth, perfect skin and wide dark eyes. Something familiar tugged at him. What was it? Calum wondered unsettlingly when he was hundreds of miles from anywhere he had ever been before.

"It was a lovely dinner, Ron," Marielle said sweetly as she folded her hands in her lap. "Thank you so much for bringing me here."

"Remember, sweetheart, the place was your suggestion. You should get the credit for that."

"Yes," said her mother. "How did you even know about it? We've never been here before."

"A girl at school," Marielle lied with an above-reproach smile lighting her eyes. "Her parents brought her here for her birthday a few weeks ago and she loved it."

As Ron and her mother exchanged a glance, and Ron whispered something to her, Marielle looked over at Pierre Moulet, who was working feverishly to tend all of the tables. The place was packed this particular evening, she thought bitterly.

Moulet had recognized her the moment they had come through the door, and Marielle had drawn great satisfaction from the complete panic on his face, the way all of the blood drained away as he had approached their table. He couldn't be entirely certain why she was here or what she planned to do, if anything. And Marielle had taken great delight in watching him wonder just that for the several hours that they had spent there.

Behind her, as Celina McInnes ordered a second coffee, Calum watched the young girl in the pale blue dress work her hand down along the side of her chair to a handbag that sat on the floor. Intently, yet without missing a beat of the story the man with them was telling, the girl worked to draw something out. As she did, she was attempting not to be noticed.

The way she did it so struck him that Calum became fixed on the girl's furtive movements. Finally, after several attempts, he watched her draw out a small, pale pink hand towel and place it in her lap. The bill had come and the man and woman who sat with her seemed taken up with that. As the man drew out his billfold and withdrew his francs, Calum was absolutely stunned to watch the girl open the towel and take out the carcass of a dead rat, then very calmly drop it onto the table behind the candle, the salt, and the pepper.

He wasn't certain why, but something told Calum that this was not merely some sort of adolescent prank. The girl he had watched all evening didn't seem the type. She was too intense. Too refined. Rather, he guessed this was to be some sort of payback. Most likely one that was deserved by someone here at La Petite Auberge.

Suddenly then, as they all stood to leave, the girl shrieked. The sound was loud and thin as she jumped, knocking her chair over backward. Calum put a hand over his mouth to hide his smile. This really was too delicious. *If she weren't so young, I'd even* . . . But then he remembered that Paris was his punishment. There would be no girls. The wild thought, along with the impossibility of it, snapped from his mind.

"What is it?" the man with her leaned across the table to ask with concern.

"My God! It's a dead rat on our table!" the girl

cried. "I never saw it! All through dinner! Oh, it is hor-
rible!" she covered her face with her hands. "Horrible!
And I actually ate here! I think I'm going to be sick! . . .
Oh, it is horrible!"

A crescendo of chatter rose up around them.
Suddenly other women were standing up, tossing down
their napkins, and even though he did not speak
French, it was quite clear that they were not going to be
spending another moment in so unsavory a restaurant
as this.

As she turned briskly to leave, and was doing it with
quite a dramatic flourish, Calum looked right at the
girl, smiled slyly and nodded. He wanted her to know
that someone had witnessed the bravura performance
and approved. It had certainly added something to his
otherwise bland Paris excursion. That brought a tentative smile to the girl's lips. Then their eyes met. Hers
were deeply brown and glittering. There was a faint
blush along the soft line of her cheekbones. Her smile
set her on the edge of being almost pretty. *I know her,*
he thought suddenly, with a jolt of certain recognition.
Yes, I do know her. But from where? . . . He had never
been to Paris. And, by the sound of her voice, what he
had heard for the better part of the evening, she certainly was not a Scot.

"Hey," Ron said to Marielle in a whisper as they left the
restaurant. Vivienne was a few steps ahead of them,
talking in a tone of incredulity to another woman about
the horror of what had been found right on their very
dinner table. "You had some great ideas with my book.
I like your changes."

"You do?"

"Yes," he smiled. "I really do."

"They were only suggestions, you know."

"I know. But I have used several of them already. Pretty surprising for an old salt like me to be getting journalistic advice from a—" He looked into her eyes, and saw the hope there. The innocence. And yet an iron core of determination. The combination affected him deeply, just as she had. "What I mean is, I think you've got some talent, sweetheart. With a little schooling and a few good breaks, I think you could make a first-rate reporter. If you wanted to."

"Do you really think so?"

He wrapped his arm around her and squeezed. "I think you could do just about anything you set your mind to. Like tonight, for example."

Marielle looked at him, her lips slightly parting. The reference had surprised her. He could see that.

"Someday you will have to tell me what horrid thing the people of La Petite Auberge did to merit such clever retribution."

"You saw me?"

"No," he chuckled with a wry arch of his brow. "You were smooth as a jewel thief." Then he paused. Suddenly, Ron Jaeger's eyes darkened as he looked down at her. "That man, the waiter. He didn't hurt you, did he?"

"My father was the only one ever to do that," Marielle said, covering a conviction that had begun to root in her deeply. "And I'll never let a man do that to me again."

"You know." He kissed the top of her head. "I do just believe you will keep to that promise."

"But I'm awfully glad I have you."

They stopped beneath a street lamp. The bright white light made his face shimmer. Marielle looked up at him as her mother bid the other woman a good evening and the two women promised to tell everyone they knew never to patronize such an unsanitary restaurant as La Petite Auberge.

"Believe me, my sweet girl," Ron sighed. "The feeling is mutual."

Barry came into the cottage in the middle of an evening thunderstorm. The sky was black, and his arms were loaded with bags of groceries dripping from an unexpected rain that was pelting Killin. It was a minute, as he drew off his rain slicker and high black galoshes, before he realized there was no fire blazing in the hearth. No familiar aroma of stew for supper. The starkness of the place shot through him. And then it left him for a moment unable to move. To think. Even to breathe.

Regan . . .

His eyes darted across the room to the old box bed, with its faded patchwork quilt they once had shared, though lately, Regan had slept alone in it again. His eyes followed a trail to her pillow where a white slip of paper sat propped. Heartache bound his chest tightly as he picked it up.

Dearest Barry,

I know it won't be easy for you, having lived with a wicked woman like me. Having me

*has cost you dearly. And for that I am sorry.
But I know you, Barry Buchanan, and you
will make your way in this world better than
anyone in this little town could guess. You've
a shining star to catch. And catch it you will.
Because your soul is so full of fire and your
heart is so full of your grand dreams.*

*You aren't to come after me. What we
had is over. My own dreams lay ahead of me
as well, with a man from Fort William I met
a few months ago. He's good to me and with
him I know I can make a fresh start. I need
that. I think we both do.*

*So, reach for your dreams, Barry. Because
they're waiting for you. Out there. Waiting for
you to reach out and snatch them.*

*A part of my heart always,
Regan*

His mind froze. And so did his heart. He didn't
love her. Not in the way he knew a man should love a
woman. And yet still the ache at her leaving was profound. Because for the second time in his life he was
once again entirely alone.

Regan had saved him. And now she had set him free.

He walked outside onto the porch, then he moved
down the steps into the rain, letting the water wash
over him, tipping his face up to the black night sky. To
the rivulets of water that beat down on him. Blinding
him. Beating at his skin. He was twenty-three years
old. And he felt ancient. As if he had already lived a
lifetime. And, in so many ways, he had.

Barry squeezed his eyes. And there it was again. An image. And the sensation. Like electricity, the way it coursed through him. A premonition. He'd had them since he was a small child. Always when something grand or meaningful was about to happen.

He had seen his mother's illness. Her death. He had seen Regan's face in his mind days before she had found him sitting among the moss-covered stones in that special place just beyond the glen. Bereft. Orphaned.

Now it was the face of another young woman that had snapped into his mind, taking it over. Lighting the darkness. She was like a painting. But with the greatest depth. Her hair was the color of chestnuts. Long and flowing. And her eyes were deep, so deep that the image of them in his mind took his breath away.

She stood somewhere—not here, but on a gray city street. Calling out. He could not make out the words. Only that there was a desperation about her. And then curiously, he also saw a large mossy stone, as a shadowy object behind her.

The strangely incompatible images surrounded him until he realized that the girl in his mind looked very like Mairi Gordon and that the object was the ancient and mystical Promise Stone. It had been a long time since he had seen Mairi or thought of her. Startled by the meaning behind her and that stone, Barry opened his eyes, walked down the few steps into the clearing, into the wet and cold. Hair fell from his forehead into his eyes. The rain pelted him. The wind was gusting. *Mairi*, he thought. How strange it was to think of her. Especially now.

CHAPTER SEVEN

Six weeks after her sixteenth birthday, Marielle was summoned by her mother to the offices of the *International Herald Tribune*. She had been told they would be going to lunch with Ron, but Marielle had the distinct impression it involved something rather more than that.

Marielle was filled with curiosity as she walked into the first-floor lobby in her best gray felt skirt and neat white blouse. Her hair was loose and neatly cropped at her shoulders, a new fashionable style. Around her neck she wore both a diamond pendant and a gold Celtic cross.

This past year, Marielle had lost the remainder of the chubby, awkward quality that had so defined her youth and which had prevented her from having the confidence Colleen had possessed as a child. But this ripening of her beauty, this transformation, was one of which she was totally unaware.

A man stood beside her waiting for the elevator. He was a big man with ink black hair and a thick, shaggy mustache. He was awkward with his large size, in the way he stood, the way he held himself. He said nothing, but she could feel his eyes on her, blue, gentle eyes. "Going up?" he finally said in a deep French baritone when the doors opened.

Marielle nodded with only a hint of a smile. They rode together in silence but she could feel him watching her. Was this what it was, she wondered, to be admired by a man? She had seen men look at her mother this way, but she had never experienced the same appreciation herself.

When the doors opened, he nodded to her and smiled. She moved out first into the reception area of the *Herald Tribune*. Seeing her coming, Vivienne stood up at her desk and came forward stonily. "We will go somewhere private, Marielle. We need to talk."

"*This* is your daughter, Vivienne?" the man said with a marked tone of surprise, recognizing the name.

"Daniel Benoit, may I present my daughter, Marielle Girard. Marielle, Daniel is our new feature editor here. He is also a good friend of Ron's."

Marielle felt herself instantly soften as she looked up at him for the first time. He was big and robust, with a barrel chest, a man who reminded her of her father. But his blue eyes were startlingly deep. They had a kindness that softened him. She smiled.

"My daughter fancies herself something of a budding journalist, Daniel," Vivienne explained with just a hint of sarcasm.

Marielle's heart slipped. How, she wondered, could her mother possibly have known that? Or have said it in the slightly mocking manner that she had now?

"Is that right," he said, smiling approvingly. His smile was as big and robust as he was.

"It certainly is." Ron seconded defensively as he stood in the doorway that separated the offices from the reception room. "And she'll be a damn good one too. *If* that is what she decides to do with her life."

"Speaking of my daughter's decision-making skills," Vivienne said in a disapproving tone to both Ron and her daughter, "will you both come with me?"

Marielle complied, but all the while she was aware of Daniel Benoit, whose eyes had never left her.

Marielle stood between her mother and Ron in the silence of Hervé Chabrol's glass-partitioned office in a corner of the busy newsroom. Her boss was out for the afternoon and this was one of the few private places available. Marielle's face was pale with disbelief beneath the harsh neon lights. Her mother's flawless cheeks were crimson with rage.

"You told her what I was doing for you?" Marielle asked breathlessly as the neatly typed manuscript lay on the desk between them.

"Ron told me nothing," Vivienne snapped. "I saw some of the pages in your typewriter in your room and I read them."

Marielle shot a stare at her defender. "Sorry, sweetheart," Ron said, shrugging.

"It makes me physically ill, the two of you working together behind my back."

Ron groaned as he took a step forward. "For God's sake, Vivienne. I've told you twice already, there was nothing clandestine about it. She was just helping me out with some typing, that's all."

"And, of course, you were going to pay her."

"Of course."

"Did I not have a right to know about an arrangement like that?"

"It really was no big deal."

Vivienne was angry. More angry than Marielle had seen her in a very long time as she shot a cold stare at her daughter. "And for what did you so desperately feel you needed to earn money that you could not tell me about, may I ask?"

Marielle tipped up her chin defiantly. Her own eyes blazed with conviction. "You know the answer to that, Maman."

The silence fell heavily between them. "Still, Marielle?"

"Always, Maman. You are not going to make me forget her no matter how much you wish it were so."

"A pity Colleen does not appear to be maintaining the same obsession."

The coldness of the shot went, as directed, straight to the heart. Marielle's face drained. "I'm sure there is a good reason she hasn't written to me. No. I *know* it."

"The reason, Marielle, difficult as that appears to be for you to accept, is that Colleen has gone on with her life. And, sooner or later, you must force yourself to do the same."

Her mother felt like a stranger now. An enemy and a stranger. There was no way she would ever understand. "I am *not* Marielle! My name is Mairi! Mairi Gordon!"

"The only name you need to remember is Marielle Girard."

"I hate you for doing this to me, Maman!"

"You had no right going behind my back with Ron! Oh, the very thought!"

"I have a right to my childhood!"

"Your father made it clear to me that you are not welcome in their world anymore."

She would not be undone by her mother's cruelty. "Even so, I have a *right* to my sister!"

"She has forgotten you—clearly, Marielle. You make a fool of yourself by struggling so frantically for a tie that no longer exists."

Marielle felt as if the world were off-center. As if she were sliding from it suddenly and there was nothing she could do to stop it. "It does exist," she said dryly. "I know what I saw in Colleen's eyes."

"Let go of it, *chérie*," Vivienne pleaded. "Just as Colleen has done."

"Never, Maman! Never!" She spun around and headed for the elevator, which had just opened behind them. "Not as long as Colleen and I are alive!"

CHAPTER EIGHT

Paris, 1996

"Just one more minute, Daniel!"

Marielle was not asking for the extension. It had been a declaration as she waved a hand in the air then buried herself back in the direction of her computer screen. She was an hour past her deadline as it was. But the story would be worth it. Daniel Benoit would be glad he had waited. Just like always. As her editor over these past ten years, he was proud of that. As her closest friend and confidant, he was proud of *her*. Even if she had steadfastly refused to take him into her bed, something he had wanted almost from the first. She valued him too much, she always said. An enduring friendship meant far more to her than the risks involved in love.

Certainly Marielle had dated through the years. Gone away for the weekend with someone a couple of times, he remembered. And he had, on occasion, seen flowers arrive at her desk. But Daniel had never known her to fall deeply or completely for anyone. Perhaps letting down her guard like that had always seemed too great a risk for the pretty, wounded bird who had become so dear to him.

Daniel looked at Marielle now from behind, reflecting on the well-proportioned frame into which she had grown so smoothly these last few years. The face that had angled and thinned into something classically pretty held eyes he did not have to see to know. Big and dark with long curled lashes, they were doe's eyes, deep with meaning. Such history and the pain of complex years were mirrored in them. So it had been for him since he had walked onto that elevator all those years ago now, and met the bright young daughter of the receptionist. And lost his heart to her.

"Dépêche-toi, hmm," Daniel urged her now, looking away from the past, and steadying himself by glancing around the vast wide newsroom. No one got special treatment here. No one except Marielle.

They went into his small glass-walled office together. Daniel closed the door and sat down. He was big in his chair, oversized. He called her article up on his own computer screen, taking a sip of cold coffee from a styrofoam cup as he read. The hand holding up the cup was thick and meaty, making the cup appear especially small.

The story was good. He knew that from the first paragraph. Marielle could have gone from this to being a superb newswoman. But something clearly held her back from real success in all areas of her life. And Daniel knew intimately, because he had loved her, and been kept at arm's length. The reality of that, her inability to care fully for anyone in return, was still something that hurt.

Daniel had known, when their working relationship had first intensified to real friendship, that what was between them was a kind of father-figure worship because he was Ron's close friend. Because Marielle could never have the man she most adored—Ron himself. And then there was that accident. A sudden tragedy that had sent Marielle ever further away from him—from anyone who wanted to care for her.

Marielle had, from that day on, built a great wall around herself, letting few past the veneer she had so neatly constructed. She focused intensely on work. Continued to live with Vivienne. Cultivated few friends beyond the walls of the *Herald*'s frenetic center—a perfect diversion from the rich life she should have had.

"This is good," Daniel said, glancing up and smiling. Marielle crossed her legs and smiled back. She didn't say anything.

After that, there was silence between them. Their eyes met.

"I'm glad you convinced me it was a story worth doing," he said.

Marielle tipped her head, smiled. "What are friends for?"

"There was a time when I hoped we'd become something more than that."

"But that was a long time ago."

"Not to me." He fingered the cup. His own blue eyes widened as he looked at her. "Do you suppose there is any chance—"

"Like I always say, why should we ruin a perfectly good friendship with something as fickle as love?"

He clicked off the computer screen and leaned

forward across the desk, clasping his hands. "If not me, *chère* Marielle, then at least there should be someone you let a little way into that tightly protected heart of yours."

Her lips twisted slightly, those dark eyes glittering at him. "I've no time for love with a taskmaster like you with whom I must contend every day."

"Ah, Marielle. Always so quick with a clever line to keep from a serious reply."

Marielle laughed. "That *was* a serious reply."

He watched her expression glaze over then, as it always did when he, or anyone else, got too close. "I'm happy with my life as it is, Daniel."

They both knew as she said it that her reply was not truthful. But a component of their long friendship was also complicity, an adherence to the distance Marielle sought to maintain. It was one of the reasons, he knew, that Daniel could still count himself her confidant. And it was a distinction he wanted very much to maintain.

After bidding Daniel good night and taking the métro away from the busy tangle of skyscrapers in Neuilly, Marielle rose out of the subway station back in the city center. She then went alone out onto the avenue Bosquet. The sun was a fiery orange ball in the Paris sky and the wind caught in her hair. It invigorated her. This was an autumn evening made for walking.

Along the way, she stopped at the Café Grenelle. Content with her own company, she sat alone at one of the outdoor tables and sipped a glass of Bordeaux, and ordered the *plat du jour* as she often did after work.

Beside her, a young couple sat locked in an embrace. A moment later she became aware of other couples, hand in hand, along the boulevard before her. Marielle was accustomed to dining alone, especially here where the waiters knew her and where they were attentive enough that she did not feel awkwardly alone. But somehow tonight was different. There was an uneasiness about sitting like this beside an empty chair.

It seemed to be a metaphor for her life. In the center of much, but always slightly set apart.

Marielle pushed away the comparisons and the reflections Daniel had stirred. Then she stubbornly opened a paperback pulled from her purse for just such an occasion. There was no point in rationalizing her nonexistent personal life again. Especially to herself. She knew precisely why things were as they were.

Work, Vivienne, and Balzac, an old, stray tabby she had befriended, they were the only things for which she felt any shred of real devotion. Perhaps one day she might find a way even to forgive Colleen for not having kept her promise, a reality that had devastated her when she acknowledged finally that her sister, the person she had sought so desperately to return to, must have forgotten her after all. Giving up the dream of being reunited had left an enormous scar.

Or perhaps she could let go of the bitterness she had for Ron, going on assignment as he had done and then dying, when she hadn't even had a chance to say good-bye.

The sudden thought of Ron made the wine bitter in her mouth. The boulevard before her was busy. Loud. The smell of diesel was everywhere.

Marielle's thoughts were thick and painful now, as they always were when the kindest man she had ever known came again to mind. Loss and betrayal had mixed inside her to form a bitter rue, something she had not yet gotten past.

Damn you, Ron, for disappointing me too when I actually started to believe you'd always be there for me! She had shouted it so many times, into her pillow—the tears staining her cheeks and her heart, that it almost didn't mean anything anymore.

That horrible day now was like a movie in her mind. Five years ago a letter had come to the apartment in New York, where they had all moved when Ron's assignment had changed. Ron was late coming home from Bangkok, and Vivienne had opened it excitedly at breakfast. He wanted them to meet him somewhere, she smiled knowingly. Perhaps London again for another family holiday. His letter would be filled with apologetic words for being late, for causing them concern. It was just another story that had taken him over, just like it always did. But that was who he was, Ron always explained. A newspaper man. The chase was a part of his soul.

Marielle stood over the table with a pot of coffee as her mother opened the letter and read it. Morning sun from outside on East Fifty-first Street streamed in through the kitchen window. Suddenly, her own joy at the arrival of the letter darkened like a stain as Vivienne began to shake and her thin frame began to fold in upon itself, and violent sobs bounded through the flower-filled apartment.

Roses. Lilacs. Irises. All wired from overseas. Everything Vivienne adored.

"He *can't* be dead!" Vivienne wailed, mascara running down her cheeks, pooling with the tears as they touched her lip and the collar of her dress. "He just sent these! Just yesterday! He just sent them!"

The letter feathered down onto the tiled kitchen floor as her mother lay like a rag doll, completely undone. Marielle glanced at the paper and saw that the writing was not Ron's. It was official. Typewritten. Impersonal. A notification.

"God, no!"

The words escaped her mouth before she pressed her hand over it, as if she didn't give a voice to the notion it could not possibly be true.

Dead. In the first heartbeat of that awful word, it had come to Marielle as something different. It was a kind of surreal distortion of things as she had watched her mother die a little death of her own, their dreams of a happy ending washing away like a chalk drawing on the sidewalk in the rain.

"Damn you, Ron Jaeger!" Locked alone in the bathroom and free to experience her own searing pain, Marielle cried out. "You were just like him after all, weren't you? We trusted you, Maman and I! We loved you! And you're gone in a puff of smoke now too!" It wasn't logical, she knew. It was pain making the rules in her heart.

Marielle had renewed her promise that day, as fearsome as all the other promises she had ever made, that no man would ever bring her that kind of hurt again. Because she would never, *could never* trust enough to love deeply ever again. The risk, and the pain, were simply too great.

Safety—that was what one should value in life.

Marielle had found herself the next morning, asleep on the cold white tile of the bathroom floor, wrapped up like a baby, in Ron Jaeger's favorite houndstooth jacket. And to this day she had no memory at all of how it had gotten there. The bathroom door was still locked, and there was no key.

Marielle had always taken it as a sign of apology from Ron, about his death, about having gone off and not given her a chance to say good-bye. And, in spite of her anger, the jacket became as dear to her as Colleen's cross. Pieces of a past she was not ready to relinquish.

A moment later, as the memory and the shock of pain began again to fade, Marielle took a sip of wine and watched the sun slowly set. What was that awful feeling in the pit of her stomach? Something totally unrelated to the memories. Things were so strangely off-center these days. There seemed a kind of discomfort in everything. She simply could not shake it. Though she was uncertain why, Marielle had begun to feel as if something unexpected was about to happen. It would have felt almost like a premonition if she believed in ghosts, or the kind of magic a place like Scotland once had stirred within her. But those were little girl thoughts. And Scotland was a wounded heart away.

"Maman?"

Marielle stood the next morning at the bedroom door as she spoke to her mother over the roar of the shower in her white tile bathroom beyond. She was not in the habit of borrowing things. They had never developed that sort of relationship. Their continuing to live together was not so much about some sort of developing sisterhood between mother and daughter as it was a function of economics.

"Mind if I borrow a camisole this morning? Mine is in the laundry, and I'm too late to construct a new outfit for work."

"*Vas-y,*" Vivienne replied loudly as the water continued to run.

Marielle took a step into her mother's inner sanctum, a room full of chintz and sweet perfume, then stopped, only just realizing she had no idea where to find her own mother's underthings. Their lives here were that separate. Since Ron's death, they saw one another even more infrequently, usually only by passing in the corridor on their way in or out of the apartment.

"Maman? Your camisole?"

When no further reply came from the bathroom, Marielle's gaze was drawn across the room to her mother's rosewood dressing table. Displayed there were several antique perfume atomizers and the only photograph still in the apartment of Ron Jaeger. Framed in sterling silver, he was standing, hands on his hips, at the foot of one of the pyramids in Egypt, happy, smiling that full-of-life smile.

Marielle moved slowly toward the image, her heart wrenching. The wound of his death was still so painful. She would never get over losing him.

Marielle sank onto the velvet-tufted stool, drawn by the square jaw and the smiling eyes. She touched his cheek. When the glass over his image reminded her that it was a face she could never see again, Marielle drew her hand away and sat back.

She inhaled a breath and looked down at the three drawers on each side. She pulled the one on the top left. Costume jewelry and a few bills. The drawer below it contained a thick collection of scarves and a bound group of letters half hidden beneath. Marielle pushed the drawer in when a postmark caught her eye. Scotland?

That seemed curious enough that she drew the drawer out again. There was no one in Scotland her mother could possibly have wanted to correspond with. She had been so firm about cutting all of her ties in a country she despised. Marielle turned back toward the closed bathroom door, feeling suddenly like an intruder, feeling her heart begin suddenly to accelerate.

"Maman? Your camisoles?" she tried again thinly. "Where do I look?"

She saw when she glanced down again that the letter was one of a collection of same-sized white envelopes all bound by a pale blue ribbon. Marielle drew them out and, as she did, it felt very like someone was holding her throat, making it difficult for her to breathe. She knew the handwriting instantly, the open looped style. And they were addressed not to Vivienne but to her. . . .

Colleen.

It felt to Marielle like that first drop on a roller coaster, swift and unexpected. She could not breathe. At the same moment, a metal tube of Chanel lipstick fell behind her and onto the tile floor. Marielle jumped. Vivienne stood in the doorway between the bathroom and bedroom, seeing what her daughter saw. Marielle's head jerked up, and she felt the horror of betrayal wrench her heart as she saw her mother face in the mirror's reflection.

"My God! How could you, Maman?"

"You had no right—"

"Colleen *did* answer my letters, after all?" Her voice was thin and pained. "You've been lying to me all of these years, lying when all along my sister had not forgotten—"

The silence that followed was taut, searingly painful with the betrayal of a daughter by her own mother. "I didn't want you to be hurt more than you already had been," Vivienne said weakly, studying her stunned daughter tentatively as she sank onto the edge of her bed, and looked back at Marielle through the mirror.

"Colleen never hurt me."

"She would have in time. Her allegiance was to Malcolm."

"She loved me too. You knew that."

"I did everything for your own good, Marielle."

"What you mean, Maman, is for *your* own good. So you wouldn't need to be reminded of your mistakes. You cut Scotland out of both of our lives so that you could pretend it never happened!"

"That's not true."

"You knew what keeping Colleen in my life meant to me." She ran a hand across her eyes. Her head was spinning. "How could you have done this to me, Maman? To your own daughter?"

"I loved you."

"You loved yourself far more, it seems!"

Vivienne shook her head. "It is a mother's instinct to protect her child. Perhaps one day you will know that kind of devotion."

"God keep me from devotion like *this!*" Marielle was clutching the letters, her hand was trembling. "And so all of these years Colleen remembers only that I wrote to her, that she replied and then, for no reason at all, she believes, I simply stopped? That I gave up on her?"

There was a silent pause, one heartbeat, then two. "That is not precisely all of it."

Marielle felt her heart begin to bleed. Was more betrayal by a mother actually possible to bear? Vivienne's voice was flat when she spoke again. She was forcing out the words. "Colleen never got your letters."

"What did you do, Maman? . . . Damn you, tell me everything!"

"Very well." They were looking at one another, tension simmering between them. Both of them had tears in their eyes. "I was acquainted with a clerk at the *poste* around the corner. I was certain that you would go there to post anything you might get a mind to send to Colleen. So I paid him to throw them away."

"I gave up writing to her because of that! I never wrote Colleen again after all those months waiting for a reply! And the reason she didn't reply was because she *couldn't!* You made me believe she didn't want me in her life any more when that wasn't true at all!" Marielle gripped her forehead as Vivienne continued to meet her incredulous stare head-on. "Och! You truly must despise me, Maman, to have done something so cruel!"

"I know you don't understand this just now, but it really was for the best."

"For the best?" she laughed bitterly.

"Yes. When Malcolm was alive he would have reminded you with every day and every letter of his indifference toward you! No child needs more of that from her own father than you'd already gotten from the bastard! Just look what it has done to your life as it is! You've never had a decent relationship with anyone!"

Silently, she stared at her mother's reflection, unable for a moment to speak. Only one portion of what she'd said now registered with Marielle. "Malcolm is dead?"

"News of it was in Colleen's final letter some years ago. She gave you few details, only that he would be buried in Fort William beside his first wife." Seeing her only child's pale, stunned reaction, the Pandora's box that had been opened, Vivienne sat silently with the bitter truth now out between them.

Malcolm: father and stranger. A man who had kindled nightmares and regrets within her for a lifetime. Suddenly now he was dead. And the barrier, like a great drawbridge, had quite swiftly and unexpectedly been lifted.

She was really nothing at all like him. Where Malcolm Gordon had been tall and stout, with a shock of fiery red hair and a full red beard, sea green eyes imbedded in small, deeply set sockets, his second daughter was strictly French. Marielle was the image of her mother: slim and petite now that the last vestiges of childhood were gone, she had chestnut hair chicly cropped at the shoulder, highlighting wide mahogany eyes. Vivienne Girard was a beauty still. And her daughter, quite unexpectedly to her, had become one.

But, as Vivienne maintained, he had left his mark on her life, nonetheless.

When the implications of everything finally settled, it felt as if there were a hot stone in the back of her throat. Marielle sprang from the small tufted stool facing the dressing table, with all of its creams and colognes, still clutching the letters.

Come back to me one day, will ye? . . .

The sweet voice in her head, Colleen's voice, was almost as clear as it had been on that afternoon the words were spoken. And Marielle had been trying to do just that, get back to Killin, for so long.

"Where are you going?" Vivienne's tone held sudden panic.

"You know the answer to that."

"Don't, Marielle."

"I'm *going* to Scotland."

Vivienne stood now, entirely defeated by her daughter's iron-willed insistence. "She's gotten on with her life, *chérie*."

That same memory filtered back. Colleen, with her long copper hair and mossy green tear-filled eyes standing barefoot on the steps of MacLaren's Bend, too afraid to wave as they left, still, her eyes had held the message. *Do no' forget me.* . . . Colleen had mouthed silently, that gray, rainy afternoon, as Marielle had looked out the rear window of the idling car. Both of them had focused their eyes intently on one another.

"Never," Marielle had mouthed in return.

Vivienne was pacing around the bedroom now, a high-ceilinged room, with its flowery *toile de Jouy* canopy over the bed and the antique wardrobe, her bare feet tapping on the parquet floor. The rhythmic sound forced Marielle back into the present.

Vivienne shook her head again. "I should have burned the wretched things."

"Then why didn't you?"

Their eyes met again. "Ron made me promise that I wouldn't."

It was almost too much. She couldn't believe that on top of all the rest, even Ron . . . dear, special Ron . . . "He knew about these?"

"I made him swear that he wouldn't tell you, and he loved me. Apparently he kept his word. But he always said that life was long and that one day you—" Her thoughts fell away. There seemed little acceptable explanation for any of this with which Marielle could ever find peace.

"Je suis désolée, chérie," Vivienne tried weakly to add, placing a hand softly on Marielle's shoulder. There was a flash of anguish in her eyes.

"I swear to you that I never meant to hurt you with any of this. In the beginning, I only wanted so desperately to protect you. And as you grew up, and the letters kept coming, well of course by then I had reached the point of no return on the subject. And I told Ron that. You would have despised me for what I'd already done."

Marielle stopped and pivoted back. Her eyes were wide as they flickered in the dim lamplight. "No more than I do at this moment," she said bitterly.

Alone at a small table around the corner at the *bar-tabac*, Marielle still felt horribly off-balance. A small, strong *express* had done nothing to blot out the vision of Vivienne's slim, elegant face with its pleading expression still so achingly bright in her mind. What was left to her now was to steady herself enough to buy a plane ticket back and try to make up what she could of the past.

For the third time, she opened the letter on top of the neat stack. The date was December 18, 1988. It was so excruciatingly full of little details that Marielle had almost memorized it already.

The images of Killin played in her mind. The quaint main street. An old bridge, with cool, white water raging beneath. And at the edge of town a vast, green glen full of heather and broom. A mist-covered place full of memories and mystery, and a sky above that looked as blue as fresh cornflowers. Wild flowers as far as the eye could see.

> *Dear Mairi—It is almost Christmas. Only a week away. But it is five years and six months since you left. That seems somehow more important than Father Christmas and a lot of gifts. I still have heard nothing. But I believed you. You will find a way back one day. You have that sort of fire in your soul, not to let life outdo you. And after all, you promised.*

"Yes, I did," Marielle whispered, pressing a single finger along the faded blue ink, a place where her sister's hand had once, long ago, touched the very same page.

CHAPTER NINE

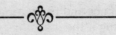

Surely no one would remember her. It had been too long. She had left as a girl and was returning as a woman. But she remembered everything. Marielle drew in a deep breath, tipped her head back, and stood still on the road into Killin, a place she had known in her soul she would one day see again.

The road she stood on was old, bordered by rhododendron bushes, their leaves shimmering in the faint breeze. There was a rushing stream nearby, a glittering sapphire which widened in places as it twisted and turned. The blue water dashed over rocks and stones, then, outside of town, it deepened, pouring itself into the great Loch Tay.

It was a world away from the frenetic, harshly lit offices of the *Herald Tribune* in Paris at which she spent most of her days, carving out stories and uncovering scandals. Or the density of her fourth-floor pied-à-terre with only a sliver view of the Eiffel Tower. Or the grime of the métro, which took her back and forth through the *rive gauche*.

Killin, by contrast, was still a breathtaking hamlet deeply imbedded in the Scottish countryside. A sanctuary from reality. There was no turning back now.

Her heart was fluttering like bird's wings. She had waited so terribly long for this.

The road ahead twisted through a grove of moss-furred beech and oak trees, their heavy branches bowing down to lush beds of ferns, dashes of foxglove and goldenrod, giving it the look of a grotto. She began to recall images:

Ye'll no' be defyin' me, Mairi Gordon! I'll no' have it! . . . She squeezed her eyes shut, but his voice filled her mind. *Ye're no' to go into that glen! Ye know that! Why can ye no' be more like Colleen?* . . .

Why, indeed? It had been the great question of her life. A haunting question.

She continued on down the two-lane road only spotty with the occasional small car or aged rider on a rusting bicycle, following along the twisted line of the old crumbling stone wall. It was all familiar.

The air was bracing, and the sky was a brilliant, cloudless blue. Marielle shivered, but she actually felt herself begin to warm with a smile. She felt good about this. Everything inside told her that it was right. Returning. And for that little shred of self-assurance she was grateful. Now, as the moment drew nearer, she was actually nervous about seeing Colleen again.

Grasping the small Celtic cross she still wore around her neck, and wrapping herself in an oversized herringbone jacket, Ron's jacket, now her favorite piece of clothing, Marielle closed her eyes. She drew in a breath, taking in the essence of Scotland, the sense of victory that finally she had done as she had promised. She had come home.

But after today, nothing would ever be the same again.

"Tread carefully, *chérie,*" her mother had warned as she had left this morning for the airport outside Paris. "Remember, Malcolm had a lifetime to turn Colleen against you."

"That would never happen."

"Colleen was a little girl, *chérie,* who loved her father."

"But she saw how he treated me."

"What she *saw* was a second child, her half sister, who defied him. Who needed discipline where she did not. I am quite certain that is how Malcolm will have recounted it through the years."

Marielle had then painfully learned for the first time, as she packed sweaters and jeans for the trip back to Killin, that Malcolm Gordon had sent his French wife a cable shortly after she had left him. It was a warning for her never to return, nor ever to try to see the other child she had raised from a baby.

Knowledge of that had not taken away the betrayal Marielle still felt for her Mother's years of lying about Colleen, and yet the intense pain was diminished. She would probably never agree with them, but she understood that Vivienne had her convictions. Malcolm Gordon had left a deep scar on her mother's heart that had changed Marielle's life forever, as well.

Marielle set her bag down in the lobby of the Dunham Hotel now, the small inn in Killin fashioned after an alpine chalet and built on the edge of the widest part of the River Dochart. It was a charming little hotel, far more so than she remembered, with bright green shutters and window boxes stuffed with red geraniums.

At the desk, a stoop-shouldered man with a ring of white hair sat, dressed in a tartan plaid shirt and gray slacks, behind the counter. He was sipping steaming tea from a blue china cup, perusing a copy of the local paper as two unruly Jack Russell terriers with short, stubby legs scampered in and out between Marielle's feet.

As she looked at the man, the realization shook her. This was Ian McShane, a man who had played cards with her father every Tuesday night for as long as she could remember. His wife had been one of the only women not to ostracize Vivienne or to treat her as an intruder on their small, idyllic town.

How Vivienne had ever settled for a rough, ale-drinking rounder like Malcolm Gordon in a town that in the main, was unreceptive to her had always been difficult for Marielle to comprehend. They were so different. Such worlds apart in everything.

Vivienne tried once to explain their meeting to Marielle. It had been the free-spirited summer of 1969, and Vivienne had been on summer break from the Sorbonne. She'd gone on a backpacking trip through the English countryside with a friend. Hitchhiking, they had taken a ride from a group of Manchester boys who had taken them up to Scotland. It was difficult for Marielle to conjure the image of her mother, long-haired, her face free of cosmetics, dressed in bell bottoms, a braless halter top, and leather sandals.

Her relationship with Malcolm Gordon had been intense and passionate. But an innocent at the time, Vivienne had confused lust with love. Malcolm had not. A widower at the age of thirty-eight, he was looking for a mother for his infant daughter, Colleen. He was most definitely *not* looking for love.

Mairi was born exactly nine months after they were married. And it was shortly after that when Vivienne discovered that her new husband had maintained a roving eye and a bad temper of which she had only seen glimpses prior to their small church wedding.

"Help ye, lass?" McShane asked, glancing over black-rimmed reading glasses that were shoved down onto the tip of his nose. The sound of the thick Scottish burr broke into Marielle's memories of her mother's story.

"Have you a room to let?"

"Aye," he smiled, pushing the leather-bound register across the counter to her. "If ye'll fill in your name and address here . . ."

Something in Marielle caught at the request. This was not a trip, but a journey. She was not ready to entertain explanations about why she had returned after all this time. At least not until she had seen Colleen. Her sister deserved to be the first to know that she had finally come back. But Girard was a name he might recall.

So a moment later, she signed the register as Marielle Jaeger.

"May I leave my bags here and see the room later?" she then asked in flawless English cultivated when she had lived in New York, entirely devoid of any French accent.

"Need directions to somewhere, lass?"

"Not to MacLaren's Bend," she smiled.

McShane was surprised. "Ye know the place, do ye?"

"I'm actually looking for Colleen Gordon. Does she still live there?"

The man seemed to pale as he slowly removed his spectacles. He never took his eyes from her. In fact, now it seemed to Marielle that he was studying her intently as he rose very slowly. He moved to the desk that separated them, then balanced his liver-spotted hands on the counter. "I'm sorry to be the one sayin' this, lass, as it still seems hard to believe, but Colleen's dead. Two years ago now."

It was a heavy, almost choking weight that descended upon her. "That's not possible."

"'Twas an accident. Or so the papers said."

Her fingers went to her lips. She felt herself flinch as though she had been struck. The words were breathless, barely audible. ". . . Oh, no."

"I'm sorry, lass. 'Tis a dreadful thing, someone so young and vital losin' her life like that. 'Twas a fair shock to the entire village, but somethin' of a mystery. Few of the details of how it happened were ever made public. Between you and me, I always thought her husband had a good deal more to do with it than what people said."

Her husband. The words were all jumbled together. *Husband. Dead. Accident.*

Marielle gripped the counter as the shock swelled up, surrounding her. Then anger met the shock inside her heart, twining like a skein of yarn as she thought of Vivienne so stubbornly keeping them apart all of that time. Precious years they could have had.

"Are ye all right, lass?"

McShane moved the black pipe from one corner of his stained teeth to the other. Then he smoothed a hand across his shirt. His words brought her back yet again, but they sounded very far off. Marielle tried to speak in reply. Her lips moved. But no sound came out. She drew in several deep breaths trying to stave off the onslaught of tears she felt pressing at the backs of her eyes.

"Perhaps ye should sit down. Ye've gone white as a sheet."

She tried to keep her voice from sounding shrill. "It just comes as something of a shock."

"Were ye friends?"

"We weren't as close as I wish we'd been."

"I'm sorry then. Colleen was quite a bonny lass."

"Yes." Marielle's voice trembled on the edge of desolation. "She was."

"Morte." Marielle said the word in French, hoping there would be more reality about it for her in the sound. For a woman who had spent the past thirteen years in Paris. Working. Writing. Avoiding life. Avoiding commitments. But never forgetting what, and who, made her who she was.

"Colleen *est morte.*"

Marielle left the hotel blindly after that. She needed some air and a chance to decide what to do next. She wrapped her arms around the herringbone jacket she wore. Ron's jacket.

An accident. "So the papers said."

Marielle flinched at the echo of Ian McShane's curiously vague indictment. This wasn't fair, not when she had only just returned. But life in general wasn't particularly fair, was it? That was what Maman always said so stoically. *Our goal,* Vivienne had preached at her, *is to make the best of the hand God, and fate, have dealt us.*

But what was she to do with this grim hand now?

She was, the realization came to her, a woman full of passion, ambition, and potential. Stymied by sorrow. Isolated from life by choice. Marielle felt, at that painful moment, like a powerhouse of emotion that had been set adrift. No husband. No lover. No sister.

But inside of her, a faint voice spoke. Suddenly, it was Ron's voice that filled her mind. An old friend coming back through time: *Keep your dreams, sweetheart, as your greatest treasure. Because they are yours, and only you can make them into reality.* Ron was watching her from above, she knew. Leading her. Guiding her.

Still, and always, her angel.

Only give me a sign, she silently pleaded. *Tell me, where do I go from here?*

Marielle walked numbly along a sidewalk spotted with midday shoppers, stout women in tweed skirts, aging cardigan sweaters and chunky, sensible, putty-colored shoes. Many of them stopped to chat with each other. Marielle glanced absently into a few shop windows, her mind still reeling. It all seemed very far away. The butcher, a stumpy little man wrapped in a white, blood-spattered apron, with silver hair brushed neatly back from his forehead, was, with smiles and chuckles, taking the long line of customers each in turn.

The shop next door, at the end of the lane, was called Ware on Earth. It was the shop of a local artisan. Marielle stood at the window for a long time, pretending to study each unique and brightly glazed piece of pottery. Many of them were striking, with objects pressed into the surfaces; the shape of a leaf. Butterfly. A slip of distinctive lace. But her mind was numb. All that registered there were a cloudy tangle of colors and shapes. Grand vases. Bowls. Long-stemmed goblets.

She still was not entirely certain what to do now. Stay? Leave? Go back to Paris knowing only that Colleen was dead? It didn't seem conceivable to just turn around and pretend she had never come here. Pretend she had never been a part of this place.

There was so much of her past here that she longed to make peace with. Perhaps instead of a reunion, her journey home could become about healing.

Marielle did not know how long she had been standing there when she felt someone watching her. She glanced up suddenly and, through the window, saw a lean man with shaggy maple-colored hair, sitting at a potter's wheel smiling at her. She held up her hand in response, giving him a tentative wave in greeting as he motioned her inside.

The little shop was warm, flooded with the melodic strains of a Brahms symphony, and stuffed floor to ceiling with pots and vases in every stage from drying clay to ones that were freshly painted.

Years in strict French schools had taught her about classical music, but in defiance against those early years back in the structure of Paris, Marielle had never come to appreciate it. Here in Killin, safely in out of the frigid autumn air, and surrounded by the strong scent of wet clay and paint, the music felt strangely right. Like a part of this place. Welcoming.

"Hallo," he said, as she closed the door that had one of those little brass bells that tinkled.

"Ye're stayin' at the Dunham?" he asked, barely looking up now from his wheel, his slim arms soaked to the elbow in wet clay.

Marielle was surprised. But still so numb. "Yes, I am," she answered blandly. "Although I suppose by now I should be saying 'aye.'"

"Not unless ye're a Scot," he smiled affably. "Besides, your speech is lovely, as it is, with that slight accent of your own."

His voice was deep. Smooth. And he was so softly spoken. Hypnotically so. She was drawn away from herself by it, and by the first mention from anyone of what she had always considered a closely guarded secret. Could he really hear something in her voice?

Marielle stopped at a rough-hewn table with several unique vases in all shapes and sizes. Pretending to be interested in a tall slim cobalt blue vase with a pattern of large leaves pressed into the clay, she picked it up and examined it more closely. It reminded her of the glen; the arc of trees overhead, the sound their rustling leaves made . . . the sound of Colleen's laughter.

The symphony ended and there was a break in the music.

Suddenly she was not looking at the pots, but at the man. Her gaze lingered a moment longer than it should have. The curls on his head were smoothed back from his face and his jaw was shadowed by what looked like a two-day growth of beard. He had the shaggy, unkempt appearance of an artist, and yet beneath it were unmistakably refined features, a long, flat nose and tapered chin and a full, sensual mouth.

She watched his reedy forearms move back and forth, the muscles, like thick honey-colored rope, flex and straighten as he worked the wet clay.

"Wherever ye've come from, welcome home to Killin."

Marielle felt a stone form in her throat. "I beg your pardon?"

He looked up. "Wherever in the world ye come from, there's a wee part of everyone who belongs to this place."

He took his foot from the pedal, then picked up a rag and began unsuccessfully to wipe what she could see were long and slender clay-caked hands. Intrigued by his quiet intensity, Marielle moved a wary few steps closer, absolutely unable to admit out loud now who she really was. "I'm Marielle Jaeger," she said instead. The name had come to her again, as it had at the Dunham, a protective mechanism, like so many of her instincts. And it surprised her, because she hadn't planned it. Hadn't planned to perpetuate a lie.

The music began again. This time, it sounded like Handel. Something from the *Etudes*. He extended his hand. "The name's Barry. Barry Buchanan."

The sound of that name crossed the chasm of time, hitting her hard. Blinding her for a moment. *What ye do fancy is that older boy who sells pots on the side of the road, called Barry Buchanan, isn't it?*

The years had done little to change him, she saw now that the whirlwind inside her mind had begun to settle. Now that she knew who he was. There were still those unruly waves of hair. The deep hazel eyes. And the mysterious poetic quality about him that Colleen had been drawn to years ago.

A stray thought crossed over her mind then, and she was suddenly cold. Would he, could *he* be the man her sister had married? The man who may well have had a hand in her death? In a town this size, anything was possible.

Free to meet his gaze, to assess the dark thought as it swirled around in her mind, Marielle studied him more closely. She saw that he was tall and very slim. He wore tan corduroy slacks and a denim shirt rolled up over his elbows. But there was a certain elegance even in that, the colors together, the perfectly accessorized maple-colored belt and the matching, slightly worn lace-up shoes. Barry must have done well for himself in what seemed a modest enterprise.

"Handsome jacket," he said. "A man's cut, though, isn't it?"

Marielle glanced down, having forgotten in that instant the precious, comforting herringbone fabric. It was a curious moment; one of her two worlds crossing into the other. *Paris. Killin . . . Ron . . . Colleen.*

She touched the lapel. "It belonged to a friend."

"Lucky friend."

"Not really. He's dead."

Barry's expression deepened. "Sorry," he said. And she knew that he meant it. "I was just about to take a cup of tea. Join me?"

It was so simply offered, his tone once again so matter-of-fact, as he turned away from her that, even before she replied, Marielle felt compelled to accept. It was all so refreshing, the way he had asked, simply, politely. Besides, she could see that it was starting to rain again.

Droplets of rain spattered against the windows, slowly at first, pattering out a rhythm that almost competed with the *Etudes,* and she was actually glad to be inside. Somewhere. Anywhere. Even here. With a stranger . . .

Who was not really a stranger, after all.

As Barry Buchanan stood with his back to her at a small table with a hot plate, teapot, and a collection of heavy earthen mugs, Marielle went back to one of the tables full of that strikingly beautiful pottery.

"How long have you been doing this?"

"Makin' tea?"

"Making pottery."

She could hear him softly chuckle. Marielle knew the answer, of course, remembering the young man who had put aside pride and done what he needed to earn a living and to survive without parents. But this had become true art.

"Nearly as long I've been makin' tea," Barry said smoothly. "My father was a potter here in town. 'Twas in my bones, I expect, to carry on with it."

"Your work is exquisite."

"And what piece is it ye fancy most?"

Marielle saw that he had turned around with the two steaming mugs and was coming back toward her in long-legged, elegant strides.

"This is wonderful," she said, picking up the slim cobalt blue vase. As a child she had never known that he had any great talent. But the beauty of these works, the luster of the glazes, was breathtaking.

"'Tis yours," he said of the vase.

Her eyes met his again. "Oh, I couldn't possibly."

Barry's sudden smile was broad and full of sincerity. He handed her the steaming earthen mug of tea, then sank easily against one of the display tables, crossing one long leg over the other.

"'Tis nothin' all that grand, Marielle, believe me." He took a sip of tea. "A simple gift to welcome a bonny new lass to town, it is. Nothin' more than that."

Marielle believed him. And she liked the way he said her name, *Marielle*, in a tone of simple, unadorned respect, as if he genuinely liked women for who they were. Not for what they might be able to give.

Still, she set the vase back on the table. "The thing is, my plans have changed rather suddenly and I won't be staying as long as I'd hoped."

"Ye heard that Colleen died." It had come as a statement, not a question, and Marielle's face blanched with shock that he had known it. He saw that. "News travels at the speed of lightnin' in a town of few diversions. And," he smiled good-naturedly. "Ian McShane, who runs the Dunham, drops by here most afternoons for a wee chat. He was here just before ye arrived yourself. 'Twas he who told me ye'd inquired after Colleen."

"Did you know her well?" Marielle forced herself to ask, not quite able to meet his gaze now when she did.

"Well enough to miss her for the rest of my life," Barry replied. There was a catch in his voice as he said it that told her it had been a great deal more than a casual friendship between them.

"And you?" he asked her then.

"We were pen friends as teenagers," she said, making it up as she went along, still feeling strangely protective of what she and Colleen had meant to one another, unwilling yet to share this new grief with any-one—even an old friend. "I always wanted to come here and meet her. But it never worked out. Sadly, until now."

"When was the last time you wrote to one another?"

"It was actually a very long time ago. But I never forgot our letters. Or her."

"She was an extraordinary woman, Colleen. I can understand that."

Had he looked overly sad when he said that? Marielle asked herself. His eyes had been so clear with sincerity. Suddenly, she ached to discover how well this man had come to know her sister—what all of these people knew of Colleen.

"Mr. McShane told me she died in an accident."

"Aye." Barry looked away for a moment, then his eyes went back to her. "'Twas a black day. One 'twill never be forgotten in Killin," Barry said, fighting to press back something brittle that threatened to creep across his deep Scottish burr.

Seeing that he was not about to volunteer any details about the tragedy, Marielle stood then and handed him back the mug. Her movement broke the intensity that had sprung up so suddenly between them. "Well, thank you for the tea. It was kind of you."

As she turned, he touched her arm and drew her back. He handed her the cobalt blue vase she had admired. "Please," Barry said. "Take it. Any friend of Colleen's is a friend to me, as well. 'Twould please me to give it to ye."

Marielle looked at him for another moment, wondering if she should ask the question that lay so heavily on her mind. Finally, the words came out slowly, deliberately. "Mr. McShane also mentioned that Colleen was married."

Barry's gaze was distant in the silence that followed. He gazed out the window and across the street toward the shimmering crystal loch beyond. "Aye, she was." His voice was suddenly very flat. "Grandest mistake of her life."

CHAPTER TEN

Marielle sat alone on the bed in the small hotel room that evening, listening to the river rush below. She was glad her sister hadn't married Barry Buchanan. He was too kind and genuine for her to fathom him implicated in her death. But if it wasn't Barry, then who had won her heart . . . and possibly betrayed her with it?

Had Colleen and this man had children? Did they look like Colleen? Did they look like Malcolm? What would she be able to discover of the precious years they had lost now that she was dead?

But she couldn't leave Killin. Ron had taught her that. There were too many unanswered questions. Too much to process.

This was not only a journey of grieving, and a chance to make peace with the past, but it had very quickly become an exploration for the truth: Had her sister's death been something more than an accident, as Ian McShane had inferred? What had actually happened to take the life of a young woman in a sleepy little town where danger didn't mesh at all with the picture-postcard image?

Suddenly she was glad she had not revealed her

identity to Ian or Barry. There would be too many questions for her, since, as Barry had put it, "news travels at the speed of light in a town of few diversions."

Perhaps there was someone living at MacLaren's Bend now who could speak of the details more easily. Perhaps she would say that her friend had told her so much in her letters about the beautiful old house on the hill, and she had hoped to see it at least once before she left Killin. Marielle ran through the conversation in her mind. She picked up the telephone receiver.

"Aye?" It was Mr. McShane's voice.

"Could you give me the number of MacLaren's Bend, please?"

"I'm no' certain anyone'll answer there. Jennie Quinn is right angry that her ma is tryin' to hire help, and most days she refuses to pick up the telephone."

Jennie Quinn . . . The name settled in her mind as she remembered the kind woman who had owned the bake shop, the woman who had given her and Colleen an extra tart more than once. Quinn's Bake Shop. That little baby daughter of the couple who owned it, a rosy little girl who had played with her mother's gold crucifix and sat happily in her arms, was living in Malcolm Gordon's house.

Marielle tried to keep her voice steady. "Could you try to ring anyway?"

"Aye, lass. Just give me a moment."

Coincidence tumbled upon fate—which seemed now to be leading her. Drawing her into something that felt as intricate as a web. The phone rang once. Twice. Three times. "Hallo?"

"May I please speak with Mrs. Quinn?"

"She's no' in." The voice was a young girl's, heavy with a Scottish burr.

"Do you expect her soon?"

"I expect precious little out of life anymore."

"When would it be best to call back?"

"If ye're ringin' after the ad, we're no' needin' anyone, it turns out."

Very suddenly, the line went dead.

Marielle gazed down at the receiver in her hand a moment more before she hung it back in the cradle of the phone. She sank onto the bed, thinking now of the Quinns, remembering how the pungently sweet tarts from their bake shop had tasted as she and Colleen ate them beneath the sunshine that filtered down through the trees. Both of them so young then. Laughing. Happy. It was the last time she could remember feeling any bit of innocence.

I owe this to you, Colleen, Marielle was thinking. *I promised.*

And very suddenly, she felt a chill at the base of her neck. It was as if someone were pressing her onward in agreement. As if someone were telling her to go forward with her search.

Marielle finally stood before the pale pink house that from its incline, looked down onto the sweeping shoreline of Loch Tay. To the north were purple, heather-clad hills that climbed silently into slow, scudding clouds. She knew it in an instant. MacLaren's Bend. *Home.* She stood in the rain for a very long time, looking up at the house, drawing in breath after breath, steadying herself. The very walls, the out-of-place front porch and the two windows above it, spoke out to her like an old friend, an estranged friend, with memories of long ago.

Ye've come back, at last. I knew ye would.

Her skin had turned to gooseflesh with the cold and the irony, but she steadied herself and moved forward. As she drew near, Marielle was surprised to see that the house was weathered now. Sadly neglected. The salmon pink paint on the eaves and the white on the shutters was chipping. There was a large fenced garden to the left of the door, now choked with nothing but weeds and drooping sunflowers folding in on themselves, on long, brown, withered stalks.

Le jardin de ma mère . . . Mother's garden.

But that, Marielle reminded herself silently, was a lifetime ago. She pulled the collar of Ron's jacket up around her neck as a gust of wind rushed up off the loch, and she moved in quick steps up the long gravel driveway. Rain was coming again. So were the memories.

Mairi! Mairi, come on, will ye? We'll be late for supper!

The pungent fragrance of her mother's French *pot au feu* set out in dishes on the blue-and-white checked cloth—beside it, their father's bottle of aged Scotch.

Marielle squeezed her eyes with a steeled determination, then opened them and marched forward. The doorbell, she found, was rusted now. It no longer worked, so she knocked. Her hands were like ice. She rubbed them together and waited. A fine mist of rain fell, and the air was bitter cold. She exhaled and saw her breath in an ivory plume.

Finally, after she knocked and waited again, a voice—that same slightly irritated girl's voice from the phone—came to her from the other side of the door. "Aye?"

"I'm here to see Mrs. Quinn," Marielle called through the closed door.

"I told ye on the phone. 'Tis no' a position anymore. Sorry ye wasted your time."

"Are *you* Mrs. Quinn?"

"No. But there's still no position."

In the space of an instant, the rain came harder and the icy wind was pushing up under the eaves, driving into her clothing, making her shiver. *I have come too far to be put off like this by some spoiled child,* Marielle was thinking. Now she *needed* a reason to stay long enough to find some answers about what had happened to Colleen.

"Look," she called out. All that had happened strained her patience. "It has been a bloody long journey, the likes of which you cannot begin to imagine! Now, could you at least have the courtesy to open the door and speak to me directly?"

After another moment, the girl complied with an audible groan.

Marielle felt an enormous stab of guilt for her tone when, as she was about to charge forward through the slowly opening door, she was met with the formidable barrier of a fragile-looking adolescent, with long kinky hair the color of fresh rust, sitting in a wheelchair gazing up at her with a startlingly vacant expression.

That sweet little girl, Jennie Quinn . . . I remember you. . . . I remember so many more things now about this place and all of you. . . .

"So now that I've opened the door, as ye've asked, will ye be takin' your leave?"

"I had no idea," Marielle breathed.

"A fine thing indeed. Another pityin' stranger." The girl rolled her eyes. "'Tis lovely to make your acquaintance, as well," she drawled sarcastically. "So, ye've gotten what ye've come for, your close-up look at the town cripple. Now if ye'll just be on your way, I can get back to—"

Marielle blocked the door with her foot just when the girl tried to swing it at her. "At the very least, you could invite me inside until the rain lets up."

"'Tis only October," she sniped, her reedy soprano rich with that Scottish burr Marielle usually loved. "That could well take till May."

Marielle leveled her eyes on Jenny. "Well, that'll be fine. I've nothing particular to do. And I do mean to see your mother."

The room into which Marielle pressed herself, dripping and shivering after that, had changed little in the years she had been away. The parlor was still large and warm, and stuffed nearly floor to ceiling with the same heavy Victorian furniture and fringed velvet draperies, the color of ripe, green Spanish olives, as it had been when she was a girl.

On two walls were cabinets bursting with Wemyss Ware pottery and old jars painted with bordello-bright ladies' faces. Others were emblazoned with images like the London Bridge and the Brighton Pavilion. Marielle remembered that Vivienne had kept her prized collection of delicate French Sèvres porcelain in their places. *One piece of which Marielle had grabbed to strike her father the day everything had come undone.* The memory stung.

Still, it really was a lovely house that lay beyond the formal foyer, a home with planked floors jutting out from beneath Turkish carpets and a collection of antique birdcages. A bit dusty and tired looking around the edges, inside as well as out, but full of history and the secret welcome it had extended silently to her.

Marielle turned back to the girl, who was gripping the wheels of her chair and looking up now as if she were trying to fend off an evil marauder. Stubbornly, Marielle prepared another tack.

"Perhaps you could simply tell me when your mother will be returning, then you and I can call a brief truce."

"I've nothin' against ye 'twould require a truce other than I do no' wish to have ye keep house here or stay with me."

"I've always favored blunt honesty." Marielle smiled. "I think, until this moment."

"In my case, what ye're seein' is what ye get."

"Well, since I'm already here, I am Marielle Jaeger." Marielle extended her hand, going for broke and breaking the awkward stillness that had settled in between them in the echo of the girl's retort. "I also knew Colleen."

The girl glanced up again, flashing eyes that were wide and sea green, and in which for the first time Marielle saw a hint of vulnerability.

"Oh, very well. For whatever it's worth to ye then, the name's Jennie Quinn."

"I'm pleased to meet you, Jennie." She held the girl's small hand in her own just a moment longer than she might have someone else's, trying to say through the connection, *It's all right. You can trust me. . . .* But Jennie retracted her hand and pressed it back onto the chair wheel, firmly reestablishing their distance.

Marielle glanced at her watch. It was after six. "And your mother? Do you expect her soon?"

"'Tis rather unpredictable, that. She runs the bake shop, mostly alone. 'Twas my da's enterprise. But he's dead now, ye see, and my ma's determined to keep it, even if it leaves me to the mercy of strangers, and sends her to an early grave alongside him."

Marielle felt a sudden burst of sympathy for Jennie, with her gorgeous mass of pre-Raphaelite hair. Jennie felt powerless over her destiny. She was lashing out, not at Marielle particularly, but at the control that was being taken away in her life. She understood that more profoundly than Jennie could know.

"I'm sorry about your father."

"He's been dead a long time and my ma was remarried anyway. Though he's dead now, as well. 'Tis nothin' for you to be sorry about."

"I lost my father too suddenly when I was a girl. Not having a strong figure like that is a loss in a young woman's life that never leaves you."

Marielle watched as color patched Jennie's pale face. "Now I'm the one who's sorry."

"Well, at least on that score," Marielle said honestly, "we understand one another."

They heard the front door open then and the sound of rain rushing in on a gust of wind from outside. The door clicked quickly to a close. The sound of shoe heels followed, coming across the floorboards. They softened to spongy footfalls on the worn, slightly frayed Turkish carpet that Janet Gordon, Colleen's mother, had long ago bought. It was strange, Marielle thought, recalling that just now.

"In here, Ma," Jennie called.

A moment later, she saw a stout, rawboned woman with a square chin and wide rosy mouth, who was smoothing back her wet short silver curls with one hand. With the other hand she was removing a scarf as she came in through the swag of green Victorian draperies. The years had changed Catriona Quinn. Only her sweet-toned voice and her smile remained the same. "Why'd ye no' phone me, Jennie, to tell me we had a guest?"

"She was a friend of Colleen's who's come about your ad."

Marielle stood and extended her hand. "That's not entirely true, Mrs. Quinn."

The wind rushing up the hill rattled the windows as the rain went on beating against them. Catriona looked closely at her then, and as she did, her face paled. But her tired eyes were alive suddenly with a kind of recognition Marielle had not counted upon.

"Saints above . . . Can it be?" Marielle was silent as the breathless question settled uneasily between them. Catriona glanced down at Jennie, her face still expressionless with shock. "Be a good lass and put a kettle on for tea. Let me speak with our guest privately for a bit, hmm?"

At first Jennie did not move. She seemed to be considering whether or not to comply. Finally, with a more than obvious air of reluctance, she placed her hands back on the rubber-coated wheels, sighed, and began to move herself forward with angry little thrusts.

"'Tis true, isn't it?" Catriona said once Jennie had gone. "Ye're Mairi Gordon, all grown up."

"I'm called Marielle now," she conceded to the woman whose tender heart, which she still remembered, made her want to be honest.

"Ye've changed into so bonny a lass that I'd no' have recognized ye if 'twas no' ye lookin' the very image of Vivienne. Well, welcome home indeed," Catriona said, a broad, friendly smile finally dawning on her full, crimson-patched face as she drew Marielle into a grand and awkwardly tight embrace.

A moment later, they were parted again and Catriona's expression was still one of surprise. "Ye've no' had the fortune of seein' the place for a very long time."

"No. But it is exactly as I remember it."

Catriona sank into one of the turn-of-the century velvet sofas, never taking her gaze from Marielle. Her face was still kind, Marielle saw, as the older woman shifted, moving into the light of one of the glowing Tiffany lamps. It was a soft face, fleshy with a hint of the rosy blush she had had as a much younger woman. Her deeply set gold-green eyes were full of such a staggering warmth that Marielle felt strangely protected here—safe, in her father's house, for the first time in her life.

Finally, Marielle sat down on the sofa beside her.

"I tried to contact ye myself after Colleen died," Catriona said, her smile now fading with the seriousness of the revelations coming between them. "There seemed no reason to keep up your da's barrier by then, him havin' passed a good year before that. But I had no address, ye see, no number to ring. 'Twas a difficult time for all of us here."

"Thank you at least for trying."

Catriona reached for her hand and squeezed it. "I'm sorry for how ye were treated, child. I tried in my way through the years to soften his heart about all of it. For Colleen's sake especially. She missed you and Vivienne frightfully at first. I loved him dearly for most of my life, and in the end he came to love me, as well. But there was no changin' the heart of my husband, no matter who it was that tried."

Marielle felt the weight of sudden realization like a stone in her throat. Catriona and Jenny had not leased the house. Instead, this kindhearted woman before her had become her bitter father's third and last wife.

"Did ye come here finally, then, not knowin' what had happened to your dear sister?"

Marielle was pulled back to the moment by eyes heavily upon her and a question that felt almost painful. "I'm not certain I do know. Ian McShane said it was an accident."

A huge clatter beyond the closed kitchen door just then stopped their dialogue. A host of expletives muttered by Jennie filled the silence, and Catriona glanced at Marielle. "She's needin' to do more for herself, but she's none too happy about the fact," Catriona said in an apologetic voice.

"I would imagine it would be very difficult for someone her age to make peace with her limitation.

"Since it happened, Jennie has fairly well decided to insulate herself. She's built a wall around herself and let no one in."

Jennie's instinct after a tragedy, drawing into herself, was something Marielle understood only too well. She forced up a smile of sympathy.

"So tell me, Mairi. Did you and Vivienne stay on in Paris after ye'd gone away from Killin?"

"We were in New York for a while. But we always kept our apartment in Paris."

"Ye know Colleen tried to write to ye there, but 'twas never any reply. We rather thought ye'd moved on."

"An illusion my mother cultivated," Marielle said, struggling to keep that new, raw bitterness from creeping up into her voice. "My mother never got over how things had gone for us here. She kept Colleen's letters from me, believing it was in my best interest. I never had any idea until yesterday that my sister had ever written to me."

"Oh, lass." Catriona was still holding Marielle's hand. She squeezed it tightly again. "And so now ye've come home again after all of these years only to find her gone."

Marielle shifted, leaning forward, feeling the desperation for all that she had lost swell now inside her. "Tell me, Mrs. Quinn, please. How *did* Colleen die?"

Marielle felt an odd and sudden tension spring up between them then. Catriona clasped her hands at her lips, pointing them like a steeple, and paused. "I'm no' certain I still know all of the details of it myself, Mairi, nor that I even want to," she finally said. "'Twas such a dark time to live through. What I can confirm is that it was indeed an accident, as Ian said. Colleen's car went off the Dwelly Bridge just outside of town one night. By the time help arrived, 'twas too late to save her."

Marielle felt a shiver blossom at the base of her spine and work itself upward. Images of water at night, cold and unforgiving, flashed through her mind. How horrible. Her sister had drowned! "But surely Colleen knew the bridge. She'd lived in Killin all of her life. How could something like that have happened?"

"No one talks about this, Mairi. There's no point in darkening her memory now. But she was your sister, and ye've come a long way for such grand disappointment. So the truth of it is, I'll tell ye, she'd begun drinkin' quite a lot in those final days. Especially that night. 'Twas only a horrible miscalculation of a few feet that cost dear Colleen her life."

Marielle was stunned into silence. The various levels of shock were almost too much to take in. Her sister's marriage to someone she didn't know, the drinking, then her death.

Finally, Marielle stood on shaky legs. "Well, thank you, Mrs. Quinn, for your kindness. And for your honesty."

"Now, ye're no' leavin' already! Ye've only just come back!"

"I'll be staying in Killin for a while. At least until I can make some sense out of all of this."

"Then ye'll be callin' me Catriona and ye'll be stayin' right here at MacLaren's Bend!"

"That's very kind of you, but—"

"No matter what has gone on through the years, child, this is still your home. I would no' feel a'tall right knowin' ye were down at the Dunham all alone."

"Honestly, I quite enjoy my own company."

Catriona's eyes shimmered with sudden tears. "Colleen would have wanted ye here, I think. She'd have been as angry as a hornet knowin' that I let ye get away."

Marielle conceded that much. Catriona was trying her best to welcome her back, to make amends in some small way for the losses Marielle had suffered. It would have been wrong, going against the knowledge of that. "Well, all right then. If you're certain it wouldn't be any trouble."

"No' a bit. And, frankly, ye'd be bonny company for Jennie when ye were around the place. I'm down at the bake shop so much these days. She gets a bit lonely."

As they walked together through the doorway into the kitchen, Marielle stopped again. Her face was full of conviction. "But I *do* have to ask one thing of you, Catriona."

"I believe ye know I'll try to help ye any way that I can."

"Then for a while, at least, I'd prefer people here think of me as Marielle Jaeger, Colleen's pen friend during our school years. Under the circumstances, I'm really not ready for all of the questions and whispers the truth would bring up."

Catriona was surprised. "And Jennie?"

"It would be easier for me if only you knew the truth."

"I've never lied to my daughter about anythin', Mairi."

"I'm not asking you to lie. Just don't tell her all that you know of my past."

"What if someone else in town should recognize ye?"

"I was a child when I left here. If you hadn't loved my father for all of those years, and still think of him so often even now, do you suppose *you* would have made such an immediate connection to Vivienne?"

Catriona shook her head. "I'm just no' certain what the need is for the secrecy, lass. Malcolm's gone now. There's no one left in Killin for ye to fear."

Marielle wasn't altogether certain either. But so much of her own nature these past years had been solitary that she could not have managed her grief and shock just now in any other way.

"Please understand, Catriona. I had no idea what to expect, coming back here. But it certainly wasn't this. Now, for as long as I can avoid it at least, I need to have this be *my* journey. And a private one. I need the time and solitude to make peace with the past. I need to grieve in my own way. I just can't have a lot of people asking me questions about where I've been all these years, what my own life has been. Please, tell me you can understand that."

At last, Catriona patted her shoulder in a kind, motherly gesture. Marielle could see her eyes light again. "Very well, dear lass. I'll keep your secret as long as we can. But I would no' go expectin' your anonymity to last forever. The truth has a way of comin' out eventually."

Thinking of Colleen and not herself, Marielle's lips turned slightly upward into a grim smile. "That's what I'm hoping for."

"Now, then. Before we have our tea, shall I show ye to your room?"

Marielle stood in the open doorway for a long time, clutching the doorframe with a trembling hand, as

Catriona drew back the draperies, opened window shades, and lit the small ivory-colored ceramic lamp between the twin beds. The busy wallpaper, large pink roses with moss green vines of ivy, jumped out at her from the past, drawing her in. Frightening her.

"Oh, go to sleep, will ye, Mairi? We've got school tomorrow."

"Won't ye tell me just one more story, Colleen? Please? Just one more."

"Count the roses on the wall if ye canno' sleep. 'Tis what I always do. . . ."

Voices echoed through the years. Time and loss, shook her. Even the matching bedspreads, faded pink eyelet for Colleen's twelfth birthday, were the same. A tear lingered on Marielle's smooth cheek, dropping to the top of her lip, where she swiftly wiped it away. *I cannot stay here. Be in here where the memories are like hobgoblins. Taunting me . . .*

"I thought ye might find bit of that peace ye're after here in the room ye once shared with Colleen," Catriona glanced around. "Do ye remember it?"

"There is very little about this place I could ever forget." Her tone was bittersweet.

"Well, it still has the best afternoon light in the house and the same lovely view of the back garden."

The aroma of pipe smoke, an aroma from long ago, was suddenly heavy in the air. Her father's pipe smoke. Marielle shivered. "What is that?"

"What's what?"

Her mouth was dry suddenly. "Can't you smell it? The pipe smoke."

"Is it, now?" Catriona chuckled. "'Tisn't very likely,

that, with Malcolm gone and he the only one in this house who ever smoked."

A shiver shook her, but Marielle pressed it away with a stubborn determination that was ages old. She would not be undone by vivid memories of a man whom she had despised, who had despised her. A man who was dead. *Of course it's not likely,* Marielle scolded herself. *He can't hurt you anymore. You're just tired, that's all. And it has been a shock coming into this room again. It's probably just wet earth outside from the rain. It's an old house. Things smell. Things creak. Of course that's all it is.*

"It really is as lovely a room as I remember," Marielle managed to say, ignoring the pungent aroma that had made her skin grow cold. She drew in a long, slow breath, willing the strange fear of being here away.

Still, gloom welled inside of her. *Oh, please let me be doing the right thing,* Marielle silently pleaded, yet feeling, even as her mind formed the thought, that in so many ways, here at MacLaren's Bend, she was playing with fire.

Marielle sat staring at Colleen's untouched bed. Being here, the circle it completed, went very deep inside her. She touched the smooth quilt her sister had once so loved, then sank back onto her own small bed, remembering the warm feelings and the comfort she had once found in this room.

"Ye're the only one, Colleen. The only one in the whole world who's no' remindin' me that I'm as plain as I feel. . . ."

"Ye're beautiful, Mairi Gordon. . . . Beautiful in your heart. The rest'll come in time. I know it. . . ."

A squall hit the window, making it rattle. It was cold outside, raining hard. Marielle straightened. She was shivering. The room was strangely cold suddenly. And then again, there was the strong aroma of pipe smoke.

"Go to hell, Malcolm! Like it or not, I have a right to be here!" she growled angrily, before she realized what she was saying, and to whom, feeling foolish. Wearily, she climbed into the twin bed. Her own bed from a lifetime ago. It had been an unbelievable day, and she was exhausted.

It took only a moment for her eyes to close and the dream to pull her. A dream . . . *or was it?* She sat up again in the small bed, rubbing her tired eyes, sensing someone in the room with her. Her mouth was very dry. She drew the covers back and swung her legs over the edge of the bed.

"Who's there?" She groped for the light switch on the table lamp, but the bulb seemed to have burned out. "Damn. I said, who is it?"

The odor of pipe smoke was cloying now, thick and full of memories. In the dark, Marielle went to the door and tried to open it. She twisted the handle, but it was stuck. Outside, the wind gusted, rattling the window glass. With a shudder, she pivoted back, her eyes rooting back to the beds, fear pulling her.

"You don't want me back here, do you, you old bastard?" she called out to the dark space before her. "You never did! Well, Colleen wants me here!" Her heart was beating very fast as she did her best to face her demon. "Colleen would have wanted me to know what happened. And I am *going* to find out!"

Another gust of wind shook the house, rattling the windows, frightening her. But Marielle squared her shoulders. She was not the impotent child who had gone up against a cruel, angry man many years ago and lost. Things had changed. *She* had changed.

"Now, if you are quite finished, I would very much like to get some sleep!"

A moment later, the odor that had drawn her from her bed was gone. The wind had died away too, and the old house was quiet but for the beating rain. She crawled back beneath the covers and drew her pillow to her chest, her heart still pounding, and forced herself to close her eyes.

Ye'll no' be defyin' me, Mairi Gordon. I'll no' have it!

She heard the words in her head then, the angry, taunting from her little-girl memory. But there was something eerily current about them, and against that she entirely rebelled. "Sorry about that," Marielle said in a defiant whisper. "It appears that I already have."

Marielle knew when she woke that it had been a dream.

The cold, white autumn sky, as she gazed out of the bedroom window and stretched, had a crispness that made her feel a little foolish for having been, even for a moment, afraid to be back here. The aroma of her father's pipe smoke had been something that had made a deep and lasting impression. Something tied up tightly with this old house. She had forgotten about it until she returned. Like so many other things.

Marielle touched the Celtic cross still at her neck. A talisman of love and promise, she could feel its strength against her fingertips. This was probably foolhardy, what she was going to attempt to do here, to stay among most of the people in this tiny, closely knit town as a stranger. And she hadn't been entirely honest with Catriona about her reasons for it. Yes, she needed to keep her anonymity so that she might make some peace with her past. But the reporter's instinct she had cultivated had been piqued by Ian McShane's comment and by Catriona herself. Something very strong inside her said that Marielle did not yet know the whole story of her sister's life in Killin. Or of her death. And before Marielle could go home to Paris, she was absolutely determined to find some answers.

CHAPTER ELEVEN

After supper the next evening, after Jennie had rolled out of the dining room in a huff, Marielle and Catriona went together into the salon. They took with them two cups of tea and a plate of sliced Dundee cake, a local favorite, brimming off the sides of a large silver tray. Catriona sank into Malcolm's easy chair with an audible exhalation of breath.

Marielle looked away for a moment from the old and heavy piece of furniture that had remained in the same spot, and covered in the same dark leather, since she was a child. Images flashed in her mind: Malcolm's bitter eyes cast disapprovingly at her, pipe smoke swirling around his red-gold hair.

Her gaze caught on the mahogany buffet in the dining room where her own mother had laid out Christmas pudding, her carefully crafted *coq au vin*, and even that Scottish lamb she had taken so much pride in mastering. The buffet was now covered with a sea of knickknacks, a garish replacement for the elegance that Vivienne's fine things had brought so briefly into this old house.

Marielle took her tea and went to the Adam side table crammed with small tarnished silver picture frames spread out on ivory-colored lace. She studied each of the faces. There was a wedding picture of Catriona and Malcolm.

Like Catriona, he had aged a great deal through the years. His red hair and beard had gone white. But his hateful eyes, green and hard, had remained unchanged. He had not smiled for the photograph. Not even on his wedding day. His third wedding day.

Beside it was a large silver framed image of Jennie that was probably a year or two old. Her hair was much shorter and she was standing. Marielle picked up another. She looked more closely at the image of a very young man who appeared just out of his teens, with dark hair windblown down into his vivid black eyes. He was standing down by the edge of the loch, a large fishing boat dwarfing him in the background. Instantly, Marielle saw something familiar about him, though she was not certain what it was.

"He's a nice-looking boy."

Catriona moved to see which one had interested her. "Ah," she smiled. 'Tis ancient, that photograph. He's grown into quite a grand and sturdy man from the young lad there. Do ye no' remember him?"

Marielle looked up. "Not entirely, no."

"My nephew, Calum." She took a sip of sherry. "He's my sister's son. But the two of us have been close since he was a wee bairn. I'm certain there was a time or two ye ran into one another at the bake shop back in those early days. Every time the poor lad would find himself in an embarrassing scrape, or on the wrong side of town, his ma, my sister Celina, would send him here to the country as punishment. Calum, ye see, was somethin' of a renegade. In some ways, I suppose he still is: Goes against the grain of most things."

Marielle smiled back, thinking of some of the things she'd done in her own life. "It happens to the best of us," she said.

"Calum was also Colleen's husband."

Her heart felt as if it had stopped. It was a blow she hadn't seen coming. . . . *I've always thought that husband of hers had somethin' to do with it.* . . .

She glanced down at the photograph again. It was not difficult to understand why Colleen, as an adult, had been drawn to him. Even as a boy, he had the potential to become a gorgeous man. "They didn't have children?"

"Calum dearly wanted wee ones, ye see, but he and Colleen were never blessed by the good Lord."

Catriona's proud smile dimmed at the memory. "He was a solicitor over in Crainlarich. But after Colleen died, he lost his heart for the work. He could no longer concentrate, he said."

Catriona's voice grew softer, and it was tinged with sadness. "And then Jennie still needed a lot of special things after the accident, and since her da was gone, and Malcolm as well, Calum took the duty on. But the work he sought was mindless. Helped out with everything. We could have gone to my sister in Glasgow who has more money than any woman needs. But he wouldn't hear of it for some reason."

Marielle was surprised. "Surely the government pays for what Jennie needs."

"Not for what *he* insisted upon. To Calum, no expense was to be spared. 'Twas his obsession that

Jennie get the best of everythin'. And that he should find another way than being a lawyer to pay for it."

"He sounds like quite a wonderful man."

"Colleen was dead, ye see, and I think he really put all of his grieving over on my Jennie. Her situation was somethin' I expect he felt he still had some power over. So he found her a fancy wheelchair. A special imported bed. And, for a while last year, there was an Italian physical therapist. Concetta cost a small fortune, I can tell ye. 'Twas drainin' him quite dry until Jennie and that temper of hers chased the woman off."

Marielle could not help being impressed. "There aren't many young men, in the middle of the sort of personal grief he experienced, who would be so faithful to their families."

"Even so, 'twas difficult to watch him give up his dream, and then come face to face with a mountain of debt for Jennie's sake."

"Could he not go back to his practice one day? Build it up again?"

"Calum has been toilin' away on one of the fishin' boats down at Mallaig Harbor since Colleen died, and he insists he has no plans to stop any time soon."

From solicitor to fisherman for grief—and family honor. For someone who had begun life as a renegade, her nephew had put quite a noble finish to that. As she looked at the image of the handsome young man from years past, it made her think of other people, other pictures, that should have been here at MacLaren's Bend.

"Are there no photographs of Colleen?"

"They were all brought down after she died, I'm

afraid. We none of us, Calum especially, could bear to be reminded every day of our loss."

Marielle felt the sting in that simple statement. *Our loss . . .*

The good Lord—and Vivienne—had taken away her right to know what Colleen had become and to miss the things about her that the people of Killin did. That was a painful truth, like so many others here.

"Are there any of the photographs, perhaps put away, then, that I could see?"

"Oh, of course, lass. How thoughtless of me. Let me have a look." Catriona went into an old oak sideboard and, a moment later, drew out a small photograph framed in dark wood. She handed it to Marielle.

The image was startling, and Marielle suddenly felt weak. It was a photograph of two girls, Colleen and Jennie at sunset, standing against a car. The girls were smiling, and Colleen had her arm around Jennie's shoulder. *Like two sisters,* she thought achingly.

Time had changed Colleen more than she had expected. Her older sister had grown into a tall, beautiful woman, with long, thick copper hair pulled back at the top, highlighting a perfectly oval face with those same wide, expressive green eyes. Her body was willowy and clearly sensual. The joy of life was written across her face.

Marielle looked back at Catriona, her heart squeezing. "They were close?"

"Aye. In spite of the difference in their ages, Jennie and Colleen grew to be thick as thieves." Catriona smiled, and sank down beside her studying the photograph with Marielle. "It was her way, I think, of tryin' to replace what she'd had with you."

Marielle struggled to keep her voice. "Was she angry that I never wrote?"

"Sad, I think. Colleen went through a lot of years convinced that ye would, and no one could tell her otherwise. 'Tis terrible when a marriage comes apart like that. It seems it's the children who always suffer the most."

Marielle glanced down at her sister's image again. The smiling face. The bright eyes. So full of life. A life that had been snatched up far too early.

"I'd like to ask one more thing."

Catriona's face was full of kindness as she patted Marielle's hand. "Ask what ye will."

"How did Colleen feel about you marrying Malcolm?"

"'Twas a difficult time for her at first. Vivienne and Colleen had been close, as ye remember. The only ma she'd ever had. For all of your ma's city airs, she was good to the lass, and Colleen held on to that part of her heart with the same stubborn insistence that Malcolm had for things."

Headstrong. Passionate. Colleen had grown into a woman she very much wished she had known. Her wounded heart felt battered now, hearing that.

"Did things ever improve between the two of you before she died?"

"We did get on better after a time. But there remained that garden standin' outside there as our greatest barrier. 'Twas a silent reminder to us both of the way things could never be again for her." Catriona glanced out the window at the scrappy piece of earth that once had bloomed so beautifully beneath Vivienne's careful hand.

Marielle wasn't surprised to know what it had come to mean to Colleen.

"Come on, Mairi. Let's pick the bluebells out of the garden for Ma. She's always givin' them away to everyone else. Let's put them on her own bureau for a change. That should make her smile after Da's tirade last night. At least for a little while."

"She fancies ye callin' her that, ye know. Ma."

"Sometimes I actually forget she's no' my real mother."

"I think she'd like to have been."

"Don't tell Da this, all right, Mairi? But I wish the same thing."

"Aye. Out there was dear Colleen," Catriona sighed, bringing Marielle back to the moment with a jolt, "tendin' that garden every day, fussin' over it, no matter what the weather, as if she were a caretaker for somethin' precious—and I suppose, to her, she was just that: a caretaker, of her own precious childhood memories.

"You didn't like her, did you?" Marielle asked.

"Your ma?" Catriona tipped her head, considered that. "She was wrong for Malcolm, that much I'll say. High-strung and shrill, like a pedigreed cat. People here always thought she looked down her nose at everyone."

"And did *you* think that?"

Marielle could see that she was considering again whether or not to answer the question. "Please, Catriona. I really would like to know what you thought."

"All right, then. Had Malcolm not been lookin' for a mother for Colleen, he'd never have married her.

'Twas what I thought." Then she smiled again and braced her hands on Marielle's shoulders, softening the blow. "But that does no' mean for one moment, dear, dear, Mairi Gordon—child of these hills and glen— that your da should no' have considered you every bit the blessin' from God that Colleen was to him."

Marielle felt the sting of Malcolm's rejection as sharply as ever. "I never remember him looking at me with anything but pure contempt."

"You were wronged by Malcolm Gordon, and by your ma, 'tis certain. And I mean to do whatever is in my power to help ye heal that part of yourself now that ye've come home again."

The truth will do that, she was thinking. But she didn't say it.

After Catriona had gone up to bed, Marielle rinsed off the dishes, then went into the small bedroom that still brought back too many memories. In the night silence, she opened the bedroom window that looked out onto the back garden and let the room fill with the crisp rush of air.

She stood for a moment, hands braced on the window casement. This kind of quiet was deafening. She had forgotten that. Even now, so soon after she had arrived here, the sounds of the city, the incessant clamor, had ceased to exist for her. Marielle turned around and leaned against the windowsill, smiling as she once again lifted two fingers to the Celtic cross at her neck and felt the reassuring curve.

Perhaps the bright light of this quest should have dimmed with time, she thought. *But it hasn't. And the*

memories are still there too. Yellowed. A bit faded. Like
old photographs in an album, long unseen. But their
presence, the essence of them, is never forgotten. They
have drawn me back here, Colleen. Back to you. And
to unexpected connections to all of these people who
were a part of your lovely, complicated and all-too-
brief life here near our glen. The one we never quite got
to explore together as we planned. . . .

Like the petals of a lush, fat rose, Marielle
thought, the layers of her sister's life were very slowly
being opened to her. As she went to bed and drifted off
to sleep, however, Marielle thought not of that, nor of
the dark dreams she had begun to have in this room.
Rather, her mind was taken up by thoughts of the
handsome renegade Colleen had married: Catriona's
nephew, Calum, the man Ian McShane had so unsettlingly implicated in his own wife's death.

Marielle walked back up the sloping gravel driveway
with a heavy heart the next morning as the sun went
behind a dark cloud. A sudden wind gusted up off the
water. She had spent the morning wandering the paths
and lanes she had walked through long ago with
Colleen. Reliving moments. Conversations. Trying to
make her sister seem alive again. But it had been a
futile exercise that had left her exhausted and even a
little angry.

"Well, now. 'Tis high time ye were back."

Marielle felt the fist in her stomach tighten as she
closed the front door, then hung her jacket and scarf
on the antique hall tree beside the door. While
Catriona did everything in her power to make Marielle

feel at home at MacLaren's Bend, Jennie did the opposite. She did not want her here. As she had with the nurses and therapists Calum had hired for her, Jennie Quinn was doing everything in her power to make *that* abundantly clear.

Whenever they found themselves alone, Jennie had been demanding and spiteful. *Do this for me, Marielle. . . . Do that. . . .* until Marielle thought she would go out of her mind from the desire to give her the proper tongue-lashing she needed.

Marielle opened her mouth, feeling pressed to lash back boldly, as she knew she could so well. But prudence once again stopped her with a firm hand. Marielle was not the sort to be baited. She took a breath then calmly said, "What is it that you need, Jennie?"

"'Tis time to change my colostomy bag. I need help. Ye're here so ye're elected."

"Your mother told me you are perfectly capable of doing that chore yourself."

"If I've got to have ye hoisted upon me like this, do ye no' think ye might as well make yourself useful?"

The glint in her eyes, suddenly, was pure malice, and Marielle felt a chill spiral up from the base of her spine. Marielle knew this was a point of reckoning between them. Now, clearly, it was time to have it out.

"In my opinion," Marielle said calmly, remembering her resolve, "it would be good for you if you learned to do a few things for yourself. Taking care of your own hygiene seems to me like a proper place to begin."

"Ma always changes it for me."

"Well, your *ma* isn't here now. Is she?"

They were glaring at one another, entirely at an impasse. The only sound was the howling of the wind that rattled the windows and even the heavy front door like a menacing stranger. Then suddenly, Jennie took the full bag up and held it out like a weapon. Her eyes narrowed combatively. "I asked ye to take it for me. 'Tis full."

"And I said, Do it yourself, Jennie. You are perfectly capable."

"I'll no'."

"Then I suppose you have a problem, don't you?"

Marielle turned to walk into the kitchen when she heard a sudden *splat* on the hardwood floor and the room was instantly filled with a putrid odor. Marielle shot back around in horror, eyes blazing, her mouth agape.

"Now look what ye've made me do!"

"Why, you little—" She bit off her words at the tip of her tongue. Jennie Quinn was proving to be a better opponent than she had expected. Marielle had absolutely no idea what to do now. She certainly couldn't leave the filth there. But to capitulate and clean it up was tantamount to admitting defeat. And her journey in Killin was far from over.

Marielle took a deep breath. "I'll get a bucket and rag. Then I will help you clean it up."

"I'll no' be doin' that!" Jennie spat out an incredulous little laugh. "*You* are the one here with legs."

"Then it can sit there and smell up the place until your mother comes home."

Jennie's face paled suddenly with that. Marielle had finally struck a cord. "Ye would no' dare."

"Oh, wouldn't I?" She waited a moment, considering her words. "Now, I'm going to help you onto the floor, get us a couple of rags, and we'll both take care of this mess."

"To the devil with ye!"

"Fine. *After* we get this cleaned up."

Marielle reached over and, as forcefully as she could manage, locked her arms around Jennie's middle in the way that Catriona had showed her to do when her daughter needed to be transferred to her bed or the bath. But this time Jennie resisted, thrusting at Marielle with such force that she too tumbled forward until the chair tottered off-balance, knocking Marielle, Jennie and her chair into a heap on the splattered floor.

"Just what in blazes do ye think ye're doin' there?"

Marielle sat up, her head whipping around in response to the boom of a deep male voice, rich and thick with the Scottish burr. In all of the commotion, she hadn't even heard anyone come in through the front door. Yet now, behind them, was a sturdy man in a leather jacket and jeans, his deep black eyes piercing hers accusingly.

"Well, if it's any business of yours," she said as she struggled to her feet, "I am *trying* to get her to help me clean up a mess she made."

"I don't know who ye are, lassie, or how ye got yourself into this house, but one thing is certain, ye'll no' be speakin' to Jennie like that!"

Marielle stood, strode forward, and looked at him more closely, taking in the sudden and unexpected briny scent of the sea. He was a very powerful presence, with tousled dark hair and deep, dark eyes, both the color of ebony. Unfortunately, all of it came packaged with an unattractive chip on those very square shoulders.

"So who the devil *are* ye then?"

Marielle pressed her hands onto her hips and faced him directly, his attributes snapping from her mind like a bubble that very suddenly had burst. "I might ask *you* the same thing."

"Name's McInnes," he sarcastically revealed. "Now, *if* 'twould no' be askin' too much—"

"Name's Jaeger." She delivered her name in the same manner and the same cool reserve that he had. Marielle did not feel inclined to elaborate beyond that with someone who was glaring at her as if she had just revealed herself to be the very reincarnation of Lucrezia Borgia.

"So then, lassie. Why don't ye be tellin' me what the devil are ye doin' in my aunt's house?"

Marielle swallowed her shock. Colleen's husband. "*You* are Calum?"

"In the flesh."

He took two purposeful strides, in heavy dark boots, to where Jennie sat on the floor surrounded by her own urine. He didn't seem to notice it or care, rather, he stroked her hair lovingly and kissed the top of her head. Then he stood protectively with one hand anchored to her shoulder. "And now that ye know my connection, what might be *your* reason for bein' here?"

"I knew Colleen. I am here at your aunt's invitation."

"Not very well-mannered for one of Catriona's invited guests."

Marielle felt hot blood rush up into her face. "Mr. McInnes," she shot back fiercely, leveling her eyes on him, "it was your niece who was out of line."

"Is this how ye return their hospitality, Miss Jaeger?"

"You have no idea what has been happening here."

"My cousin, Miss Jaeger, is an invalid! I do no' need to know much more."

"Your cousin can't walk, Mr. McInnes. That does not give her license to treat her mother's guests like the hired help!"

"Oh, take me to my room, would ye Calum," Jennie said with a dramatically weak flourish. "Suddenly, I'm needin' to lie down for a bit, after I change."

Calum shot Marielle another accusatory glare, as if her insensitivity alone had somehow reduced Jennie to such a state of exhaustion that she now required this sudden period of very dramatic repose.

Marielle watched without knowing what she could possibly say, as he then scooped Jennie up into his powerful arms and, like some sort of white knight, did not place her back in her wheelchair but instead whisked her off to the safe harbor of her bathroom.

Once they were out of sight, Marielle went to the kitchen for the bucket and rags. As she waited for the bucket to fill, she brushed the back of her hand across her brow and leaned against the sink.

Like the paint that was peeling away from the eaves and the shutters outside, Marielle's optimism for this trip into the past, and what it could bring to her, had already begun to chip away. Few things in

Killin were going as she had expected. And she still knew very little about how and why her sister had died.

Just now, the entire situation felt hopeless.

The mess was cleaned up when Calum came back out and stood, strong and solid, over her. She could sense him there, so she didn't bother looking up. "Well, then. She's cleaned up and restin'."

"How lovely."

In spite of her clipped retort, his tone was softer. The harshness and the edge previously in his voice was gone. "Look. I'm sorry about all of this, but ye simply canno' go treatin' Jennie as if she's like anyone else." Calum stopped, then started again. "Ye do no' know what she's been through."

Marielle scrubbed hard at a patch that had hit Janet Gordon's Turkish carpet. "I have a pretty good idea."

"The loss is likely permanent."

"So I have been told."

"Then how can ye be so hard on the poor lass?"

Marielle finally looked up and dropped the cloth into the foul-smelling water. "That *poor lass,* as you call her, has worked me like a pro. And I don't mind telling you that I have just about had it with Scottish hospitality according to Jennie Quinn."

"Well, you Yanks are no' full of much pluck. . . . You are a Yank, aren't ye?"

Perhaps it was the way it sounded, especially with that same accent, so much like one of her father's barbs. Perhaps it was because she physically ached at the thought of her sweet sister married to an insensitive lout like Calum McInnes. But at his words and their inference, Marielle felt something inside her suddenly snap. She shot to her feet, her cheeks filled with the blood of hot rage.

"Well, Mr. McInnes, if you Scots know a better way to teach a girl who is wallowing in self-pity about self-respect and independence than cleaning up her own damned shit, of which she is perfectly capable, I wish you the very best of luck!"

Without waiting for another of his retorts, Marielle stormed into the small room behind the kitchen. She slammed the door but with the force she had used, it swung open again. Marielle didn't notice. Instead, her entire focus was on flinging her suitcase onto the bed, thrusting open the dresser drawers and tossing clothing in the general direction of her bed and the two suitcases on it.

Marielle didn't know what to do now to find out about Colleen. But at the moment, this entire excursion into the past felt like a disaster.

Impulsively, she tossed her blue jeans and sweaters onto the bed and then went into the second drawer, where she had neatly placed her underthings.

"Are ye not bein' just a wee bit hasty, lass?"

Once again, Marielle did not bother turning around. She just kept tossing things into the suitcase, wanting, foremost, to be away from this brutishly handsome, infuriating man. "I don't believe so. And I most certainly am not your *lass!*"

"Aunt Cat will be livid, ye know, if she thinks I've chased off one of Colleen's friends."

Marielle stopped, turned and looked up for only a moment. "Oh," she said sarcastically, placing a hand to her chest in a dramatic gesture, "you mean you'll have to tell her your considerable charms had no effect on the compassionless Yankee lass?"

"I expect I deserved that."

"Believe me, that wasn't anywhere near my best shot."

"It hasn't been easy for Catriona," he confessed, shaking her a little with the sincerity suddenly in his voice. "She has no' had much time for friendships."

"Well, everything in life has its price, Mr. McInnes," Marielle said, intentionally disregarding this new tone. "Even defending your niece. I really don't think you can blame this on me."

"I wish ye'd be callin' me Calum."

"It's much easier to be angry at someone with whom I'm not on a first-name basis."

"Then I'll be *insistin'* ye call me Calum."

Calum's sly smile just then wiped away the brooding intensity she had seen at first. The change brought to the fore the most attractive man who had ever taken a second look at her. Marielle had not been prepared for that. In the face of his smile, she felt the anger begin to fade.

A moment later, she sank onto the corner of the bed. "Look, Calum," Marielle said, pushing his name out awkwardly. "I've tried with Jennie. But she has made it abundantly clear that she does not want a stranger tending to her."

"She needs a good deal of understandin'."

"What she *needs* is a good spanking."

"Jennie's no' a child."

"Well, she has certainly been behaving like one."

A new silence, thick and taut, fell between them. Marielle watched the muscles in his square jaw tense as he suddenly glared at her. "I would no' have figured you for an expert in spinal injuries."

"Maybe I'm not. But I *do* know about self-pity. And believe me when I tell you that it can destroy you if you let it."

"An outsider like yourself really can have no idea what she's been through."

"I don't need to read every chapter of this story to know how the book is going to end if someone doesn't help her off her pity pot."

He gripped the doorjamb, turning his knuckles white. The smile was gone. So was the very brief moment of concession. "Well, I'll be leavin' ye to make your decision, then," he said tartly. "If ye're wantin' a lift to the train depot, I'll be right glad to take ye."

With the firm termination of the last act in a play, Calum then turned on his sturdy, dark boot heels and walked out of her room. Marielle sank back onto the bed feeling as if a powerful storm had just knocked her down completely.

As much as she wanted, at this moment, to leave Killin and return to the predictability of Paris, Marielle reminded herself that she would do so without closing an all-important chapter of her life. She would lose the chance to make some sense of a loss that had marked her deeply.

Safe to say ye'll screw this up, as ye've done with everythin' else.

Marielle stopped on the road down the hill from MacLaren's Bend, her heart slamming into her ribs.

The breath froze in her throat. That voice inside her head very clearly had been her father's.

"Bastard!" she shouted. "Leave me alone!"

She waited stubbornly for a reply, her mouth dry with fear. But there was nothing more. After a moment, she wrapped her arms around her waist, lowered her head, and walked alone down into the center of town.

"Get a grip, Marielle," she muttered to herself.

It was the frustration over Colleen, she decided, and being back in Killin with all of her dark childhood memories of Malcolm. Of course that was it. Yes, of course.

Marielle wasn't certain where she was going now. All she knew was that she needed to get away from that house, with all of its memories and tensions, for a little while. Try to make sense of things before she did something rash. And Jennie, quite clearly, was in good hands now that her great, infuriating champion had come home.

Moments later, Marielle found herself walking back into town toward the main road. She hadn't even realized that she was in front of Barry Buchanan's shop until she saw him sitting again at his potter's wheel.

Barry wiped his hands on a gray cotton cloth, stood, and greeted her with a hearty smile. Marielle wondered as he looked at her if there was anything about her that seemed familiar to him. He certainly didn't appear to recognize her real identity. But then it had been such a long time, and they had both grown from children since she had gone away.

"'Tis bonny to see ye again," he said with his deep, slow voice and that same easy charm.

"I was just out walking and—" She looked at Barry

for a moment. The depth in his eyes made her feel foolish for trying to sound light. "Oh, to be truthful about it, I needed some time to rethink my decision to stay these few days in Killin."

It surprised her to hear him chuckle as he leaned back against one of the display tables and crossed his arms. "So Jennie McInnes has gotten to *you*, as well, has she?"

Marielle suddenly felt defensive. "She's just a very difficult and unhappy young woman."

"And apparently she's no' met her match yet."

"Excuse me?"

She looked at his face then, but what her mind conjured was an image of Colleen. As she had been when they were children. Looking at Barry, Marielle remembered clearly how her sister had admired his intensity and sensitivity. Perhaps he was right about Jennie.

"I meant no offense," Barry said quickly. "'Tis only that Jennie could use a spark of hope. And you bein' from a sophisticated place like New York, a reporter and all—"

"How did you know that about me?"

"Ian and I are friends. And, as I've said, 'tis a small town here."

"Well, in any case, there is very little that will get past that exceedingly sour uncle of hers, when he's home from the sea."

Barry's eyes changed, darkening. He waited a heartbeat, then two, to respond. "Ah, yes. Calum."

"Catriona told me that, in his grief, he had sold his law practice and then took up fishing on a trawler to pay for Jennie's extra expenses after her accident."

He watched her thoughtfully for a moment. "What else do ye know of Calum McInnes?"

"I know that Colleen married him. Beyond that, very little, actually. Our meeting just now was a bona fide disaster, and Catriona has spoken of him in only the most glowing terms."

"That does no' surprise me. Catriona Quinn sees the best in most everybody."

She ran a hand through her hair and looked out onto the street spotted with shoppers. "I really don't know what to do," Marielle sighed. "Killin certainly is everything Colleen always wrote to me that it was. And since Catriona has been so nice and has offered me a room at MacLaren's Bend, I thought I might stay for a few days more. But I really can't do that where I'm not wanted."

"Oh, but ye *are* surely wanted there at MacLaren's Bend," he said in a thoughtful tone, the openness and sincerity swiftly returning. "And needed, as well."

She was surprised. "Needed? What could *I* possibly do for *them*?"

"Time will tell ye that, Marielle. 'Tis better to make life's discoveries on your own. The meanin' is deeper that way."

"Well, if they need me, Jennie and Calum have the strangest way in the world I've ever seen of showing it."

His hazel eyes widened. Marielle saw them glitter. "And what does your heart tell ye to do?"

"At the moment, I don't honestly know."

"Then ye're no' listenin' closely enough."

"And how would you propose I change that?"

Barry smiled suddenly, then pivoted around and

was moving back across the room in those graceful, long-legged strides that seemed almost to define him. He was not classically handsome, she thought, but he possessed a kindness that softened that image, a gentleness of spirit that drew her to him in a curiously intense way.

"My da was poor as a church mouse, but a wise old man he was, Marielle. And he taught me a long time ago that when ye're needin' to listen to what your heart is sayin', ye've got to get out where there are no distractions. 'Tis the only way sometimes to really hear the truth in the words."

She couldn't imagine what he was talking about as he plucked two worn, dark anorak jackets from an old brass coatrack in the corner. "Come."

Marielle glanced through the windows at the torrent coming down outside now, sheets of white, cold rain. "Where are we going?"

"To listen to your heart, of course."

"In this weather?"

"This is Scotland, Marielle," he chuckled. "Ye'd best grow accustomed to that if ye mean to stay. We Scots do nearly everythin' in the rain!"

How curious it was to feel that she could trust this man she barely knew—*any man,* when she had spent so many years running from those sorts of connections. That was the first thought she had as she and Barry Buchanan walked together toward the edge of town, he so tall and full of self-assurance, beside her smaller, less commanding frame.

Marielle hadn't liked strolling in the rain since

she was a little girl. There was simply too much of it in Paris. Now she happily slogged through little peat brown puddles along the road out of town just to keep up.

Then suddenly, as she looked ahead, her heart stopped.

Before her, a muted vision, like a Monet water-color, was there. Vaulting back from her memories. Vivid. Unchanged. The heathery moor sloping down into a broad, green glen. *The forbidden glen of our childhood.* It was the one place she had avoided on her walks since she had been back, afraid to confront that fragile recollection. Yet it was the very first place that Barry brought her now.

As a sudden gust of wind drove the rain, the smoke gray stems of the wine-dark heather bent with it, all shining like polished satinwood. Marielle slowed to take it in, this breathtaking painting—drawing in air that was sharp and clear. She could see herself and Colleen again. Feel it. The breeze blowing their hair, their gauzy dresses back . . .

"Come on, Mairi!"

This was the place. Their secret place. The stuff of her most precious memories.

When Barry and his long-legged strides gained too much distance ahead of her, Marielle broke into a slight jog just to keep up. Colleen's voice filled her mind, her vision, and her heart, as she ran. *Look at that, Mairi, will ye! . . . How wonderful! Mystical!*

Now he was passing through a little break in the crumbling stone wall and moving into a field peppered with black-faced sheep. As they went deeper, ever deeper into the glen, Marielle glanced back at Killin, remembering how she had held up her limping sister and helped her back along that same path to MacLaren's Bend.

I ache for what we missed, Colleen, she was thinking. *I ache for all of this.*

For a moment, the driving rain slowed to nothing more than a fine mist. The clouds hanging heavily over hillcrests suddenly parted and a pale ray of sun sliced through. The quiet instilled in her such emotion that she felt a flurry of tears pressing at the back of her eyes.

They moved onward, further than she had ever gotten with her sister, nearing a little stone bridge that crossed over the mud brown river and led to a tall bower of cedar trees.

Again Marielle glanced back at the little hamlet of Killin, smoke from its many chimneys hanging thick and motionless in the biting air, looking like a slightly dark, idyllic Victorian painting of the way the towns of the world once had been.

Then ahead of them, tucked deeply into a cluster of evergreens, she saw the rest of the cottage she had only seen glimpses of on that long-ago afternoon. It was small and tightly sealed, with a thatch roof, a front porch, and a bright blue door, all of it bathed in emerald green ivy. A stone chimney, green with moss, shot up from the roofline, and there was a woodpile beneath it.

"Caretaker's cottage for centuries," Barry said simply, as he kept moving deeper, ever deeper into the lushness of the secluded woods. "'Tis my home now."

They passed the stream that twisted along above it as the icy water slipped smoothly over little piles of silvery pebbles. The air now, in late afternoon, was sweet and cold with a pungent earthiness. He did not speak again as Marielle followed him steadily through the dense trees and the wet, browning bracken, until she saw the unexpected spire of sandstone and the tower of a ruined Gothic abbey. Marielle slowed as it came majestically into view, framed and protected by low-hung branches and a thick gray mist, making it look far more like an apparition than something real.

Finally, Barry stopped too. Both of them were gazing up.

"It's magnificent," she breathed, suddenly hearing the trickle of water echoing through the trees.

"I had a sense ye'd find it so."

She looked up at him, smiling, happy to be here.

"'Twas destroyed long ago by rebels. But even burnin' could no' take away the essence of the place. People still come here, even as it is, most of them searchin' for their own answers." Barry stopped talking and stared up reflectively again at the lone spire, magnificent and proud among such violent ruins.

"So. How did you come upon this place?"

"The cottage belonged to someone once dear to me. Her father was caretaker of the abbey."

Ye're no' to go into that glen! Ye know that. . . . A wicked woman lives that way.

Marielle tipped her head, chasing away the harsh sound of her father's voice.

So that was indeed why they were always forbidden to go into a sinful place where two innocent girls might happen on to the orphaned young man and his lowborn lover. *We all do what we must to go on, to survive,* she thought. Marielle had. And so had Barry.

"Caretaker over the ruins of a cathedral?" she smiled wryly.

"'Tis a lengthy story indeed. But suffice it to say that his father before him came to believe 'twas the responsibility of the sons of Maitland to protect what was left of the abbey, so special was it."

She bit back a weak smile. "But your friend was a woman?"

"Aye. That did prove a bit of a complication."

Marielle touched a fern. "So then you've lived here for a long time?"

"Since my father died and Regan Maitland took me in. But the abbey was always the place I'd gone to work things out on my own before that. 'Twas where Regan found me years ago," he gestured, "sittin' forlorn on that very stone, and she with no one left to care for her either. 'Twas fate in it, we both knew."

"It seems there's a lot of that here in the countryside."

"'Tis an ages-old piece of earth we're sharin', these hills, this glen, full of wonder and even a bit of magic."

"And ghosts?"

Barry turned to her. His smile blossomed again. "Anything is possible here."

Marielle shivered. She didn't want to believe in her father's ghost. But something more was at play at MacLaren's Bend than her simply returning. She felt now as if Colleen too had called out to her since her death, willing her to return. And Malcolm, the essence of a bitter man, was intent on keeping her away. Yes that was it. Not ghosts perhaps, but some sense of the past breaking through to the present, forcing her to deal with it all.

Sensing a change in her, Barry said, "Regan taught me somethin' very important, Marielle. Do no' fear the magic that happens here, embrace it. 'Tis peace in acceptin' what will be anyway."

Marielle liked that, felt comfort from it. "She must have been very wise."

"Aye, Regan was that. In spite of what people believed."

"I'm honored that you would want to share something so personal with a stranger."

Barry gazed down at her, his slim face lighting around deep, soulful eyes. "'Tis just the point, Marielle," he said smoothly, in a voice that suddenly made her shiver. "In a curious way, ye're no' a stranger here a'tall, are ye?"

Did he know? *Could he?* "How do you mean that?" she asked carefully.

"Only that there is somethin' about ye that belongs to this place."

"I'm beginning to feel that way too."

"Then always know it's here for ye. Just as it is for me."

His voice was like a gentle incantation as he took her hand then to help her over some loose stones and they went together inside what was left of the giant nave. There was a thin mist clinging to the massive skeleton of moss and stone as they carefully stepped. When they were near what had once been the altar, Marielle sank onto a large sandstone bolder, feeling breathless and a little overwhelmed. It had been years since she had been inside of a church. Even the remains of one. Since the day they had buried Ron. Now, suddenly, it felt good to be here.

The books were right, she thought. . . .

There really were miracles to be had in Scotland.

And it was a miracle too that Barry Buchanan had come into her life just when she was on the verge of giving up this crazy, impulsive thing, this ruse, she had begun in Killin. She sensed that Barry was a guide of sorts, someone to help keep her from straying too far. Because of him, Marielle suddenly had a renewed spirit for what she wanted to do here.

Marielle gazed up at the soaring, once-great monolith, such faded grandeur, such magical beauty all around her. "I suppose I really don't *want* to leave Killin."

"No," Barry said, as if he had known that was what she would say.

They looked at one another and, as naturally as every other one of his movements, he reached over and carefully lifted the collar of the anorak up against her neck against a fresh breeze that stirred around them.

The nearness of him didn't bother her. It was not sensual, but strangely welcome.

There was reassurance in it, a feeling that she was on the right path at last.

"They need ye at MacLaren's Bend, Marielle," he said, calmly then.

No, not sensual at all, she decided, looking up at Barry. But the gentleness of him, the sincerity, was something very powerful in its own right. She still could not quite believe there were men in the world left like that. Forceful, yet gentle . . . honest. He reminded her of someone from another time, another age.

He was a man, she realized, very like Ron.

Marielle chuckled softly, nervously, hugging her arms around her chest, in a situation that was foreign and even, somehow, a little frightening to her. "I'm not so sure any one of them but Catriona would agree with you, Barry."

"Then ye're task is to *make* them agree. 'Tis inside ye. Let them know that ye're needin' to become a part of this place for a while. In the same way it has already become a part of *you*."

How did he sense that about her? Or did he *know* it? Marielle tipped her head, her nervous laughter fading to nothing more than a wan smile. That haunting kind of Lord Byron quality about him reared up again just then and made him attractive. Suddenly, she almost wished he recognized her.

"How did you become so wise, Barry Buchanan?"

His gaze held hers. "Experience is not always wisdom, ye know."

"Well, in your case," she said, still smiling, "I have a feeling it probably is."

Marielle closed her own eyes for a moment and drew in another deep, contemplative breath. The air on her face was cool and wet. She felt calmer now, more at peace suddenly than she had for days. Maybe longer than that. Yet what a day this had been. You never quite knew here what strange experience or what curious new person lay just around the corner.

From the sullen intensity of Calum to the wise, free-spirited Barry. From Jennie's curious bitterness to Catriona's kindness. And, unforgettably, there was still Ian McShane's haunting accusation: *I always believed that husband of hers was involved.*

It all was such a great deal to reconcile, what Marielle had found here. But it occurred to her, as she sat calmly like this, eyes closed, that if Scotland really was the land of magic and dreams, then perhaps her sister's spirit could work a bit of that magic and help her uncover the truth of how and why she had really died so suddenly.

Barry had brought Marielle back to his shop, the place where their journey began. Now he watched through the bay window as she walked away. It had stopped raining. Gentle silver threads of sunlight came gleaming through a bank of heavy white clouds that still pressed themselves oppressively from the sky. They were so similar, she and Colleen. Marielle had her essence. Strange, he thought, and sad, really.

After all this time. After she was out of his sight, the bell overhead tinkled lightly. Ian McShane ambled in, hands shoved casually into the pockets of worn, gray corduroy slacks and an unlit pipe clamped between his teeth.

"Barry." He nodded.

"Afternoon, Ian."

"I see we've got ourselves a bonny new lass in town," Ian casually observed. "Certainly has been a while."

"Aye."

"She's no' married."

"No?"

"No weddin' band, anyway."

Barry grinned. "I thank ye for thinkin' of me."

Ian gazed out the window at the passersby again.

The two men were silent for a moment. "Sure asks a lot of questions, though."

Barry looked at him. "And what did you tell her?"

"Only the wee bit of truth I knew. About Colleen."

"And which truth would that be?" Barry asked.

"About that husband of hers and all of the mystery concernin' the way she died. No one around here knows all of the details, to this day."

"So what did you tell her about him?"

"That I could no' prove it, but I always thought he'd played a part in her death."

"'Twas better left unsaid, ye know."

"Perhaps. But she knew Colleen."

"So she's said."

"Well, I had the feelin', by the look on her face when I told her Colleen was dead, that at some point the two of them had been fair close."

"Aye," Barry said.

"I just thought she deserved to know."

CHAPTER TWELVE

Marielle sat alone on the front porch at MacLaren's Bend the next morning, wrapped in a Scotch blue plaid blanket as a thin, soft rain began to fall on Killin. The black road beyond the steep gravel driveway glistened as droplets fell from the pewter sky and from the two thinning elms, their steady spray of leaves fluttering across the horizon like crimson and golden-brown butterflies.

She had always loved the morning, but here in Scotland it was especially glorious. Marielle took a sip of hot black coffee from a clay mug, then leaned back in the fraying white wicker rocker, her sleepy gaze fixing on the gray veils of mist settled down on the town before her. Suddenly, into that pungent earthy fragrance of wet grass and new mist, streamed the sharp, competing aroma of kippers cooking.

Last night, her reporter's instinct had taken over and Marielle had concluded that what these people were not able to tell her about Colleen she would need to uncover for herself. Certainly stories had been printed about the tragic death, complete with details. *I didn't come all the way back here to leave without knowing the truth,* she had resolved.

But the only newspaper serving Killin was a train ride away in Oban. Marielle sat up and raked the hair back from her forehead. She turned around and looked at the house. *You hold so many secrets, don't you? If only you could talk, instead of that bitter old goat of a ghost!*

Finally, she went back inside and stopped at the archway into the kitchen. The rich aroma surrounded her. She was surprised to see Calum, dressed in tight-fitting jeans and an ivory Aran sweater, sleeves pushed up to his coppery elbows, standing at the stove in front of a black cast-iron pan.

Before she could turn away, he glanced up. "Hungry?"

Marielle was still wary of Calum McInnes. "Actually, yes," she said cautiously.

"I hope ye fancy your eggs fried."

"That's fine."

"I see ye've already got coffee."

"I've been up for a while." Calum turned back to the pans on the stove, intent on his goal of conjuring up breakfast. "Is anyone else up yet?" she asked after a moment.

"No, but I find this works better than any alarm clock when I'm in town. Catriona'll be out here before I've got it on the table." In spite of herself, Marielle smiled. That surprised her.

She sank onto one of the oak kitchen chairs. Her eyes and her attention shifted to Calum as she watched him cook. He moved in smooth, strong pivots and turns, from the stove to the counter top, where the blue earthenware bowl of eggs and the clear glass pitcher of milk sat, and Marielle saw how different he was from Barry, in temperament and especially in build.

As she sat holding the warm clay mug, his back to her, Marielle's eyes were free to play over the curves and angles of his body. Where Barry was slim and lithe, almost like a willow tree, Calum had the broad-backed sturdy bearing of a young oak.

Marielle squeezed her eyes and opened them again as Calum faced the stove. She was surprised at herself for even having had the thought. This was, after all, her sister's husband.

"I was hoping we could declare something of a cease-fire," she suddenly blurted.

Calum did not turn away from the stove to answer her even though her words and their quickened tone were unexpected. "I've nothin' particular against ye."

"That wasn't the way it looked yesterday."

She watched him divide the eggs and kippers onto two of his aunt's blue willow plates and set each one on a beige lace placemat at the little oak breakfast table. He hadn't seemed particularly struck by her words, she thought, nor by her attempt at making peace. Calum McInnes was exasperatingly composed—when he wasn't being snide. He was certainly hard to peg. What, she wondered, would happen to that well-honed composure if she were to tell him just now exactly who she was?

Calum set a rack of dry toast between the four plates, then pulled out one of the empty ladder-back chairs and settled into it across from her. As he lifted a fork to his mouth, without looking directly at her, he finally said, "Ye're Catriona's guest. Ye're no' too hard on the eyes. Let's leave it at that, hmm?"

Calum's comments came at her like a sudden slap, as if she were being brushed off like a stray scrap of lint from his sweater. Making her feel the way her father had, like most handsome and self-assured men always had, insignificant. And certainly dangerous to know.

Marielle stiffened further still and lifted her mug to her lips to take a sip of cooling coffee that she didn't want. "Fine with me."

"Good."

"Good," she echoed sharply.

A moment later, Catriona was at the door yawning, with the back of her hand across her mouth, still in her long floral bathrobe and slippers. It was Sunday, Marielle remembered, and the bakery was only opened in the afternoon. It was the one morning a week that Catriona had to herself.

"Coffee?" Marielle asked.

"I've got it," Calum intercepted, snapping up and grabbing an empty clay mug to fill it. Marielle sank back into her chair.

"It does smell delicious in here." Catriona smiled as she sat down and yawned again into her fist.

"I've made your favorite."

"'Tis a splendid thing indeed to have ye here, Calum. Even if I would favor seein' ye back at your law practice."

Marielle watched a shadow of something pass across his face with that. But before she could identify it, the shadow was gone. He picked up his fork again and took a bite of egg. "Jennie awake?"

"Just barely."

"I'll be puttin' her plate in the oven, then, so it'll stay warm."

There was a moment of strained silence while Calum's flippant comment to her still churned inside her head. Finally, Marielle dotted her mouth with her napkin and stood. How could he be two such different men? Marielle wondered. There was such a rough carelessness that kept clouding over the instances of humor and kindness. It was as if he were purposely trying not to be liked.

"If you'll excuse me," she said quietly. "I need to get some air."

Before she got halfway down the hall, she heard Catriona huff and a whispered conversation follow. "I'm tellin' ye, Calum McInnes, if ye've offended the lass, 'twill no' be an easy thing to forgive."

"So what is it ye want me to do, then?"

There was a small silence. When Catriona began again, her tone of voice was softer, less combative. "I understand ye, Calum, and why ye are as ye are. But even so, 'tis none of it Marielle's fault. Still, ye've been as sober with her as a rector on Sunday. Apologizin' to her for forgettin' your manners, I think, would be a grand place to start."

CHAPTER THIRTEEN

Catriona felt horrid about not having told Mairi the whole truth when she came back to MacLaren's Bend. About Jennie. About Calum. About what had really happened. Neither of them was making it particularly easy for the sweet young woman in their midst who, in spite of the protective distance she liked to keep and the sophisticated city airs, was still as fragile as a piece of Edinburgh glass.

But like Malcolm had always said, *Some truths are made to be spoken and others are best left to lie. . . .*

Catriona had watched Calum wrinkle his face at her suggestion, reminding her of how Malcolm had looked at the end. Bitter and sour as old fruit. She had tried her best to make a difference in her husband's life, as she had done for Calum. But sometimes the wounds were just too deep. She had learned that the hard way in those last years. Like Vivienne, she had never fully measured up to Malcolm's beloved first wife.

Calum had shot her that brooding look of his as he thrust his chair back and followed their houseguest out of the kitchen. Hopefully, to apologize.

It was the last thing Catriona wanted for her

nephew, to end up like this before his life had really even begun. Angry. Spiteful. Blaming the world for what had happened. Yes, Calum had faced an unspeakably dark episode already in his young life. Catriona had to make allowances for that. But, even so, she wasn't about to let him ruin this return for the nice young woman, a strong woman with determination and fire, who had come back to battle demons of her own.

She had promised Calum, hadn't she? In her own way she had vowed him her silence. The whole town had. Not to delve too deeply into what had happened that awful night.

Because she loved him like a son, Catriona wanted to go after him now that he had charged out the kitchen door, to say that she was sorry to have pushed him. But maybe it was better this way. Maybe he and his wife's sister could find some common ground anyway.

Catriona wondered if she had done the right thing, agreeing not to tell anyone who Marielle Jaeger really was. Especially Calum. A part of her thought he, of all people, had a right to know. After all, she would have been his sister-in-law. Perhaps knowing that would have made him a bit more tolerant while she was here.

But Catriona had promised, and the poor young woman did deserve not to feel as if everyone in the world in whom she had placed a trust would betray her.

Calum stood at the front bay window watching her.

Marielle Jaeger was the most genuinely confounding woman he'd ever had the misfortune to meet. Or was it *fortune* that she had dropped into their lives as she had? The single thing that made him ask himself the question now was the dull ache at the center of his chest as he watched her. She was hunched over outside in the old, weed-choked garden, petite and slightly fragile. But Marielle was fiercely determined, for some unknown reason, to pull up all of the dead stalks and leaves. As if she belonged here. As if that garden meant something to her.

It was a sensation, watching her alone outside, something that he hadn't felt for a very long time. *Since Colleen.*

He'd never thought a great deal of Americans. Most of them seemed too brash to him. Too forward. But Marielle was certainly in a league of her own. A rich combination of determination and vulnerability. And if you could get past those acid retorts of hers every time he said the least little thing, she was actually, well, she was fair bonny. . . .

Liar! his conscience snidely taunted. All right, he silently amended. Beautiful. She was beautiful. And there was something actually familiar about her. Although he could not place it, he found himself wondering if anyone else sensed it.

Calum watched a moment more, her cheeks pink from the cold, her chestnut hair blowing in the wind as she worked the dirt intensely. Someone else's garden. A stranger's garden. Calum felt his heart expand. He didn't want to go outside, to speak with her as Aunt Cat had urged. But something greater inside him compelled him to do it.

They couldn't possibly have gotten off on a worse footing. She had just looked so irritatingly confident yesterday. Uncompromising, when she didn't know all of the facts. But wasn't that part of what also made her so different? *Special* was probably the word those who loved her would use.

Calum hadn't realized how long he had been standing there watching her until he heard footsteps behind him and the front door click, then close, knowing it was Catriona on her way to church. Still praying for him, no doubt. Jennie, who refused to go to church on Sunday since the accident, was probably still in bed.

He was alone now with his conscience.

What a lummox he had been, with his own crisp retorts and icy manner. She seemed nice enough with those smiling eyes, the color of mahogany. Damn, but they held something familiar. It was strange, he thought, unexplainable really, that this woman, this stranger, should actually remind him of Colleen.

After the door closed, and Catriona had gone out, the house stilled again.

On impulse, Calum tossed on the black leather jacket that had been hanging on a peg of the hall tree and walked outside, down the front steps and over to the side yard where the sad remains of the garden lay. It was a garden once tended by Colleen's stepmother, he remembered her telling him, then by Colleen herself, in tribute to the only mother she remembered.

He stood next to Marielle for a moment, hands shoved into his pockets, watching her, before she was aware that he was there. Close up, she reminded him of a colt, that wide-eyed beauty, he thought. Sleek and very smart, but a little skittish. Someone not altogether comfortable with her beauty, as if she hadn't always possessed it.

Calum exhaled a breath, leaving a plume of white air just as she turned around and glanced up, her eyes fastening onto his. "Ye're no' likely to find much of beauty that'll grow out here this time of year," he said.

She looked at him critically for a moment, her face pink now, iridescent, especially her small, perfectly shaped nose, her dark eyes sparkling. Then she surprised him by, unceremoniously, turning back to the dirt. Only then did she say, "I like working the soil. It's one of the few things that appreciate my hard work and doesn't talk back."

"Ye're no' goin' to make this easy for me, are ye?"

"Even if I knew what *it* was, I don't imagine that I would."

He couldn't help it; his jaw clamped shut.

The words *I'm sorry* had always stuck like a fish bone in his throat. That impenetrable Scots pride. That's what it was. But it was especially difficult now to bring those particular words across his tongue when this lass, this Marielle Jaeger, was so ruddy flip. So quick to toss a line back at him.

Pretty as a rose, he thought—and sharp as a thorn.

Then it felt as if something unseen were actually pushing him quite forcefully until he surrendered, crouching down beside her. "The woman who first planted this garden was French. She used to fancy hollyhocks and foxglove here, I was told. People in Killin still talk about how beautiful it was."

"I don't know much about either of those flowers," she said, in a voice softer than the one he'd expected. "My own mother used to like violets. She had a real way with them. Everyone in our neighborhood envied

her, the way they sat on our windowsill, always bloom-
ing like crazy."

Suddenly, she looked up at him, and Calum realized that they were very close. He could actually feel
her warm breath on his cheek. The realization of that
brought a sudden sensation, as if he's drunk a dram of
Scotch too fast. He was off-balance, wanting to be
nearer to her in spite of his reserve.

*Never again. . . . No, never again! I canno' care for
anyone like that! Not in that same all-consuming way!
Especially after what it cost me!* He closed his eyes for
a moment, giving in to the censuring voice inside his
wounded heart. And when he opened them again he
was intentionally looking back down at the ground, the
place where she had been digging. *Looking away from
her.* As if, perhaps, he was studying the composition of
the soil. Anything to steady himself. To set him right
again on his course.

Being with Marielle Jaeger, he thought, was a little like that sensation the first time he'd been on a fishing boat. So incredibly groundless. Unsteady. Not ever
quite being able to get your bearings no matter how
hard you tried.

"Isn't there anything that would grow here?"
Marielle suddenly asked.

There was a flash of something when he looked
up, the tone of her voice as oddly familiar as the rest of
her, drawing him back to the moment. Their eyes met
again.

"Plants," she amended. "What sort did the French
woman manage this time of year?"

Calum rubbed his square chin, where there
remained a dusty stubble of beard from the day

208 DIANE HAEGER

before, and felt a tug of anxiety. It was as if what she wanted to know actually mattered.

The sad fact, he realized, was, as much as he wanted to answer her, he didn't have a clue about gardening. All he knew anything substantive about were legal briefs and, of course, these days, fishing trawlers. And he knew that winters in Scotland were harsh. He looked at Marielle again and saw a leaf settle suddenly into a fold of her hair near the corner of her eye. It lay lightly, a slip of tarnished gold, fluttering softly, and Calum had the overwhelming urge to reach out and brush it away. To touch her.

He felt something very hot surge up inside him at the thought, and it was another moment before he realized that it was desire.

He was so focused on Marielle and on what to say next—that stray leaf still fluttering in her hair—that he hadn't heard anyone else. Before he could say anything, Jennie was coming down the ramp and moving near in her wheelchair, her face as red as Catriona's fresh beet salad.

"Get away from there!" she was shrieking. "'Tis no' to be touched, that garden! I'm tellin' ye both, get away!"

Calum came to his feet, brushing off his jeans at the knees, but Marielle remained as she had been, looking up at Jennie.

"What are ye yellin' about?"

"*You,* of all people, ought to know better, Calum McInnes! 'Twas Colleen's garden! 'Twill stay as she left it. Now get her away from here!"

Marielle was coming to her feet then, although reluctantly, and still holding onto the small silver spade. "I think together we could help make this garden something Colleen would be proud of," Marielle said, stubbornly forcing the tremor from her voice.

"I do no' care what *you* think! Ye're no' a part of this family, and ye were no' a part of hers! Ye're a stranger, here by my ma's good graces alone, and I'm sure I do no' recall anythin' in her invitation about gardenin' privileges!"

"I only thought—"

"I told ye, I haven't a care what ye thought! The garden here is to remain as it is! 'Twas Colleen's from her childhood! 'Twas sacred to her!"

"Enough, Jennie!" Calum said strongly, and then there was silence.

He and Marielle both saw the shock register on Jennie's face, first in the way her bare pink lips parted. A moment later her curved jaw slackened, and he felt a sharp little knot of disloyalty thread its way up his throat. A week ago there was nothing in the world that would have made him raise his voice to Jennie.

"'Tis a lovely thing to know whose side ye're on now."

"I'm no' takin' sides. I only think ye might give Marielle a bit of a chance."

Jennie's pale green eyes, as she glanced up at her new companion, were flat and unsmiling. "Sorry, Calum, but this mornin' I'm fresh out of chances."

He glanced at Marielle just then and felt his heart do a little flip. The expression on her face was one of hurt masked over lightly with that same chin-lifted pride, and he felt a wild surge of something actually urging him to defend her further.

This is foolhardy! Ye barely know her! But Jennie here before ye is blood!

It didn't matter. Somehow, though, Calum knew now, with a curious little burst of recognition, what her friends and family must know: that Marielle Jaeger was someone special. That she deserved better than she had gotten from him since she'd been in Killin. And she certainly deserved better from Jennie.

"Ye know well that I understand," Calum said evenly, pacing his words. "But how ye're seein' fit to treat Marielle is where we part if ye're of a mind to continue."

"I wonder where ye'd be today if I'd adopted *that* particular stance myself," she shot back cryptically.

He saw that Jennie knew what line she'd crossed by the way she averted her eyes, then opened them wide again, daring him to push her into saying something further that neither of them wanted to hear. As she looked at him, her face was full of bitterness. "I just don't know why she had to come here and stir things up!"

"Jennie! 'Tis no' like ye atall, speakin' this way!"

There was a little silence, and Calum helplessly watched her sweet, rosy face strain to withstand the oncoming tears. Suddenly, she was sobbing, wiping at her cheeks as he looked into eyes that were branding his with their sorrow. "I just want things to be the way they were, Calum! I want my legs! Oh, God! And I want Colleen back!"

"Well, we canno'! None of that is ever goin' to come back to any of us! We've got to deal with what *is*! We've all of us got to try!"

He could feel Marielle watching them as Jennie surrendered her face to her hands, the sound of her sudden keening wail filling the still, cool morning air.

Then it started again. Like it always did. Like it always would. Guilt seeping into every pore of his body, taking him over, a heartbeat at a time.

Marielle took a step forward. "What can I do?" she asked, pressing a gentle hand onto his shoulder.

"I'll just get her inside. She'll be all right in a bit," Calum said, managing to sound like he meant it—as if anything in the world would ever really be all right again.

She watched him help her back up the ramp that had been fitted beside the stairs, and Marielle felt a burst of sympathy for the embittered Jennie, knowing that she would never be able to climb the steps again. Her entire life, like that ramp, was about alteration and change. That Jennie had not yet made her peace with it, or with what had happened to take that vital freedom away, was understandable.

But what *had* happened? People in Killin said almost as little about that as they did about Colleen's death.

Marielle heard a bedroom door close down the hall and, after a moment, Calum reappeared. She was still standing in the center of the room, waiting for him. "How is she?" she asked, meaning it.

"Jennie's lyin' down and has taken one of her pills. She'll be fine after a bit."

She could see that his face was troubled. Even beneath the handsome features and the forced pleasant expression there was still that spark of grief. Life had brought him great misery. Recognizing that helped her soften to him. Calum was a far more complicated man than the one she had seen at first.

"I'd like to know what happened, if you'd be

willing to tell me," Marielle said tentatively, her voice pitched low.

"'Tis ancient history now."

"Not to Jennie, I don't think."

A look unfolded on his face, a falling away like layers of a camellia, revealing something profound underneath. His eyes, *the windows to his soul*, were suddenly sad.

Marielle stood very still. Waiting. In the foyer, the tall clock chimed the hour. She didn't realize for a moment that she had actually been holding her breath as she looked at Calum, seeing some piece of what was really inside of him. It felt then as if something powerful was about to happen.

Her voice dropped even lower, wanting now to be soothing somehow. "Maybe if I understood what went on, it would help me make fewer mistakes with her while I am here."

"'Tis nothin' personal, Marielle," he finally said, not looking at her directly any longer. "But rootin' round in the past serves no purpose."

"Neither does hiding it."

"I'm sorry," Calum said with firm sincerity.

Still, Marielle felt the sting of his rejection again and, in its wake, she fought everything inside of herself not to counter with some further quick retort. Her defenses against men, and their ages-old ability to wound her, still ran deep. She meant nothing to this dark, brooding Scotsman. Why on earth would he choose to reveal the past about Jennie to her?

Still, as she watched Calum put his jacket back on and walk again out of the front door, Marielle was entirely taken up with the tormented vision before her, a man with a powerful presence and a dark secret, perhaps as complex and heartbreaking as her own.

"Sorry, lass. No trains from here on Sunday."

Beneath a cool and cloudless blue sky, an old drinker with rotting teeth sat with a near-empty pint between his knees. He was alone on the stark platform at Crainlarich, in front of the sealed ticket window. An hour after she left Calum and MacLaren's Bend, Marielle's heart sank at the sound of his slurred pronouncement. A crumpled slip of paper and an old paper cup, driven by the breeze, tumbled along the ground between them in the silence.

"None?"

"First one again is tomorrow mornin'."

"Another day is an eternity!"

"So goes the way of the world," he said, waxing philosophic.

Marielle felt the weight of disappointment heavy on her shoulders as she walked away from the platform. "One step forward, two steps back," she sighed. It was what Ron had so often said. "Just keep at it, and eventually you'll get where you want to be."

But right now she felt as if that was the furthest point on earth. Knowing why her sister had died, discovering the details and making sense of something so premature, was the only thing in the world that could give her any peace at all.

Marielle woke that night to the thunderous sound of water very near.

Dazed and a little surprised at a booming, unexpected sound cutting into the stillness of the night, she sat up and squinted at the clock, not really certain at first that it actually did say three in the morning. But the sound she heard was not rain, she finally realized, it was the shower in the bathroom between her room and the kitchen.

She looked up at the dark ceiling and remembered the supper they'd had last night.

While there was conversation and occasional laughter, the meal had crackled with undercurrents. Jennie's smoldering anger and Catriona's impatience with her daughter had been balanced by Calum's curious intensity.

Throughout the meal, Marielle had found her gaze continually wandering across the table, and settling on a man who had seemed to have little use for her. But each time she realized what she was doing, she had quickly looked away. The last thing in the world she needed was this attraction. Good Lord, Calum had been her sister's husband, she reminded herself again.

And she was here in Killin about Colleen. About their past. Not about any sort of fantasy romance she had so long denied herself, especially with a handsome, brooding Scot. Marielle lay back against the cool linen sheets, wondering now if the sound of water, the shower, had been something she'd dreamed. She didn't hear it any longer. She didn't hear anything. The old house was still.

Marielle tried to fall back to sleep but couldn't. She was wide awake. What in heaven was she supposed to do now? It wasn't yet dawn. After a moment, she gave a little defeated huff, tossed back the covers and dangled her feet over the edge of the bed. She was actually glad when they touched the floor because the shock of cold floorboards beneath her toes drove away the persistent images of Calum McInnes plaguing her mind.

She drew her white chenille bathrobe over her shoulders and decided on tea. She could take it into the salon with the novel she had been reading and then watch the sun come up. There really were the most incredible sunrises here in Killin.

Marielle moved out of her room quietly in bare feet and took two tentative steps into the darkened kitchen when a shaft of golden light from the slightly open bathroom door, shot into the kitchen. Her heart lurched. Someone really was up. She hadn't dreamed it.

Sinking back against the doorjamb, unsure of what to do, she held her breath in the darkness. Then slowly, ever so slowly, she turned around. Nothing, she thought in a little burst of panic, could ever have prepared her for what she saw.

Her heart vaulted into her throat.

It was Calum who was standing at the white pedestal sink, his back to the slightly opened door, clutching a gray bath towel, his body as bare and chiseled as a Roman statue as he bent slightly to dry off his expansive thighs. The rest of him, still wet with shower water, glittered like bits of crystal in the pale golden light.

She knew she should look away, but she could not. The image before her, and the illicit view of a man she barely knew, drew her to examine the arms, all muscled and corded like thick braid. The broad tanned back that tapered into tightly formed, cream-colored buttocks, leading down to sturdy, developed thighs. It was a worker's form, she thought numbly, honed by long hours of stretching and lifting, endless days on the ocean, drawing nets, pulling rope.

Marielle must have gasped, because she watched him suddenly straighten, then turn his head to the side, but not fully back around, as she shrank into the shadows.

The memory of the other men she had seen unclothed in her life were a stark contrast now to the supple, tanned mass of flesh standing before her. Then, with a sudden shift of his eyes into the mirror, Calum saw her watching him. By then it was too late for Marielle to shrink back again—to pretend that she wasn't there, watching him, naked and golden.

Her heart slammed into her ribs as the reflection of his eyes in the mirror held hers. She wanted to turn and run but she was riveted to the moment. There was something very powerful and yet curious in this awkwardness. It was curious most of all because Marielle wasn't particularly ashamed that he knew she had seen him like this.

On legs that were weak and unsure, she took a step forward closer into the light, knowing that he could see precisely who it was behind him. Then something changed.

It was an instant full of more than his powerful physical presence. There was a connection that went beyond the moment. Beyond time or sound. Or her own breathing. And yet she wasn't drawn to make it more than that. It, whatever *it* was, just seemed important somehow, suspended in time, like a rich Renaissance oil painting branded indelibly onto canvas. Filled with detail. Evocative. Yet only that. An image. A little reluctantly, with him still standing motionless, open to her, and meeting her gaze through the bathroom mirror, Marielle finally did shrink away, melting back into the night and shadows.

She had gone back to her room after that and was afraid to turn on the light. Sitting alone on her bed, with her knees drawn up to her chest and her heart still pounding, Marielle had finally calmed and fallen asleep again.

When she woke a second time, she was a bit disappointed that there was no aroma of breakfast cooking. The house was still quiet, as it had been in the darkness of an early Monday morning, even though a grainy beam of sunlight burst through her bedroom window telling Marielle that finally it was morning. She opened her eyes, rubbed them, then gazed up at the ceiling. . . .

And then she remembered. *Oh, damn! Damn, damn!*

How was she going to face Calum McInnes in the broad light of day? He really was different from anyone she had ever known. No matter how gruffly he spoke or how frustratingly sullen he could be, there was still a genuine warmth that had bled through in the garden yesterday when he had risen to her defense.

Then last night, in the dark, there was that unsettlingly intense moment between them. It had felt like a fantasy. But now, when daylight took away dreams and hid fantasies, Marielle was simply embarrassed. What must he think of a woman gazing at him so wantonly? It was so humiliating.

Oh, grow up! she chided herself. *You've faced worse things in your life than this. Remember that evil old crow, Pierre Moulet, and how you handled him? Yes, of course you can do this. . . . You'll just face Calum, smile, say good morning, and the awkward moment will be over. You will make it be over.*

Marielle moved warily out into the kitchen, having dressed quickly in blue jeans, an old sweater and sneakers, then run a brush quickly through her hair. Her heart was thumping with anticipation that felt more like fear. But no Calum. Someone was up and present, however. It was Jennie.

"Well, now. I was wonderin' when ye'd be after joinin' me for breakfast," Jennie said. And, although the words held her typically caustic tone, they were not delivered on that familiar bed of harshness that Marielle had come to expect.

Was it actually the first chip in her granite veneer? After what she had seen yesterday in the garden, that peek into a little corner of her heart, Marielle thought perhaps the confused young girl before her might actually be coming around.

"Well," Marielle said, smiling, "here I am." She wasn't a great cook but she had mastered the finer art of oatmeal, enriching it with raisins and walnuts and then covering it over with a layer of brown sugar. "I'm no culinary expert, but if you'll take pot luck, I'll make us both something."

"'Twould be fine. Thanks."

Civility? Marielle's hope swelled. She reached down for the large kettle and the tin of oats and turned toward the stove, lighting the pilot with a match from a box sitting between the burners. "Your mother gone already?"

"At dawn. Like always."

Marielle poured the oats into the water and began to stir them with a wooden spoon. "How about your uncle? Is he up yet?"

"Hours ago, I expect."

Marielle did her best to sound nonchalant. "Then while I'm getting this together, would you go tell him breakfast will be ready in a few minutes?"

"I do no' believe this chair of mine'll make it all the way down to Mallaig Harbor."

Marielle pivoted back around. "He's gone?"

"I'm surprised ye did no' hear the shower goin' near your room in the wee hours. Boat pulls out of the harbor at dawn."

She turned around and looked at Jennie. "Why would Calum use my shower when it's so far from his room?"

"Nearest to the water heater. It takes a lot less time to heat than the bath upstairs, and he hates to wait when he's got to get out of here before the sun comes up."

Marielle tried to ignore it, but the disappointment was swelling inside her chest. Why on earth should it matter that he had gone so suddenly? Or that he hadn't bothered to tell her he was leaving? After all, why should he? She meant nothing to him.

Foolish. This was absolutely foolish.

Suddenly, a spasm of hot pain shot through her,

and Marielle bolted back, dropping the wooden spoon with a little shriek. She had forgotten completely about the oatmeal, and it had boiled over onto the handle of the pot.

Marielle gripped her own hand at the wrist. *"Merde!"*

In a flash, Jennie rolled her chair quickly to the sink, grabbed a dish towel and shoved it into the water. She wrung it out and spun the wheelchair deftly back around, coming to the stove in two short wheel strokes. "Here. 'Tis cold. Put it on the burn straight away or ye'll scar. I'll fetch some ice."

Marielle was too surprised to move, watching Jennie whisk back to the freezer, open the ice tray and dump the white cubes into another towel in her lap. It wasn't so much the pain that shook her as the realization that her instincts about Jennie had been right. The girl was far more self-sufficient than Jennie herself believed.

Silently, Marielle took the ice and put it onto her wrist as she sank into one of the kitchen chairs. "I canno' imagine there'll be much of a scar now," Jennie said.

"Thanks for your quick thinking."

"I'm only useless from the waist down." The silence that followed was a brittle, unexpected thing. *"Merde,* that's French, isn't it?"

Marielle felt her face flush. "I speak several languages, but I only curse in French," she tried to joke.

Jennie stopped. The silence continued on, thick and uncomfortable to Marielle. "My ma's second husband, Malcolm, was married to a French woman once," Jennie finally said, cutting into the tension. "He called her a vile creature. Selfish. Wild. Like all the French, he said."

"I don't know that I'd agree with that assessment," Marielle carefully defended.

"The woman berated him continually, they said. Ma always pitied him over that. She said even though he could have the most sour temper at times, 'twas one of the things that made her accept his proposal. He needed someone to take away the bad taste from the woman named Vivienne."

"People who are bitter often tell tall tales."

"'Tis true enough that Malcolm Gordon was bitter. The man never cared for much beyond his own daughter. He and I never did get along properly. 'Twas clear enough that I was nothin' a'tall like his beloved Colleen."

Jennie had introduced the seemingly forbidden subject, and Marielle's mind swam with what to say next. She took great care with the tone of her question. "No one seems to talk much about Colleen now, or about her marriage to your uncle."

"Her death hit hard in Killin," Jennie said with a strange note of caution creeping up into her voice. "'Twould be better if we all just remember the good parts of how she lived, Ma says."

"So they weren't happily married, then?"

Jennie frowned. There was a moment before she answered. "'Twas complicated, I'd say."

"I don't mean to pry." Jennie was closing down again as suddenly as she had opened up, and Marielle could not press away the sensation of suspicion. "It's just that I've missed not knowing much about Colleen's life these last years."

"'Tis a raw wound, still."

"At least can you tell me if you ever suspected something more happened that night than just an awful accident?"

Jennie's eyes narrowed as they settled on Marielle. "What are ye implyin'?"

"I'm not sure."

With Marielle so mired in the intense moment, the ringing of the phone in the kitchen with them sounded very far off. But then Jennie was picking it up, cutting off the conversation as she said, "Hallo?" A moment later she glanced up and held out the receiver to Marielle. "For you."

"There must be some mistake."

"No mistake."

Marielle hesitantly drew up the receiver as Jennie watched. "Yes?"

"Marielle? 'Tis Barry Buchanan."

"Oh, hi. How are you?" she asked. His kind face was suddenly tumbling over thoughts and images of Colleen, and a lovely warmth settled inside her.

"I'm sorry to be ringin' ye up like this, out of the clear blue. Sounds a bit as if I've caught ye at a bad time." There was a small pause. His lovely, deep voice had taken on an awkward tone. Marielle's heart began to slow.

"No, it's all right."

"I wondered how ye were gettin' along there at MacLaren's Bend."

"Much improved," she managed. "Thanks to your lovely encouragement the other day."

"Sounds then as if I just may have a chit to call in with ye."

She could hear the wry tone in his voice, that lovely sense of humor that, just like the day they'd met, was causing her suddenly to smile. "It does sound like it, doesn't it?"

"Well, on to the second point of my call, then."

Marielle felt her own relieved smile widening.

"I'd like to convince ye to join me for lunch today. Nothin' high like ye'd have in the States, of course. Just a bite down at the Dun Whinney, the café over on West Street. Sheila there makes a fair bonny vegetable stew at Monday lunch."

The Dun Whinney she knew well. It was the place she'd had her last cup of tea with Colleen before she and Vivienne had left Killin for good. Her heart squeezed a little at the memory.

Marielle had planned to take the first train into Oban this morning to talk to someone at the newspaper office and maybe even the police station, but she knew from experience that the more details she had in hand, the better. Perhaps over lunch, where things would be more relaxed, she could search out a few things about Colleen and Calum's life together from someone who had known her sister well. After all, there were trains every two hours today. She had checked.

"What time?"

"Half past twelve?"

"That would be lovely."

There was another little pause, a charming hint of hesitation. "Well, all right. Splendid. Until then."

"Until then," Marielle echoed, and hung up the phone. Then she turned back around, forcing an easy smile onto her face. "So. You were about to tell me what you thought about Colleen's accident."

"Was I?" Jennie gave her a withering look.

"Please. It would mean a great deal to me to know something of the details."

Jennie looked at her, the fern green eyes widening in a plea. "I do no' want to be a part of that. I've my allegiances, ye understand."

Marielle turned quickly back to the stove, not wanting Jennie to see her face, the frustration there. From her years as a reporter, she knew well that there was always more than one avenue to finding information. But someone who had been so close to Colleen would have been invaluable.

"Well, then. Let me see what I can do about salvaging some of this oatmeal."

"I'm no' very hungry any more."

Marielle shot her a twisted smile as she pivoted back around. "I've already got the oatmeal made. After my war wound here, the least you can do is humor me."

"I'm not really much about oatmeal myself," Jennie said, interrupting her. "Actually, I believe I'd like some of that barley bread Calum made, spread with a bit of jam."

"Hey, you're not talking to the local café cook here."

"What's it take to slice a bit of bread?" Jennie pushed into the silence.

Marielle snapped back around from the stove. "Well, you certainly know where your Uncle Calum's bread is if you want it that badly. And after what I saw this morning, you don't even need to waste your breath telling me you can't at least do *that* for yourself."

"Taskmaster!" Jennie clipped with the surprising hint of a smile.

When she looked back, Marielle saw her lowering her head at the table, biting her lip and trying not to smile. "Very funny."

Then they exchanged a complicitous little glance and even Marielle could not help but feel her lips being drawn upward. It was almost, *almost*, as if they were becoming friends.

Marielle realized that in the few days she had been in Killin, not one girl, nor young man for that matter, Jennie's age had come to visit. And Jennie certainly had not gone out. All day long, she stayed like a prisoner, reading or watching television in that small, dimly lit bedroom, mostly with the draperies drawn. Didn't she have any friends her own age? Marielle wondered. She must have known kids before her accident, she must have had friends who cared enough to—

Jennie was wheeling back with the loaf of bread and a jar of jam in her lap and she still actually had, wonder of wonders, that slight, friendly smile on her face.

It's a good thing I'm already sitting down, Marielle thought, swallowing a laugh as she sipped her coffee and sank back against the chair, watching her.

Her hand was smarting from the burn, but she didn't actually feel all that bad, considering. This was something new before Marielle. Something fragile.

After they'd eaten breakfast, Marielle wrapped her arms around her waist and moved slowly through the parlor back toward the grand bay window, having grown already to adore the view. Wonder of all wonders,

Jennie was actually drying the breakfast dishes without a struggle. It really had been quite a morning, all the way from their newfound understanding to the increasing mystery of Colleen's apparently troubled relationship with Calum.

She felt a little shiver bubble up as the image of Calum's slippery golden skin and taut body came alive again in her mind. She pushed the image away. It felt too much like a sin. Even though her sister was dead, it would be wrong to feel anything for the same man Colleen had loved and married.

But try as she might to make it seem as if Calum didn't matter—and that he shouldn't matter—Marielle felt another little jolt of disappointment that he had left this morning. She had no idea when he'd be back.

Of course, on the other hand, she reminded herself, it wasn't as if either of them had been prepared, in the dark of night, him bare, and her standing there taking it all in, to engage in a conversation including dates and details.

She fought a little smile. It really had been quite comical.

Marielle nonchalantly touched a corner of the heavy velvet draperies, and with that a sudden shock coursed through her. On the broad windowsill sat half a dozen small, potted violets and, above it, a special purple light had been installed, like the one her mother had always used. Plants that would grow even in Scotland's inclement weather, she realized, thinking back to the advice she'd asked of him.

Is that where Calum had been yesterday after he had disappeared? She hadn't seen any sort of nursery anywhere near Killin. Could it actually be that he had done this for her?

Fighting a disbelieving smile, she moved closer still until she saw that, tied to one of the pots, was a small white envelope with her name on it. Marielle took it and tore it open.

Now at least you can have your own garden while you're here, to remind you of your mother. I didn't realize until we met how much I'd missed the sight of flowers.

It was not signed, but of course there was no need for that. Marielle clutched the note tightly, fighting the feelings of flattery. But she could not undo the ridiculous smile she felt on her face. She could not remember ever having allowed herself to smile at the overtures of a handsome man, a man who, in spite of their poor start, seemed to have taken a liking to her.

Jennie rolled up beside her then. "What are these about?"

She put her hand on her hip and sighed. "Well, it appears to be something of a peace offering. This is just like the violet garden my mother had when I was a little girl."

"Where'd they come from?"

Marielle sighed. "Actually, they came from your uncle Calum."

"Not much to rally the guard about."

Marielle tipped her head quizzically.

"I mean, 'tis no' much of a surprise. Uncle Calum certainly has lost that scowl since ye've been here."

Marielle's face held genuine surprise, and Jennie reacted to it.

"Oh, come on. Now do no' go tryin' to tell me that ye haven't noticed."

"You're completely wrong." Marielle tried feebly to pass off the notion.

"He's a lad like any other," Jennie smiled impishly. "And ye are fair bonny to look at. But then I'm certain ye know that."

How odd that felt to hear in Killin, the one place on earth where she was made to feel as unattractive as a mud hen—where her insecurities had begun. Marielle drew in a breath. "I think a very large part of Calum's heart is still broken over the loss of his wife."

"Well, now. They do say the best way to heal an old love is with a new one."

"Some wounds never heal."

Jennie seemed undaunted. "And sometimes life has a lovely way of surprisin' ye," she smiled. "I certainly think ye've surprised *him*."

CHAPTER FOURTEEN

An hour after their lunch at the Dun Whinney, Barry Buchanan and Marielle Jaeger became something of an "item" in Killin. The things she heard whispered as they walked to Barry's car made Marielle laugh a little. Life in a small town, and the lightning speed with which people inferred things, was such a world away from Paris. But she was also surprised how easy Barry was to talk with, so open and without complication. About everything and nothing. The only subject he seemed to avoid was Colleen and Calum.

"So where to?" she asked, taking his hand as he led her through a grove of lichen-covered beech trees that grew more dense the further along they walked.

"I've another secret place I want ye to see."

"Are there really so many around here?"

"Oh, lass," he chuckled that kind, rich laugh of his that always seemed to make her smile, "the countryside here is full of wee places that are wonderful hidden jewels. Ye need only know where to look to find them."

Through a light mist, Marielle followed him, tromping on mud brown bracken and heather, spindly now and losing its tiny yellow flowers to the oncoming chill of a Scottish winter. A sudden cool wind drove the mist arching and dipping through the birches, rattling the last few autumn leaves, but already she was beginning to adapt. Even though she was shivering, the cold felt invigorating to her.

Suddenly, the trees thinned again as Marielle and Barry neared the sound of rushing water. Another step, then two, past the branches of two thick emerald ferns, and it was there: a waterfall cascading over the rocks, surrounded by another little grotto of ferns, white stone, and tangling ivy, protected from the rest of the world as it fell into a deep, sapphire pool.

Marielle bent down and dipped a finger in the water. It was warm, even soothing, with the effervescent feel of a mineral spring. What a surprise, up here, hidden like this.

"'Tis my other little piece of heaven," Barry said as the mist from the waterfall fell softly through the trees. Marielle was breathless.

"I had no idea there were places left like this on earth, much less beyond that glen."

"They are all here for *you* now, as well."

Marielle looked up at him. "So tell me, why is it that you're being so kind to me?"

"'Tisn't any other way I know to be with someone who's soul is as pure as yours."

"What if I'm not so pure as you think?"

"'Tisn't possible."

"Oh, I don't know," she demurred, sinking onto one of the huge white rocks and then pulling absently at a little corner of fern which hung softly across her shoulder. "People sometimes are forced to do things . . . the wrong things, even if they are for the right reasons."

"'Tisn't so much what ye *do* in this world as what ye *are* at your core that matters."

"Do you really believe that?"

He sank down beside her, all bones and tousled maple hair. "With all of my heart."

The gentleness of him, the continued simplicity of Barry's goodness, even without the physical attraction, was a powerful draw to Marielle. She glanced around. "Are you able to come here often?"

"Often enough."

"And do you, what? . . . swim here?"

A slow smile broke across his face and for an instant she felt as if his warm gaze was actually touching her. "The water's quite warm, even in autumn, but it's as pure as if it came straight from heaven. Are ye wantin' to go in, then?"

"Now?" she gulped, looking back at the water through that thin, fine mist.

Barry's grin was wide and sincere. "Life is short, Marielle. So are most of its pleasures."

She'd never had a particular madcap spirit for adventure. In fact, Vivienne had always told her she had anything but that. Methodical, she had branded her daughter. Careful. Marielle could barely believe it, but she was actually considering a spur-of-the-moment swim in cold autumn air simply because it was something she'd never done.

"Oh, why not?" she smiled tentatively.

"Aye?"

"Aye!" she parroted, beginning to tear off her windbreaker, then her boots, and only then realizing that as much as she liked Barry, she was not quite prepared to make this an afternoon of skinny-dipping.

As if he'd read her mind, Barry chuckled. Then he said with a clever smile, "Of course, I'd expect ye to be a proper lass and wear your knickers, because I know ye'd no' be the sort to do otherwise."

Marielle felt her face color. She pursed her mouth to push away the smile she felt. "If I didn't know better, Barry Buchanan, I'd bet you could actually read minds."

"Now what fun would that be, knowin' things before they happen? I quite fancy livin' a life that's full of surprises."

"Well, meeting you has certainly been a surprise for me," she said honestly. "It's actually been an awfully long time since a man has shown me such kindness. And"—she smiled, remembering the precious years she and Vivienne had spent with Ron Jaeger—"such fun."

His shaggy brows merged beneath unruly hair that he frequently tossed from his eyes. "'Tis a shame if that's true. I'd have guessed the lads would be queued up at your door," he said as he bent then and stripped down to his own baggy plaid boxer shorts and white T-shirt without so much as a shiver. "Come on, then. Let's make a real afternoon of it!"

A moment later they were waist-deep in water that was warm and soothing. Somehow, this little grotto was protected from the wind and the cold. For so long, her life had been defined by her losses. Her career and the self-protective mechanism she had so firmly set in place. Fun was something other people had. But now, suddenly Marielle was giggling uncontrollably, the frigid air above the water making her shiver as she laughed and splashed Barry like a child—and, wonder of wonders, for these few blissful moments, she was feeling carefree.

After she was completely numb, and they had dried off as best they could, Barry made her cover up with his jacket as well as her own as they scampered like children, wet-headed and giggling, back through the grove of beech trees.

"'Twould be best to dry off here," he said as she stood shivering beside him on the porch and he opened the front door. "Or the old ladies of Killin'll have a scarlet letter on ye before mornin'."

Inside, the tiny cottage where Barry now lived alone was just as she'd imagined it since she had first seen it from a distance. It was a single room with a large soot-stained hearth taking up one entire wall, and an old black iron stove on another beside a box bed. The place was rustic and earthy, smelling slightly of wet thatch and damp wood. Simple and pure, something from another time. Like Barry himself.

And Marielle trusted him. Yet for her to admit the truth was growing more difficult each day. Because things here were certainly growing more complicated.

She stood beside the door, a little uncertain, as Barry moved to a drawer in the bottom of an old pine sideboard and drew out a large tartan blanket. Then he wrapped it around her. There, holding the blanket together at her chest he said, "Would ye fancy a bit of a fire while ye're dryin' off?"

"That would be lovely."

Stripped of her wet underthings and wrapped in that wonderfully cozy blanket, she sank into an old cane rocker near the hearth, watched him strike a match, and a small blaze soon kindled beneath it.

Marielle watched his long-limbed deliberate movements. They matched the smooth hands of an artist. Barry was different from anyone she had ever met. So poetic-looking. He was certainly blessed with a wonderfully dry wit and an endearing sage quality. And he was safe, like no man since Ron had been. All of those things together had started something inside her. A feeling for him. It made her want to go on spending time with him.

"Tell me more about this wonderful old place," she said as he stood at the black iron stove, putting a kettle on for tea.

"The cottage belonged to the Maitlands for generations. Regan, was the last of them. She lived here with her husband for a while. But he ran off to Ireland with everythin' she had. It devastated her for a long time. She was no' an educated nor a skilled woman. She could no' find a proper job in town, ye see. I suppose she should have moved on. Gone somewhere else. But for a very long while she tried to stay here, put up a fight for this—"

Marielle knew what he was going to say. And she wanted suddenly to make it easier for him. "We all do what we feel we have to do to survive."

"Aye."

"I don't suppose it helped your reputation much, living out here with her like that."

"Regan had a kind heart. She took me in when I was still a lad. She gave me a home. Saved me. And I cared no' one wit more then than I do now what people in Killin thought of me for what happened between us."

"You must have loved her very much."

"No. Not the way *you* mean, anyway. And eventually we both moved on in our lives."

"And in your hearts."

He turned to look at her. "My heart has not yet belonged to any woman, Marielle."

She felt a shiver at the absolute conviction in his voice. Marielle curled up on the rocker, drawing her legs beneath the blanket as he added what looked like a dram of Scotch to the mug of tea and then handed it to her.

"Did *you* care for Colleen?"

Marielle warmed her hands on the mug, in the same style of pottery he made at his shop, and waited for him to answer a question she knew had come as a surprise. He sank down onto the hearth before her.

His words and tone were simple, as understated as he was. "Aye, years ago. But 'twas a lad's way of lookin' at love. No' a man's."

Marielle watched his slim face tighten ever so slightly. Even so, his winsome smile never quite faded. "But you were friends?"

"Dear ones, aye."

She took a sip of the potent tea, then leaned back. Marielle wanted so much to know about Colleen, and she trusted that Barry was the sort of man who would be honest with her. "I'm sorry if I was prying. It's just that it was such a shock to find out that Colleen had died."

"Her death was a shock to us all."

"Naturally, I have questions about it, questions no one here seems particularly interested in answering, which in my line of work makes me all the more curious."

He leveled his hazel eyes, studying Marielle for a moment. Suddenly, his own expression became one of knowing. "And ye were hopin' I'd be the exception."

"Yes."

He was smiling, unfazed by the force in her tone, but he said nothing.

Suddenly, with those rich, kind eyes still upon her, Marielle felt apologetic. "Look. It's not like I'm a total stranger here, you know. I knew Colleen."

"So ye've said."

"Then will *you* be the one to give me a few of the details about her death?"

"It means that much to ye, does it?"

"Yes, it does." He seemed to be studying her in the silence. Marielle felt her heartbeat quicken.

"'Twas a car accident that claimed her. Colleen drowned in the loch. I arrived just in time to see the police plunging down into the black depths. 'Twas an eerie sight, the moon on the water, people cryin', shakin' their heads. The sound of their weepin' stayed with me for a long time after that." Barry stopped for a moment. The words had come with difficulty. "Those were dark days, Marielle. It took a long time even to reconcile in my mind that someone so special was gone so suddenly. I think many in Killin felt that way."

Marielle nodded her understanding. It was all she felt she dared do with them so close, as if the truth of her identity could seep out in a glance held too long between them. They drank the rest of their tea in a charged kind of silence then. After a time, Barry broke the tension a bit by reaching over to check their underthings. "Dry as a bone," he pronounced, examining the bottoms of her silk long underwear first.

Marielle stood and took the two pieces from him, feeling curiously unfettered, as if she'd known him all of her life, as if there had never been those interrupted years. She found herself wondering if Colleen had felt the same thing for him, the same intensity, and then knowing that she must have. His essence of goodness was simply too strong for it to have been otherwise.

"I suppose we should be going. I've got some things I want to check out before supper."

Then, just as she moved to turn away, Barry very gently hooked a finger beneath her chin and pulled her toward him until their lips met. It was a sweet kiss. Chaste. But not at all unwanted. And when it was over, he took a step back, assuring her that he meant to press her no further.

"Ye're special, Marielle Jaeger," he said softly until his deep voice almost broke. "No matter what ye've believed of yourself in the past . . . *that* is the truth of your future."

Not his kiss, nor even his nearness, engendered a pulse racing, heart-hammering sort of thing. And yet still Marielle felt she could have stayed here like this forever, listening to Barry's calming voice. Surrounded by him and this place. Drinking that wonderfully spiked tea. And, little by little, even sharing their secrets.

Perhaps it was how he looked at her. As someone precious.

"I'll leave ye to dress," he said simply, then turned and walked outside.

Marielle stood still like that, as she had been when

he'd kissed her, her mind whirling almost too much to move. Very suddenly, surprising her, an unexpected image of Calum rose in her mind. It was as vivid as if it were he who had been standing there before her only a moment ago. She remembered Calum's solemn face, lightly bearded. Eyes, intense and dark. His firm, square jaw. A body that was purely male. And, at the thought of seeing him bare as she had that night, her heart did then begin to race.

But attraction was something altogether different than real affection, she told herself.

Wasn't it? Now suddenly, she was confronted quite boldly by both—but in two different men. And Marielle felt entirely inadequate in dealing with either experience.

Marielle put on her underclothes and then dressed again. She ran a hand through her hair and felt that it now was dry as well. The afternoon was over. She went outside a little reluctantly and found Barry standing on the porch gazing over at the ruins of the abbey shrouded now in a thin mist.

"I don't really want to go," she said.

"They'll be other times. If ye'd like."

"I would like that," Marielle said, meaning it.

But he did not try to kiss her again, nor did he touch her, even hold her hand, on the long walk back out to the main road. "I'd fancy ringin' ye tomorrow if ye would no' mind," he said when they reached the bottom of the drive at MacLaren's Bend.

"Actually," she said as the cool wind tossed her hair. "I'd like that quite a lot."

❖   ❖   ❖

Barry went back to the cottage after he had seen Marielle back to MacLaren's Bend. Pulling off the tartan plaid jacket he had hastily put on, he tossed it on the peg beside the door. He then went to an old tin box near the fireplace hearth.

Solemnly, he knelt and lifted the lid, bringing out a photograph of Colleen. It was one taken a month before she married Calum McInnes. Her hair was long, eyes wide as she gazed directly into the camera. Her mouth was turned up into that ever so slight, beguiling smile. Then he closed his eyes and sank back onto his heels.

"'Tis her, isn't it?" he whispered into the stillness. There was nothing but silence for a moment longer. "Aye. I felt that pull from the first. She's bound to find out what happened, ye know," he said deeply, opening his eyes again and gazing down at the image of a woman who was imprinted forever on this heart. Then the room was still again. "Help me lead her to the truth, Colleen. Without hurtin' anyone when I do."

There was no answer. Just as there had been no answers for so many things between them. But there would be, he knew. When the time was right, Barry would know what to do.

Two hours later, Marielle stood inside the doorway of a small, musty police station in Oban. A low watt bulb with a tin shade hung overhead. There were two desks, both covered with a sea of papers, files, and styrofoam cups. Against the wall were three old metal file drawers and a copy of a painting, in a cheap frame, of a historical figure who looked like Rob Roy.

After what seemed an almost rude duration, the inspector, a short, beefy man with a bloated face, glanced up. "What's it ye need?"

"I'm trying to find some information about the death of a young woman two years ago in Killin. Her name was Colleen McInnes." Marielle watched him shuffle a collection of papers, taking his time. She noticed a sign on his desk that said *Inspector Bainbridge.*

"Killin, was it?" He looked at her vaguely and with a clear disinterest.

"There can't have been too many accidental deaths of beautiful young women around here in the past couple of years. You must remember it."

He leaned back in his swivel chair and did not bother standing. "Aye, well, I do no' specifically have anythin' about that at the ready."

"I can wait."

When he lowered his eyes on her, his chin doubled. "Look, lass. I'm up to my ears in paperwork here. If ye could just come back. Maybe tomorrow I'll have the time to—"

Now it was Marielle who was irritated. "Inspector, Colleen was my sister. My *only* sister. And it has taken me thirteen years to 'come back,'" she said, tilting her chin and meeting his gaze head-on. "Now that I have made it, through obstacles you cannot begin to imagine, and I find that she has died, you say you're too busy to tell me how and why it happened?"

He tossed his pen onto the desk. "Look, lass. 'Tis no' that I canno' find some sympathy for ye, but we've a small enterprise here. Myself, a couple of other lads, and Mrs. Bainbridge who types up the reports—"

"I can wait."

"Och, Jesus, Mary 'n' Joseph," he mumbled out the curse. "Rohan! Get over here and finish the report for me, will ye? I've got to be dealin' with this!"

Marielle watched with some small satisfaction as the surly little man stood finally and went to one of the old brown file cabinets in the corner, muttering beneath his breath. When he had found the file, he motioned for her to come and sit in the chair beside his desk. "All right, then. What is it ye're wantin' to know?"

"Was her husband ever a suspect?"

He looked at her appraisingly with tiny, dark eyes. "A suspect in what?"

"Colleen's death."

The inspector looked at the file again, his lips moving silently as he read. "Ye've been watchin' too much of the telly, I think. Poor Mrs. McInnes drove her own car straight off the Dwelly Bridge. 'Twas a tidy little tragedy. Open and shut."

"Did you ever interview her husband, ask him any questions?"

He glanced down again at the open file. Marielle leaned across the desk, trying to make out the words upside down. Bainbridge snapped it away. Their eyes met again. His were stern and red-rimmed. Hers were unflinching. "As a matter of fact," he said indignantly, "since he was the first one there, Mr. McInnes was the first witness my constable spoke with."

"Witness?" Marielle felt an icy hand lay across her heart. "Do you mean Calum was there at the scene . . . the night she died?"

"So says the file."

"Did he give your constable a reason why he was there when it happened?"

He read further. *I always thought that husband of hers* . . . Marielle felt a cold sickness growing as the silence lengthened.

"It says here in his statement that they'd quarreled that night. The lady had been drinkin', so he went after her. His statement at the time was, "I went after her, I just could no' get to her in time.""

"Was he distraught, does it say?"

Bainbridge cocked a bushy eyebrow at her. "Lass?"

"There should be something there about Mr. McInnes's state of mind. Was he upset? Tearful? Were his clothes wet from diving into the water after her?"

He balanced his pasty, white elbows on the desktop, and then leveled his gaze on her. His expression was sickeningly condescending. "Now look here, lass. I understand ye lost a sister in it, and I'm fair sorry ye did. But for your own sake, do no' go makin' it more of a drama than it was."

"I don't think *that* would be possible."

"'Twas an accident. We did no' find anyone responsible for her death but Mrs. McInnes herself. Why do ye no' try to do your grievin' as ye must, then make whatever bit of peace ye can with that?"

The only peace for Marielle lay in knowing the whole truth.

Sloughing off the inspector's explanation, she sat in the hauntingly quiet back room of the library in Oban. She was studying the front page of a two year old issue of *The Stirling Observer,* the newspaper serving Killin. There was one article in particular. Marielle held the book up to the lamplight. The bold headline shook her.

CAR PLUNGES OFF DWELLY BRIDGE.
LOCAL WOMAN DROWNS.
DRIVING TEEN SURVIVES.
CIRCUMSTANCES CALLED MYSTERIOUS.

Driving teen survives . . . Colleen hadn't been alone that night. Her sister hadn't faced those last terrifying moments of her life without someone beside her.

Then the emotion shifted, and Marielle felt that same strong ache of longing surge through her. *If only I'd been here sooner. I might have been the one . . . I might have been able to . . .*

Even before she read further, she knew that the teen the headline referred to was Jennie. Marielle strained hard against the shiver that was gripping her as the words of the article made those dark, last moments cruelly real.

A car belonging to Mrs. Colleen McInnes, daughter of Malcolm Gordon of Killin, plunged off Dwelly Bridge sometime after midnight Saturday. At the scene, and questioned by authorities were Mrs. McInnes's husband, Calum, and Mr. Barry Buchanan, also of Killin.

So Barry and Jennie had been a part of that awful night, as well. They were facts she would have known days ago if she'd been able to get to Oban. If the surly police inspector had been forthcoming.

Marielle's heart felt swollen. Battered. Like it had felt when Ron died. She was wounded all over again by the details of her sister's death. Marielle wiped the stream of tears with the back of her hand. She struggled to regain control of herself. To read on. She needed to read the words. She *needed* to know everything.

> Rescued, and in critical condition, was the reported driver of the vehicle, Miss Jennie Quinn, daughter of Mrs. Gordon. Her injuries are reported to be severe. Police call it an unfortunate tragedy, and will file no charges.

Marielle sank against the chair back. Its creaking was the only sound in the nearly vacant library. There was almost too much, in that first blinding moment, to reconcile. Poor Jennie had lost the use of her legs that horrible night—but apparently, according to the police report at least, Calum had played no part, after all.

The unbearable weight in her chest began to ease. Marielle's heart had told her he could not possibly have been involved in something so unspeakable. Now the detective and the newspapers were saying that as well. She felt for the cross at her throat. Touched it. It was a gesture that still brought comfort. It would have been too awful to bear, thinking that the man her sister had loved, trusted—the man Colleen had married— had betrayed her in that ultimate way. Thank God that at least she had uncovered that much.

❖   ❖   ❖

Marielle tossed a fresh log into the grand old soot-stained fireplace hearth back at MacLaren's Bend. After the flames took hold, she went to the windowsill, to the collection of potted violets. Then her heart skipped a beat when she saw a few dead blossoms on one of the smaller, more fragile plants of the collection. Marielle hadn't noticed anything out of the ordinary this morning, and she quickly checked the soil to see if the soil was too dry.

Why on earth it should matter, Marielle wasn't at all certain. But it did.

Damn! It was dry, probably too dry. Her mother had always had such a wonderful way with these fragile little things.

She went to the kitchen and filled a measuring cup with water, then brought it back through the house. Carefully, she added a few drops to each of the plants. Later, when they were moist, she would add an extra drop of that special fertilizer Calum had left. Then she checked the light. It was fine. Perhaps it was her. Perhaps she really did have the brown thumb she'd always believed. And who was she, anyway, to think she could keep violets growing in the middle of Scotland in October?

Ye're a useless child, Mairi Gordon! Good for next to nothin' much that I can see but to your ma!

The memory of Malcolm Gordon's voice was suddenly so vivid in her mind again that she dropped the measuring cup, splashing water on the hardwood floor and up onto the corner of Catriona's antique rug. Marielle dove onto her knees in an instinctive jerking movement, trying to mop the worst of it with the corner of her baggy sweater. Like the time she had spilled her father's cup of tea on the hooked rug that Colleen's mother had made.

How could ye be so careless? If ye've ruined this one, wee lass, I can tell ye there'll be hell to pay!

"You bloody bastard!" she growled. "How you and this place haunt me still!"

"Whoever the man was, he must be a real fine piece of work to get your back up so."

An icy panic sliced through her at the sound of Jennie's voice behind her. Marielle sat back on her heels and very slowly turned around as her heart beat its way up into her throat. "You weren't meant to hear that," she said tentatively, seeing Jennie, in her wheelchair, gazing at her.

"No, I do no' suppose I was."

"I'm sorry if I woke you."

"No one woke me. I was only lyin' in my bed to pass the time. Truth is, I do no' much fancy sleepin'."

Marielle fumbled for the measuring cup and stood back up, pulling the damp corners of her sweater back down around her hips, feeling a little foolish for having panicked like that over a bit of water. "If I'd known you were awake," Marielle said in an apologetic tone, "I'd not have gone out."

"There would no' have been anythin' for ye to do here anyway."

"Maybe we could have played cards or something. At least passed the time."

"I don't much fancy cards. If I do play, I do it for Ma's sake."

"And what is it you do for yourself, Jennie?"

"This grand piece of metal fairly limits my options," she said slapping a chair wheel as a trace of bitterness crept into her voice.

"Oh, I don't know about that."

Jennie's copper brows merged suddenly, sending more of a barrier up. And, in that, she reminded Marielle suddenly of Calum. "What could *you* possibly know about bein' an invalid?"

"There are all kinds of paralysis, Jennie," Marielle said gravely. "Personally, for a very long time, I was paralyzed by loss. Maybe not physically. And I wouldn't even try to compare what you've been through with my situation." Then thinking of her father's cruel voice, the hate in it that came through the decades, she said, "In many ways, my memories of my past ruled my life."

"Is that why ye came to Scotland, then?"

"In part, yes."

Jennie's full lips lifted slightly. "Well, I'd say, between Uncle Calum and Barry, ye've found a wee bit more here than memories."

"Barry Buchanan?"

"I saw him leave you out at the front gate. He fancies ye, Marielle. Almost as much as my uncle does."

Jennie's lips lifted further still into a wry smile and Marielle felt her cheeks warm. "All right, you." Marielle said suddenly as she set the empty measuring cup down on a little side table. "Get your coat."

But Jennie didn't move. "I do no' understand."

"What part of that wasn't clear?" she asked light-heartedly.

"I'm no' up to goin' anywhere, Marielle."

"Well, *I* disagree." Marielle put her hands on her

hips and turned back around fully, her own smile broadening. "And, as I see it, a splash of color on those pretty young cheeks of yours is more than a little over-due."

"But I've—What I mean is that—"

Marielle gazed down, feeling her heart give a little tug at the suddenly unsure, vulnerable tone in Jennie's voice. "I know it's been a long time since you've been out," she said more softly. "But I only want you to go with me into town for some milk and coffee."

"Oh, Marielle, I don't know."

"Just the market. That's it, okay? Every journey starts with one small step, Jennie. Believe me, I know."

"I do no' want folks gazin' after me with their pityin' stares."

"Did it ever occur to you that they might be look-ing at you with affection and concern?"

"In this thing?"

"Yes, in that thing. These are people who have known you all of your life. And, seeing what I have of the people of Killin, as I am starting to, they are prob-ably people who care about you a great deal."

There was another little silence and, much to her surprise, Jennie actually seemed to be considering the venture. Marielle held her breath, hoping Jennie would follow, as she moved toward the door and began buttoning the same jacket she had worn earlier in the day when she'd gone out with Barry.

Now that she was this far enmeshed in things, Marielle very much wanted to see Jennie make some progress before she left Killin. Much to her surprise, Marielle had actually begun to care what happened to Jennie Quinn. And she wanted very much to help her back to a place of confidence, the way Ron Jaeger, once long ago, had helped her.

"All right," Jennie said as Marielle turned the handle on the front door. "But just to the market. And do no' go gettin' any bright ideas that this is goin' to become a habit."

"Of course not," Marielle lied, biting back a victorious little smile. "I wouldn't dream of it."

CHAPTER FIFTEEN

Picnicking in the rain was a new experience for Jennie. In spite of her vigorous protest against joining Marielle and Barry the next afternoon, Marielle used their experience at the market the day before as the impetus.

Surprisingly, Jennie smiled quite happily at the novelty of sitting beneath the outer eaves of the ruined abbey and munching on smoked salmon and cucumber sandwiches.

As Marielle sat with her shoulders wrapped in another of those wonderful tartan blankets, sipping hot black coffee, she watched with a kind of ease she could not recall since her own childhood days with her mother and Ron, as Barry slowly drew Jennie out of her shell with his laughter and jokes and his comical attempt at catching raindrops on his tongue.

"These are really lovely," Jennie smiled as she swallowed another bite of sandwich. "Especially for how dreadfully ladylike they sounded."

Barry smiled and took a sip of hot coffee. "All of life is an adventure, lass. No matter how things seem to ye at times, ye've just got to reach out and take off a bite to see how grand it all can be."

Marielle glanced over at him as he teased Jennie, and both of them began to giggle about something she hadn't heard. But it didn't matter. There was a kind of centered calm she felt being with him. A warmth. Peace. Such strength of character. Now that was a commodity that couldn't possibly be overrated. And Barry had *that* in spades.

After the rain had stopped and they walked together, pushing Jennie, back to MacLaren's Bend that afternoon, Barry's arm came to rest gently upon Marielle's shoulder. And she did not object. For a moment, the first she could recall, it was actually good to feel close to a man who liked her. A good man. A safe man.

They stopped at the bottom of the drive that led up to the house. The rain had stopped, and silver rays of sunlight came streaking through the clouds in that wonderful way she had only seen here in the country. Jennie looked up with a glorious, ruddy-cheeked smile.

"Thanks for the picnic, Barry."

"'Twas my pleasure, lass." Barry nodded, and it was an almost courtly gesture.

"I hope we can do it again soon."

Marielle's heart caught at the way Jennie was looking up at him, her small face so full of admiration, needing the kind of father figure she had not had since her own had died. And she too had been faced with Malcolm Gordon. The moment reminded her, achingly, of herself and Ron in those first early days.

"I'd like nothin' better, Jennie."

"Can we catch raindrops again?"

"Oh, indeed," he chuckled. "Indeed we can."

When Jennie had gone into the house, Barry took

Marielle's shoulders and gently turned her until they were facing one another. "I had a lovely time too," she said, feeling a little awkward. Nervous. Not quite certain what he meant to do now.

"There's a *ceilidh* in town tomorrow night," Barry said deeply, that voice of his breaking the still surroundings of Killin.

"What's that?"

"I expect you Yanks would be callin' it a barn dance." He settled his eyes on hers. "Go with me?"

"I'd love to go with you."

"'Tis for everyone. We'll bring Jennie with us, if ye can convince her to go."

"I think she just might. Today she actually smiled."

"Aye, I saw that."

"That was thanks to you."

Barry smiled. "Ye both have helped me, as well." He settled her chin in the palm of his hand. Then his kind face stilled to something very intense. "It's been a long time since I've looked forward to bein' with anyone as much as I do you."

"Thank you," she replied, unable to manage anything more.

"Until then." Barry smiled, leaning over and pressing a feather-light kiss onto her cheek.

Marielle went quickly up the steps to the house after that, not realizing until now how late it had gotten and how long they had all been gone. When she came through the front door, a little breathless, she was stopped in her tracks, jacket and gloves in hand. Catriona and Jennie were collected around Calum who, scruffy, windblown and lightly bearded, looked himself as if he'd only just arrived. As she came through the front door, everyone glanced up smiling, clearly glad to see her. Especially Calum.

"I didn't know you'd be back today," Marielle tried to say casually as she attempted to hang her jacket on the peg beside Catriona's navy coat without dropping it or knocking something else onto the floor.

"'Tis little predictable about the sea. When the boat's full, we come back in."

"Makes sense, I suppose," Marielle said.

It was strange standing here, still in the glow of the wonderful afternoon with Barry. Yet she was faced now boldly with the raw power of Calum. It was a power so new that it banished everything else.

Yet, in spite of the moment between them in the dark of night—the moment that had ignited this within her—it was a contrary kind of intimacy they shared. There were miles between them in terms of what they knew of one another. Calum sensed it too, she knew, because he looked directly at her for a very long time before he spoke again.

"I've brought ye a bit of somethin' for supper," he finally said to Catriona. He broke the connection between Marielle and himself by handing his aunt a fishy-smelling brown bag that obviously contained a portion of his catch.

Catriona smiled and thanked him, then carried it off into the kitchen. "Rough seas, Uncle Calum?" Jennie asked.

"No' bad."

Calum raked a hand through his wild, windblown hair, then went over to the sofa. Marielle could see how tired he was as he sagged against the folds of the old forest green velvet. It was still difficult to imagine him a lawyer, as he sat here in well-worn jeans and a denim work shirt, with a unshaven jawline, and him smelling so like the sea. But knowing that Calum had once led such a contrary life, one he had abruptly abandoned, made him that much more intense and intriguing.

It fascinated her, really, what had caused him to make such a sweeping change, and she couldn't help wondering: Had it been his grief, exclusively, over losing Colleen, or had something more been involved?

Whatever it was, Marielle now had a strong feeling that it did involve Jennie. They had a closeness that was curious, something more than it should have been.

"Come on, Ma," Jennie called over her shoulder as she wheeled toward the kitchen. "Let's get to that supper."

When they were alone, Calum came back to his feet and faced Marielle. The silence was strained as evening shadows played between them. "Ye've done quite a fine job with the violets," he said, glancing past her to the windowsill that held them.

"You really didn't have to do that."

"Oh, but I did. 'Twas the only way I could think to let ye know I was no' a total lout."

She laughed at that, softly, a little unsure. For the first time, she thought he looked slightly awkward. He seemed more vulnerable than he had when they'd first met, when she had been so certain she despised him. This was, she imagined, the side of him that Colleen had seen. The side of him she had loved.

"They're difficult to grow, you know. My mother's the only one I've ever seen who could do it."

"You seem quite determined when there's somethin' ye want. I expect ye'll be surprisin' yourself about that."

"Actually, I hope so," Marielle said, glancing at the flowers again, afraid of the intensity between them and wanting to break the hold his deep black eyes had on her. "Now that they're here, I'm already growing kind of attached to the little things. They're so delicate. It is, I think, what makes them so beautiful."

"The lad at the garden center over in Fort William told me they're a good deal heartier than they look. Beneath the care of a tender hand they'll thrive. They're a lot like some people—special ones—that way."

Her heart quickened again when she looked back at Calum, the echo of what he'd said filling the room and her head like some earthy, ancient perfume.

"How long will you be staying this time?"

He paused a moment, still looking at her. His face was more tanned, she realized. The color of fresh brick now. His eyes glittered more brightly, it seemed. It was difficult to take her gaze from him too, from that raw physical essence that was so much a part of him.

"Long enough," he simply said.

She didn't ask him what he'd meant by that. Still, Marielle found that she was glad that Calum was back at MacLaren's Bend.

After dinner, Marielle went outside onto the front veranda. She drew in a cool breath of evening air that carried with it little woody wisps of smoke from nearby chimneys and the faint fragrance of mist-laden heather from across the glen. She stood there like that, leaning over the banister, lost in the sensations as screeching gulls dashed over the loch nearby.

She ran her fingers through her hair again, seeing Vivienne in her mind. Her elegant mother. The short, stylish hair. The same mahogany-colored eyes with long lashes. The fashionably tailored Chanel suits. Always with pearls.

Oh, how much Vivienne had come to despise Scotland since they had left here. Everything about the way she lived her life now was a statement against that. She imagined how little of this beauty Vivienne had seen because of the man who had colored it all so darkly when she had been his wife.

The rain had stopped as quickly as it had begun, and everything now was very still. With the stars and the moon the only things lighting her way, Marielle wrapped her arms around herself and walked quickly down the hill, away from MacLaren's Bend.

In the distance, she heard the hoot of an owl. The sound echoed into the darkness, and she felt her heart quicken. Her footsteps slowed as she walked toward a thick of pine trees. The woods around Killin were lush and evergreen.

She had not realized until this moment, her mind so full of memories of her mother and the life they had left behind, that she had come to the Promise Stone. Marielle stopped and touched the surface for the first time since she had done so with Colleen; the sensation of it was bittersweet. The promise had been kept, just like the legend said. She had returned to MacLaren's Bend. Suddenly, she felt uneasy. Marielle glanced around. Her feet crunching pine needles was the only sound. The sense of someone else nearby was very great. Marielle spun around. Her mouth was dry.

"Who's there?"

Marielle stood still, wondering if she should run back up the hill to the house. Her heart now was beating very fast. There was a shadow that looked like a man's. And again there was that unmistakable aroma of pipe smoke blotting out the smell of the pine.

Malcolm.

Not again. Marielle froze.

She heard Barry's words in her mind. *Do no' fear the magic that happens here, embrace it. 'Tis peace in acceptin' what will be anyway.*

Still, she had to be imagining things, the stress of all that had happened here lately. But something deep inside her pressed Marielle to treat this moment as if it were real. And this was a magical place, as Barry had told her. As Colleen too had believed.

"All right, then," she said, her voice thin in the cool night silence. "If it *is* you, then let's have it out!"

What came from her next was something she didn't realize until this moment that she had waited years to say. "All right, you old bastard! Come on! I know it's you! You were a lousy father and you're an even lousier ghost!" The air around her felt suddenly more frigid. Marielle shivered at what felt like a response. Whether or not she was imagining this, the urge to run now was very strong. She spun around instead, the pine trees above bristling suddenly.

"Okay. So you don't want me here. Well, you know what? I wouldn't be here if it weren't for Colleen! I know you always hated me! Well, it cannot possibly be any more than I have hated you!" She spun around, glancing up into the darkened trees and the night sky, its stars suddenly not quite so bright.

Marielle stood still again, waiting, as a lifetime's worth of tears filled her eyes. She wiped them away with the back of her hand. "Well, it's your loss, Malcolm Gordon!" she said bitterly.

A gust of icy wind came up just then, startling her. But Marielle laughed through her tears. "Not too fond of the truth, hmm?"

She couldn't smell the pipe smoke any longer. But the wind was still gusting at her. "I survived in spite of you! In spite of your indifference! And, in spite of the scars, I've turned out pretty damned terrific!" Marielle tipped up her chin. The wind blew. Her tears dried on her cheeks. "And more important than that, I am loved! No thanks to you, *I am loved!* So, go to hell, Malcolm Gordon—if you're not there already!"

She stood there, defiantly, gazing up for another moment at the trees, watching them bristle overhead, watching the silvery stars. A moment later, the wind stilled. The woods were silent again. Marielle felt like she had finally vanquished a lifelong opponent.

Then, suddenly, at the base of the tree just to the left of the Promise Stone, something shiny caught the starlight. Marielle bent down and brushed away the dirt. It was a small tin box buried only loosely there. She clutched the metal handle and drew it out slowly, dirt falling away around it. The initials *C.G.* emblazoned on the top were rusted. Still, she knew them. She knew this box. It had been Colleen's. A chest she had kept jewelry and special things in long ago.

A shiver pulsed through her as Marielle looked up at the night sky.

"Did you lead me here?" she called out, the shock of an unbelievable revelation pulsing through her. "To *this*? Some sort of recompense, is it?"

When no reply came, Marielle sank onto her knees and opened the small box. Inside was an old cameo that had belonged to Janet Gordon. Beneath it were two other items: a train ticket, unused. Marielle picked it up. One-way to Glasgow from Crainlarich. The date was May 19, 1994. Two months before her sister had died.

Along with the ticket was a newspaper article: GLASGOW'S FAST GROWING ART COLONY. Was this just a coincidence or actually a clue to something that Malcolm, of all people, had shown her? And then the thought came, blotting out the question. Perhaps he had not despised her after all. Perhaps this solitary, rather unbelievable moment in the quiet of the Scottish countryside had not been her own reckoning so much as it was *theirs*—a father and a daughter. Contrition. Healing. Was it possible? Did it even matter now?

And more than that, if this was about more than a wounded daughter's fantasy, what was Malcolm trying to tell her from beyond the grave?

"Penny for your thoughts."

Calum's voice rocked her and she jumped back. "Sorry. I did no' mean to startle ye. Ye'd just been gone for a while and Aunt Cat was worried. I volunteered to find ye."

Marielle looked up at him in the moonlight, feeling that same powerfully unsettling attraction. "Why?"

"We were no' certain ye were safe, no' knowin' your way around out here."

She brushed Colleen's chest back behind the tree

trunk with a deft foot. "And what sort of harm could befall me in these lovely woods?"

"These woods are fair full of mystery, Marielle. Much of it better left alone, I've long been told."

"And what about the magic? Do you believe these woods are full of that as well?"

"Magic is fantasy," he snapped. "And my own life's been far too full of reality." After a silent moment, he said, "So then, do ye take that penny?" She didn't remember what he meant. He could see that. "The penny for your thoughts just now. Ye looked fair far away."

"You wouldn't believe me if I told you."

His smile was slightly devilish. "Why do ye no' try me?"

"Honestly, what I'd like is to get away from the house for a while."

Hearing that, Calum took her hand with the sure grip of a man who had done it a dozen times before— even though it was the first physical connection between them.

It was a powerful, callused hand that led her, trembling nervously, back into the house—a hand that seemed to take possession of the rest of her as well.

"Get your scarf," he said in a voice that was surprisingly gentle in its command. "We'll be goin' for a ride."

In all of her life, Marielle had never been on the back of a motorcycle, and this one looked as if it had fallen off the celluloid frames of *Easy Rider*. It was a big chrome and leather bike that sounded like a small truck and rattled like one as well when he started it up. *Harley Davidson,* it said on the gas tank. *Expensive bike,* she thought, especially for an import, as Calum wrapped a red bandanna around his head and she wrapped her arms around his waist.

Marielle had no idea where they were going, only that they'd told everyone they wouldn't be long. Yet they were certainly leaving Killin as the old road dipped and turned on its way steadily out of town.

She saw it first as they rounded the old road that stretched right up to the watery banks along Loch Tay. Polished brass lamps lit the long gravel drive. And at the top of a crest was what looked like a grand stone manor, lights blazing from all of the windows.

Calum parked the motorcycle in the courtyard next to a sign in gold lettering that read *Kilkenny Inn*, and after a moment, a young carrot-haired boy in a black suit and tie came sprinting down the front stone steps to greet him. "Evenin', Mr. Quinn. Will ye be stayin' for dinner?"

"Not tonight, Brian," Calum said as he unwound the bandanna from his dark hair, then smoothed it back from his face. "We're just after a drink."

"Very well."

As the young man motioned where he was to park, Marielle got off and went up the front steps. She waited for Calum at the carved mahogany doors and they went inside together.

"Ah, Mr. McInnes. How bonny to see ye."

"And you as well, Anne," he said, placing a gentle hand at the small of Marielle's back. She felt his touch and the little jolt of excitement—even at this tentative connection between them. "We're just stayin' for a drink."

"That table beside the window is nice."

"Splendid," he smiled broadly and led her into the lounge.

The gray-haired lady in the red sweater and tartan skirt at the desk had been right. It was a quiet evening. There was one man, a local-looking older gentleman, fatherly in his gray cardigan and well-worn dark worker's pants, drinking a pint of dark ale at the bar.

There was a battered walnut piano in one corner and only one other couple, young honeymooners, they appeared, huddled together at a small table near a blazing fire. But the room was filled with the most haunting Celtic music that Marielle had ever heard. Sounds she could have listened to forever.

"It's so warm and lovely here," Marielle said as they sat down at the window table with a view of a dining terrace, empty now but lit with candles on every table and a glass partition to stop the wind up off of the loch.

"Would ye fancy a wee dram of Scotch, since we're here?"

A barrel-chested man with a bushy gray mustache, the bartender, came to the table. "Evenin', Calum."

"William."

He laid two white cocktail napkins before them. "What can I be gettin' for ye this evenin'?"

"A wee dram of Glenmorangie would warm my soul nicely."

"Miss?"

Marielle looked up at him. "Fine."

"Two then, William . . . And could ye open the windows here for us and let a bit of the night air in?"

William nodded, complied, then turned and headed back to the bar.

After they had gotten their drinks, Calum waved to the man at the bar and excused himself from Marielle for a moment to greet him. And she watched him walk away from the table, still not understanding why she was allowing herself to be drawn to him when she had so artfully avoided similar attractions in the past.

He could be so sullen, so vague and abrupt. But something about him always took her breath away. *A diamond in the rough,* she thought. Yes, very like what her mother once thought of Malcolm Gordon. When they first met. *Heaven help you!* her mind taunted at the very moment the thought came, and she shivered, remembering the reason she had wanted to be away from MacLaren's Bend in the first place.

Malcolm. A ghost, a spark of Scottish magic. What had that really been tonight? Was it only her wounded heart's longing for a father who was no father at all? The question was too painful after what had happened out there in the dark. She needed suddenly to be outside on the well-lit terrace, in the fresh air. She needed to try to get her balance, make sense of things . . .

She needed to see if there was a clue for her in all of it.

Marielle thought about the buried chest she had found. Had Colleen been going away to Glasgow with Barry after all, so that he could pursue his art in the city? It had to be that Barry was involved in her life more deeply. Who else could she have known who had an interest in the art world?

But why a single ticket? When she considered it for a moment, there were a handful of explanations. Perhaps Colleen had meant to go on ahead, make the break from Calum, and Barry was planning to join her later. Yes, that was the most likely.

Barry had told her there had been nothing romantic between him and Colleen. But who really understood relationships, anyway? Certainly not Marielle. She only wished he had told her the truth. For some reason, his honesty mattered.

Marielle saw that Calum was still talking to the man at the bar so she went alone out onto the empty veranda. Candles glittered in hurricane lamps on tables neatly set with pink linen behind a barrier of glass to keep the wind away. It was a place to feel safe. *Good Lord,* she thought, glancing back at him, *Colleen's husband!* Even with her sister's death, this attraction still felt wrong—as wrong as her parent's marriage.

When Calum came out suddenly behind her, Marielle wrapped her arms around her waist and turned away. It was that protective mechanism that was ages old. But Calum took her shoulders and turned her back around. "Can I help?"

"No one can."

"Now," he murmured, "I do no' believe that."

"My life is complicated. You shouldn't get involved."

The expression in his eyes pleaded for her trust. But he said nothing. Only his hands held her locked beneath their powerful grip. She flinched and grew rigid beneath his touch. It was beyond frightening to her, acknowledging what her body felt—what she had closed herself off to for so long.

"Oh, Calum. I really don't think—"

But he pushed her words away with the feather-light touch of his lips beneath her ear, along the line of her jaw.

Calum kissed her then, very suddenly, and Marielle forgot completely about trying to break free. His lips moved against hers, gently at first, then more urgently. As she tasted him, felt him surrounding her, the hesitation began to melt away. Still trembling, her body fell against his, and he only pulled her in more tightly. As if he could take up all of her, shelter her from everything in the world that was bad—from her fears about men, fears about passion. And the fear of letting go.

Drawn into his arms like that, his solid, hard body pressing against hers, she was breathless. "Ye can trust me, Marielle," Calum whispered, his mouth brushing her cheek.

This is too strange and wonderful, she wanted to cry out. *When it was the last thing I wanted to feel.* But this attraction, in spite of how she had gone though life avoiding it, felt now like a kind of possession.

Calum pressed his lips gently against the bridge of her nose, then to each of her cheeks before he straightened. Beneath his deep, soulful gaze, Marielle felt as if she were becoming a part of a powerful thing.

"Well, whatever brought ye to Killin, I'm fair glad of it. But only tell me this: Are ye hidin' some dreadful secret, the truth of which would be my undoin'?"

"Would it change things if I said yes?"

"I'd only be wantin' to know ye the more."

She heard a seagull cry in the distance as a light rain began to fall beyond the terrace eaves and a fresh breeze stirred. "Everyone has their secrets, Calum. Maybe we should just leave it at that."

"I do believe I'd likely kill the likes of any man who'd ever try to harm ye," he said in a strong voice that, yet, was surprisingly still.

Strange, she thought, *that he should say it quite that way.* It struck her sharply, but then he kissed her again, and his words were forgotten beneath the power of the moment. Taste, touch, the way he smelled, virile and entirely male. All of it was a new sensation. Powerful. And so intoxicating. She wrapped her arms around his neck, and felt his own arms lock her in more tightly. She could feel how deliciously hard and excited he was. "We'd better stop this before we do something we'll both regret."

"'Tisn't anythin' under the sun I could do in your arms that I could ever regret."

Marielle caught her breath. *Don't be too certain of that,* was what she was thinking.

"Are ye wantin' me to take ye back to the house, then?"

"I think that would be best."

As she tried to take a step, he stopped her, taking her face in both of his hands. Those large, rough hands held her as gently now as if she were precious glass. "If I have anything to say about it, lovely Marielle, the complications of your life are behind ye."

Marielle wanted to cry all over again. Calum McInnes was the most handsome, passionate, and yes, most confusing man she had ever allowed even this small way into her life. And he was worlds apart from Barry in what he brought out of her. But surrendering her heart, as Calum made her want to do, taking a chance standing here in the mist and the darkness, would be dangerous. Especially with the entire truth still a barrier between them. Between her and most everyone in Killin.

CHAPTER SIXTEEN

The ceilidh was to be held in an old barn on Frazier Carnegie's sheep farm just outside of town. Everyone from the area was involved with some aspect of the event. Catriona had gone early to help the ladies set things up. It seemed to Marielle to be so wonderfully old-fashioned. Cookies, cakes, punch for the children, and plenty of free-flowing Guinness and wine for everyone else.

She hadn't seen Calum at all during the day. And by afternoon, Marielle was glad to have accepted Barry's invitation. After all, Calum hadn't even asked her. The defense mechanism around her heart had convinced her that it was just as well.

The far-off droning of a television and the intermittent laugh track drew her from her thoughts of two very different men. Jennie was alone in her room again. Marielle walked down the hall and knocked.

"Aye?"

Marielle opened the door partway and stuck her head in. Jennie was sprawled on her bed in the dark, propped with pillows.

"How are you doing?"

"Fair." Then she turned and looked earnestly up

at Marielle, standing in a cone of light from the hall. "So how come ye're no' gettin' ready for the ceilidh?"

"Oh, I will in a few minutes. There's still time. Mind if I come in?"

Jennie hit the mute button on her remote control. "Come if ye like."

Marielle sank onto the edge of the bed. Colors flashed across the dimly lit room as Jennie stared at a television, now with no sound. "Aren't you coming?"

"I certainly canno' dance," she said without looking away from the silent screen. "So what'd be the point of it?"

Marielle was careful. She could see a flash of something raw as the question came—the vulnerability that sometimes slipped beneath the protective coat of anger for only a moment or two. "Well, for starters, you might see some of your old friends."

"They do no' interest me any longer."

"Isn't there anyone in Killin you care about seeing?"

Jennie shook her head.

"No one?"

She finally looked up and Marielle could see, even in the dim light from the lamp beside her bed, that her face was wet and puffy from crying. Her own heart twisted for the girl with her barrier of false pride.

"'Twas fair nice of ye to *seem* carin' and all, Marielle."

"Would it surprise you so much if I really did?"

"What?"

"Care about you."

Jennie's eyebrows merged in a disbelieving frown. "We're strangers."

"We live in the same house."

"Familiar strangers, then."

Marielle chuckled, remembering the little girl who played with a gold cross at her mother's neck. "Score one for the lass."

"Ye'd give me one without makin' me work for it, now would ye?" Jennie's lips suddenly lengthened in surprise.

"You really do have quite a sense of humor when you feel like letting people see it."

There was a little silence, but Marielle could feel that wall between them breaking down each day they spent together.

"Was it difficult?" Jennie suddenly asked, her eyes wider, her tone honest.

"What's that?"

"Carryin' on after your da died. With your family and friends, actin' as if it hadn't happened when they canno' bear to say how sorry they are another time . . ."

Marielle was cautious, but she wanted to keep this new and fragile connection between them. "Well, I don't have many left there in either category, friends or family, to be honest with you."

"Ye don't have to go to the other side of the planet for that to happen."

Marielle knew that she was talking about herself now. "Friendships take work, Jennie. It's like my violets." *My mother's violets.* "I can't just leave them sit there on the windowsill and expect that they'll keep growing."

"Well, I canno' go to the *ceilidh*, if that's what ye're meanin' by this interest ye're showin' me."

"Would it be so awful for people who haven't seen you in a long time to come and ask you how you are?"

"They know fair well how I am. They can see that if they've got eyes."

"I think you underestimate the people of Killin."

"I canno' bear their pity."

"I asked you once before if it might not be pity but concern?"

"Ye do no' know what ye're talkin' about."

"Oh, I think I do." Marielle's voice went lower, and she leaned in a little closer toward Jennie. "You know, I won't have any friends there tonight either, besides Barry Buchanan and your mom. And you of course. *If* you'd agree to come."

Jennie looked away. "Do no' be askin' that of me."

"It's been hard to come here, expecting to reconnect with a friend, finding out that she has died so young. These people don't know me, don't care about that."

"Ye're tryin' to compare your situation with mine?"

"I'm only saying that you're not the only one who could use a little compassion."

The risky tack she had taken seemed to be working. Marielle could see, as she sank back against the bed pillows, that Jennie was actually considering it. "I've nothin' proper to wear."

"Oh, I'm sure we could find something."

"Well, I will no' be stayin' past a few minutes. *If* I go, ye understand."

"I understand."

"Just long enough to see ye settled in with some of the local lads. 'Twould make it fair interestin' for my uncle and Barry Buchanan to add a bit more spice into *that* stew."

Marielle bit back a victorious smile. "You just tell

me when you're ready to leave and I'll bring you home
myself. Agreed?"

There was another little silence as the television
continued to flash colors across the dim, tightly cur-
tained room. But then suddenly Jennie looked directly
at her and smiled. "Fair enough."

It was a big victory Marielle had fought hard for
these past days. One she'd earned. She lifted herself
from the bed then and moved toward the door quickly
before Jennie had a chance to change her mind. "I'll
be back in a few minutes to help you find something
pretty to wear."

"Do ye suppose I might be borrowin' that beige-
colored sweater of yours?" she asked as Marielle
pulled open the door and a stream of refreshing
golden lamplight from the hallway flooded the tiny
room. "The bonny one with the tiny pearl buttons."

"Sure," she said. "I don't see a reason in the world
why not."

The old barn, smelling of hay and musty wood, was
strung with white lights and bursting with people
when they arrived. Barry was dressed neatly in a red
plaid shirt and corduroys the color of melting butter.
His wavy hair was tamed back.

He had stood waiting at the bottom of the hill at
MacLaren's Bend a few minutes ago, bearing a bouquet of slightly wilted white roses tied with blue ribbon. Marielle had felt surprisingly like a teenager on
her way to the prom. She had thanked him, then let
him help her into the back seat of his battered old
Morris Minor, and watched as he put Jennie into the

front seat. Marielle's mind flashed for a moment on the last time she had gotten into a car with Barry Buchanan, all those years ago. How much life had changed them both. It had left her scarred, made her wary. But adversity seemed only to have enriched him.

No one spoke as they drove in the rain through town, and Marielle felt a wash of relief when they finally arrived and were ensconced in the rousing music and the chatter of other townspeople, many of whom already were dancing. Barry offered to get her a cup of punch, ale, or a glass of wine, and something for Jennie.

"Wine would be nice," Marielle said. Jennie asked for punch.

Marielle smiled at the courtly way he acknowledged them, nodded, and moved into the crowd. Then she glanced down at Jennie. Her expression was tense, poor child, and her face was the color of flour. Coming out like this was really difficult for her. "I'm awfully glad you came," Marielle bent down and said softly.

"Ye owe me for this one, Marielle Jaeger."

"A debt I will gladly pay," Marielle chuckled and squeezed Jennie's shoulder supportively.

Marielle watched a young woman approach them. She was slimmer than Jennie but her hair was the same long curly copper. Her eyes were wide and full of her smile. "Jennie!" she said as she stooped beside the wheelchair placing her hand on Jennie's knee. "Lardie, I'm glad to see ye here! No one thought ye'd come, or we'd have asked ye to help with the food or somethin'."

"I was no' goin' to come."

Marielle heard a little strained silence. After a moment she was relieved to see the good-natured girl smiling again. "Well, I'm just so glad ye did. Roddy's here somewhere. I know he'd want to see ye."

"I'm sure no' the girl he used to know."

"Roddy never cared about stuff like what you mean. Ye know that."

"Well, I will no' be stayin' long, anyway. 'Twas a favor to Marielle here, ye see. Me comin' out like this."

"Well, if ye ask me, 'twas long overdue."

"Do no' expect it to become a habit."

"Now, that'd be a sorry thing. Ye've been missed by everyone."

Jennie glanced back up at Marielle with a tentative expression. Marielle stooped over again and whispered, "Remember, we can leave any time you want."

Before she had a chance to reply, two more people who looked about Jennie's age, a girl with corn-colored hair pulled away from her face and a dark-haired boy with freckles and a hook nose, came up behind the other girl.

"Jennie Quinn!" the girl squealed with surprise. "No one told me ye'd be here!"

"How are ye, Jennie?" the boy asked more seriously.

Marielle watched protectively. But these were friends. Good friends. The boy especially had meant something to Jennie. Their tone and their interest were sincere. "Still near as ornery as you, Roddy McFee," Jennie said with a twisted smile.

"'Tis a shame then ye've no' been around much. There's no one near as fun to spar with as you."

"Well, she's back now. 'Tis all that matters," said the first girl who had come up. "Come along, Jennie. Ye've got to be listenin' to all the sordid tales of what your old mates have been up to. And Mary'll never let us hear the end of it if ye don't let them brag a bit, as well!"

Marielle proudly watched Jennie wheel herself off into the crowd with the awkward and gangly Roddy McFee by her side. It really was the best medicine in the world. Just as Marielle had always suspected, there were people who cared for her, who were concerned. One in particular.

"It's been a long time since I've been to one of these," Barry said with a smile as he handed Marielle a glass of wine. He looked out at the dancers doing a traditional "knees up" while the onlookers rousingly clapped in time.

Marielle, in a pair of blue jeans and a white silk blouse, looked over at him. "Don't they have them very often?"

"Oh, all of the time. I just haven't been much inclined. That is, till I met you."

Barry settled his eyes on her then. He was smiling. And Marielle felt a pure and growing affection for him. But in their private silence, one surrounded by music and laughter, the giggles of children dancing, she knew he wanted more, something she was not certain she could give him.

As proof that he understood, Barry came around behind the refreshment table toward Catriona when a new tune began. It was *her* thick, reddened hand, not Marielle's, that he took and squeezed with an open affection. "If ye'll be excusin' us," he said with a wink at Marielle, who chuckled and nodded her overwhelming approval. "But this next one is *our* dance."

Then Marielle watched them, knees up Scottish

style, twirling in time to the new upbeat Celtic tune. Children were dancing as well. Parents, grandparents. And Marielle thought in that moment how special this world was. How different from what she remembered when Malcolm Gordon was alive. And, at this moment, she was glad to have come back here. Glad that she would have more to take back to Paris than only the loss and tragedy that had greeted her at first.

Marielle gazed out at Barry, so kind to the stout, twice-widowed Catriona, and she felt her heart expand. A gentleman in the truest sense of the word.

A firm hand on Marielle's shoulder pulled her suddenly from that thought and back to a moment of pure physical awareness. She turned around to see Calum standing behind her, in slim, worn denim jeans and a slightly wrinkled blue plaid shirt. His dark hair was windblown, and he still had the same slightly wild bit of beard she'd seen last night.

"I didn't know you were coming to the dance," she said above the music, glancing guiltily over at Catriona and Barry.

"I did no' know that I was either."

She wanted to say that she was glad he was here. But something stopped her.

She was Barry's date, after all.

"Ye're no' dancing?"

Marielle felt his eyes on her as the question lay between them, and a tiny shiver threaded its way up her spine. Marielle wanted to look away but she couldn't.

"I'm here with Barry Buchanan."

"Aye. But it appears that he's taken up at the moment."

Marielle glanced again at Catriona and Barry, dancing and laughing with everyone else. As she watched them, Calum watched *her*.

"'Tis only one dance I'm askin' for." His voice was low. Coaxing. "I'm leavin' again in the mornin', and ye'd at least be givin' me somethin' bonny to think about besides the fish."

She smiled at that, feeling his eyes play over her face as he stood stone-still, a presence stronger and more commanding than any she had ever encountered. Marielle could hardly catch her breath. "Well, I suppose in that case, just one dance wouldn't hurt."

He clutched her hand firmly and led her onto the dance floor, when suddenly the music changed. The soft strains of a harp filled the old barn, and a young girl singing a melodic tune stood bathed in a pale blue spotlight. "You knew they were going to do that," Marielle said as he wrapped his arms around her.

"Aye," he smiled rakishly, and his dark eyes glittered.

She bit back a little smile herself. "So will you be the one to tell my date that you got me out here on false pretenses?"

"Believe me, Buchanan there is a lad who can fend for himself," he said bitterly, as he pulled her close to his chest. His solid arms went around her then, and his firm body pressed tautly against hers. It was a seductive movement, even in a crowded barn. "I hope ye'll be forgivin' me, Marielle. But I'd rather no' talk about anyone else just now."

His voice was still low, and they were so close. Touching. She felt her heart racing.

"What *do* you want to talk about, then?"

He ran a hand, feather light, across her cheek. It was warm. Commanding. "I only want to look at ye, here like this. Up close."

Suddenly, they might as well have been the only two people on earth. Marielle felt herself giving in a little more with each quickened heartbeat to the power Calum McInnes had over her. The raw sensuality of him. "You make me want that too," she said softly so that only he could hear.

"Meet me outside when the tune is through."

"I can't. I told you, I'm with Barry tonight."

"'Tisn't where ye're meant to be."

He hadn't said it arrogantly nor possessively. But there was a rightness about the statement that made Marielle shudder. "He's been kind to me."

"And I've been more than a little pigheaded. We got off to a poor start. I'd fancy a chance to mend that."

Marielle's heart soared as she pulled away and looked at him, at those penetrating eyes that could make her forget almost every promise she had ever made to herself.

"Last night, you caught me when I was at a weak point," she tried to protest.

"What happened between us last night was perfect."

"You can't begin to understand. But I'm afraid, Calum." Her words came in a whisper. She was shaking as he held her, as they moved to the music.

"Ye needn't fear what's meant to be."

Marielle felt the pressure of his hand at the small of her back. She watched his mouth, knowing then that he was going to kiss her, right here in front of everyone. And then, just when she could feel his breath on her face, a solid force jerked him back with one powerful thrust. It was Barry, his eyes blazed with anger, his fists were raised in combat.

"Oh, no ye don't, Calum McInnes! Ye'll no' be takin' another brilliant young life down with ye!"

"Can ye no' see I'm dancin'?"

"Song's over. So's the rest of it."

"Ye'll no' be tellin' *me* what to do, Buchanan. Ye ruined enough of my life as it is!"

"Oh, give that up, will ye, man? I tell ye, McInnes, if ye still believe she was the kind of woman to have done *that* to ye, then by God, ye never knew Colleen a'tall."

Marielle glanced back at Calum. His teeth were clenched, his handsome features hardened to a mask of rage. He did believe Barry and Colleen had cheated on him. Barry was denying it.

Only one of the two men she was coming to care about was telling the truth.

"Marielle, perhaps ye'd like to leave." A chill hung on the edge of Barry's clipped words as well. The gentle man she had come to know seemed to have vanished. Marielle was shaken by the quiet vengeance that lit his eyes. It was the same way that Calum looked back at him.

Marielle swallowed hard. Her words came out weakly. "I told Jennie I'd stay until she was ready to leave. I can't go now."

"She can go on home with Catriona. Or with Calum when she pleases."

"Barry." Marielle dropped her voice, realizing now that everyone else was staring. "It was just one dance. There's been no harm done."

Barry turned away from her then and shot Calum another rooting look. "Ye're forgettin' that I know the whole truth, Calum McInnes. So let's no', the two of us, be talkin' here about who ruined whose life. And, for that matter, I'll tell ye straight away, lad, ye're no' to get a chance to snuff out Marielle's existence now as well!"

Everything stopped with that, and a cold, hard knot settled in the pit of her stomach, the accusations and revelations making her ill. Like Ian McShane, Barry too believed Calum had caused Colleen's death.

Yet again her mind wound back to him. She saw the flowers, tiny delicate violets Calum had left for her. A kind act following days of heart-numbing harshness.

How cold he could be. And yet how passionate his kiss. How warm his touch. Calum McInnes was a man of such unsettling contradictions. All of it tumbled around in her head in that moment, each of the images fighting one another. Was he kind? Or cruel? Was the real Calum the man who had brought her flowers? Or a man who had somehow caused his own wife's death, after all?

Calum was looking at her now, and his deep, black eyes were silently asking her to do as he had bid her earlier. To come away with him. To make a stand on his side.

"Perhaps ye should all calm down a bit here," Catriona interjected into the taut silence. "Take a wee dram and—"

Calum's eyes narrowed. A moment later, when Marielle said nothing at all, and when she did not move toward him, Calum was forced to take that as her answer. In the stony silence, he turned, stepped into the stunned crowd, and slipped quickly out of sight.

But Barry remained, as she knew he would. Still, it was clear to her now, painfully so, that she was not the only one keeping secrets.

The music began again. The tension of a moment ago was eased now by laughter and voices that had risen up. Barry clutched Marielle's hand and led her outside. The night was cold, the air biting. They sat on an old log that had been fashioned into a bench and gazed out across the pitch black field where the Carnegie sheep grazed.

Confused and a little angry at the behavior of both men, Marielle had come outside for one reason only: she needed to know about Calum and Colleen. She hoped that at last it would lead to the details of how her only sister had died and why there were still whispers that her husband had been involved.

"So, what just happened in there?" Marielle asked firmly, her spine stiff as she turned to him.

Hearing her tone, Barry laid his head back against the barn wall and gazed up at the stars. There was a long silence. Finally, he turned to look at her. "Very well, then." His face was tight. Determined. It was another beat, then two, before he began. "'Tis a fair amount of history between Calum and me."

"Apparently so."

"As I've told ye, Colleen and I were friends. Dear friends."

Marielle was thinking of the train ticket to Glasgow and the article about the art world that she had kept as something special. "And that's all it ever was between you?"

He raked a hand through his hair and once again looked out at the still, dark night. "Not in Calum's mind. He was a jealous, possessive lout who held his wife so tightly that in the end, it broke her. I know her spirit was gone."

"Oh, Barry. I'm not certain that you can blame everything on—"

Barry cut off her sentence. He turned to her, took both of her hands and held them tightly. His eyes were startlingly serious. "Trust me about this."

"About what?"

"Tell me, do ye trust me, then?"

"Of course. I mean, you're not like anyone I've ever known. But—"

"Then believe me when I tell ye he's no' the man to belong to."

"I don't *belong* to Calum," she said stubbornly, that tough, ages-old, independent side of her surging forth.

"He's got secrets, Marielle."

"Doesn't everyone?"

"No' like Calum's."

Barry's tone, the deep conviction behind it, resonated, and it was unnerving to her. "I really do think you're getting a little ahead of yourself. Calum hasn't said a thing to me about a relationship."

"No' yet. But it's clear that he wants ye."

"That takes two. And I'm not inclined to be anyone's possession."

"No. I canno' imagine you as a possession," Barry said deeply, his eyes shimmering in the moonlight. That face, the lines of it, were so intense.

"And what do you imagine of me, Barry?" she asked, wondering in that little moment what he would think if he knew *her* great secret.

"I do no' imagine it. I *know* what I see: a lovely woman with a heart of gold, but one who's vulnerable. A woman who's lettin' the past lead ye straight into somethin' ye canno' possibly deal with when it comes at ye headlong."

Marielle sprang to her feet, wrapping her arms around herself, feeling cold again and a little panicked by everything that had happened this evening. It was too much to accept. Too much to consider. "I'm sorry I asked."

He stood up beside her. He was bracing his hands on her shoulders as she turned away. "I was hopin' ye would no' say that, no' if ye really do trust me."

"It's getting harder and harder to know who to believe." Marielle pivoted back around. Their eyes met, his deep and soulful. Hers were tinged with panic. "Tell me one thing more," she said as her heart raced.

"Anythin' I can."

She felt the anger again. "It's about time someone was honest with me about all of this."

"'Twill be me, if I can."

"Do you honestly believe what you said in front of everyone . . . that Calum was involved in Colleen's death?"

Barry looked at her again just then, the blackness in his eyes were full of a sudden bitterness. "All right, then. He killed her, Marielle. The truth is, Calum McInnes killed his own wife."

She was breathless. Marielle felt her mind spinning

at the harshness of the accusation. "But *you* told me yourself that it was a car accident."

"'Twas before I knew he meant to have ye next. Before I thought ye could be in danger. But for more of the truth than what I've already told ye," Barry said stonily, "ye'll have to confront Calum himself."

CHAPTER SEVENTEEN

It was after midnight by the time she'd said good night to Catriona and Jennie and collapsed into one of the overstuffed, velvet-covered chairs in the dark salon at MacLaren's Bend. Marielle couldn't possibly have slept. Her mind was still whirling. Now was the first peaceful moment she'd had to think—to process it all.

Then suddenly it came to her again. Now it was not a random thought, but one full of great precision and truth: The two men who had cared for Colleen, who had both been a part of her life, both of them were now fighting for *her*, here in this same small Scottish village where it had all unfolded for Colleen.

Had her sister ever felt the same conflicting emotions Marielle did for these two complex and mysterious men?

Barry. Her thoughts tumbled back to an image first of him, standing before her at the *ceilidh*, smiling that handsome, gallant smile, caring for her in that quiet, understated way. He was the kindest man she'd ever known. So full of compassion. That infectious, slightly Bohemian zest for life. A man who could make her happy . . .

If not for what she felt when Calum touched her.

"He told ye about Colleen and me—about her death then, didn't he?"

A gruff whisper pierced the darkness. Startled, Marielle shot to her feet. Before she could answer, Calum came toward her, cloaked in shadows.

"He said that you were responsible."

"And did ye believe him then?"

She waited a moment, thought about the question. What would she do now? Who should she believe? "I have no reason not to."

"Ye have what ye feel for me. Could ye no' trust that?"

Marielle stood and waited by the chair until he came to her, nothing but shadows and that earthy fragrance of him in the darkness. She was firm in her anger that someone was lying to her. "Are you saying that Barry is not telling the truth about your involvement?"

Calum drew near until they were a breath apart, his firm, fit body half in shadow, half in shimmering light from the slip of silver moon coming in through the bay window—the place where the potted violets sat. Her eyes were wide. He could see that she was on edge. "I'm sayin' that she was my wife. Aye, Colleen was that. And he wanted . . . No matter what he tells ye, Marielle, the truth is Buchanan had long wanted her for himself. I've seen enough of the world to know how powerfully that can cloud a man's mind. And at the end I think he almost had her, with all of that carin' and concern he heaped on her. Apparently, he's no' forgiven me for the fact that she died *my* wife and no' his."

It made a strange kind of sense.

She remembered the way Barry had looked at Colleen when they were much younger. And yet would Barry lie about Colleen's death as some kind of revenge because they never got to act on his plan to go away to Glasgow together? It didn't seem like Barry, not the man she was beginning to know.

Marielle looked at Calum squarely in the shadows. "Were you responsible for Colleen's death?"

He didn't respond quite so quickly this time. The accusation was harsh, and the air between them was suddenly full of the tension it brought. Calum was so close in that silence that she could feel him draw in a breath then let it out.

"'Tis no' easy to speak about," he said in a hoarse whisper. "Even with someone ye've come to care for."

"Try."

"Colleen and I had our problems. I'll no' deny that to ye."

"Thank you at least for being honest about *that*."

"She did drown that night, Marielle . . . a horrible accident. Anythin' more heinous than that is pure fiction, somethin' of Buchanan's mind."

"But Mr. McShane . . ." she haltingly confessed. "He implied the same thing as Barry when I first came to town."

"Buchanan and Ian McShane are great mates. Surely ye've seen McShane sittin' in the studio there, both of them takin' their tea. Seems natural for the man to side with a mate, especially when matters of the heart are involved."

Her tense muscles softened. He touched her face tentatively then, and Marielle melted against the warmth of his palm. Calum's plausible excuse hung between them in the still night air. He sank into one of the chairs then and Marielle knelt before him. "We've come this far. . . ." she persisted. "Please, Calum. I need to hear it from you. I believe you that Colleen did drown that night. But tell me yourself you had nothing at all to do with it."

Calum's eyes searched her face in the shadows, trying to reach into her thoughts. "Ye continue to ask, so a part of ye must still believe that I could have."

"Choosing *not* to believe Barry is hard."

"And why is that?"

"Because I have begun to feel something for him—almost as much as I feel for *you*."

Her last words were like a confession between them. Calum drew her up suddenly then, and Marielle hadn't been prepared for the swiftness of the movement. Always so strong. But now there was desperation in it.

A flutter inside her chest strengthened. She could see the softly shadowed features of his face in the moonlight when she looked at him then.

There were so many other questions she longed to ask. So many things she wanted to know about him. About the details of what had happened. But, in the power of the moment, she forgot them all because never in her life had so incredibly sensual a man as Calum touched her. Kissed her. Ignited her.

He wrapped a hand around her neck and pulled her close until their lips met. Marielle was surprised this time to feel his mouth tremble against hers. The taste of him had been so raw and powerful that first time at the Kilkenny Inn. But there was still that little sliver of vulnerability about Calum that drew her inextricably. Beneath the bravado and the facade was someone else—a man who had known the same love and loss in his life that she had. Who had been scarred deeply by it.

Tasting all of that now, the fear and the hesitation about him, about *this* with a man, simply floated away. Now she was not a part of his past, or her own. This was everything.

Calum drew her onto his lap and moved against her. He was so full of desire for her as they kissed that she could no longer catch her breath. There was a starved part of herself coming alive beneath those warm, powerful hands—a woman whose passion had been imprisoned.

His fingers were on her breasts then, moving down and back up beneath her sweater. She felt his hands beneath her bra as his mouth took hers again and again in powerful, endless kisses. "Not here," she whispered shakily.

Calum picked her up, still kissing her, a hand still beneath her sweater, the other cradling the bend in her legs, as he took her out into the cool night air behind the house, down the mossy brick path, toward the small secluded potter's shed, covered in ancient ivy.

So slowly, carefully, she was sure she was dreaming, Calum lit a single candle and tossed a heavy tartan blanket onto the floor while she waited tentatively beside him. Not moving. Barely breathing. Her heart racing.

Then he came back, pressing her against the cold plank wall beneath a shelf stuffed with bags of fertilizer and little brick-colored pots of mulch. His arms curved around her again, wanting, seeking. Her heart climbed into her throat at the way he touched her. Had she ever been touched this way? Had she ever even imagined anything like this? Marielle felt alive suddenly. Freed from a prison of her own making and hungry to be loved like this.

Calum's hands cupped her bottom as he pressed himself against her. He was so hard, his chest, thighs, the rest of him felt like granite. But warm. *So warm.*

Wordlessly then, he backed away only enough to pull off her sweater. When he tore off his own shirt, then pressed himself against her again—his muscled chest meeting her bare breasts—her skin turned to gooseflesh.

Trembling with a pleasure so exquisite that it felt almost like pain, Marielle's eyes rolled to a close as he fell to his knees before her. In a haze of a passion, she wrapped her arms around the broad expanse of his back and let him lower her onto the blanket. Before she could catch her breath, Calum began again to lift her back to a place where she had never gone before tonight, as endless as the sky, driving into her, touching her, tasting her . . . her name, *Marielle . . . Marielle,* in the French manner, the only sound on his lips.

She hadn't realized she'd slept, but when she turned to touch him in the darkness, Calum was gone. She lay there in the potter's shed alone for a little while, thinking perhaps it had not been real. Only a dream could have been that wonderful. She sat up and saw that the candle had nearly burned out. She missed him already.

Marielle dressed and walked quickly back up to the house. She needed coffee. Great volumes of it. But she went instead alone into the salon where Calum had come to her and she sank back into the same chair. It was nearly five o'clock.

She waited like that, alone in the dark, filled with the essence of him, knowing he was not going to return to her now. Calum had told her that today he'd be leaving again for the sea. And so he had. In the flat gray of early morning, once again her mind reeled with unanswered questions.

Was Barry telling the truth? Was Calum?

Unable to stop herself from feeling the curiosity that was consuming her, it was nearly dawn when Marielle crept up the darkened staircase toward Calum's bedroom. Carefully, she opened the door, gazing in at the neatly made four-poster bed, the simple, unadorned dresser, and the wicker rocking chair wedged into a corner.

Marielle felt short of breath, knowing it was wrong to be in here, as she closed the door, then flipped on the small table lamp. But something drove her forward.

She sank onto the edge of his bed, picturing him in her mind, so roughly sensual. His touch came back to her. Tender. Vital. She was still able to taste him on her lips. That was not a man capable of murdering his wife. But, with the same certainty, Marielle could not believe Barry had lied. After a moment she rose and went to the dresser, pulling open each of the drawers, seeking some little bit of the truth. *Calum's truth.*

White underthings. Shirts, neatly folded. The bottom drawer full of denim jeans. But beneath them, something else. A tattered album. Marielle lifted it out and brought it back to the bed. She opened the cover, doing her best to ignore the wrenching in her stomach. An old photograph gazed back at her from the first page. The pretty face, softly freckled smiled at her hauntingly. *Colleen.*

Marielle carefully lifted the photograph from the four corner pockets that held it. Then she turned it over. Her hands were trembling.

To Calum, on our wedding day. We're going to make it. The worst is past and we have the future ahead of us now. It's going to be wonderful! My love always, Colleen.

Marielle put the photograph back, then turned the page. Dried flowers pressed behind a piece of wax paper. They looked like daffodils. Beside it were two ticket stubs for the Dover ferry over to France. She turned the page again.

"Interestin' readin', is it?"

The album tumbled to the floor as Marielle sprang to her feet, startled by the sudden voice that came at her in the darkness. In the doorway before her was Jennie.

"How did you get upstairs?"

"Lift in the back of the house. Did you no' know we had one?"

"I didn't even hear you. I was just—"

Jennie rolled her chair forward, cutting Marielle off. "Just tryin' to uncover the truth?"

"Yes."

"Well, there's a bit of the same I'd certainly fancy uncoverin' from you." Her eyes narrowed suspiciously. "Such as, who are ye *really*? And what are ye after here in Killin?"

CHAPTER EIGHTEEN

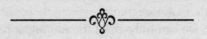

Marielle struggled to catch her breath. She averted her eyes, knowing what her gaze would reveal. "I'm not sure I know what you mean."

"Oh, I think ye do."

There was a moment when Marielle's mind actually searched for some way to perpetuate the ruse she had begun here. There was so much more invested in it now that things didn't appear so cut and dried any more about the way Colleen had died. But looking at Jennie, whose expression now held more interest than accusation, she realized that carrying it on would be pointless.

"All right," she said reluctantly. "My name is not Marielle. Not my given name, anyway."

Jennie rolled forward and closed the door. "I knew it."

"I was born Mairi. Mairi Claire Gordon."

"Mairi Gordon?" In a flash of recognition, Jennie's eyes flared brightly. "Your mother's name is Vivienne?"

"Yes. When we returned to my mother's native country of France, after she left my father, Vivienne was bitter. She changed my name to sound more French. I have been called Marielle for a very long time now."

"Och, saints preserve us! Colleen was your sister?"

"Yes."

"But why on earth the grand charade?"

Marielle spoke slowly. Each word was controlled. "This trip home for me unexpectedly became one of grieving, Jennie, when I found out that my sister was dead. I've not been a person who opens up easily." Marielle watched Jennie's face pale. "My memories of Colleen—reconciling all of that was an intensely personal journey, and your mother respected that."

"Ma knows?"

"Yes."

The next silence stretched on for what seemed an eternity and a shiver ran up Marielle's back.

"And does my uncle know, as well?"

"No."

"But he was married to Colleen! He knew your sister better than anyone!" Jennie's face colored. "And now the two of *you* are into it deeper than—"

"I can't tell him, Jennie. Not yet."

Jennie's eyes glittered in the dim light. "Would ye no' say he deserves to know?"

"Yes. Just not yet. And I am asking you, *please,* not to be the one to tell him." Marielle struggled to hold the reins on her emotions as Jennie sat incredulous in the silence.

"Ye've been kind to me since ye've been here," Jennie finally said, her words coming slowly, deliberately, as she gazed at Marielle. "Ye've certainly treated me better than I treated you."

"I've become fond of you, Jennie. That has nothing to do with Colleen, or why I came back to Killin."

They waited silently. Moments passed. The two

women looked at one another then. Jennie's expression was thoughtful. "I believe ye. And I'll no' be the one givin' away your secret."

Relief washed over Marielle at that moment like a great warm wall of water. "Thank you, Jennie."

"I had a bonny time at the ceilidh last night. I had no' expected that."

"I know."

"What I *did* expect never happened."

"Sometimes life has a way of surprising us."

Jennie looked back at the album lying open on the floor between them. Then she glanced back at Marielle. "As it has for you with my uncle Calum?"

"He's a very complicated man."

"In that, he's a lot like Barry Buchanan, isn't he?"

Marielle knew what she meant. Jennie had seen, firsthand, much of the time she had spent with Barry. And yet there was no way for her to have missed the intensity of what was between her and Calum whenever her brooding young uncle came back from the sea.

"'Twas the same dilemma Colleen faced once. The two of them lovin' her, Barry takin' advantage, tryin' to woo her away from Calum when they started havin' problems."

Marielle ached at the ironic comparison. "Do you honestly believe Barry was in love with her and not just maybe trying to help a friend make it through a tough time?"

"They spent time together before she married Calum, that I know. And he always seemed to be around afterward, when things had begun to go bad."

"Do you believe that they were actually having an affair?" Marielle asked.

"All I know for certain is that Barry seemed to be around her an awful lot toward the end of Colleen's life. What that was about, only the two of them knew."

Why did each revelation make things more complicated? The room stilled as Marielle looked back at Jennie, hoping for a small miracle. "Now, I have trusted you with my greatest secret. We trust one another. Please, Jennie. *Please*. You were there. Tell me about the night Colleen died."

She looked away. "'Tis no' my place."

"Trust is a two-way street."

Jennie glanced down at the album. "I can see ye've already been through the memories that Calum keeps."

"It only tells part of the story."

"Ye'd best be askin' Calum for more than that."

She felt increasingly desperate. "But why do you refuse me when you were there? You know as well as he does about the last moments of my sister's life."

"I've never spoken about that night. No' with anyone."

The desire to add more pieces to the puzzle that had been Colleen's life and death became very strong. Especially with her own feelings tied up so intensely with the two men who were there. The box she had found buried and had taken away only added to the mystery. Marielle leaned forward, crossing her arms over her chest. It gave her a moment to collect herself, to lower her tone. "When Colleen and I were children, we played in the same hills and fields you played in. Malcolm—my father—never wanted us to go into that glen down the road that leads into town. Do you know the glen I mean?"

"Of course."

"Colleen and I thought it was such a special place. It was an adventure. We never got to go all the way in together. We never got to share that. And so much more. I never got to tell her how much I wanted to come back to her through the years, to know about her life. To share it with her, as sisters do. It hurts that I will never have that chance now. For so many things."

"I'm sorry."

"It may have been a long time ago. But Colleen and I were close. As close as any two sisters could be. And I never once stopped thinking about her. Or about wanting to come back here. She is a part of me, Jennie, still. And now I can never ask *her* how she died." Marielle drew in a painful breath to steady herself against the tears she felt stinging her eyes. "At least tell me if Calum had anything to do with it."

Jennie was wary again. Marielle waited. It felt like forever.

"Aye," she said finally. "I suppose 'twould be the only answer, that he did."

The silence stretched on.

"Tell me, please, Jennie," Marielle said softly, the plea coming on a ragged breath.

"All I can say for certain is that Calum was a man fair full of frustration. He thought he was better than this place. But he'd had a poor start to things with his work and he could never quite manage to put things together for them in Glasgow, as he'd always promised her he would. It made him bitter toward the end of Colleen's life."

"His frustration must have been very difficult for her."

"Her defense against it was to drink. And after a while, the two of them did a whole lot more fightin' than anythin' else."

"She lived with a lot of pressure," Marielle realized sadly.

"From her father. And from Calum. Still lovin' her with that powerful, silent way of his. I guess, for all of her tryin' to avoid it, she married a man just like her da."

Marielle was almost afraid to hear the answer. But she had to know. She had to understand. "And the night she died?"

Jennie's voice went lower. Again Marielle waited. "'Twas a Saturday night. Colleen's birthday. Calum was up in Glasgow with some of his old mates. He'd told her he'd be back in Killin on time. When he was no' and the house was full of guests, she was embarrassed, a bit angry as well. So she drank. She drank a lot that night."

Marielle's heart felt as if it were being twisted in two, and she struggled to remain silent. Still, every word was painful. Because, as Jennie spoke, it made Colleen alive again. Not the bright, beautiful Colleen she remembered, but a troubled young woman who covered over her problems with alcohol rather than dealing with them.

"When he finally did come home, Calum and Colleen had a bitter row. Colleen left her own party in a state. 'Twas quite a scene. I don't think he knew how truly drunk she was."

"But you did."

"Aye. I went after her when she headed for her car. I had hopes she'd let me drive. I thought 'twould be safer until she calmed down. But she'd have no part of it." The pace of Jennie's confession slowed. The words came with more difficulty. "I crawled in beside her, hopin' to get her to stop." Jennie's eyes filled with sudden tears as she gazed down at the photograph again. "And the next thing I knew they were pluckin' me out of Loch Tay . . . and tellin' me Colleen was dead."

Marielle waited a moment. She was careful with her question. "But the paper said that *you* were driving."

She wiped her tears. Sniffled. "*That* I did, for my uncle."

"You told them *you* were driving the car when you weren't?"

"'Twould have been no point in harmin' Colleen's memory that way. Lettin' everyone think that this"— she touched the wheel of her chair—"was her fault. And I thought my uncle'd already dealt with enough in the way of guilt for how they had fought."

Marielle was speechless. This young girl whom she'd so misjudged, who she'd believed was nothing but self-pitying, had acted in the most selfless of ways. Not only that night. But after.

So that was what had bonded the two of them. She had sensed from the first that there was something. It was their knowledge of that final fight—and a realization that Colleen's recklessness had been at least in part responsible for her death. Marielle felt a shattering jolt of compassion for the two people who had sought to protect her sister's memory. Compassion for all they both had endured after that night: Jennie's paralysis and Calum's grief that had cost him his career.

How Marielle wished he were here. That she could go to him, hold him, as she had last night. She wanted to tell him that she understood. She wanted to tell him that in spite of his wounded soul and the way he tried to push her away at times, she still cared for him. Marielle wanted him to know that she believed him.

She was suddenly angry at Ian McShane for his harmful inference that first day when things were so clouded in her mind. It certainly shouldn't have been seen as Calum's fault, the tragic consequences of a marital spat, Colleen's flying off and trying to drive when she had been drinking. The poor man had obviously done enough blaming himself for letting her go, in the two years since her death, for everyone concerned.

Marielle thought that fate had been cruel to have taken his wife from him at that particular moment in time, with anger still raw between them. Never to be reconciled. How like things between her and Malcolm. Wounds open, permanent. And a final chapter never to be written. No wonder it had altered Calum's life so profoundly.

This encounter with Jennie had been pivotal on two levels. She now also had to believe, sadly, that Barry's feelings for Colleen had driven him to implicate Calum in this horrible tragedy. But Marielle was left to wonder what Calum felt for her. He had left her alone again, without any sort of declaration of his own feelings, and gone back to sea.

In a strange way, she felt like she had as a child with a father she had never understood. Off balance. Vulnerable. Frightened by feelings that could wound her deeply. And she was so very tired of living a life like that. She wanted something stronger now. Something enduring. She didn't want what Vivienne had with Malcolm. Nor what Colleen had known with Calum. Something torrid, full of passion and anger.

"So you *are* French, then?" Jennie's question jolted her back.

"Half."

"I believe I've changed my mind, ye know." Jennie smiled. "I don't believe ye're like Malcolm said the French were, wild and selfish."

Marielle managed a weak smile in return. "Thank you for that."

There was another little awkward moment between them. But there was a bond being forged. Something both of them felt. "I do wish ye'd be after tellin' my uncle the truth, though. After all, he was married to your own sister. Come to think of it," Jennie tipped her head and her eyes glittered as a smile lifted the corners of her mouth, "we're almost related, you and I."

"So we are."

Jennie seemed genuinely pleased with her realization. And her smile faded only slightly before she said, "Don't let it go on too much longer though, hmm? Someone else might get hurt if ye do."

Marielle felt her heart tug at the way that had sounded. "You knew them both. You saw them together. Do you think, if Colleen had lived, she and Calum would have stayed together?"

"Who can say for certain? He loved her, though. That much I know. And they were fair passionate about one another. Good passion. And bad. But sometimes, they say, don't they, that all of that crazy, wild stuff like in the movies just isn't enough?"

Marielle thought of her own parents and the impossibility of what she had begun here with the man Colleen had loved and married. "Yes," she said. "They do say that."

CHAPTER NINETEEN

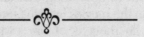

Barry and Marielle pushed Jennie along the road beside the glen the next morning. Autumnal mist surrounded them all in knee-high streaks of silver. The morning sun above struggled through a veil of clouds as thin streamers of pink and lemon yellow lit their path.

The air was brisk as it came off the shoulders of the great aubergine hills, its jagged peaks and splintered terraces lying directly ahead. But somehow, more and more, this cold seemed invigorating to Marielle. *Right.* The beauty here, the endless field of browning bracken beside them, and the silvery stems of heather bent by the wind, was almost celestial as they walked. They were heading toward the neighboring town of Crainlarich and the fish market there.

They did not speak about the ceilidh—about what had happened between him and Calum or about the distorted version of the tragedy Barry had told her because of his feelings for Colleen. And Marielle did not confront him with it. Perhaps, in Barry's mind, she reasoned, Calum was responsible because it was their argument that had so fatefully forced her into the car that night.

"We could have taken the car," Barry said suddenly.

Marielle shivered at the irony of how her thoughts and his words had crossed at that moment. She looked over at him, the cold air stinging her face. "Now, what fun would that have been? Besides," she said, as she pushed the wheelchair, "this is wonderful for Jennie. I haven't seen so much color in her cheeks since I've been here."

Barry's smile was slow and appreciative. It lit his deep, hazel eyes, crinkling them at the corners. "I was hopin' ye'd say that. Truth is, I wanted ye to see all of this and be beside ye when ye did."

"The stomping ground of a true Scot."

"Aye."

"Well, it's magnificent. All of it."

She could see, as he smiled, that Barry was pleased. "'Tis a part of ye now, the magic of this land, hmm? Just as it is me."

More than he could know. Scotland was always more deeply imbedded inside of her than France had ever been, because the moments here had made such a deep impression. And there was still that unfinished business with Malcolm that kept rearing up, begging to be dealt with.

Yes, she was a part of this place. But Marielle knew acknowledging that—making Barry think she might stay—would be giving him hope. She had a life in Paris. Her mother. Her work. And then she thought of Calum again.

Would it make a difference if *he* were the one wanting her to stay?

But he wasn't, Marielle reminded herself as she

saw that Jennie had stopped her wheelchair and was sitting stone-still. Ahead was a large stag with a full set of antlers and a shaggy chest, lying in what was left of the heather.

"Will ye look at that!" she called out softly when Barry and Marielle were near enough to hear.

"A stag, lass. And a bonny thing he is too," Barry chuckled.

Barry and Marielle exchanged a little glance, both of them windblown and smiling as they pushed Jennie carefully forward. Marielle was thrilled to see Jennie happy, able to savor a bit of life after the tragedy she had endured.

They remained silent together for a moment, the three of them, watching the deer look up, wide-eyed. Silent. Not particularly in fear, simply in acknowledgment. It really was so extraordinary. But then it had begun to surprise her less and less, this world into which Barry was slowly drawing her. The gentleness. The beauty. And it was at that moment that Marielle realized this time with Barry had begun to feed a very different part of her soul: her need for kindness. For the sweet, sweet things life had to offer.

It startled her, the acknowledgment of that.

She'd known so many other elements of living: loss, joy. Certainly great tumult. But never the simplest of pleasures. Passion and inner peace. Until suddenly, from out of the blue, they were there. Bright and glittering.

But they glittered in two different men.

They all went on from the fish market to the fresh vegetable stalls nearby. Stout, rosy-cheeked women in tartan skirts and Aran sweaters. Smiling. Chattering. Men in suspenders and plaid shirts.

Barry bought them all ripe red apples that they ate as they strolled. As a rousing Celtic harp from a street group filled the background, Marielle took a turn pushing Jennie, and the two of them began to giggle at something unimportant but which, aloud, sounded like a private, childish secret.

It rained as they left Crainlarich, and when they heard it wasn't going to let up anytime soon, Barry and Marielle quickly wheeled Jennie into a pub called The Merchant to wait out the downpour.

It was a dark and cozy place, with rough dark beams overhead and a blazing fire in a stone hearth that dominated one entire end of the place. Jennie joined a boy who was sitting on a stool near the fire as he played intently with a pocket computer game. Marielle had never seen Jennie look so happy.

"I've had a wonderful day," Marielle sighed as she sank into the high red leather booth beside Barry.

"I'm glad," Barry said deeply, taking up her chilled hand in his own so forcefully that, for a moment, she shivered. Especially when he drew it up and kissed her knuckles tenderly, seductively, like a lover would do.

"Oh, Barry, I—"

"Now, I'm not askin' ye for anythin'," he firmly stopped her, drawing back a little. "'Tis just time to let ye know what I've come to feel for ye."

She calmed at that. At his tone. The assurance in his eyes. She believed him.

After that, they ordered two drams of Scotch and two coffees, then watched Jennie and the boy sitting near the fire talking together and laughing about something indistinguishable. Marielle felt deeply relaxed and rejuvenated.

"Inviting Jennie was so thoughtful. Thank you, Barry, for being so nice to her."

"'Tisn't hard to do."

Marielle tipped her head, looked directly at him. "Did you ever want children of your own?"

"A house full. And I'd still like them," he smiled, his eyes bright and glittering in the firelight. "*If* I'd be havin' them with the right lass, of course."

She shifted in her seat. Marielle felt the weight of her deception suddenly heavy on her chest with his clear-eyed honesty so boldly between them. She needed to be candid with Barry. He deserved that.

"You asked me the other day if there was anything else I wanted to tell you about myself."

"I remember."

The waitress, a girl with a braid of fiery red hair down her back, brought a wicker basket of warm bread for them just then. For a moment, the intrusion threw Marielle off her stride. She glanced back at Jennie. There would be no truth harder for her to tell than this. Quite likely, it would change everything between them.

I am Colleen's sister. . . . You knew me once as you knew her, and I have lied to you. . . .

"I wasn't really Colleen's friend. The truth is, she was much more to me than that."

"And ye're no' really Marielle Jaeger, are ye?"

His smile was gentle. Knowing. It rocked her completely. And she felt like a small child who had been found out. The crimson rose on her cheeks and she looked away. "I don't know what to say."

Gently, he reached up and, with a solid hand, touched the Celtic cross at her throat. It was something so much a part of herself that she forgot most of the time that she was even wearing it.

"'Tis no' American jewelry. And it surely is no' new. T'was a hunch that grew from seeing that." He sank back against the booth. His eyes were rooted on her, and his mouth bore a hint of a smile, as if he were looking at the most wonderful woman in the world. "I asked myself the first time I saw it around your neck why ye'd really have come to a place like Killin. I found the answer when I truly looked into your eyes. Ye must know ye've a face that's the mirror image of your mother."

Marielle realized that his hand, still wound in hers, was oddly comforting. Warm and strong. "I never forgot the wee lass with the determined eyes who asked me for help and a ride, one long-ago afternoon."

Barry was looking at her deeply. "You knew who I was all along?"

"Nearly all along."

"Why didn't you tell me?"

"'Twas your story to tell, sweet Marielle. In your own way and in your own time."

"But I was lying to you." She shook her head. "It has all been a lie."

"Not your smile. Your laughter. Not what I see when I look in your bonny, bright eyes."

Her voice caught in her throat. "I feel like such a fool."

"Mairi Gordon had a difficult life here. Colleen told me all about what ye went through. About how your da treated you and your ma. The rows, the beatin's, much of it because he did no' fancy ye were the beauty she was. Colleen said she could never get that out of her mind. That she could never forget you, nor stop wonderin' where ye'd gone. If ye were all right with your ma, if ye'd found happiness at last."

Marielle's eyes slid away. She could feel tears coming. "Colleen spoke of me to you?"

"Quite a lot. That part of her childhood was a dear subject. Playin' with you. Sharin' secrets. She kept that physical image of you alive in *my* mind as well."

"I tried so hard to get back here for so long. How I wished I'd known her."

"You did know Colleen. Ye knew the essence of her. Believe me, that much never changed," Barry said deeply. The pain that those words brought to her was softened by the gentleness in his tone. "She was the same sweet lass she was as a child. And, in spite of the demons that came to haunt her more and more, she was so, until the very end."

Marielle leaned back and drew in a ragged breath. "I'm glad she had you in her life. It must have meant a lot to her in those last months, to have that when things weren't good with Calum anymore and she was drinking too much."

It surprised her that he stiffened almost imperceptibly then. But she was near enough to feel the change. "I'll no' wager 'twas Calum who told ye that."

"It was Jennie."

"Ah, yes." He cast a glance toward the hearth. "Jennie. Well, I suppose a lot of us tried to help Colleen at the end. She and I had many conversations about her leavin' Calum, goin' somewhere to start a new life. I believed then as I do now, 'twould have been the only way to get her away from the Scotch. The only thing that could have saved her."

"So Colleen's drinking was what really killed her. Not her husband."

"She drank because of him. 'Tis a difficult thing for me to keep the two as separate thoughts."

Marielle broke the awkward stillness that had fallen between them by reaching up and taking his hand, which lay resting on the tabletop now. Marielle took it with both of her own, trying to anchor him for what she was about to say. "I'm sorry I couldn't just take your word for it, but I had to find out for myself that Calum was not a suspect with the police."

"And ye've done that."

"Yes. It must have been awful for Calum to have had anyone in Killin really believe that he had been involved."

Barry's eyes were dark with seriousness as he turned and settled them on her once again. "About that, I spoke out of turn," he said in a voice she suddenly did not believe. It was the first time she had ever suspected him of being anything less than genuine. "'Tis a subject that makes me quite irrational. Colleen was too young to die and it was a tragedy of the greatest proportions that she did."

"We both lost her too soon." As she looked at him, Marielle realized that she was still holding his hand in both of hers. "I would like very much to see Colleen's grave before I go back to France. I think it would help to finally put an end to things."

"I'll take ye to the marker tomorrow if ye'd like. But there's somethin' else—"

She stopped his words with a finger to his lips. His

eyes held her with such tenderness it made her want to weep. "You have been so kind and so patient with me, Barry, and now you've brought me to this wonderful place. And you know what? At this moment, I think I would rather savor that, just for a little while. Tell me the rest after we finish our drinks, all right?"

Once the rain stopped, they hitched a ride back to Killin on the back of a hay wagon. The driver put Jennie up front. Barry gazed at the sky as the cart gently swayed down the twisting, single lane road. "I'm sorry for deceiving you," Marielle softly said. "You deserved better."

"People change, Marielle," he said in a philosophic tone. "'Tis part of livin' on this earth. And people grow. Sometimes, so do their hearts." He looked at her then. "I should no' have tried to turn ye against Calum. I'm no' certain what I was thinkin'. Ye're a grown woman, and 'tis your decision to make, if Calum McInnes is the man for you."

The night sky was clear and cloudless. A deep, fathomless black. He tipped his head up. Gazed at the moonlight, a silver beacon above them. "I know ye say ye're goin' back to France," Barry said, his words breaking once again into the silence. "But I'll warn ye, I'm no' above tryin' to convince ye to stay."

Marielle could feel her heart slipping at that. It was full of such tenderness for Barry. But it was still not the wild, unexplainable hammering she felt for Calum. Tonight, like this, after everything they had shared, after the thoughtless way Calum had left her, Marielle felt quite ashamed of herself for that. And she actually wished that this newfound awakening to passion within her was something she could change.

When Barry bent his neck to kiss her this time, Marielle tilted her head up to meet him. She wanted this. She wanted something to ignite inside her. As his kiss deepened, she parted her mouth, twined her arms around his neck. She felt herself resist then as he pulled her closer, as she felt his arms move up around her.

He smelled good. Different from Calum. Slightly sweet. Like tart green apples and rich ale, she thought. And his lips were strong and far more commanding than she would have guessed. Still, Calum and the questions about what was really between them were tugging at her heart. Pulling her away from the moment. As the thought bloomed in her mind as well, the kindling of what she had begun to feel now with Barry snapped like a twig.

Marielle pulled back. "I really have had the most unexpectedly wonderful day."

A knowing expression, a kind of slight, lopsided smile, crossed Barry's face, both of them forgetting that there was something more he had wanted to tell her. "I've got time, Marielle. I've got all the time in the world to convince ye they could all be days like this."

CHAPTER TWENTY

Calum leaned over the bow of the ship as it dipped into another wave, chugging its way slowly back into Mallaig Harbor. He drew in a deep breath of briny salt air and gazed across the dark, unending sea. The last time he was in Killin, he had been given a glimpse into that little corner of heaven he thought he'd never see again.

That moment in Marielle's arms had given him the first bit of peace he'd felt in a very long time. He had hated leaving her as he'd done, while she slept, without saying good-bye. But he had needed time to think before any promises were made. Before he had looked once more into those beautiful, dark eyes and forgot everything else.

So Barry wants her too, he thought as a stain of bitterness darkened his mind. He'd seen that much at the ceilidh. First Colleen. Now Marielle.

Things might have gone so differently if Buchanan hadn't inflicted himself into his marriage at the end. He was always around, stirring things up. Offering consolation, friendship, and only God knew what else. And since leaving Killin this last time, Calum had asked himself if he had the strength now,

two years later, to fight the same man for another
woman who had captured his heart.

The old fishing trawler groaned when they crested
another wave, then dipped as the cold wind sliced
through his jacket and bulky Aran sweater. Calum took
a sip of lukewarm coffee from the styrofoam cup he'd
gotten in the galley, then gazed out again as dusk bore
softly down along the horizon. He pressed his hand to
the folded letter crinkled in his breast pocket. He had
read it so many times he knew each line without needing to look.

> Dear Mr. McInnes,
>
> Dr. Phillips is pleased to inform you that a
> consultation has been scheduled in the
> name of your niece, Jennifer Ann Quinn,
> for November third, here in our Glasgow
> clinic. The doctor greatly looks forward to
> meeting with both of you and hopes that
> your niece's condition is compatible with
> our new and encouraging technology.
>
> With sincere regards,
>
> Constance Morgan
> Assistant to the Director,
> Phillips Institute for Spinal Injuries

It was what he had waited for. Prayed for. Giving
Jennie a second chance. Now finally, she would have
that. As the boat was heading into Mallaig Harbor, that
was what he must concentrate on. Not on Marielle or

Barry. Nor on the mistakes that had forever changed his life.

An hour later, wrapped in his black leather jacket, Calum's Harley rumbled slowly along the banks of the loch, crushing the carpet of russet, brown, and gold autumn leaves that spread from skeletal tree branches down to the water's edge.

As he drove, the sky darkened. Rain fell. Thin, slanting and cold. Killin lay before him as he rounded the corner, its tiny houses and shops, many of them ancient now and softened by trees, were lit with golden light through the pane windows. White smoke puffed from rows of brick chimneys. The streets were bare and wet, but welcoming.

Then he saw her standing there on the veranda, her small frame a wispy, black silhouette, looking out across the garden. For a heartbeat, he thought it was Colleen.

Seeing him, Marielle held up her hand in a tentative wave, and the moment passed. Calum pulled up the hill at MacLaren's Bend and turned off the engine. His headlight dimmed, brightening the lights up in the house beyond the grand bay window, illuminating her face. She was waiting for him, as Colleen had done so many times. That ache never seemed to lessen.

So much of it had been his fault. He had been sullen, bitter about the way his life had turned out. Finally, in the years without Colleen, he had come to take responsibility for the part he had played.

Calum had become, after all, what his mother had most feared, a simple country solicitor, with no prospects for anything better. Wrongly, he had taken much of that out on his wife, whose ties to Killin, to the country life, were greatest. It was easier, his wounded pride had reasoned, than admitting that for so long he had put careless expectation ahead of diligence. He had never been able to accept that he deserved the unspectacular life he had earned. For her devotion to a man who was so filled with the frustration of an unrealized life, Colleen had paid a high price. And for that he would never forgive himself.

That people in Killin, even his own Aunt Cat, believed he had left his paltry career willingly, out of grief, made the drubbing only somewhat easier to bear. In reality, he had failed even as a simple country lawyer, drawing up wills and divorce decrees.

Six weeks after Colleen's death, and with his small law practice deeply in debt, he had closed up his office and taken the job at Mallaig Harbor just to pay his creditors. But no one had known that, thank the Lord.

Calum sat there for a moment, watching Marielle—thinking of new beginnings. That night at the Kilkenny Inn flashed in his mind. How vulnerable she was, some unknown secret of her own tormenting her. But she was a fighter, feisty and full of fire. He drew off his leather gloves and pressed them into his jacket pockets, then he walked slowly toward the house.

Marielle came down, meeting him halfway, the night sky lit only by a cloud-covered moon. She did not seem to mind the rain as Calum took her hand. Marielle raised her eyes to meet his. "You didn't say good-bye."

"It was wrong. I'm sorry."

They stood there in the silence for a moment more, the cool autumn wind and rain playing through both of them. Ruffling their clothes. Feathering back the ends of their hair. Both of them feeling the same thing. Neither saying anything. They walked back up onto the veranda together where it was dry, where the wind could not touch them.

Calum led her to a secluded corner that was dark and private. He touched her hair. Then, very suddenly, urgently, he pressed her back against the outside wall. His fingers were warm and rough but tender on the nape of her neck. His thumb moved along her shoulder as his mouth came powerfully down on hers.

He bent his head then and kissed her neck. She twined her fingers into the thick tangles of his hair. They sank down together onto the antique rattan sofa, emerald green and covered with an oversized cushion.

Then Marielle drew away from him. The move was unexpected. "What is it?" he asked her, pressing a hand in against her back, to keep her close.

"I need to tell you the truth," she said haltingly.

Marielle paused. This was different. More difficult than telling Barry. With Barry, she had felt safe. Free to confess the past. Now the words froze in her throat.

There was a moment after that when she was not certain what she actually said. There were only his eyes widening as they rooted on her. And a small muscle in his jaw flexing as she spoke. The silence seemed to go on forever, after that. Painfully intense.

And heavy, as if a shroud had fallen down around them.

"*You* are Mairi Gordon?"

Marielle only shook her head to confirm it.

"I canno' believe ye deceived me!" He was in a sudden rage. "And ye did the same to everyone in Killin!"

The moment, and the intimacy between them, had vanished. Suddenly, he reminded her of Malcolm. The realization angered her. She would not make Colleen's mistake. She would not fall in love with a man like their father.

"Look, Calum, it was a great shock coming and finding that the only sister I will ever have in the world is dead. You must understand, I needed time just to process everything without people asking me a lot of questions."

"Well, I do no' understand! My God, woman! Colleen was my wife! You were her only sister! And knowin' all of that, still ye let me care for ye! Let me—" She could hear the pain and the pride in his tone. He did not finish his sentence. But she knew what he meant.

"That just happened between us. It had nothing to do with Colleen."

"Everythin' ye did had somethin' to do with Colleen! Ye did no' care about me! About Jennie! Certainly no' about Catriona's hospitality! Ye were thinkin' only of yourself when ye worked your way into my aunt's house. And into *my*—" Again he let the words fall away as they looked at one another. As his anger burned between them.

"Barry didn't have a reaction like this. He understood why I needed some time. . . ."

The air went very still again. But Calum's eyes still blazed. "Buchanan knows who ye are?"

"Yes."

"When? When did ye tell *him* that you are Mairi Gordon?"

"It is only important that I did. Isn't it?"

His eyes fixed hard on her. "Gallant Barry. Dashing Barry. Always there like some great white knight. Especially for the women he loves. Women who do no' love him in return."

She felt a bubble of unease work its way up her throat as his eyes narrowed. As a blue vein stood out in his strong, thick neck. It was that ugly, troubling side of him again, a side that once had frightened her. Didn't he know that Barry and Colleen had only been dear friends, lifelong friends? That Barry had done what he could to help a friend dealing with alcoholism and a failing marriage?

"That's enough, Calum."

His hand shot out and his fingers tightened on her shoulder in a surprisingly hard clasp. Suddenly, a cold sliver of that same fear pierced her heart. "'Tis enough, Mairi Gordon, when *I* say it is."

He had said her real name mockingly. Angrily. And she was afraid of him again now. Afraid of how he had changed from a man of tenderness to one who seemed capable of great violence.

"So who else knows your little secret?"

"Catriona and Jennie."

He was suddenly speechless as Marielle struggled to free herself from his grip. She felt herself grow cold all over, impervious to what she once had felt for him. She was halfway to the door before she spun around and looked at him one last time.

"They know, Calum. And, like Barry Buchanan, *they* have been able to accept me, as well as my reasons for doing what I did. Perhaps you should look to your own heart to see why that is not the case with you!"

The warmth of the old house engulfed her quickly as Marielle dashed inside. Calum came in behind her, slamming the front door with a thud that shook the pictures on the walls. Golden light pulsed through the room, casting shadows into the far corners. There was the pungent aroma of lamb roasting and only the sound of floorboards creaking as Catriona saw the trouble between them and came to her feet. Jennie remained where she was, playing solitaire at the old table near the fire.

Marielle glanced at Catriona with an expression full of hurt and confusion. Catriona went to her and put an arm around her shoulder. Her voice was low. "So ye've told him then."

"Yes."

"Don't try to speak to him just now, lass. Let him calm down a bit first."

Calum did not look at Marielle again. There was not the slightest hint of softness about him. And now, tonight, she knew with an aching clarity what kind of life her sister had faced at the end, and with a man startlingly like their father. She understood how the bright and beautiful Colleen she remembered had changed. Now, tonight, she also understood why.

Marielle excused herself from the supper ritual, unable to sit across the table from Calum without her own anger building at the force of his response. But later, when he and Jennie were in the kitchen washing the dishes, Marielle could not help taking in their conversation just beyond her bedroom door.

"I've got some news, finally," Calum said.

"I canno' imagine how 'twould effect me."

"I've heard from the clinic in Glasgow." Marielle came to the door of her bedroom and stood in the shadows. "It seems we've got an appointment at last."

Jennie sagged back against the back of her wheelchair. "Oh, Uncle Calum, no' that again."

"Ye knew I'd been waitin' to hear from them."

"And *you* knew how I felt about it. 'Tis castin' your money to the wind."

"Why don't ye be lettin' me worry about that."

Marielle took a tentative step forward into the light, unable to keep herself from intervening. "You're taking Jennie to a clinic about her legs?"

Calum gritted his teeth, then pushed the acid words up across his tongue. "'Tis a family matter, Mairi Gordon. It does no' concern ye."

"Calum!" Catriona gasped as she came in from the dining table carrying two empty wineglasses.

"She's a stranger here."

"Och! Ye certainly know that's no' true now, don't ye, lad?"

"The fact remains, 'tis none of her affair."

Disappointment flickered in Marielle's eyes as those last cruel words lay there between them. "The appointment is the day after tomorrow," Calum went on, turning now to his niece, her jaw clenched, her eyes slowly narrowing.

"Well, I'm *not* goin'!" Jennie stubbornly proclaimed, crossing her arms across her chest with a little huff.

"But why?" Catriona asked.

"'Tis *my* life, Ma!"

"One Calum is tryin' to improve."

"False hope is all it is. And I don't want it. None of it. Ye hear?"

"Well, we're *goin'* to Glasgow!" Calum shot. "After that, ye can live any bloody way ye like!"

Jennie stiffened and shot her uncle a glaring, angry look. "I'm *no'* goin'!"

"If I have to tie ye up and toss ye across my shoulder, by God, oh, ye'll go, Jennie Anne! Ye'll go!"

Green eyes wide again and suddenly bright with tears, Jennie darted a desperate glance at her mother. Then at Marielle. It was clear she was looking for an ally in this. But what Marielle saw was not hostility or anger. Not defiance. But pure fear. If she didn't try to walk again, she wouldn't need to face the potential disappointment.

"Well, for what it's worth, I don't think you should go either," Marielle observed.

Calum scowled at her, but she turned away and closed her eyes to him. After all, this was not about her and Calum. This was about a confused and frightened young girl who, after an act of bravery two years ago, now needed a friend—and maybe, too, a clever bit of psychology.

Jennie's eyes suddenly cleared. "Ye don't?"

"Absolutely not. You're old enough to know if you want the chance to walk again and if you don't, I personally don't believe anyone should force you."

"Oh, who asked ye?" Calum growled.

"I don't hear Jennie objecting to hearing my opinion."

"Well, ye sure as hell can hear *me!*"

"Calum, please," Catriona said calmly. "Let's listen to what she has to say."

Calum looked at his aunt then rolled his eyes. "Oh, for the love of Mike! Have ye any idea what it's taken to get this appointment? The wait I've had?"

"This isn't about *you,* Calum!" Marielle burst out, feeling her personal anger bleed into the tension. "Anyway, I certainly don't blame you, Jennie, for not wanting to go. It's a long trip and a lot of upheaval just to hear someone say, in all likelihood, that they can't help you walk again."

"'Tis what he would say, ye know," Jennie said.

"I suppose you're right. A lot of time has passed. And no miracle can give you the time you lost, can it? All this clinic can promise you is a chance."

The word came carefully from Jennie's lips. "Aye."

The silence which followed was thick and taut. "Well, it *is* only a consultation."

"Oh, of course. Right. But Dr. Phillips is world-renowned, and I'm sure he'll have you imagining before you leave that there actually *is* a chance that something can be done. . . . But you're happy as you are. Isn't that what you said?"

The next silence stretched out. The mantel clock above the fireplace tolled seven-thirty. "'Tis no' as if I don't *want* to walk again."

"Well, as I said," Marielle reiterated calmly, hoping now that she could possibly be a part of a lasting difference in a young girl's life, "I really wouldn't bother. Not when you can stay home here with your mother where it's safe and predictable. Where at least you don't have to take any chances that could bring you more disappointment than you've already endured."

Jennie's eyes narrowed again suddenly, and her softly arched brows merged as she searched Marielle's very best impassive face. "I know what ye're doin', ye know."

"What's that?"

"Ye're tryin' to change my mind. . . . Only I will say ye're a fair sight more round about it than Calum."

Gazes darted like fire, everyone looking at everyone else in the next long, uncomfortable silence. The rain outside began to fall heavier now as the fire in the hearth crackled and popped. Marielle exhaled a breath and realized suddenly that she had been holding it in anticipation. Certainly it was a long shot, and a great risk for her in facing potential failure. But, like Calum, if there was any chance at all that Jennie might one day walk again, they should know it.

"Would *you* go with us, then? . . . *If* I were to decide to go to Glasgow, I mean."

"Me? Oh, Jennie, I really don't think—"

"Out of the question!" Calum cut her off before she could tactfully decline.

"Well, I canno' be goin' only with you, now can I, Uncle Calum? Ye don't know the first thing about tendin' to my female needs. Ma has taught Marielle everything since she's been here."

"She has a point," Catriona said calmly, cautiously.

Suddenly Marielle was trapped by her own well-meaning intentions, as his open rejection of who she was only just then began fully to settle in her mind.

"Well, ye've changed your mind," Calum said

cutting into the next uncomfortable silence as he glanced down at Jennie, "and I'm fair glad of it."

"I meant it, Uncle Calum. I *want* Marielle to come."

"Two hotel rooms are all I've arranged and all I'm goin' to arrange."

"Perhaps your uncle is right," Marielle said softly. "This is something between the two of you, after all."

Jennie's glance shot upward, fixing on Calum. Defiance was suddenly bright and alive again on that softly oval, lightly freckled adolescent face. "Either Marielle comes with us or I meant what I said. I'm *not* goin'!"

With those final words hanging like a punctuation mark in the slightly smoky air, Jennie turned the wheels of her chair swiftly, unceremoniously, and rolled herself back down the hall.

"I'll go after her," Calum flatly said.

Marielle looked at him and when their eyes met, for only a moment, she was startled by the dead expression there. *As if they truly were still the strangers as which they had begun.* "Maybe you should let me talk to her."

Frowning, he said, "Suit yourself, Mairi Gordon."

Marielle searched his eyes one more time, then angrily pivoted away and went down the shadowy hall after Jennie.

"I'm really very flattered, Jennie."

Marielle stood in the doorway to Jennie's dark bedroom. She was gazing at the girl and her wheelchair, both in shadows from the single dim light on her night table.

"Suit yourself."

"People in your family say that a lot. I only wonder how many of you really know how callous it sounds."

"We all are grand at self-protection."

"It's just a lot more complicated than me not wanting to go with you, Jennie."

"Aye? Like what?"

"To begin with, your uncle knows now that Colleen and I were sisters. And he feels that I have betrayed him."

She turned her head slightly, held it for a moment, then turned back to the window.

"'Twould be too much to ask, I suppose, for both of ye to put *me* ahead of the romance and all of that tension that's been boilin' up between the three of ye for days."

"I just don't think it would help things, us being that close together."

"I'm no' askin' ye for the moon, for Lord's sake! All I want is a bit of moral support! Ye're good at that. Ye know ye are. A comfort even. Ye make me think I can do things."

Marielle felt an instant spark of shame. Like it or not, she was a part of the lives of these people now. She cared for them.

There was another silence. They could hear the floorboards creaking out in the corridor. Muffled voices. And that interminable rain beating down heavily now on the roof, and against the windowpanes.

Marielle could see Jennie shifting in her wheelchair. But still she refused to turn around. "I love my uncle Calum," she finally said. "I think, after what I told ye about what happened that night with Colleen, ye know just how much I do. Truth is though, I'm just no' ready to be alone with him."

The old iron bed creaked and the mattress buckled beneath her weight as Marielle sank onto the edge, waiting, hoping, that Jennie would trust her enough to turn around and explain that. That strange confession made no sense. What on earth would she have to fear from the man she had spent two years trying to protect?

"Might I ask why?"

"We've never spoken about it directly, ye see," she finally said, that same vulnerability she'd heard on that early morning of confessions now bleeding through that staunchly guarded tone of hers again. "About the night Colleen died. 'Tis enough to see the sorrow and regret in his eyes every time he comes into this house."

"I think Calum needs to have you do this, Jennie. As much for himself as for you."

"I knew all along ye thought I should go."

Marielle smiled. "You're a very bright girl, Jennie."

"Ye want to know the grandest reason I was hopin' ye'd go along?"

"That would be nice."

She turned her wheelchair around and finally came across the room to the corner of her bed where Marielle sat. "Ye do no' treat me like I'm so different. Ye do no' look on me like an invalid."

"We have certainly had our differences about that."

"Aye. But ye make me feel . . . what? Normal. Like I could be normal if I wanted."

"I believe you can be." Marielle took Jennie's shoulders and held them. "Whether or not you ever walk again. But only *you* can make that choice for your life."

"Come to Glasgow with us, Marielle. I'm askin' ye. *Please.*"

There was a tremor in her tone, not a pleading sound exactly, but a vulnerability that tore at Marielle's heart. How could she refuse Jennie?

"I'll speak with your Uncle Calum and then I'll decide, all right?"

"If that's the best I can get from ye—"

"For now it is." Marielle reached out and took Jennie's hand then gave it a little squeeze. "We'll talk more about it in the morning."

Moments later, Marielle stood at the bay window, watching Calum outside on the front porch. So handsome and complex. Her attraction had been overwhelming, blinding almost. That night in the old potter's shed she had put aside everything. Especially her loyalty to Colleen. She had taken some small comfort in discovering that their marriage had been in trouble, that they might even have sought a divorce—if Colleen had lived.

Calum sat unmoving in a battered old wicker rocker, one denim-clad leg crossed wide over the other, as the rain came down from the eaves in long white sheets. Behind her, the last of the fire sputtered and popped.

Marielle flung her jacket across her shoulders and went outside.

She knew he'd heard the front door close, but Calum did not look up or acknowledge her. Marielle felt the same sting she had earlier but she pushed past it, sinking into the empty rocker beside him.

"We need to talk about this."

"Ye're no' goin' to Glasgow, no matter what Jennie said."

"My, my. Aren't we full of ourselves tonight."

His head jerked around and his mouth snapped open for what she sensed was a stinging retort. Then, to her surprise and confusion, he simply sank back against the chair and looked ahead again out into the rain and the night. "It does no' matter what ye think of me. Ye were right when ye said goin' to Glasgow was somethin' between Jennie and me."

"And were *you* right when you said I was still a stranger?"

Marielle watched him grimace in the rain-shattered silence. But the eyes that glared at her then, in the buttery backlighting through the bay window, were slitted and uncompromising. "That night was a mistake. One thing is certain: I'd no' have been with ye if I'd known you were my wife's sister."

For a moment, she was silent. "Well, Jennie still wants me to go along for moral support. What am I supposed to do about that?"

"Ye tell her no. Pure and simple."

"Well, I'm sorry, Calum, but I am not quite so good at cutting off my emotions as you seem to be."

The slight was a direct hit. She saw him flinch then look away. "Ye're good with words, Marielle. Far better than I. But it does no' change the facts as they are. Ye're no' a part of this."

Something very stubborn began to bubble up inside of her now. An anger that she hadn't felt since those first years in Paris when a brazen restaurateur had tried to use her. Marielle set her shoulders squarely then, and glared back at him. "I'm sorry you don't think this has anything to do with me, but while you've been away, your niece and I have become friends, and *she* feels a need to have me come. I am not going to disappoint her about something as important to her as this just because you choose to be pigheaded and selfish. Like it or not, I am coming with the two of you to Glasgow."

The challenge in his eyes was hostile. "Well, I'm no' arrangin' any more hotel rooms."

"Calum McInnes, I wouldn't take anything else from you if you were the last man on earth!"

"Good." Calum said flatly, not looking at her any longer. "Because I'm no' offerin' anythin'!"

"*That* is only too apparent."

"Well, I've said all that I mean to say," Calum said flatly, not looking at her any longer. Marielle grimaced at the harshness in his voice. Then she bounded down the steps and out into the rainy, pitch black night, not certain where she was going, or to what.

CHAPTER TWENTY-ONE

It took her half an hour to walk the dense and muddy path to Barry's cottage in the woods, the gusty wind and rain blowing her hair and jacket. Only when she stood at his doorstep in the shadow of the blazing lights inside did Marielle realize that she had been drawn here.

She hadn't even knocked when Barry opened the door and a soft rush of Mozart met her. He had a book in hand and curious expression on his face, something like a half smile, that said her coming here now was not a total surprise.

"Come in."

She did, and then went to a chair near the fire. Barry sat down across from her, balancing his hands on his knees. The small room, bathed in golden firelight, smelled gloriously of cooking stew, herbs like basil and oregano, twining with the fragrance from the burning logs. Barry waited for her to speak, but now that she was here, Marielle had no idea of what to say or why she had really come. But he had drawn her, she knew that much. Perhaps it was the safety of him, she thought.

"I've nothin' fancy to offer, but ye're welcome to stay for supper."

Marielle realized that with what had happened back at MacLaren's Bend she hadn't eaten and, after their drinks in Crainlarich and a long walk through the woods coming here, she was famished.

"Thanks."

Barry smiled at her then, and she felt the warmth of it flow through her veins. She sank back in the chair.

"You're not going to ask me why I'm out by myself tonight?"

He went to the stove across the cozy room. "Ye've proven yourself a woman who knows her own mind, Marielle. Ye'll tell me if ye like."

She hugged her knees. "I told Calum who I am."

"Did ye now?"

"He didn't take it very well."

"Ye'd like me to be surprised at that?"

Barry brought her back a glass of red wine, which she took a sip of gratefully. "I guess I was hoping he would have been more like you about it all."

"We're very different lads, Calum and I."

"So I am discovering, daily."

The music in the background softened. It sounded like Chopin now. Barry took her hands and sat back down. His eyes settled on hers. "Personally, I'd like nothin' better than if ye did discover the whole of it."

She couldn't look at him for a moment. "I'm so confused, Barry."

"And I'll no' add to that."

"It's just that my life, well, I haven't really lived it the way I suppose I should have. The truth is, I've been alone a lot. Avoided things. Relationships."

He touched her cheek, and her eyes lifted to his. "Are ye frightened of me?"

"No. That's just it. I'm more comfortable with you than anyone else, I think. Well, since Ron."

He sank back, letting go of her hand. "Ye do no' talk about him; the man with the jacket."

"Ron Jaeger was my mother's lover, not mine. And he was as close as I ever got to a father's love, before he died unexpectedly. Like Colleen."

Barry's face was shining in the firelight. "There are no guarantees, Marielle, if that's what ye're after, with love."

"It has been quite an awakening for me here in Killin. On so many levels. The point is, I'm not sure I know *what* I want."

"Then ye've got to keep lookin' until it finds ye."

"What if what I want—"

He finished her thought. "What if it is no' Barry Buchanan?"

Marielle turned toward the fire, but he brought her face back around and came off of the chair to crouch before her. Barry took both of her hands again, but this time he brought them to his lips as his eyes held fast to hers.

A heartbeat later, he said, "Then I'll live with that."

"Will we still be friends, do you think?"

"There are no conditions here, Marielle. I've offered my heart to ye freely. It does no' mean ye need be givin' yours in return."

Gently, Barry touched her lips with a kiss. His mouth lingered there for only a moment, then he stood once again. "Now. How about some border stew?"

"Really?"

"It's been done for ten minutes."

She bit back a smile, thinking again, with a little spasm of regret, that he was all the things a man should be. All the things she *ought* to want. "I meant about your heart."

"I'm a different sort, Marielle. I suppose 'tis for you to discover whether I'm the sort who can keep your heart, after all."

Early the next morning, she stooped in the cold wind at a grave. Barry stood behind her. Watching Marielle. The flowers she held, the violets Calum had given her, fell from her limp hand onto the marker. *Colleen Mary McInnes. 1964–1994. Beloved wife, daughter & friend.* The inscription was simple. What she would have wanted, Marielle knew. Honoring those who had loved her.

But not *all* of those who loved her.

"I wish it could have said 'beloved sister,' too," she whispered. Then Marielle sank onto her heels.

Barry hadn't been able to bring himself to come here in months. To be faced so boldly with the termination of a life only partially lived, that sweet and gentle girl with the lovely moss-green eyes, so full of dreams unmet.

He pushed the images of that night back now—the last time he had seen Colleen. The things she had said. *I'm ready to do it, Barry. I'm ready to leave him. 'Tis frightenin', but I want my dream more. . . . I need a different life than this. . . .*

Then everything had ended in the water of Loch Tay. He had raced there with a half dozen others, arriving in time to see Jennie alone brought back out of the wet, cold darkness, and Calum standing eerily at the water's edge. Not weeping. Not shedding a tear for his own wife. Just gazing blankly into the black depths.

Something had happened before he and everyone else had arrived. He knew it down to his bones. Those premonitions he had had since childhood had plagued him almost nightly since Colleen's death. He could see her face, full of panic, at the wheel of her car. Racing away from something or someone. And he could hear Jennie crying, *"Stop! Please stop this! Ye're frightenin' us!"* But before she ever said a name, or finished the plea, the vision always ended.

Of course it had been Calum. But when Barry had asked, Jennie claimed she remembered nothing about those last awful moments. Her mind had blotted it out, and everyone thought it was just as well.

Everyone but Barry.

Now Marielle was falling in love with a man who was responsible for something he could not prove.

He watched her trail a hand along the marker, brushing away a bit of mud until Colleen's name shown brightly again. Glittering almost. *How I do miss your friendship, sweet lass. I did what I could,* Barry thought. *Your imprint will be on my soul forever. . . . I only wonder what ye would have thought that it was your own sister who'd be the one to finally capture my heart?*

Barry felt a little spark of guilt now for desiring Marielle, for thinking about that in a place like this. He smoothed the hair back from his forehead and gazed up at the cloud-heavy sky. Now there was only the rush of cold wind. The hollow whistling. And the silence.

When she was ready, Barry took her hand to help

her back to her feet. Then he put a firm arm around her. "It didn't help the way I thought it would," Marielle said achingly. "Thinking about Colleen lying here forever, beneath this soil . . ."

Barry's face changed. "Would it help to know that she's no' really here?"

Marielle tipped her head. "I don't understand."

"This is a marker, not a grave, Marielle. 'Twas what I began to tell ye yesterday at that inn. Until ye spoke of comin' here, I thought Catriona or Jennie had probably told ye."

"Told me what?"

"That they never pulled her car up out of the loch."

Her face drained of its color. "My God, why not?"

"It seems that Calum thought 'twas best that poor Colleen lay buried where she had died."

"But surely the police—"

"They went along with his request."

Marielle shook her head. Her face was pale. "God . . . I can't believe that."

"Since they did no' suspect any foul play, the police honored the wishes of the distraught husband."

Marielle felt as though an icy hand had clamped over her heart. "Something is not right about all of this."

Barry looked at her quizzically, his mind only beginning to comprehend what she was asking. "There's no question that she was in the car, ye know. There were half a dozen people who saw her drive away from the house that night and another handful who saw that very car melt deep into the reeds and silt."

"Oh, maybe you're right." Marielle finally shook her head, the possibilities simply too awful to examine any further. "Sometimes it's hard to give the reporter in my head a rest."

Barry kept his grip around her shoulder, leading Marielle back to his car. She sat stone-still as he walked around to the driver's side and climbed in beside her. "'Tis no' about livin', this place."

"I suppose not." Marielle lay her head back against the seat, feeling defeated and exhausted. "But I had to see it before I go back to France. It's a part of completing things."

"I know."

They were looking at one another. He still had not started the engine. A few stray leaves, gold and brown and russet, were landing on the windshield. Marielle had wrapped her arms around herself in the silence, trying to stop the shiver she felt. But that was more from the moment than from the cold.

"Where did she like to go? A favorite place, somewhere that made her happy?"

"'Tis easy enough to show ye that," he gently smiled, starting up the engine.

The car hummed as they followed the curving single lane dirt road beneath a heavy bower of evergreens. As he negotiated the twists and turns that led them up a hill and down another and over a fairy-tale brick and wooden bridge, Marielle glanced across at Barry.

She studied him, in his black turtleneck sweater, jacket, blue jeans, and boots. That tousle of maple-colored hair. He looked more striking to her today than ever. More long and lean. And even desirable.

What, she wondered, did the rest of him look like? Warmth crept into her cheeks as she began to question the extent of those long sinewy lines of his face and arms. Suddenly, an image came that she could not press away: Barry beneath a rich plaid quilt in a grand oak-framed bed somewhere. Perhaps the cottage. Wind howling. Rain and branches slapping the windows. For the first time, it was an image that seemed enticing to her. Because of his goodness, perhaps. Or because the fantasy of Calum had begun to fade a little.

Barry stopped the car behind the familiar glen, beneath a shading grove of evergreens. Marielle realized only then that they were parked facing the ruined abbey.

It was so cold, and the wind was howling. Barry helped her out of the car and led her quickly through a stone arch, an old church entrance, and into the cavernous nave of the abbey.

There was little left. The stone foundation. Two massive walls. A few soaring arches overhead. An eerie skeleton. They moved forward to the place where the altar had been. There was more shelter here. Less of the raging wind.

To the left of the altar there was another stone doorway and, beyond it, steps leading down, curving steeply into darkness. Barry plucked a taper that had been placed on the wall in a rusty iron sconce, and lit it from a lighter from his pocket. The cellar beneath them began to glow a deep gold. Marielle's stomach clenched into a hard fist.

"Down there?"

"Aye," he nodded.

She followed him carefully on the well-worn stone steps, a little in awe that a dark and secret place like this could still exist, considering the destruction of the rest of the abbey.

At the bottom of the steps was a locked wooden door. Barry moved a brick from the wall that was loose and drew out a long, ancient key. Then he slipped it into the lock. A moment later, they were standing in a huge room with a low, coved ceiling. Marielle touched a finger to her lips as Barry went about lighting a dozen long white tapers in brass sconces and on tables around the room.

"I can't believe it."

"'Twas what Colleen said the first time she saw the place." Marielle looked at him and was silent for a moment. "But your sister loved the solitude here. And the privacy."

On the walls were watercolor prints tacked onto rough wooden frames. Delicate images in pale pastels, outlined in ink. A stooped old woman feeding pigeons. A young man who looked like Barry. Richly detailed. Very artistic.

The breath caught in her throat. "Colleen was an artist?"

"A much finer one than I. 'Tis why I stick to fashionin' pots." He smiled tentatively.

"Your pottery is beautiful."

"But Colleen's watercolors had a true soul. Ye can see that, I'm sure. She was self-taught, but she had true talent, I always told her, if she had only found the courage to follow her dreams." Barry paused a moment, then moved behind her, placing a hand on her shoulder. "This one was her favorite."

Marielle advanced as he motioned. Her arms were wrapped around her waist as they had been almost entirely since they had come away from the cemetery. But even so, she could not stop the trembling. The breath left her lungs now in a single dizzying rush. It was a stunning watercolor work before her, lit by candlelight, half of it glowing, half in shadows. Two little girls, running, holding hands. One of them slightly behind. The wind blew back their long hair. Their skirts. Both of them with heads back. Laughing.

"She called this 'The Joy of My Youth.'"

Marielle turned around. Stunned. "It's Colleen and me."

"Aye. I told ye she never forgot you either."

Tears filled her eyes. "But this is so much a part of her. Why did you not bring me here when I first told you who I was?"

"All things happen in their own time, Marielle," he said gently, but with a wisdom that shook her. "So it is with this, as well."

"Did Calum know about this place?"

"She did no' work much after they first married. I never had reason to believe he knew about it. Or what she kept here."

Marielle slowly surveyed the watercolors, each of them separate in its beauty and theme. "She was so talented."

"I told her that many times. But Colleen did this work for herself. She never had much belief in anythin' about herself."

"That, I'm sure," she said bitterly, "was Malcolm's doing. A way to keep her close."

"I'm sorry to say that Malcolm Gordon was a bitter man who had lost his own dream and could never put much stock in anyone else's."

"Bastard."

"I always thought of him as pitiful."

Marielle spun around, her eyes wide and sparkling in the candlelight. "Funny. I always thought of him as evil incarnate."

"Ye had a right, I'd say."

She sank onto a bench before a table littered with long white tablets, watercolor palettes, brushes, and a paint-stained smock left on top. As if Colleen had been here just moments ago and had left her things precisely as they were. Marielle picked up a paintbrush and looked at it, still spattered with colors. *Her* colors.

Then Barry went to an antique wooden box near one of the easels, and drew out a small leather diary. "This was Colleen's. When things with Calum began to go bad, she asked me to keep it for her. Colleen'd come here nearly every day, write in it. She said being alone here gave her some sense of peace."

Marielle looked at him, wondering why she hadn't buried it along with the train ticket. But then a diary was something one would probably want access to every day. "Have you read it?"

"'Twas no' my place. But ye were her sister and there might be some sense of peace in those pages for you."

As he moved to the stairway, she rose. "Wait!"

Barry turned. "'Tis your journey, sweet Marielle. I'll wait for ye near the car. Take as long as ye need."

After Barry had gone back outside, Marielle turned back to the diary. With trembling hands, she opened it and gazed down at words written in delicate, sloping blue ink. The first entry had been written on May 8, 1990. . . .

> *I think Calum is going to ask me to marry him tonight. I believe I will say yes. It's also a way out of Da's house, and all of that bitterness about Vivienne he can't seem to get past. Calum is going to be a big solicitor in Glasgow. His ma doesn't favor me much. Thinks I'm not grand enough for her only son. But we'll have a fine life. All the things I always wanted.*

> *May 15, 1990*

> *It's finished. And I think I've done my best work yet. I've decided to call it "The Joy of My Youth." An image of Mairi and me. It was hard to remember exactly what she looked like. Her face was the hardest part for me to paint, since Da won't give me any of the photographs back. But I think I got close. Barry's eyes sparkled as he looked at it. He wants me to show it to someone down in Glasgow. A professional. I told him I couldn't possibly. But there was such faith written all across his face that it made me want to cry. Maybe one day somehow I will have a career.*

July 30, 1990

> *Yesterday was Mairi's birthday. What would she think of me now, I wonder.*
>
> *She's on my mind so often these days. My dear sister. I wonder how she and Vivienne are. If they are back in France. Happy. Mairi promised me she would come back to Killin. And there aren't too many days that go by that I don't look at each car that comes around that bend near the loch. Looking, hoping, Mairi might be in it. I don't think she's forgotten me. No, I know she hasn't.*

Marielle crossed her legs, shifted, and kept reading. Entry after entry.

December 2, 1990

> *Calum and I were married last night. We didn't intend to. At least I didn't. Even now it seems too soon. Maybe it was the Christmas spirit. But Calum insisted. He has been pressing me for weeks. He was desperate, he said. Desperate for us to start a life. It's a chance to start a life away from Da and his sour thinking. All of that is fair bleeding me dry. And I do love Calum, I think. He wants us to go back to Killin. Start a life. To have a baby. And so do I . . . don't I?*

For a moment, Marielle stopped. Suddenly it was too much. The words, Colleen's words, were too real. Her heart felt scorched.

In the beginning, Marielle had wanted so much for the recollections to bring her sister back to life. Now it was too painful—because it had done just that. She felt as if Colleen were right here with her. Marielle too had felt so many of the things Colleen had felt. The insecurity with her talent. The devotion to and disillusion with her single parent. And of course the self-doubt.

Colleen had been so confident as a child, so beautiful. The world should have lain open for her. Ironically, it was Marielle, Malcolm's ugly duckling, who was on the threshold of a bright career in a thriving city like Paris—a woman whom men had begun to see as beautiful.

Marielle ran a finger along the smooth, cool surface of the small book and drew in a breath. Of all the recollections from Catriona, Jennie, and Barry, even Calum, none had the pungency nor the truth of Colleen's own words. Marielle glanced down and pressed back the front cover of the diary again. Then she thumbed forward, opening it to the page dated July 14. It was, Marielle knew, three days before her only sister had perished in the icy waters of Loch Tay. . . .

CHAPTER TWENTY-TWO

July 14, 1994

Our battling is worse now. We can't agree on anything. I know it's his business failures, all the things he thought he'd be by now. But I can't change that for him. I can't be a refuge for him—and I guess, after everything I'd hoped, he can't be one for me.

And Calum certainly doesn't fancy my friendship with Barry now that things are so bad. But that is about the only thing that brings me joy anymore, his belief that I could still make something of my painting. Barry thinks I should go to Glasgow. Just run away if I have to. But can I? Begin again with nothing and no one? I'm just not strong enough for that.

If I could just find the strength to escape to Glasgow somehow, run away. Just begin again. My painting is all that there is. When I work, I paint the past—but I still see the future.

It was the final entry.

Marielle felt herself grow cold. Her eyes were shining with tears. The words of confession were there before her in Colleen's own hand.

Marielle felt as if the floor had been pulled out from beneath her. There had been no warning. She sat there frozen. Her eyes unblinking. Feeling as if, inside her, she were coming apart. Splintering.

It seems that Calum thought 'twas best that poor Colleen lay buried where she had died . . . The police went along with his request.

"Good Lord . . . is it possible?"

They were holding hands after Marielle had collected herself and come up and out into the gray daylight again. They were both silent after that as they stood in the cold, battering wind. Barry faced her, then wrapped his arms around her shoulders before she could think how to react.

"Thank you, Barry. You've given me a great gift."

"I wanted Colleen to live for ye for a little while, Marielle. She was a special woman who was troubled at the end," he finally said in that deep and steady voice. "I cared for your sister and tried my best to help her. But I was never in love with her. I want ye to know that."

She felt her heart squeeze, there in the wind. Wisps of hair whispering against her temples. Her nose and ears were stinging and frozen with cold. She wanted to tell him suddenly how no man had ever been for her what he was. "Thank you for that," she said instead, not ready to consider the implications of her deepening feelings.

He settled his eyes on her then, his maple-colored brows merging above them. Barry took her chin with a single finger and drew her near. The power and possession in his gentle kiss made her want suddenly to weep.

"So ye're still goin' to Glasgow with Jennie and Calum."

"Yes," she answered him.

"And will ye be comin' back to Killin?"

"I don't know."

"Believe it or not, I'm glad ye're goin'," Barry said after a moment. "Ye need time with him."

Marielle raised her eyes. They both knew whom he meant.

"When do ye leave?"

"Early tomorrow morning." Marielle straightened her shoulders and blinked away new tears. "I'm glad we came here, Barry," she said haltingly as the wind still tossed her hair, the lapels of her windbreaker, and ruddied her cheeks again. "I'm glad you showed me all of this. It helped."

He gave her a gallant look. "'Twas the only purpose in it."

"I want to tell you something else, Barry."

"More truths?" he asked, his eyes sparkling, as the wind still battered them.

"Yes. And, since we spoke once of magic, you are the only one I would tell this to." Marielle drew in a breath. The wind blew. "Okay, here goes. I think I talked to my father a few nights ago."

"'Tis normal enough, I suppose, with so much unfinished between ye."

"That's not exactly how I meant it. I think he might

have been listening." Marielle watched him for signs of a smile, a mocking of her revelation. But Barry's face never changed. "Well?" she finally asked.

"Ye're wantin' me . . . what? To say ye're daft?"

"I'd rather know what you think."

"Ah, but ye already do." He steepled his fingers, touched his chin. "Or ye'd never have told me to begin with."

"Is it really possible, do you think, that Malcolm Gordon's spirit somehow reached out to me?"

"Did it help ye to consider it a possibility?"

"Yes, it actually did."

"Then 'tis *that* ye must dwell upon. No' what the rest of the world would tell ye is surely no' possible."

"I waited for so many years to have it out with my father. But I never got the chance."

Barry's gaze was suddenly intense. "Until now."

"Yes. Until now. It's strange, but I think he wanted to make peace with me." She drew Colleen's chest from her coat pocket and handed it to him. "Malcolm led me to this."

Barry seemed to know the small wooden box with the rusted initials. "She told me she'd buried it somewhere that no one would ever find."

"You knew about this?"

"Aye."

"And about what she kept inside?"

"No' that. Why?"

"When I came to meet you today, I was hoping you might give me some clue about these things, but now I think I understand a little better." He opened up the chest with clear hesitation and drew out the cameo, train ticket, and newspaper article.

"God bless her," he said sadly, holding up the train ticket as though he'd been struck. "Dear lost angel. So she was tryin' to do it, after all. Of course this was different to her than the paintin's. 'Tis why she buried these. She would no' have wanted Calum to have a road map for the plans she was doin' her best to make."

"So she was absolutely going to leave him?"

"I honestly did no' think it'd sunk in to that beautiful, troubled head of hers. I told ye about all of that, of course."

"Yes."

"She just kept tellin' me 'twas such an awfully grand step to leave a husband."

"I guess your opinion of things mattered more to her than you realized."

"'Tis only a tragedy that she never got to use this ticket."

"Yes." Marielle looked at him. Again there was that strength. "But I'm proud of her that she tried."

"Ye've no' shown this to Calum?" Barry asked of the chest.

"I've not told anyone about it but you."

She watched his lips move then as if he were about to say something more. Or as if he might kiss her again. And for the first time Marielle was surprised to realize that she truly wanted that.

For a moment longer they lingered, his gaze holding hers. But he didn't kiss her. And he didn't say anything else. Finally Barry put an arm on her shoulder and led her back to the car. Marielle felt a pang, wondering if she had made the right decision, going with Jennie and Calum. But it was all decided. It was too late now to change her mind. Jennie was counting on her support. And she wasn't all together certain things were really over between her and her sister's husband.

As Marielle walked into the small police station in Oban late that afternoon, she slammed the door behind her, startling the portly inspector who sat hunched over at his desk again, this time stuffing a piece of scone into his open mouth. The sound of the door startled him and he jumped back, knocking over a cup of tea. "Blast it, lass! Don't ye know better than to sneak up on a man like that?"

Marielle ignored him. "Why didn't you bother telling me you never recovered my sister's body?"

To wash down the scone, he took a swallow from what was left of his tea. "Did no' seem much point in it," he said, not surprised to hear the discovery she had made. "Knowin' it would no' have brought her back to life."

Marielle was furious. "Maybe not, Inspector. But it would have been some part of the truth that I had a right to know!"

"Look here, the poor lad had just lost a wife. He asked us to let her rest in peace where she died. As it happened, 'tis a deep and silty area of the loch, that. Swallows things up like quicksand. 'Twould have required Herculean efforts to raise the car. That in mind, I made a judgment that night. Wrong or right. I saw no problem givin' a poor grievin' husband his wish if there'd be some comfort in it for him."

"Did you ever consider that there might have been some foul play involved?"

"Foul play?" he mockingly repeated. "Lass, 'tis no' some program on the telly here, blood and guns, that sort of thing. 'Twas a man's real-life tragedy. A sad, sad accident."

"Did you realize that *that* man and his wife, the victim in this case, were having problems?" she flared. "That she was thinking of leaving him? That she had even purchased a single one-way train ticket that she never got to use?"

She saw his eyes narrow. He hadn't known it. Finally, he leaned across the counter and glared at her. "So what exactly are ye tryin' to imply?"

Marielle thought about the question in the face of his angry gaze. She was honestly not certain what she thought. But something was not right about all of this. And it definitely had her on edge.

"I need to know that you looked into every possible avenue you could."

"Well, it appears ye have your answer now, don't ye? More might have been done, perhaps. But it was no'. We did the best that we could at the time." After a moment, Marielle turned and walked toward the door. "So then," the inspector called out, "are ye finally givin' up this quest, lass? Lettin' your sister rest in peace?"

Marielle glared back at him, lifted her chin, with a lifetime's worth of hard-won stubborn insistence, beneath it. "I will never give up on anything having to do with Colleen. And you should be ashamed, closing your eyes to real possibilities, and then calling yourself an inspector!"

CHAPTER TWENTY-THREE

They hadn't spoken a word on the ride into Glasgow. Marielle sat behind Calum and Jennie in a train car that brought them into the Queen Street station. The city sky was a gray tangle of church spires and plain brick buildings, cars and noise, as their taxi wove in and out of the thick midmorning traffic.

True to his word, Calum had booked a small hotel nearby for only himself and Jennie. Marielle was forced to make her arrangements on her own at the front desk while they were shown to their accomodations.

A few minutes later, she walked into her own room a few doors away and tipped the bell captain who had insisted on bringing up her single small bag. After he had gone, Marielle pressed the room key into her jacket pocket and felt another. It was the key Barry had used for the abbey cellar. He had slipped it inside Ron's old jacket without her knowing it, because he felt it belonged to her now.

Marielle's heart sank, thinking of that. Of him. Of the pieces of Colleen's life he had shared with her, more precious than any jewel. Priceless. There was a lump in her throat. Suddenly, she was missing him.

Marielle walked to the double bed with the bold floral bedspread. She switched on a table lamp. *If I could just find the strength to get to Glasgow, I know I would be different. . . . My painting is all there is. It is my hope. Glasgow is my hope. . . .* Marielle closed her eyes but the haunting words had filled her mind, and her heart. *I paint the past but in it I can see the future.*

Impossible, she was thinking. Still, it was the way her reporter's mind worked. She couldn't help it. They had never recovered Colleen's body, had they? "Come on, Marielle, what are you saying here?" She sank onto the bed in the cone of grainy light from the city skyline that filtered in through the large window. It was cruel even to consider it, and she couldn't take any more disappointments. Not on a day when Jennie was so likely to face her own.

Barry picked up the telephone after the third ring.

No one knew he was still in the studio. Especially at this late hour. He had locked the door early, pulled the blinds, and then sat amid the clay and the stunning vases of a life's work. The painful memories of Colleen in this place, the dear friend he had lost, brought back to life in his many conversations with Marielle, still stung him now. He hadn't slept at all last night thinking about two sisters cruelly kept apart. The irreparable damage done to both of their lives.

She didn't know it yet, he thought. But like Colleen long ago, Marielle had already made her choice for Calum. By going with him to Glasgow, she was following her heart, even if her mind was not yet allowing her to see it.

They were alike as women, these two sisters who had touched his life in such different ways. Both were kind but headstrong. And fiercely devoted. He smiled at the thought. Neither of them ever wanting to hurt anyone. Both of them drawn inextricably to the sort of wild, mysterious man Calum McInnes made the rest of the world believe himself to be.

He knew about Calum. The air of entitlement with which he had come to Killin. The careless way he had treated his mother, and later his wife. Expecting everything—working for little. And he knew about the failed law practice, the way Calum was able to cover it up with his grief, making it seem a noble gesture to his dead wife that he had instead become a fisherman because his grief had stolen his ability to concentrate. But it wouldn't have been right to tell Marielle. This was her path to follow, her own walk toward growth.

Barry had sat for a long time yesterday on a rock at the spring after Marielle had gone. Alone. Reflective. The wind rustling his hair. His clothes. The cold numbing his face, his hands. His mind. Water cascaded down the cliff and over the rocks in a loud rush before him, covering him with a fine, cool mist. In a single moment, his world had tipped, changed forever with her going.

Ye should have fought harder for her, an angry voice inside him taunted. But that was not the answer. He had followed his heart in loving her. And he was following it now. Regan he had cared for as a boy does, with a naive passion that had come through a rose-colored veneer of romance. The way he loved Marielle was more complicated. Rich. More full of layers. More realistic. He had come to love her very swiftly, and with a depth that startled him. Marielle had changed him. Made him better. Sadder. But better.

And he could live with that. He would have to.

"Hallo?" he said in a voice that was weary and flat, as he put the telephone receiver to his ear.

"Barry?"

It was Rory McBride, his Edinburgh agent. He'd forgotten about his call. "Aye."

"Ye do no' sound a bit like yourself, lad. Everythin' all right?"

Barry washed a hand across his face. Opened his eyes. "I'm tired, Rory. 'Tis nothin' more than that. So have ye the schedule for us, then?"

"'Twill be a challenge at best, old lad, I'll warn ye straight out. We begin in Paris tomorrow evening, on to Budapest Friday, then on Saturday you're in Amsterdam."

An image of Marielle rose suddenly in his mind, her standing before him, outside the abbey. Her cheeks ruddy. Eyes, dark and wide. Her shape, slender. That sleek, chestnut hair moving like a sail in the breeze . . . And the way her lips set as she looked up at him in that last moment. She felt something for him. He had seen that today.

It just wasn't what she felt for Calum.

"Are ye up for it, then?"

"Fine with me," Barry said a little sadly. "When is it that I leave?"

CHAPTER TWENTY-FOUR

Marielle met them an hour later in the lobby of the small, fashionable hotel, One Devonshire Gardens. Calum and Jennie were sitting at a cloth-draped table in the hotel's small, lattice-covered patio. The whir of an espresso maker steaming milk in the bar nearby was the only sound among the sedate business crowd who had gathered there. Jennie sat in her wheelchair sipping a glass of orange juice, and her uncle had his face buried in a copy of *The Scotsman*.

Jennie smiled brightly when she saw Marielle and gave her a little wave. It was an encouragement, considering Calum's total lack of regard for her inclusion in all of this.

"So then. What time is the appointment?" Marielle tried to ask casually.

"One o'clock."

"Do you know where we're going?"

"They told Calum 'twas in an area near a place called Queen's Park."

Marielle's eyes widened. "At this time of the day it'll take at least half an hour to get there."

"Ye sound as if ye know this city right well for a French girl," Calum growled.

"There are a lot of things that I imagine would surprise you about me, Calum."

He stiffened. Folded the newspaper. Calum then rose to his feet, wearing the first suit Marielle had ever seen him in, dark and stiff with a navy-and-red striped tie. He looked uncomfortable. He crossed alone back into the lobby, then stood in the doorway. "Well," he grumbled, "are the two of ye comin', then?"

Dr. Phillips's office was just off Queen's Drive. It was situated in an elegant, three-story yellow stone building that had once been the office of a Scottish diplomat. It was decorated like a stately Georgian home, with antiques and long crimson draperies, except for the overly modern smoked-glass reception desk and silver and leather guest chairs in the foyer, which now functioned as a lobby.

Calum stood near the black lacquer door, wringing his hands. Marielle sat beside Jennie's wheelchair, holding her hand as they waited on elegant black and white marble tile. Dr. Phillips was already thirty minutes late. The receptionist had refused to apologize for him, which had set off an already anxious Calum. He was beside himself. Marielle could certainly see that.

The thought triggered a memory, the only really good thing her mind could conjure about Calum any longer. The value of the violets he had left for her, like a shy, adolescent offering, had faded beneath anger and indifference. He was a tormented man whose heart she had *almost* reached.

When he finally emerged, Dr. John Phillips did so briskly and in a thoroughly businesslike fashion. He was a small man with a long thin face and small, dark eyes set behind heavy, black-framed glasses. He was wearing a white lab coat, dark houndstooth slacks, and scuffed black shoes.

Phillips shook Calum's hand. Then he turned to address Jennie. "Well, then. Are ye ready, my dear?"

Calum and Marielle were shown to a waiting room leading out onto a little covered garden and instructed to wait there. The doctor had been very firm that it was an examination he would conduct privately. Calum had made a showing of disapproval but it had done absolutely nothing to dissuade the equally strong-minded Phillips.

They sat across from one another for almost a quarter of an hour before either of them spoke. "Are you ever going to talk to me again?" she finally asked. "Or is this wall between us just going to get higher and higher until there is nothing left?"

Calum's head dropped forward into his hands. A moment later, he sat up again and raked the hair back from his face. "I haven't been the most chivalrous of gentleman here, have I?"

"Nor in Killin. But then, who's keeping score?"

"I expect you are. And ye should be." Their eyes met finally. Calum drew a breath. "Ye deserve better, Marielle."

"*You* deserved honesty. I was wrong to keep the truth from you. I know it was a shock. It's just that I've never been very good at this thing they call human relations."

"Join the band."

Marielle softened. It was difficult to be too angry with someone who, on some level, related to her weakness. "It's just that when I got to Killin and found out that Colleen was dead, well, I just sort of wanted to retreat into myself; I didn't want to share any part of that with anyone until some of the shock of it lessened a bit."

"I'm sorry for overreacting. Ye just broadsided me with it." She could see the tension in him suddenly ebb. "But the fact remains, we're vinegar and oil, you and I. Ye're a big-time reporter and I'm workin' on a fishin' trawler. 'Tis what my life has become."

"That seems strange coming from a man with a big-city education and important parents."

He sighed deeply. "'Twas what Colleen always said. And I can tell ye, she said it with the same look of disappointment."

"So what did you tell her?"

"I told her 'twas too late for fantasies. I'd done too many things to ruin my chances with a career that could make her proud. Or make *me* proud of myself."

"What happened?"

"I was a cocky lad, to be frank with ye. Rich and foolish. Things had come to me so easily for so long I got to feeling 'twould always be like that. I did no' try hard enough at bein' a solicitor and I guess I did no' try any more than that at bein' a husband. When Colleen realized it, we made one another miserable."

"And you really believed she was having an affair with Barry Buchanan?"

"For a time toward the end Buchanan seemed the only one who could ever make her smile. I always thought that conclusion was logical."

Marielle sat silently, listening to the rest of the story: how her sister had fallen in love with him. How they had ended up married one night after a bitter fight Colleen had had with Malcolm. And how the marriage had begun slowly to fall apart when Calum's jealousy and unrealized dreams had come between them.

"So, do ye despise me then?"

"I think I understand things a little better now. And that is more of a gift than you can imagine. Thank you."

Calum took her hand and ran a finger back and forth over Marielle's palm. Then he drew her forward and kissed her deeply. "'Twas no' honest when I said if I'd known the truth I never would have made love to ye that night. I wanted ye from that first moment at MacLaren's Bend, Marielle. And I want ye just as much now."

Marielle wanted to believe that. In spite of everything that had happened, being near him still overwhelmed that long-dormant part of herself. "I don't know, Calum. Sometimes you just pass a point in relationships. Maybe it's not that different than what happened with you and Colleen."

"Do we have any chance, you and I?"

"I honestly don't know."

Calum looked at her. For a moment, he studied her expression. "Shall we have it all out between us then, and hope for the best?"

"All right." She looked straight at Calum and tipped up her chin. "Then tell me why you fought so bitterly with Colleen the night she died."

He didn't seem surprised she knew about that. "I'll

be makin' no excuses for it," Calum said evenly. "I went straight out of control about her and Buchanan—seein' them whisper out in the drive that last night, like lovers. I was losin' my wife to him and I could do nothin' to stop it. But the force of my anger was wrong, and I paid the dearest price there is for it."

Marielle was afraid to ask. "Then do you ever feel responsible for what happened?"

"'Twas a passionate marriage all the way 'round. The love. *And* the battles. But I had no idea she'd drive off like that . . . and straight off the bridge."

Marielle wanted desperately to believe him. And that he was not involved in her death. She knew she still needed to trust him. Needed to because Calum had taken a part of her heart she had so fiercely guarded for so long.

Her question came haltingly. It was filled with reluctance. "What were you doing, the first one there at the loch that night?"

Calum took up Marielle's hand again. The paneled door opened then and Dr. Phillips pushed Jennie in her wheelchair out into the waiting room. The expression on his face was impassive. "Would you follow me to my office, please?"

CHAPTER TWENTY-FIVE

"I'm sorry." Dr. Phillips stopped speaking. Then he began again once they were facing him across the smoked-glass desk, littered with papers and files. A filtered sunlight came in across the desk, blinding them all a little. "Mr. McInnes, I'm afraid there is nothing that can be done. Jennie will never walk again."

Calum jutted forward across the desk, his fingers splayed out on the rich oak. "Nothin'?"

Phillips glanced at Jennie, who had been crying. Then his eyes settled across the desk on Calum. "Mr. McInnes, the conclusion reached by your primary doctor was accurate. Her cord was severed at the eighth thoracic vertebrae. It cannot regenerate."

"Ye're fair full of it, Doctor! Where in blazes did ye get your degree?"

"If you will please sit down."

Marielle could see the blood flooding onto Calum's face, the weight of disappointment behind it. Jennie was still crying. "Now, I am more than happy to refer you to a very competent physical therapist who—"

"No! Absolutely not!" Calum bolted to his feet, a steel rod shot with fury at the continued inference.

"There's nothin' wrong with her spine that a *competent* doctor could no' mend!"

"Calum!" Marielle could not help herself. The name flooded out of her in a rush of shock.

At the same time, Jennie reached up, very calmly placing her hand on his forearm. "Uncle Calum. Please—"

"I said no, Jennie."

Marielle looked over at him. Calum stood, ramrod straight, clenching and unclenching his fists, looking too much like Malcolm Gordon, as Dr. Phillips made silent notes in the file he had opened once again. Jennie shook her head and sat in silence as her last chance came abruptly to an end.

Marielle went with them back to the hotel after they left Dr. Phillips's clinic. There, she helped Jennie onto her bed. She was asleep before Marielle covered her over with a loose melon-colored blanket. Then she and Calum went out along the Great Western Road. It was primarily a residential area, and a street lined with trees. They spoke very little in the cool autumn air, but Marielle let him take her hand. Still shaken and pale, he seemed to need her. After their disappointment, Marielle understood that.

They walked a long way silently and finally stopped for a drink at the Ingram, which was full to bursting with a crowd. The place was loud, the mood jovial, as American music pulsed through the collections of men in white shirts and ties and a few women in tartan skirts and sweaters.

Calum nursed a pint of ale and barely looked up at

Marielle for what felt to her like an eternity. Finally he touched her hand. It stayed there. It was a connection, powerful like all the others between them. Then their eyes met. The music seemed to go away as the understanding came, silent and deep.

"It won't help things, you know," Marielle said softly. But Calum did not reply. He only drew her up and led her out of the pub.

They walked into Marielle's hotel room together a few minutes later and she quietly closed the door. She leaned against the jamb, watching him in the same grainy, filtered light that seemed to permeate the whole of Glasgow in autumn, as he sank onto the edge of the bed, then looked up at her.

They were both escaping something in this. But knowing it changed nothing.

This time, unlike the last, Marielle allowed herself to lie beneath him and give in completely to the delicious sensations he aroused within her. Arching over her, Calum kissed her eyes, her temples, the tip of her chin. And he caressed her with his big, skillful hands. Marielle had never felt desire so intense.

He undid her shirt and bra, then moved down, sliding his lips slowly over each of her breasts, tasting the soft flesh. He bore down then suddenly with hard, tantalizing kisses that drew her into an oblivion she had known nothing about only a few short weeks ago. And Marielle responded, touching him everywhere.

Drowning in a sensual whirlpool, Marielle wrapped her arms around his neck, clinging to him, pulling him deeper. Pure pleasure. Without love. Wild. Dark. A deep kind of opiate that blocked out everything else.

Especially that she was no longer a victim of the past, but a vital woman. One who had survived.

Calum turned onto his back. He looked over at Marielle then and saw that she had closed her eyes. Her breathing was sweet and shallow. Watching her like that, his heart surged. She was a woman he could love. Deeply. Perhaps a part of him already did.

He turned then and stared at the ceiling as his own ragged breathing began to slow. It had been like this with Colleen once. In the beginning. Wild and powerful.

Before he'd let go of his own dreams. Before he'd lost his pride. Before he had made her miserable with his temperamental moodiness.

But here was a chance to begin again. With his wife's sister. Moments ago, the tantalizing aspect of that thought had excited him. A way of bringing a bit of Colleen back. Maybe even a way of undoing the part he had played in her loss.

Fool! Colleen was gone for good. Marielle was an entirely different woman. And the past was the past.

Sometimes it was also the very best place to keep the most bitter truths.

The phone rang loudly beside her, rousing Marielle with a sudden jolt. She could tell by the shadows cast across the hotel room now that she had fallen asleep. But this time when she glanced beside her, Calum was still there. He lay beside her, perfectly still but with eyes wide open, staring across the room dotted with antiques and chintz.

"Hello?" she said into the telephone receiver.

"I hope ye do no' mind my callin'. I gave myself a dozen reasons not to. But with so much ridin' on the outcome for her, I wondered how things went with Jennie."

Marielle felt her heart quicken at the sound of Barry's rich voice so filled with that sincere concern. "No, of course I don't mind." She felt the smile turning up the corners of her mouth. She was surprised how happy she was to hear from him in a moment that could not have felt more awkward. "But I'm afraid it wasn't what we'd hoped."

She heard the crumpling of sheets as Calum turned. "Oh, Lord. I'm so sorry," Barry said at the same moment. Then there was silence and a faint static on the line. "When are they to come home?"

"I don't know yet."

"And you—are *you* all right?"

Marielle felt a sharp stab of guilt at the question, for how another man, still in her bed, had awakened her body to pleasure. "I'm fine," she managed. But Marielle was surprised to find herself cupping her hand over the receiver then, hoping that Calum wouldn't speak out, that Barry wouldn't realize she was not alone.

In spite of her attraction to Calum, there was still that intense pull to Barry. She wanted to ask him how he was, but that seemed inappropriate. The silence lingered.

"I'll ask Jennie to call her mother later. Catriona will fill you in, I'm certain."

"'Tis Buchanan, is it?" Calum's question had come on a ragged breath as he shifted again onto his back. He felt strangely invasive to her then. She didn't want him here when she was talking to Barry. *What's wrong with me?* she was thinking as the charged silence lingered on. *You've just made love to this man. A man who had a devastation today. An honorable man who gave up everything for Jennie.*

"I need to get going," she said.

"Aye."

"Talk to Catriona in the morning, all right? She'll fill you in on the details then."

"I'll do that."

There was another long pause. He seemed to want to tell her something. She waited, hoping that he would. Finally, when he did not, she said, "I'm glad you called."

"Good-bye, Marielle."

"Good-bye, Barry."

And it came to her only then, in a flash of deep and undeniable disappointment, as the line went dead, that she did not care for Calum in the same way she cared for the man whom she had just let go. Again.

Calum McInnes was the man who had been her awakening. A powerful passion in her life. But he did not possess her heart. The acknowledgment of that—what she had done here with a man she did not love—was sharp. Lethal.

Marielle sat up, feeling the heat of a terrible blow.

"What is it?" When she didn't answer, Calum raked a hand through his hair. His face was stricken. "Have I done somethin'?"

Marielle got out of bed in the silence and drew on

her jeans and an old sweater. A siren sounded outside beyond the closed window blinds. Bile rose in her throat at how she felt now. Ashamed. Foolish. "I need some air."

He bounded off the bed. "I'll go with ye."

"I need to go alone. I'll see you at breakfast tomorrow. I want to be alone until then."

Calum moved to object. But seeing the powder pale expression suddenly on her face, he thought better of it. Instead, he got himself dressed. Then, when they were at the door, Calum took her shoulders and held her at arm's length. His face was filled with intensity, his deep eyes rooted on her.

As she took up her jacket, Marielle wanted to tell him there was nothing wrong, that when she returned, things could go on as they had been. But in that horrid moment of realization, she had passed across a threshold. It was a place from which she could never turn back.

She was in love with Barry Buchanan.

Calum touched her cheek but did not try to kiss her, and Marielle was glad of that. Her mind and heart were full of too much. Outside and alone, she sank against the wall of the hotel as a wave of bile rose again in her throat. The sense of shame was deep and overwhelming. Her attraction to Calum had blinded her. She had been vulnerable to that for far too long. Still, it was no excuse. And Marielle had never felt more alone in her life.

Tears filled her eyes, forcing their way onto her face. She brushed them away.

Then she steadied herself and walked alone past Kelvin Bridge and onto the busy Woodlands Road.

The wind blew her hair as she crossed to the other side of the street. A light mist was falling. The sensation was freeing, and she needed to be free just now of so much.

She walked on and on. Past a neat row of Victorian town houses with black wrought-iron gates. The streetlight turned red, and she waited. Her mind was reeling. A car rushed past, spraying her ankles with the mud from the gutter. She brushed the hair from her eyes. Marielle had no idea where she was going. It only seemed important to keep moving.

The wind was stronger, bringing wet autumn leaves and another heavier rain. It cooled her face, which had felt on fire since she had realized the truth. Marielle stuffed her hands into her jacket pockets and kept going. The Victorian houses began to be dotted with storefronts, all filled with dress shops, antiques, and art.

Things changed quickly in Scotland, and her cheeks now were achingly cold. She was shivering. Ron's herringbone jacket was too light for the turn of the weather, but there was no going back. It came to her then how similar this sudden twist with Calum and Barry had made her life to Colleen's short life. How she too had fallen for Calum, been befriended by Barry. Cared for them both—needed to be away from Calum.

Marielle walked along a row of storefront windows, her eyes catching on an antique easel, then they drifted up to a watercolor painting standing there. Children, girls, smiling, holding hands. Carefree. The street around her tilted and reeled.

She stood still for a very long time, rooted by the

startling image as people hustled around her, nudging, brushing past. Rain pounded her now, it beat against her cheeks, her shoulders. The cold was still biting. But the image held her. On a scrolled gold antique easel, was an image almost identical to the one she had seen only yesterday. Two young girls in a distinctive pen and pale watercolor style. They were holding hands as they stood in an open field rimmed with poplar trees and spotted with heather. It was a field that looked like the glen of her youth. And the girls looked shockingly like herself and Colleen.

CHAPTER TWENTY-SIX

She tried to turn the door handle of the Old Print Shop, even banged on the glass windows, hoping someone would let her inside. *You can't be closed! It's the middle of the afternoon!* she thought in a haze of panic that mixed with shock and disbelief. *There has to be someone here who can tell me who painted that picture!* But an independent shopkeeper could do as he pleased and this one apparently did. She waited there for nearly half an hour to make certain he was just not very late returning from his lunch. But no one came. So she had gone on walking, in a daze after that, random sentences clotting her thoughts, making her dizzy. *If I could just find the strength to get to Glasgow, I know I would be different. . . . My painting . . . it is all that makes me feel alive. . . .*

Alive.

Marielle shook her head. This was insanity to think, even to imagine in her most wild moment of longing. But it was, nevertheless, the way her mind worked. She couldn't help it. She was a reporter. Yet the plausibility of what this made her think . . . God, it was impossible. *Wasn't it?*

She didn't want to go back to the hotel. The probability of seeing Calum just now led her instead to a small, dark pub nearby called the Royal Arms, down a narrow and twisted cobblestone alley. She ordered a double Scotch, then went to the public telephones to try to call the art shop. As she suspected, a telephone recorder picked up the call after the fourth ring.

"Sorry we're no' in to take your call just now but we'd be delighted to ring you back." Then a long, shrill beep.

Marielle drew in a breath, then waited another moment before she spoke into the receiver. "I'm interested in the watercolor you have in your store window. If you could call me at the first possible moment I would be very grateful. Marielle Girard, and I'm staying at One Devonshire Gardens. Thanks."

She held the receiver for a long time after the machine had beeped again and disconnected her. By the time Marielle went back to the small table, her drink had arrived and was sitting on a crisp white paper napkin. She sipped it several times, then sank back, feeling dazed and out of breath.

*What am I doing? Wishes can't make dreams like that come true. . . .*She thought about the painting again, saw it vividly in her mind. The similarity of the brush strokes, the ink outlines. The little girls . . . *If I could just find the strength to get to Glasgow . . .* This time her mind brought the words to the fore in Colleen's own voice. Marielle squeezed her eyes. Life could be so cruel.

The bartender brought the old white-haired

man sitting beside her an ale, and it was the first time she had noticed either of them. "So, Denny, how's the art business?" the bartender asked.

"I'd have better luck at the lottery, these days," he chuckled and then coughed.

Marielle perked and turned toward the two men. "Pardon me, but you wouldn't happen to know the owner of that shop down the street called the Old Print Shop, would you?"

"I'd know him well as ye're lookin' square at him, lass."

She felt her heart accelerate again as the bartender walked away and the man turned to face her. "I've just tried to phone you," Marielle said.

"How fortunate I am, indeed, that my lunch today is of the liquid variety, or I'd have missed meetin' ye." There was something lecherous and drunken about him, she thought, yet she didn't care as long as he could answer her strange and unexpected query.

"I was asking about the watercolor in your shop window."

"Bonny, isn't it? One of a series, but I'm afraid I hadn't the space to take them all on. The artist is new, ye see, and my generosity is only so grand as the space I've free in the shop."

"Who is the artist?"

The man picked up his drink and put it onto Marielle's table as he inched nearer.

His breath was bad and he needed a shower. "Name's Janet Farrell."

Marielle felt a surge of disappointment that was almost painful. "Are you certain of that?"

"'Twas the way she signed the contract. Are ye interested in buyin' the work, then?"

"Perhaps. But I'd like to meet Miss Farrell first."

"I'm afraid 'twould no' be possible, lass."

"Why not?"

"She's no phone to ring her on. Lives a fairly Spartan life over near Strathclyde. That's the other university in town, ye know."

"Have you an address there?" Marielle was feeling desperate again and she knew that it had bled into her voice.

"Janet Farrell is a talented loner. If ye'll permit me the observation, she's a bit too much the eccentric artist for so bonny a lass."

"She's young, then?"

"About your age, I'd wager. Maybe a wee bit older."

Marielle was feeling queasy. She hated these coincidences and how they made her want to believe in a miracle. She took a sip of her Scotch, wanting to keep the conversation going long enough to glean any other little shred of information that she could. "Well, I'm very interested in Miss Farrell's work. I've a large house in Paris that I'm redoing and I'd really like to speak with her about purchasing the entire series."

She had hit her mark with that. The gleam in his eye was unmistakable. "I'm just rememberin' now, as luck'd have it, that Janet'll be by to pick up a payment tonight."

She wanted to ask so much more: What did Janet Farrell look like? Was she brunette or blond?

Had she ever spoken about being from the country? But Marielle had already waited a lifetime, and it was really only a few more hours. "What time?"

"Tonight at six."

Fear and anticipation soared within her. "I'll be there," she said.

Marielle went back to her hotel room, took a long and very hot shower, trying to clear her head of all that had happened. But as she wrapped herself in a bathrobe and sank onto the edge of the bed, her weary mind filled quickly. It was not an image of Colleen she saw this time, nor even Calum. But rather the one she thought of was Barry.

How she wished he were here, suddenly, wished she could share with *him* what she had so wildly begun to suspect. There was no one else she could have told, would have told, but Barry. It was a bond they had. She realized that fully only now.

Marielle glanced over at the dresser on which she had placed the piece of pottery he had given her that first afternoon. Its stark, graceful lines stood out in the shadows and half light from the open window beside it. The piece had an understated sensuality she hadn't noticed before. She still wasn't certain why she had brought it with her when she had packed so little else. But as she had gathered up her things for Glasgow she had only known she could not leave it behind.

She missed so many things about Barry now. His laugh, his sense of humor. The way he was always able to surprise her. The way he spoke to her, as if she were the most wonderful woman on earth.

Marielle realized now how happy he had made her in the little time they had been together—before she had gone away with someone else.

She glanced at the telephone sitting on the end table beside her, beckoning her, it drew her to pick it up and make a call to Killin. But so much had already happened. Maybe too much.

She swung her legs up onto the bed and propped her still-wet head with a pillow. Then she stared up at the shadows on the ceiling. It became a canvas for her mind. She saw so many things then. Like scenes from a movie. Small moments in so brief a time with Barry. Suddenly she was remembering that day he had taken her into the glen. Held her hand and led her firmly, surely, into a little piece of heaven. To the warm, hidden spring.

A tear slid down her cheek when she thought of the gentle manliness with which he had kissed her that first time inside the cottage. The respect he had shown her, not pushing her beyond that, when he could see that she was not ready for anything more. Again, it made her think of Ron Jaeger, how much Barry and he were alike.

A pounding on the hotel room door roused her suddenly then, a frantic, heavy booming that rattled the windows. "Marielle! Are ye in there? Marielle?" It was Calum's voice pitched into a shrill panic.

At first she considered not answering, unsure of whether she was prepared or not to see him yet. Unsure anymore of how she felt for him at all. But then something, a feeling at the base of her neck, told her this was not about her, not about *them*. Something was very wrong.

She went quickly to the door and drew it back. Calum was standing in a ring of yellow light from a wall sconce in the hallway, his hands and chest spattered with blood. His face was pale with fright.

Her heart leapt. "My God, Calum! What have you done?"

"'Tis Jennie!" he wailed. "She's tried to slash her wrists!"

CHAPTER TWENTY-SEVEN

Marielle was still holding one of Jennie's bandaged hands, and had been for hours, as she lay chalk white and motionless in the emergency room of the Western Infirmary. Calum stood beside Marielle, both of them bloodied now, their clothes and hands stained red, from the ordeal of trying to revive Jennie and ride with her in the ambulance.

"I should no' have forced her to come. Selfish of me . . . Thoughtless, selfish dolt!"

It was the first thing Marielle had heard him say since they had come in beside the stretcher, amid a team of white-clad doctors and nurses. Marielle turned around as the heart monitor blipped between them. "You can't blame yourself."

"The hell I canno'! She did no' even want to come to Glasgow."

"You were trying to help."

"Well, the whole bloody world is paved with good intentions now, isn't it?"

He turned away. There was a green curtain between them and the bed beyond. Marielle took two steps and stood just behind him. She put a gentle hand on his shoulder. He was so bereft that the tension between them, and the estrangement over what had happened in her bed earlier, had melted away.

"The doctor's finding was a shock to her. She just needs time to deal with the reality of things."

"God forgive me, but I actually thought that if I just found a specialist—"

"You did your best."

"Well, I did no' do any more smashingly for her than I did for Colleen, did I?"

Her sister's name—*his wife's name*—flared between them again, and Marielle felt a twinge of something strange. For an instant, she thought about telling him what she had suspected. But to carry through on it would be impossible. Colleen had drowned, tragically. Jennie had been left permanently crippled by the same accident. She couldn't possibly go spouting off now with her far-fetched suspicion that could only add to everyone's heartache. . . . Nor, on the other hand, could she let go of that very strong urge to go back to that art gallery on Woodlands Road.

Marielle glanced suddenly at her watch. It was ten minutes to six. Six! Her heart jolted her chest. *She'll be back by at six this evening to pick up a check. . . .* Marielle knew the city. She had come here for journalist conferences. She could never make it back to the art shop at this time of evening when the traffic would be at its heaviest. But she had to see the face of Janet Farrell for herself. She had to put this wild notion to rest.

Marielle snatched up her purse and dashed through the emergency room, running out onto the street, searching wildly for an open taxi. There weren't any, and she was suddenly frantic. A man in a dark business suit was stepping into a small green Ford. "Could I get you to drop me somewhere?" she asked in an out-of-breath voice. He only paused for a moment, looked at her curiously, then got in and started up the engine.

A dented, red Vauxhall was pulling up under the hospital's canopy as the other car roared away. Marielle poked her head into the open passenger window, appealing to a white-haired man with a neat beard and spectacles. A yellowing poodle sat panting over his shoulder.

"Excuse me, but there isn't a taxi in sight, and I'm desperate. Is there any chance at all that I could get you to drop me over on Woodlands Road?"

The man checked his watch. "Aye. I've got time, as it happens. Get in."

Marielle smiled. "Oh, I can't thank you enough."

The car was old and dirty. The windows were thick with a coating of dog saliva and dust. The dirty poodle licked her cheek. Marielle grimaced, trying hard not to mind. The point was seeing Janet Farrell for herself, and this stranger was doing her an enormous favor.

The man didn't speak to her, but Marielle preferred it that way. Her stomach was twisted so tightly with anticipation that it hurt. Jennie. Janet Farrell . . . Everything that had happened, good and bad, with Calum. It was all coming at her at the same time. Marielle leaned out of the window and drew in a breath. The traffic was heavy and it was just six o'clock now.

The man wove his Vauxhall through traffic, dodging cars and pedestrians with the ease of an Italian. Still, the distance was too great to ever make it in time.

She was wringing her hands as the man pulled off of busy Argyle Street onto a shady, tree-lined lane spotted with orderly houses. Marielle looked at him. "Is this the way to the Woodlands Road?"

"Shortcut, lass."

"I honestly *do* need to get there. You could almost call it a matter of life or death."

The man's pale lips turned up at the corners for only an instant. But he did not look at her. "Ye'll get there."

Marielle's body was suddenly rigid, sensing danger. Only now was she aware of her discomfort with this man. This stranger. She looked at him again, seeing a face beneath the neatly clipped beard that was gaunt and pocked, and eyes that were frighteningly vacant. The Vauxhall began to slow, and he pulled over to the curb. Marielle's heart leapt.

"What are you doing?"

He touched her knee, turned to her. His eyes were still vacant. "Call it payment for the lift, if ye like." His hand moved rapidly from her knee up along her thigh. But it was a wave of anger, not fear, that vaulted through her then.

"Not today, you lecherous old bastard! Not even close!"

He lunged toward her, but Marielle pushed him back, and in the same wild movement full of angry determination, she grabbed the dirty little poodle out of the back seat. Marielle clasped a hand around the dog's neck, thrusting her best wild-eyed expression upon the man. She wouldn't hurt the dog. She had never hurt an animal in her life. But the lecher beside her didn't know that, and at the moment it was the only defense she had. "Touch me again, even think about it, and I'll wring this scrawny little neck in a heartbeat!"

Marielle saw genuine surprise, and even a little spark of panic, finally light his limpid eyes. Marielle's anger galvanized her. "Look, whoever you are, I'd just as soon get out of this old wreck right here and now, but I can't do that. I've *got* to get to Woodlands Road, and it seems that you've been elected to take me. So when I get there, you get the dog back in one piece. Understand?"

The old man studied her for a moment, and she thought it seemed he was trying to decide whether it was worth it to press her again. Marielle tipped her chin up defiantly beneath his assessing gaze, never taking her eyes from his—daring him as she very firmly held his dog. Finally, he turned back to the steering wheel and started up the engine again. He dropped her in front of the art shop at ten minutes after six, rumbling away from the curb with the poodle safely on his lap.

Marielle's heart sank when the man she had met at the pub came to the door. "Ye've just missed her, I'm afraid," he said, glancing down the street.

"When did she leave?"

"No' more than a minute. Two at the most."

"Did you see which way she went?"

He glanced to the left and Marielle broke into a run before he could even speak out the direction. She wove in and around business people coming home from work, her purpose focused. Intense. Everywhere was a whirl of briefcases and business suits. Women walking dogs. Heels clicking evenly along the sidewalk.

Two boys laughing and weaving about. She had no idea even whom she was looking for. She had never asked for that description of Janet Farrell. *Oh, please take me to her, Lord,* she was thinking in a rising panic. *Just let me look into the eyes of the woman whose art is so hauntingly like Colleen's. . . .*

Marielle's shoe heel snapped off as she dodged between a man and a woman pushing a baby carriage. She grimaced as her ankle twisted with the sudden movement. She slowed enough to tear off her shoe as a ribbon of hot pain shot up through her calf. Marielle was limping now, running and limping. There was such a sea of people on the street before her, finding one particular woman seemed impossible.

As she searched the backs of those walking briskly before her, hoping for anything that would seem familiar, Marielle's eyes settled on a slim woman in a black trench coat with long copper-colored hair that hung straight beneath a glen plaid scarf.

"Miss Farrell!" Marielle called out loudly, her tone rising shrilly. "Pardon me, Miss Farrell!"

The woman kept walking. Marielle's ankle was throbbing. "Miss Farrell, please! Is that you?" It was starting to rain again as Marielle tried to keep pace with the crowd that carried the woman along. Marielle watched her open a black umbrella as she walked. Her heart was slamming against her ribs. The pain in her ankle was piercing.

"Miss Farrell . . . Oh, God—*Colleen? Colleen Gordon?*"

The woman stopped suddenly and very slowly turned around in the wind-battered rain. As she did, the blood left Marielle's face. Her heart seemed to stop. Everything in that strangely vivid moment came in a kind of slow motion, each movement seeming bolder, more deliberate. Marielle was shaking uncontrollably as she looked for the first time in over thirteen years into the face of the person most dear to her in all the world.

"My God," she murmured. "It *is* you!"

CHAPTER TWENTY-EIGHT

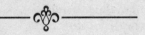

It took far longer to convince Colleen who she was than for Marielle to believe the truth of what she was seeing. Marielle had known her sister from the first full glance.

But, in return, utter disbelief had marked the drawn face that had looked back at her on that rain-soaked street. It was a face that was still remarkably beautiful, and yet one which had been aged now by time and trauma. There were fine lines and dark hollows to Colleen now, where Marielle could only remember ruddy cheeks and sparkling eyes.

A life unfulfilled, a life of disappointment was all in that first expression between them. Colleen stood on that street for what seemed a very long time, gazing at her, seeming unable to process what was happening.

"No!" Colleen cried when the recognition hit her. "It canno' be you! It canno'!" She was trembling violently, wrapping her arms around herself. Then she sank, limply, onto the wet pavement. Her face was parchment white. "Why now, Mairi? Why have ye come back *now*?"

Something about her sister's painful pleading, the tortured expression on her face, and the brittle vulnerability it conjured, brought Marielle to tears as well. And Marielle sank down too. Both of them sat there on the sidewalk, with people gazing down at them, whispering, some brushing past, as Marielle put an arm around Colleen's shoulder.

"I've been looking for you since the day I left Killin," she pleaded to an older sister who had once meant the world to her. "I swear it!"

"But I wrote to you, and you never answered!"

"I know," Marielle wept. "I know."

"How on earth did ye find me *now?*"

"I think it was magic," she sobbed now. *Barry's kind of magic,* she was thinking.

When the light rain beating down on them became a sudden thundershower, they helped one another back to their feet. But Marielle's ankle had begun to swell, and Colleen saw it.

"Well, if this isn't history repeating itself," she remarked with a grim half smile as she supported Marielle this time and they hailed a cab to take them to an old Victorian house with a small sign posted at the door that said ROOMS TO LET.

They walked inside and up two floors of a walnut staircase to a large room with a bay window, a brass bed, a wash basin, and a bureau. Colleen closed the door. There was a water heater for tea, two cups, and an open box of Tetley's on the scratched and battered antique bureau.

Thunder shook the house as Colleen took off her black trench coat and sank onto the edge of the bed. Marielle was still standing, having forgotten the pain in her ankle for the bittersweet emotion that was battering her heart.

386 ₧   DIANE HAEGER

This time—with years between the moments—it was Colleen who brought ice and a cloth to soothe a sister's turned ankle. In the silence, and on a sea of tiny memories, as that furious intensity of emotion slowly faded a bit, recognition of the moment flowed through each of them.

"I'm no' sure I know what to say," Colleen said, looking up at her finally, her green eyes still bright with tears. "This is all quite a shock."

"They told me in Killin that you were dead. I think I might have a lead in the shock department."

"Aye," Colleen conceded without smiling. "I suppose ye would have, then."

"But why haven't you told anyone that you survived that night? Jennie and Catriona, Calum especially, they're all still grieving for you!"

"'Tis no' easy to explain. Ye were away a long time," Colleen said, going over to the bureau and filling the heating pot from the wash basin beside it. It was a movement that seemed full of nervousness. Her hands were shaking badly. "Will ye have some tea with me, then?"

"I would if you'd have anything strong to go in it."

"I do no' drink liquor anymore, Mairi."

She had quite a problem with drink toward the end. Jennie's words coming at her just then were jarring. "I'm sorry."

Colleen turned around again. "Ye need no' be. I'm actually better for it all now."

"Because everyone thinks you're dead?"

"Because I'm no' possessed here," Colleen corrected, a bit of pride rising in her tone. "By drink or anything else."

"Or anyone . . . like Calum?"

"Aye, like Calum. And Da as well. I'll tell ye they were difficult years for me, to say the least, after you and Vivienne left for France."

Marielle heard the sudden shift in her tone, the veiled accusation in the words, as though Colleen had been intentionally left behind, forgotten, and her own heart ached. "Colleen, I need you to understand something." Marielle leaned forward on the corner of the bed. She braced her elbows on her knees. Her face was full of seriousness. "What I said was the absolute truth: I tried for years to get back to you. I only discovered a short time ago that my mother had kept your letters, and saw that mine were never mailed to you. All of this time, I thought it was you who had forgotten *me*."

Tears fell onto her cheeks again as Colleen leaned back against the dresser for support. She looked so fragile to Marielle. So beaten by life. The smile had left her once-beautiful eyes.

"There was no' a week, nor even a day that went by, Mairi, that I did no' think about ye, wonder about where ye were . . . or believe ye'd be back. For a very long time, ye'd been such a source of support to me when we were wee. I never realized, I suppose, until ye left, how much I depended upon ye. The laughter—the friendship. It took away the pressure from Da of bein' Janet Gordon's only child."

"Oh, Colleen—"

"And then when ye would no' write back to me, and Da was worse than ever, makin' me his whole life, I found Calum. He was like a refuge. And I thought *he* was my strength then—enough so that I found my way out from under Da."

"And then he married again."

"Catriona," Colleen said. "Isn't it ironic?"

"I am more sorry than you will ever know that I couldn't keep my promise."

"I should no' have invested so much in you—nor in anyone. Things were just so jumbled up back then."

Colleen came with two mugs of tea, tears running down the length of her face that she did not bother to wipe away as she sank onto the edge of the bed beside her sister. They were still so awkward with one another. Such familiar strangers. Finally another grim smile touched her eyes and mouth. "So then. 'Tis no' much to look at, this place of mine."

"That's not important in the least."

"Come to think of it, I'm probably no' what ye expected either."

Marielle thought of the changes again in her once carefree and beautiful sister. "It had been a long time. We've both changed, Colleen."

She saw her sister's expression lighten at the response. "Have ye been happy, then, Mairi? Have ye liked livin' in France?"

"Paris feels like my home now. But it has been a life with a very large piece missing. *You* were that piece. And not having you to grow up with changed a great many things for me."

Marielle put her hand atop Colleen's and realized only then that, in spite of her smile, her sister was trembling. For how their lives had appeared to be heading when they were children, things had changed dramatically. Gone was the carefree, confident girl of their youth; the elder sister with the looks and the promise. Colleen was a woman adrift now, living a grand lie, alone in a boarding house in Glasgow, and Marielle was the woman from Paris, in the midst of discovering the depth of her beauty—and her own inner strength—at last.

"Calum is here with me."

Colleen's face went suddenly ashen. She sank back on the bed as though she had sustained a very deep blow. "Does he know where ye are?"

"No one knows that."

"Ye canno' tell him. Ye must promise me now that ye will no'!"

Her sister's vehemence, the utter conviction that suddenly patched Colleen's pale face with red, was jarring. What horrible thing had happened to tear two people apart in so desperate a way, people who had married one another? It was not unlike Vivienne and Malcolm, she thought. People who one day had stood before God and everyone to proclaim their vow. People who had gone on to despise one another.

"But he's still your husband. He has a right to know you're still alive, doesn't he?"

"Calum has no right to any part of me, Mairi, believe me. Besides, Colleen does no' exist anymore. I've grown quite accustomed here to bein' Janet Farrell."

"But you are living a lie."

"Aren't we all to one degree or another?"

Marielle thought how she had gone back to Killin, intent at first in no one knowing who *she* was. Engaging in an affair with Calum without telling him the truth of her own identity. Suddenly, the guilt about that as she looked at Calum's wife, her own sister, became strangely intense. "I need you to know something," she said slowly. "Before you do decide to go back or someone else tells you."

Colleen took a drink of tea. She paused a moment as her expression became reflective. Marielle could see that somehow she knew. "He's a very attractive man, Calum. Very sensual," Colleen said. "And wasn't it me who said, long ago, ye'd turn into a lovely woman one day?" she smiled. "'Twas bound to happen, with both of ye together, there at MacLaren's Bend."

"I didn't know you were alive. And now, well now, it's just over. That's all."

"I'm glad." Colleen's lips stretched upward again, but the expression was not quite a smile. "Not for my sake, Mairi, but for yours. Calum's a dangerous man to love."

Was he? Marielle still wondered that. Or was he just complex, wounded? Bitter? Perhaps he had been a man with too many intricacies for Colleen to balance. After all, a poor match was really no one's fault. It happened. As it had, she thought, with Malcolm and Vivienne.

The two sisters talked for a long time after that, the moon and lamplight dappling their faces with shadows. And Marielle, even though she knew now that she did not love him, was unable to completely condemn Calum, as Colleen had. They spoke about anything and everything. Their adolescence. Their father. Vivienne. Even about Barry Buchanan. But always they steered clear of the reason Colleen had felt desperate enough to allow the rest of the world to believe that she was dead.

Their conversation was interrupted after a while by a soft rapping at her door. "Come in," Colleen called.

They both turned as a tall man with bright blue eyes and a shock of carrot-colored hair that swept back from his forehead stood suddenly in the doorway, his hands on the jamb. He was overly lean, wearing a tartan shirt with rolled-up sleeves and denim pants.

Marielle saw her sister's face. A small glimmer of the beautiful light returned. "'Tis all right," Colleen motioned. "Ye're bound to meet sooner or later. Mairi, 'tis Gerry O'Connor. Gerry, 'tis my very beautiful sister Mairi Gordon ye're blessed to be lookin' at."

Marielle watched his surprise. Gerry obviously knew much of the story and it made her happy in that instant to know that Colleen had found a confidant here in a vast, impersonal city the size of Glasgow. And perhaps she had found something more. "Your sister, is it?"

"It seems she found me."

"A mammoth task for anyone from Killin, I always told her."

"Well, you weren't wrong," Marielle smiled as she stood up and extended her hand. "There was something fated about our connecting again. I'm still not quite certain how it happened."

"I'm only glad it did," Colleen said.

Gerry came into the small room and sank awkwardly onto an edge of Colleen's bed, where they all had sat at different moments, for lack of proper chairs. "We were just havin' a bit of tea, Gerry. Will ye join us?"

"I've just come from tea at the Colonial. But thanks."

Marielle watched them exchange another glance. He was asking Colleen with his eyes if she was all right.

He cared for her, Marielle could plainly see. She pressed her advantage. "So, how are the two of *you* acquainted?"

They looked at one another again, surprised at the direct question, and Marielle thought the air between them had a bit of the purity of adolescence about it. "Gerry's an artist here in the city. Ye might say he saved my life when I first arrived."

"Ye did no' need savin'," he interrupted. "Just someone who recognized true talent."

"I was fortunate indeed, Mairi," Colleen said. "He helped me get this place and Gerry's also gotten my work shown at several galleries around the city. I truly canno' imagine where I'd be if he had no' found me."

"Works both ways, Colleen," he said deeply, and their eyes held one another's for a moment.

Colleen went to him then, sat beside him and took up his hand. "We have more than our art in common, Mairi. Gerry's an alcoholic like me, ye see." She kissed his cheek gently, placing a hand beside his chin. Then she looked back at her sister. "We've come through the worst of it together."

"I wish I could have been there for you, as well. Maybe none of it would ever—"

Colleen stopped her in a serene sort of way that Marielle had not seen until now.

"We are all where we are meant to be. It's about the journey. That's what Gerry and I are learning."

Reluctantly, Marielle glanced at her watch.

"I've got to leave. But I don't want to go."

The sisters stood together then and linked hands. Gerry stood as well. "'Twas lovely meetin' ye, Mairi," he said. "Hope I'll have the opportunity again."

"Me too."

After he had left, Marielle turned back to Colleen. "The truth is that I'm afraid if I leave, you will disappear, and this miracle will all have been a dream."

"Then stay a while longer. I'll order out for some supper."

"I'd like that more than anything. But I can't."

Marielle told her then about Jennie, about the other tragedy that had happened that night she had disappeared from Killin. Then she told her about the bleak prognosis from the Glasgow doctor that had led her to an impulsive act. Colleen was shaken by the stories. Her eyes were misted again with tears. "I had no idea," she said just above a whisper.

"I was sure you didn't."

"I might have been some comfort to her or Catriona through all of it."

"There's still time, you know. They certainly can use it, now more than ever."

"I'm dead, Mairi, and I need to stay that way. As much for my own sanity as for anythin' else."

"I'd really like to understand what happened." They were still holding hands. "What made you feel desperate enough to do what you did."

"There are things, Mairi, bits of our lives, that we are never goin' to be able to share. 'Tis sad, I know, but that much canno' be changed."

"I'd really like to tell Catriona and Jennie at least that I've seen you."

"Ye promised ye wouldn't."

"Then it's a promise to you, at last, that I can keep."

Marielle leaned over to kiss her sister's cheek and

the Celtic cross at her throat rocked forward, flashing in the lamplight. "So ye kept it all of these years, I see," Colleen remarked with a pleased smile.

"You'll probably never know how important to me you've always been. This cross was a symbol to me of that."

Marielle stood and collected her jacket, realizing then that Ron was a part of her life Colleen knew nothing about. They had a ways to go. Leaving now seemed almost as painful as it had years ago, even knowing that she would be able to return whenever she wanted to. But allegiances ran deep inside Marielle. And just now, Jennie and Calum needed her at the hospital. And more of a reunion with Colleen would have to wait.

Marielle sat with Catriona by Jennie's bedside. Catriona had taken the train in and had arrived an hour ago. Jennie was still sedated and very pale. Calum had gone down for a breath of air. Marielle thought about Calum now, the hopeful way he had smiled at her when she had come into the hospital room. She didn't love him. But he was important to her. She would always care for him for the part of herself he had helped her to see. And Colleen's vehemence confused her. Certainly the end of a marriage took two. Perhaps her sister simply had not yet come to her own recognition of that.

"No!" Jennie cried out suddenly, rocking Marielle from thoughts that were very far away from the moment. She bolted from the chair and took Jennie's hand. "Ye canno' go alone, Colleen! . . . If ye mean to go, *I'll* drive ye."

Catriona and Marielle exchanged a glance. Catriona's worried expression changed to panic. "Should I call for the nurse, do ye think?"

"Let's wait a moment. Maybe she'll settle again on her own."

"But she's relivin' the night—"

"I know."

They watched a shadow of something pass over Jennie's face in a moment of quiet, something like a frown, before it disappeared. "Stop it, both of ye now. 'Twill get ye nowhere, all of this battling. . . . Uncle Calum, stop." Then she was quiet again, and Marielle looked around, afraid the nurse would come now and stop things. "Colleen, please! We're drivin' too fast. . . . Colleen! Slow down! Oh, please, slow down!"

Catriona shot Marielle a level look, her eyes were dark with seriousness. "It's a motorcycle behind us, Colleen! Oh, no. It canno' be. . . . He's followed us! He was so angry. . . . I'm afraid, Colleen, afraid of what he'll do if—"

Jennie was clenching and unclenching her fists now. Her voice was tremulous. "It's dark out here. Oh, please don't. Please don't go so fast. . . ." There were fresh tears shimmering on Jennie's cheeks. Her body was tense, ramrod-straight as she tossed bitterly inside the hidden memories so deeply held inside her mind.

Marielle moved to stop it. "Ye're goin' onto the Dwelly Bridge, Colleen. 'Tis no' safe for cars! . . . Oh, and he's scarin' me. He's too close. . . . Stop pushing us! Uncle Calum. *Please* . . . 'Tis no' safe!"

The sick feeling inside of Marielle was growing very quickly into something agonizingly grand. "Catriona," she interjected in a cautious whisper. "I think you're right. We ought to stop this."

"Ohh! Ohh!" Jennie cried out. "Mother Mary! Ooh! The rushes! They're thick! I canno' see anything but that! 'Tis darkness all around us. *Oh!* The car is sinkin'. . . . We've gone off the bridge, into the water. Colleen! Colleen! Where are ye? I've got to get out of here! Ye've driven us into the loch! Colleen! Oh, Colleen! *Colleen!* She's still in the car! It's on its side! *Her* side! . . . I'm okay now, Uncle Calum. Go after her! Ye've got to go in again! . . . I think she's panicked! Calum, do ye no' hear me? Ye canno' just leave her there to die!"

And then, very suddenly, Jennie was quiet, spent, the recollections having faded back into the murky depths of her mind where it was safer to keep them. Where she had steadfastly kept them these past two years. All around them it was quiet except for the awful sobbing from Catriona.

Marielle sat back, stunned. Her heart was galloping, filling with anguish. She was too stunned to move. Everything that had been confusing, all of the deep, dark questions, like a long-sealed room, were blown open now, filled by a shockingly sharp and intense clarity.

A black plume of rage rose up through her chest, into her throat, choking her. So it was true. Calum was responsible for Colleen's death—or a death he fully believed had happened. He may not have killed her directly. But he might as well have, for the role he had played that awful night. She felt the tears sting her eyes. Agony like rancid fruit lodged in the back of her throat.

"Shh," Marielle tried to soothe an inconsolable Catriona. "It'll be all right."

"But everyone in town thought he'd only followed her that night. Tried to stop her from drivin' after she'd been drinkin'. 'Twas an awful accident, they said. He'd been a brave husband who suffered a horrible loss, when all the while—"

"He certainly isn't the man we all believed him to be."

Catriona tipped her head. Her eyes were still bright with tears. "What do we do now, Marielle? Should we tell someone about this, do ye think?"

"I don't know." Marielle stopped for a moment. She drew in a painful breathe. It was difficult to speak above the coldness that had gripped her heart. Knowing that Colleen was really still alive did not change the reality of what Catriona's nephew had sought to do that dark and bitter night. Nor could it change the heartbreak she felt at yet another betrayal when she had tried to trust again.

"I'm not certain I know what we do now," Marielle said flatly.

Calum was sitting alone on a bench outside the hospital entrance, head in his hands. Out in the street the traffic was heavy. That steady parade of cars. Motor scooters. Diesel trucks. Revving. Idling. Belching smoke. He raked his fingers through his hair and felt that he was barely breathing.

Jennie had been so firm. She hadn't wanted to come to Glasgow. Hadn't wanted to face the prospect of futility. Now this. More trauma. More heartache. His fault. It chafed at him. Taunted him.

He had ruined things with Marielle. As badly as

he had ruined his marriage to Colleen. And he had no one to blame for any of it but himself. He had acted by impulse and blind emotion there. And so many times before in his life. Colleen had only drawn away from him because of it, because he had not remained the man she had married. He had refused to get help in Glasgow when she had asked him.

Just as he stood preparing to return to Catriona and Jennie, Calum heard the automatic doors swing open behind him. Seeing Marielle, his heart hit his chest. The second love of his life, he thought. She was looking squarely at him, and her face was filled with anger.

Marielle charged at him then, slapping his face hard then beating at his chest. "Bastard!" He stopped her from hitting him again, but she was wild, swinging and swearing. "You evil goddamn bastard! How could you have done it? How could you have stood there and watched, and done nothing? It's like you're some kind of animal!"

Calum studied her expression as he held her by the forearms. The disgust was the hardest thing for him to see.

"Just tell me how you did it to my sister, Calum? How you did it to your own *wife?*" When he would not answer her, and the silence became unbearable, she spoke again. "I went back to Killin to fill in a void that has affected me for most of my life.

"The truth was the thing that drove me. That was my goal. But then I met you. And there was that over-whelming attraction. I stopped listening to my heart and mind. I made a mistake in that, because I didn't see that you are, at your core, an evil, evil man!"

He let go of her arms. "And what is it exactly ye're accusin' me of?"

Marielle looked directly at him now. Her beautiful eyes were suddenly hard. For a moment, they lost their depth. "Spare me, Calum. I finally know the whole truth of that last night, and the part you played."

"And what is it ye think ye know?"

She glared at him, fury fueling her in the echo of his question. "I *know* how you followed Colleen that night, angry and betrayed, not knowing Jennie was with her. I *know* how you forced Colleen off the road and into that lake because you knew she was going to leave you. Because you thought she was going to leave you for Barry Buchanan when what she was really leaving you for was *herself!* And I know how guilt about Jennie has wracked you ever since because your poor niece was never meant to be touched by your violence!"

Calum's faced paled at the sheer disdain he saw for him mirrored back in her eyes—and the truth beyond that. "I will no' be denyin' any of it."

"Say it, then, Calum. Say you killed my sister."

Calum's voice was tight. Choking. "In a crazed moment of self-pity . . . I watched that night and did nothin'. 'Twas easier to give her up that way than to have people believin' she left me."

"Then that would still make you her killer." There was that deep throb of loss in her voice. They both heard it.

"Aye."

Marielle's eyes flashed. Suddenly there were tears in them. She had cared for this man, this stranger. He had been her awakening. And he had betrayed her trust. There was silence, long and uncomfortable, before Calum lifted his tormented face to her once again. "It won't matter to ye now, but I need ye to know, even so, that I've loved ye, Marielle. As much as I ever loved Colleen."

"You're right," she said coldly. "It doesn't matter now."

Calum was still looking at her. "So then. Where do we go from here?"

"*We* don't go anywhere. *You* go back to Killin with Jennie and you do what you can to help her get on with her life. Help her recover, if you can, from the knowledge that she will never walk again!"

He extended his hand to her, then very slowly let it fall back to his side. Marielle turned away. She couldn't look at him any longer for the sick feeling it gave her, knowing that Colleen was still alive. But knowing that the man before her had gone on with his life, believing he had intentionally let his own wife die.

Marielle was still filled with anguish as she drew back the door of her hotel room and stepped inside. Then there was that stillness. Sanctuary. Safety. She did not bother to switch on a light. What she did not see at first was Colleen, there in the dark, waiting in the impersonal oak and burlap-covered chair beside the window.

"How did you get in here?" Marielle asked in surprise, more glad than surprised that her sister was here.

"I paid a chambermaid," Colleen smiled, holding

up a bottle of Glenmorangie. "I thought ye might be able to use this."

"But you don't drink."

"Right. But *you* do. And by the look on your face just now, ye could handle a dram or three."

Colleen opened the bottle and poured a water tumbler for Marielle. Then she opened a small, green bottled water for herself. "I hope 'twas all right, me comin'."

"It's more than all right," Marielle said with a strained smile that faded as soon as it came.

"The truth is I did no' want to risk losin' *you* again either." The two women exchanged a look. There was comfort in it, and Marielle felt her heart slow. "How is Jennie?" Colleen asked.

"Still not conscious, I'm afraid."

"Damn."

Marielle leaned forward. Her eyes darkened. "Why didn't you tell me about what Calum *really* did that night? About his running your car off the bridge?"

"He admitted it?"

"Jennie has been talking. Dreaming, I suppose. Catriona and I were there."

"I'm sorry that Catriona knows. She adores her nephew."

"A bit less now, I think. It was difficult for her, hearing for herself what he was capable of."

Marielle took a long drink of Scotch, then two. "God, he was such a bastard. I can hardly believe such ruthlessness."

"Was he contrite about having let me drown?"

Marielle's face blanched. It sounded so strange, the way she had said it. But Colleen hadn't drowned, thank the Lord. Marielle hadn't lost a sister forever, after all, in spite of all the obstacles they had faced. There was a chance, an unbelievable chance, for them to begin again.

"Tell me the rest, Colleen. About that night after your car went off the bridge."

Colleen considered a response. Marielle watched her face harden. She could see how difficult it was to relive it all again. "First, ye must understand that I had no idea about Jennie. If I'd known she was injured I'd probably never have had the courage to escape."

Marielle had known that, of course. Deeply.

"I'm so sorry that escape was something you felt you needed to do."

"Calum and I'd quarreled that evenin'. Badly." She spoke slowly. "Things were said, accusations made. 'Twas no' the first time. But then when he struck me and—"

Marielle felt the sound of the word deeply. Almost as if it had happened to her. "Calum *hit* you?"

"He'd thought for a long time that I was havin' it over with Barry Buchanan, ye see. Insisted on it. When I told him that night I wanted a divorce, Calum tried to implicate Barry again. It's us, I said. *We* are the problem. No' another man. But he would no' believe me. Lookin' back on it now, I don't expect I did the best job of convincin' him. I was bitter myself about the life we'd made, ye see, too far into the drink to get myself out, and wantin' *that* to be someone else's fault. When Calum told me that night that he would no' let me leave, it brought back the past too vividly."

No wife of mine is leavin'. Do ye hear me,

Vivienne? Marielle shivered. She remembered that too, and would forever.

"So I got into my car and started it up."

"Jennie along with you."

"Aye. Poor lass thought she was helpin' matters, the good Lord bless her soul. Calum was poundin' on my window, not seein' her, I'm sure. 'Tis no' over between us, Colleen!' He was yellin' that for all the world to hear, so I thought 'twas best if I just got away for a while. Let him cool down."

"But Calum followed you."

"Jennie saw the single headlight from his motorcyle behind us when we reached the edge of town. She was after me to slow down. But I knew how angry he was, and what he could do. At least I thought I knew."

Oh, please, Colleen . . . No' so fast! We're goin' onto the Dwelly Bridge! 'Tis no' safe!

Marielle was crying quietly; Colleen was too. Marielle shook her head. "It's so difficult to believe of the man I thought I had begun to know," she said achingly, thinking of the violets. Of making love.

"It was impossible at first to believe of the man *I* married."

"But it did happen," Marielle said in a wounded voice. "God, all of it."

"It was so sudden that we were in the water. The night was black as coal and everything was in the shadow of that one eerie headlight from Calum's bike. I crawled out the open window of my car and I saw that Jennie'd gone through it already. I swam for the rushes to have something to hold onto until help came. I watched in that darkness as my husband dove for Jennie and dragged her back up onto a sandbank."

She took a sip of the bottled water. "Then I waited in the water, shivering with cold, as I watched the man I'd loved, the man I'd hung my future upon, turn back around, gaze at my car. But he just stood there as the loch swallowed it up."

Marielle took a breath but no words formed in her mouth. The pain of hearing the details of something so unspeakable felt almost unbearable.

"I suppose I was in shock when I swam from there because I remember very little of what happened after that. Only that I took a ride into Glasgow from a couple on holiday. And I never looked back. I could never look back. Colleen Gordon died that night, and Janet Farrell—'twas my ma's maiden name—Janet was born again. That is why I can never go back to Killin, Mairi." Her eyes were tear-filled now, but her voice was strong. "Because that weak, painful part of myself would still be there. And I do no' honestly know if I'd ever have the strength to find my way from it again."

"I would help you."

"Ye canno' help about that."

"Would you let me try?"

Colleen turned away, gripping her waist. "The risk is too great."

"Ye'll never be whole if you don't face the past, Colleen. Believe me." Marielle was thinking of their father. Thinking of the freeing sensation she'd gotten confronting his memory so boldly outside in that cool Killin night, when she had finally been able to let go of the debilitating anger and pain that had held her back for so long. "It's Colleen who needs to tell Calum she's divorcing him. Colleen who needs to live the life of a painter in Glasgow. Not only some small part of yourself called Janet Farrell. If you don't do that, believe me, your life will be possessed by the scars, and it *will* come to control you."

After a long silence, Colleen said, "If I'm ever ready, would ye go back with me?"

Marielle smiled, wiping away her own tears. It struck her boldly then. She had become like the elder sister between them. The one with confidence. The one with promise. The one who would lead the way. "Just try to get rid of me now!"

They laughed and embraced one another for a very long time, whispering how sorry they were about the past, about all that they'd lost. Each of them gaining strength from the other. When they went out of the hotel this time, they both knew, it would be together . . . and forever after that.

CHAPTER TWENTY-NINE

It felt strange and wonderful to be back in Killin. Marielle stopped every so often along the road as she walked into the quiet village. She drew in a breath deeply. The winter air was frigid. And full of possibilities.

In the end, Colleen had chosen to go back to MacLaren's Bend, and to face Calum alone. In the weeks since she and Mairi had been reunited, she had gained enough strength, she announced, to confront the man who had betrayed her. It would not be easy, she told Mairi, but she would do it. She believed now finally that she *needed* to do it. So, they had waited for a time when they knew he would be alone in the house. Then, trembling and unsure, yet full of determination, Colleen had walked up the outside steps to the house, never looking back.

Marielle waited for her, walking past the snow-capped mountain peaks and the warm greens and gray-browns, soothing to her in its change from summer and autumn. Autumn, now, to winter. The seasons. They change. *And so have I.*

Ahead lay the church, the two rows of shops lining the neat little main street. It had been a long journey back, she thought. Weeks in Glasgow with Colleen. Time to think, to assess her life. What she wanted. What she did not. In the end, the two sisters both had come back to face a truth here in Killin.

Marielle's heart thumped like a bass drum as she neared the little pottery shop that was next to the butcher. It was odd, she realized now, that seeing Barry Buchanan, of all people, should make her nervous, when he had been the single person in all her life to bring about a kind of inner calm. A rightness to things that had always seemed confused. But Marielle understood her heart now. And she was made vulnerable by it.

Marielle moved to the door of the shop, anticipation making her heart beat like bird's wings against her chest. But what she saw stopped her into a deathly stillness. She pressed a finger to her lips. A handwritten sign was there taped to the window. Abrupt. And final: *Closed for the winter.*

Marielle shrank from the door, feeling the hope rush out of her. Certainly she had known something like this had been possible. But she had not allowed herself to actually think it could be. That she would lose this last chance with him now too.

"Is it Barry Buchanan ye're after, lass?"

The voice startled her and Marielle pivoted around. The man was old. Withered. He walked with a cane and studied her through thick gold-rimmed glasses. Lines, a map of the years, were etched into his cheeks and forehead. But he looked upon her with the same kindness and gentle smile he had when she had stayed in his hotel.

"Yes, Mr. McShane. Have you any idea where he is?"

"Pottery business."

"Have you any idea how long he will be?"

"He's had Martin, over at the post, hold his mail. I'm sorry, lass. I believe he plans to be away for some length of time."

She couldn't help it. Marielle felt the tears of disappointment pressing at the back of her eyes. And yet why should the ending be any different than this? She was the one who had made the choice. Her leaving for Glasgow with Calum and Jennie had punctuated that choice.

"Might you know if he left a forwarding address, at least? A phone number where he could be reached? In case of an emergency with the shop."

"I canno' help ye there, lass. But ye might be askin' Catriona. They're quite bonny friends."

Yes, I know, she wanted to say, as the thought squeezed her heart. But she didn't. Instead, Marielle simply smiled and thanked him. Then she headed back to her rental car, which she had parked a few doors down in front of the Dun Whinney.

She went alone through the glen after that, through the dried heather, trees bristling with the last of their dried gold and crimson leaves. Then she stood in the shade of the warm spring, watching the cascading falls. For a moment, she could almost see Barry there beside her. Feel his smile like sunshine on her face. Remember the little things he had said. The way he had charmed her.

It had been a short experience that now felt like an entire lifetime.

Marielle was not certain what she thought she would find, coming here. She knew only that she must come, sit here among the stones. The shade. The swirling, warm water.

Ye're a part of this place now, aren't ye?

Barry's words echoed back at her. He was right. But *he* was responsible for that. Colleen was too. It was the two of them who connected her to this land. Who made her want to be here. And now her fear was that Barry was gone from her life forever. A chapter, a part with no conclusion. She was filled just then with the sense of what might have been. The longing. For a lover, a friend. For a future that might have included a man who could be both.

She walked without thinking, her feet leading her toward the old cottage with the simple blue door and the thatched roof, where she knew there would be no lock to keep her out. That too was so like Barry. Simple, pure. Enduring trust.

Marielle knew she would not find him there, but still she wanted to be near what he loved. To look upon his things, if not into his eyes, for a while as a way of saying good-bye. She turned the handle and drew the door back. The same parade of memories came at her then. The time he had brought her here. The first time he had kissed her.

Marielle did not mean to intrude now, but safely inside this cottage, so full of him, she found herself touching things, holding things she knew Barry had held. It helped.

As she had once done when Ron was gone, Marielle found an old coat of Barry's and drew it over her shoulders. She ached for how much it felt like him, smelled like him, that lovely quiet strength, as she sank into the window seat and drew up her legs, burying herself in the heavy fabric. She sat in the chair before the fireplace hearth and rocked a while, the old rocker creaking, breaking the stillness. She looked out on the breathtaking glen that was his front garden. Trees. Open sky. His little piece of heaven.

How blind she had been to what was really important—to what she really needed in her life. *'Tis a part of you,* Barry had said. Yes, Marielle thought achingly. *Just as you are.*

Colleen embraced her heartily, as they stood together in the glen of their youth, cool air whipping around them. A stream of golden afternoon sunlight filtered through the bare tree branches that rustled with the breeze. This was where they had planned to meet when it was over, a place they had wanted to be in together for decades.

"Ye were right, Mairi. It needed to be done."

"Are you all right?"

"No. But I think I will be in time."

Marielle was looking into the eyes of her sister, warm, green eyes she had missed for so long. "How did Calum take seeing you?"

"'Twas, perhaps, the only solace I'll ever have from the whole affair, watchin' him look into the face of a ghost he'd buried long ago."

"But now you can move on."

"Aye. I believe I can."

Marielle smiled warmly. It was as if a dark cloud had lifted from Colleen. Her face was suddenly lighter somehow. A bit of the age, that weariness, seemed to slip away by coming back here. Then she looked around the glen and her expression became reflective. "I never came here, ye know, after ye left."

Marielle was surprised. "Then how could you have painted it so brilliantly?"

"From memories mostly, of how far you and I had gone, the memories that were most vivid."

"You've a God-given talent, Colleen. I hope you know that."

"I think perhaps I'm starting to." They began to walk back up to the road again when Colleen stopped and looked at her sister. "I loved our da, Mairi, and I tried to make him happy after you and Vivienne went away. But I was no' blind. I know 'twas he who was responsible for how ye used to feel about yourself."

Marielle's smile dimmed. "Malcolm Gordon certainly altered the course of my life." They looked at one another for a moment, their shared history a powerful link between them. "But I think I've made my peace with a lot of it now."

"Like Calum, our da was a troubled man. Not the man other people saw."

So many things here in Killin were so different than they had appeared on the surface. Even her own feelings. Marielle shook her head mutely. "No man has ever gone without disappointing me in some way. No man, I suppose, except Barry Buchanan."

They were silent then with the name between them. "Have ye seen him since we've been back?"

Marielle shook her head and gazed out the window. "How I so dearly wish I could say that I had," Marielle finally replied.

Colleen's sigh was one of recognition. "So your heart *does* lie with him. I thought as much."

"Unfortunately, *I* didn't realize it in time. I suppose today I was hoping he'd be foolish enough to wait until I figured things out."

"'Tis never a foolish thing believin' that real love will wait."

"I've just been so bloody blind about it all." Marielle shook her head. "Coming to Killin had helped me see again. But I'm afraid my great burst of true self-discovery just didn't happen soon enough."

"Because of Calum."

She looked deeply at her sister. It was still awkward to have shared the same man in that way. "I can't honestly blame things on him. There was a weakness there for me with Calum, that's true. He was the first man to ever make me *feel* that I was beautiful. For a little while, I was absolutely blinded by that. And it took time walking the streets of Glasgow alone, time to think, to realize that it had actually been Barry who had made me see *myself* that way."

Colleen shook her head. "We've lost too much at the hands of Calum McInnes."

"I was meant to know him," Marielle said. "I'm not sorry it happened. After all, he was the man who helped me realize who was *truly* important to my life."

They walked together back into town and onto the street full of people whose life had gone unchanged by what had happened to two sisters. Yet Killin still felt like a special place. To a part of her, it would always feel like home.

"I've let go of so much pain and hurt these past weeks. And now you have too."

Colleen smiled at the sound of her sister's voice. "Were ye always a stoic one like that, after ye left here?"

Marielle turned back. "Well, I certainly wasn't the pretty one. I suppose I had to do something."

"And yet look at the beauty ye've become. Inside as well as out. Just as I knew ye would. I knew it, Mairi. I knew ye'd wind up a winner." Then Colleen's smile dimmed again as she moved forward and took Marielle's chin between her thumb and forefinger. In that moment, things shifted back again. It was a motherly gesture, one Colleen had honed when they were girls. "Don't go givin' up on the love ye've found in Barry. Life is long and things can change. After all, look at the surprises it had in store for me."

They went together to the bake shop where they had gone so often as children. But Marielle went in alone at first and stood behind a line of customers. She was watching Jennie and the gangly boy she had seen at the ceilidh. Roddy McFee was serving the other customers, doing the fetching, and Jennie directing things, much in the way her parents had always done. But then she saw a little glance Jennie and Roddy exchanged. Then an optimistic smile. And she realized that something had happened to Jennie since she had come home from the hospital. When they had first met, Jennie had been angry at the world. But Marielle had a feeling that wasn't going to be a problem any more.

Things had a way of working themselves out, she thought. And Marielle was glad. Jennie deserved that happiness. And Catriona had deserved a holiday. Marielle had sent her a ticket to Majorca for two weeks on a tour with other people her age. It was the first time she had ever been out of Scotland and years since she'd had any sort of break from the bake shop.

Marielle waited for the line to shorten, a break in the customers so that they would have a chance to speak. When Jennie saw her, she wheeled her chair in front of the counter, her face brightened by a huge, welcoming smile. "I was no' certain ye'd ever be back in Killin."

"Oh, there are almost as many good memories here now as bad. I have a feeling I will *always* come back."

Jennie's smile was so warm. "I'm glad."

"Now. I brought someone to see you which is going to be a bit of a shock."

"Life is certainly full of those," she said, glancing back at Roddy.

"He's a handsome boy," Marielle confirmed.

"Can ye imagine? He says he's kept his heart for me since he was a wee bairn. And the fool could no' care less about the chair."

"Wise young man, considering the grand girl who's in it."

"So who've ye brought?"

Marielle took Jennie's hand and squeezed it. "I've brought Colleen."

The shop door opened and the little bell overhead tinkled in the silence. Colleen walked through the door in a cream-colored Aran sweater and blue jeans. Her thick hair was loose and long, and she was smiling, almost like the girl they both remembered.

"Jesus, Mary and Joseph," Jennie sputtered. "'tis no' possible!"

"Hallo, Jennie," Colleen tried cautiously.

"Ye're dead! I know! *I* was there!"

"I'm sorry, Jennie."

"But how in heaven—"

"I swam away from the car that night before it sank. I needed so desperately to get away from Killin. Away from Calum."

"'Tis all right," Jennie said breathlessly, wheeling quickly toward Colleen and holding out her arms eagerly to be embraced. "You're back . . . 'tis all that really matters now, isn't it?"

"Please believe that I had no idea the responsibilities I'd be leavin' behind. I truly did no' know until I saw Mairi again what awful thing had happened that night to you."

Jennie's voice was choking as they embraced. "Does he know . . . does my uncle know ye're still alive?"

"I've just come from MacLaren's Bend."

"Ye saw him, then?"

"I went to tell him that I was divorcin' him. That my life's in Glasgow now."

In truth, it was a life she was recovering in Glasgow. Colleen was meeting regularly now with a psychiatrist there. She was getting stronger, day by day, and she was painting. But a total healing, as Marielle knew from her own journey, would take time.

Colleen and Marielle had decided not to tell Jennie the details of that night with Calum—to what extent he had been involved. It would serve no purpose now, they decided, to bring more darkness into her young life, just when she had found a bit of light. Unless Calum decided to tell her himself. But that would be his own cross to bear, just part of the guilt with which he would now be forced to deal.

They took the train together back to Glasgow

then. And there they parted finally with another embrace and a solemn promise to keep in touch. Then, with tears in her eyes for the person she was leaving yet again for France, Marielle headed for a cab to the airport for the trip back to Paris.

It had been an extraordinary search and discovery. And Colleen had given her something to think about. But even in the face of her sister's optimism for the future, and the country magic that so surrounded Killin—a magic that had brought her sister back to life—Marielle knew she had missed her chance with Barry Buchanan. All of life's lessons had their price, she had learned, and this one had cost her dearly.

CHAPTER THIRTY

Aweek later, Marielle sat at her keyboard in the frenetic newsroom of the *Herald Tribune* and, for a
moment, lost herself in a second read-through of the
article she had just finished. It was the best she'd ever
done. She knew that. Marielle had come back to Paris
with a new sense of herself. There was a confidence
that showed in her writing. Daniel would be pleased.

She sank back in her chair and took a sip of cold
coffee. Just then, Micheline Duclos, another of the
city reporters, came by her desk and sank onto a corner. "I know it's a long shot since you keep pretty much
to yourself around here," Micheline said in French.
"but a few of us are taking Daniel out tonight for a
birthday dinner and, well, I know it would mean a lot
to him if you were able to come."

Marielle flipped off her computer screen and
swiveled her chair around. "Sounds like fun. When?"

Micheline straightened. "Really?"

"Just tell me when and where?"

"Great. *C'est incroyable, ça.* Tonight at seven at
Fouquet's." She jumped off the desk and took two
steps before she stopped and turned back around.
"Oh, and you can bring someone along if you like."

Marielle glanced up. "Someone?"

"You know, a date."

She still felt the same sharp stab she did every time she thought of that. Men. Relationships. Because, in her mind, things always made their way around to Barry. In an effort to get on with her life since she had been back in Paris, Marielle had actually let Vivienne arrange a dinner date with the son of a friend. Cedric had been pleasant enough, a stockbroker from Neuilly, who had courted her with roses. And she had actually enjoyed herself. But when it was over, Marielle kissed his cheek and told him there was no point in continuing.

"I'll just come alone if that's all right."

"It'll be great." Micheline was still wearing her shock on the sleeve of her two-piece purple knit dress. As she walked away, Micheline turned around a second time. The smile of surprise was bright on her pale, lightly made face. "You've changed since your holiday. Am I the only one to tell you that?"

"No, actually, you're not," Marielle returned the smile politely. "Must have been the Scottish air." Or love and finally growing up, she was thinking. But she didn't say that.

Marielle picked up a baguette and some cheese for breakfast at Monsieur Gaston's little shop on the rue de Amelie, then she went home to change for dinner. The apartment that greeted her was dark and cold. A note on the hall table was short and to the point.

Went to dinner with Thérèse.

Some things never changed, Marielle thought as

she went to the phone recorder, its tiny red light blinking brightly in the darkness. As she gazed at the light her heart began to accelerate. As it always did since she'd been back in Paris. Hope springs eternal. *What a silly phrase*, she thought. Marielle had no hope. Not of a happy ending like in fairy tales.

She pushed the message button. Colleen's voice filled the darkness. "Hi. Ye were on my mind today. I wanted to ask your opinion of somethin' and I thought to myself, isn't that bonnie that I can ring her and do just that? Ring me back when ye can. Love ye. Bye."

The warm sensation of her sister's voice wrapped around her, and Marielle smiled. It seemed so now like they had never been apart. The years. Pain. Loss. Healing now. The machine beeped. Another call. "I'm sorry, monsieur, but there is no answer. I've reached a recording machine. Do you wish to leave a message?"

A slight pause. "No. No message."

Click.

Thunderstruck, Marielle sank onto the parquet floor in the still darkened apartment. It couldn't have been his voice, could it? *Barry.* She'd given him no phone number. No address. She'd gone away to Glasgow with Calum without even thinking of that. Foolish, foolish!

When she could get her breath, Marielle stood, and pressed the button again. And again. Until those three simple words filled her with the sense of him. The tiny, dark apartment echoed her great sense of Barry. There was no mistaking the voice, the nuances there. In spite of the way she had gone away from Killin, he had tried to reach her, wanted to speak with her again. Her heart soared then crashed quickly.

I'm sorry, lass, I believe he plans to be away for some length of time.

She remembered Ian's words from only a week ago. There was no point in trying to return the call. Barry would not be there.

The party at Fouquet's was lovely, and Daniel's surprise at her being there had made getting out entirely worthwhile. As always, Daniel was kind and sweet and she was glad, after the way she had hurt him, that he still considered himself her friend.

Inside the sprawling terrace, closed off for the party, Marielle sipped champagne, danced, and laughed. And for a while she even forgot about Barry and the way her heart tore a little more every time she thought about the precious jewel of a man she had given up.

Like Colleen, Marielle was getting on with her life. Before she had left for the evening, Marielle had phoned Glasgow. "Gerry wants to marry me when my divorce is final, Mairi," Colleen had announced with a note of hesitation.

"And what do *you* want to do?"

"I'm no' sure I'm ready."

"Then there is your answer, I think."

"It's just that he's been so wonderful to me. I did no' see it when I first got here, so wrapped up in my own life, I was. But he's been patient. Two years he's waited. And I know that I canno' quite imagine my life without him now."

Marielle smiled as she held the receiver. "If he's that wonderful he'll wait a little while longer, Colleen."

"Do ye suppose?"

"Wasn't it you who told me not long ago that it's never a foolish thing to believe that real love will wait?"

She could hear her sister chuckle. "Ye listened to me, did ye now?"

"I heard every word. Wait with Gerry, Colleen. Wait until you *know* in your heart you cannot live another day without him."

After she had hung up the phone, Marielle thought a great deal about the wise advice she had given her sister. Strangely, it had brought her some comfort of her own. It hadn't been right with Barry when they were together in Killin. The timing had been wrong. She had not yet faced the demons of Malcolm Gordon, nor had she experienced the passion that now centered her own desires for the rest of her life.

"Dance with me?" Daniel said, bringing Marielle back to the moment at Fouquet's, full of laughter and happiness.

"Sure," Marielle smiled as she took his hand and let him lead her away from the table, blue with the smoke of Gitanes.

"I wanted to tell you privately," he said, speaking into her ear as they danced to the slow, melodic voice of Charles Aznevour.

"Tell me what?"

"I'm getting married."

Marielle's eyes were vivid with surprise. "To whom?"

"Well, it seems that Micheline thinks I'm quite a catch."

"Micheline Duclos, from the office?"

"She loves me, Marielle, and I believe we can be happy."

Marielle felt a spark of envy that Daniel, safe Daniel, had gotten on with his own life. And she had had no idea. "Daniel," she said earnestly, looking into his rich, kind eyes, "I could not be happier for you."

"Will you come?"

"To the wedding?"

"She knows about you and I . . . the way I've always felt about you," he amended, "and I think it would help her a great deal to see that we can all be amicable."

Marielle wrapped her arms around his broad back and kissed his cheek tenderly. "I would be honored to be there."

"Thanks." They danced together for another moment before he spoke again.

"And you, Marielle, how are you now that you've found your sister again?"

"It's a new world for me, Daniel. Sometimes I can hardly believe how many things have changed these past weeks."

"Well, I hope that now you are finally ready to find love in your life the way I have."

"Who knows?" Marielle smiled. "Stranger things have happened."

CHAPTER THIRTY-ONE

Marielle was as nervous as a cat.

There was so much riding on this show. She had worked for months to organize Colleen's watercolors at the Galerie des Artistes on the fashionable rue de Rivoli. The arms she had twisted. The chits she had needed to call in. And now, tonight, it would finally become a reality.

Marielle stood in the center of the gallery, wearing a black strapless sheath and a simple strand of pearls. Her hair was smoothed back from her face with a bit of mousse. Her diamond earrings stood out that way. Marielle was holding a glass of champagne. But it was still full. For the first time since the crates had arrived in France, she was really studying her sister's works.

Each of the fifteen watercolors was professionally displayed here. And dotting the white walls, between the paintings, were large black-and-white photographs of Colleen. Her smile, her eyes, shining down on the intimate gallery, for all of Paris to come to know. So beautiful. Full of life. The girl that a sister had never forgotten. And after this evening, there would be few in France who would not know the artist, Colleen Gordon.

She hated to admit it, even now, but Vivienne, with her old-money ties in the city, had helped a great deal. Vivienne was trying so hard to make amends for how she had kept the two sisters apart, and Marielle had decided to let her. Her mother had pulled out all the stops, inviting some of the most well-to-do Parisians to this all-important showing.

Marielle had been able to excite the news media, with her many stories on Colleen Gordon's picturesque rural life and work. But she had also needed the funding. For the first time since she had left Paris for Killin, she was not feeling the same anger with Vivienne for the lives she had so thoughtlessly altered. Even that wound had begun, very slowly, to heal.

"Of course I'm shameless," Vivienne had smiled when she had produced the Galerie des Artistes, one of Paris's most prestigious galleries, as the location. "I know how I have injured both of you. But part of making up for the past years of my stupidity is to do this for both of you."

So much of the circle of Marielle's life had begun at last to close.

She understood herself now. What had motivated her with men. The miscalculation she had made with Calum. And there had been an enormous healing in that. Even if it was too late for her and Barry, whom she could never quite seem to forget.

He had not called again nor left a message from any point on his trip. There was not even a forwarding phone number with anyone where he might be reached. But why would he have? He had taken her at her word. And at the expression in her eyes that cool, misty-gray afternoon. A man of honor, he would move on with his life and interfere with hers no further. She knew that's what his going away like that had been meant to convey.

"Are you ready then, *ma chérie?*" Vivienne asked her daughter in French.

"I've waited a long time for this," Marielle replied, as she glanced across the room, finding Colleen who was laughing and talking with Daniel. Kind Daniel. Dependable Daniel. Her editor and friend. A man not so unlike Barry. "It means everything to me to help give Colleen the fame she deserves."

"You have worked very hard these past months. You have a right to be proud."

The invited guests began filing into the gallery as Vivienne stood holding her daughter's hand, trying to calm her. She wanted so very much for this night to be a success. Marielle smiled as they walked slowly among the works, sipping champagne and talking in low, appreciative tones.

And suddenly, as if from a dream, there he was.

Across the room, standing in an elegant white dinner jacket, black bow tie and black trousers, speaking with Phillipe LaMartine from *Le Monde*. Tall and lanky, he was leaning against a marble column, one hand nonchalantly in his pants pocket. The other holding a glass of champagne. And he was smiling that smile she knew so well. The one that had comforted, made her laugh, and won her. Yes, so entirely.

Barry.

But how was it possible that she was not dreaming? This was Paris. A world away from Killin. From *him.* From what they had almost become. Before she had ruined it all so miserably. Marielle felt as if the room were spinning suddenly, like a great, brightly colored top, and she could not gain her footing.

How could she possibly face him this evening, of all evenings? Her stomach churned as she saw him turn, then and begin to sift through the throngs of elegantly clad guests moving toward her.

In spite of how crowded it had become, and the chatter and laughter that had risen to a crescendo, now there was no one in the gallery but the two of them.

"Hallo, Marielle."

The voice was familiar, deep and comforting. The way it called to her from her other life. Where she was not Marielle but Mairi Gordon. Where someone there had finally, and truly, loved her.

She leaned across to him. He was smiling, radiant in his confidence. Then she let him kiss her cheek. Marielle was shaken by how tenderly he did so. The months apart slipped away.

"What on earth are you doing here?" she managed to ask.

"I was invited here this evenin' by the owner of the gallery, who's an old friend of mine. He was one of the first to show my own work and for some reason he fancies me an asset at these things."

"I had no idea when we—" Her mouth was dry. She began again. "When I first met you that your work was so widely known."

"I still canno' get used to the idea, but apparently there is quite a market for it."

Marielle felt a pang. She should have known about it. She should have been able to share that kind of success with him. Marielle felt selfish again, suddenly, and small. To have been so taken up with her own world. She tried hard to smile, remain confident. But it was a false and strained expression. Seeing him, all she wanted to do was cry. Then she saw one of the photographs of her sister on the wall, and she remembered.

"You know about Colleen, then?" she tentatively asked. "That she's alive."

"It was quite a shock bein' told by the owner here that Colleen Gordon from Killin was the artist he was showcasin', I'll admit. At first I thought it must be some sort of retrospective ye'd arranged."

"You've seen her, then?"

"Aye. We spoke by phone for a long time last night. But I saw her again only just now. 'Twas quite a sight to behold. Colleen has no' looked so at peace in a very long time." He leveled his eyes, those rich, hazel eyes on her then. "I hear she owes a great deal of that to *you*."

"A lot has changed since we said good-bye that last afternoon in Killin, Barry."

"'Twould seem so."

"I'm sorry I wasn't the one to tell you about Colleen."

"When I returned home, I heard ye went to my shop. I'm sorry *I* was no' there."

Marielle felt nervous and very tentative. She could see no one else but Barry. "When *I* came home one night, I heard your voice on my phone recorder. I'm sorry *I* was not there either."

Vivienne put an arm around her daughter's shoulder then, tearing them from a moment Marielle had dreamed of for months. "It has been a long time, Monsieur Buchanan."

Marielle glanced at each of them, her mother and the man she loved, surprised that Vivienne remembered a boy, now a man, from so long ago. "Aye," Barry said. "And ye're lookin' magnificent as ever."

"My, but you've grown gallant since I left Killin."

"No' gallant enough to have won your daughter, I'm afraid," he replied, smiling in a courtly way, but not looking at Marielle for any sort of reply. Still, there was something in the way he said it, a hint of something. Her heart began to beat very fast. Was it possible that he still cared for her? That they still might have a chance? Her heart soared. A woman came up behind Barry then, placing her hand gently on his shoulder. There was a nuance in the movement, something intimate. Marielle looked at her. She was small and beautiful, with blond hair wound into an elegant chignon and pinned with a diamond clip. "If I might see you for a moment," she said to him with a smile. She was English. Probably from London. And it was very clear to Marielle that they had known one another for some time.

Have I been replaced so quickly in your heart? she wondered with an excruciating little burst of jealousy she had no right to feel.

"Excuse me, will you?" Barry nodded, first to Vivienne, then to her. His tone had changed quickly. It was polite. Certainly polished. But his look conveyed the sense that they were strangers. That there had never been those walks through the glen. Private stories of a delicate and painful past. Or kisses deep with promise. That there had never been anything between them before this very formal moment here in a Paris gallery.

Marielle nodded in reply, then watched Barry
melt very steadily back into the collection of other
Parisian guests. The tears she had been pressing back
since seeing him rose hot and choking, and Marielle
felt as if she could not breathe.

"I've got to get some air," her voice cracked.

"I'll go with you, *chérie*," Vivienne offered.

"No. I need to be alone." As she turned to leave,
Vivienne held her, forcing her to pivot back. Vivienne's
long fingers were pinching her wrist. There were tears
now running down both of Marielle's cheeks.

"Monsieur Buchanan is more than a friend to you,
isn't he?"

"No," she said achingly. "Thanks to me, that's all
there ever was between us."

Marielle drew in a breath of air and wiped the tears
from her eyes with the cocktail napkin. She stood out
on a balcony that faced the Seine. There was a small
wrought-iron table, two chairs, an English ivy potted
in stone, and a half-full ashtray.

She watched the cars rushing by out on the busy
boulevard before her.

"Marielle . . ."

It was Barry.

She jerked around as an unexpected battery of
goose bumps barraged her. "How did you find me out
here?"

His smile was the same calm, slow upturn of his
lips that could so quickly warm her back in Killin. Now
he seemed familiar, more genuine than the man
before her a minute ago. "Ye never left my sight from

the moment ye arrived. By now I'd have expected ye to figure on that."

"I had no idea that you were going on any kind of publicity tour. That seems like such a big thing to leave out."

"Early on, the way things were beginning to go for us, I actually fancied that ye might consent to join me."

"But then, like a fool, I went to Glasgow with Calum—" The self-deprecating words died away. "When I got back to Killin I did go to your shop. But it was not just to tell you about Colleen."

He tipped his head. His eyes were deep and rooted on her. She felt their intense power and it hurt to be looked at that way. "What else would ye have told me, Marielle?"

It was difficult now to confess it. The words felt like a stone in her throat. *Barry has gone on,* she was thinking. There was someone else now. She glanced back into the studio and caught sight of the lovely blond in the black halter dress, laughing and speaking with Vivienne. So beautiful, tanned and full of self-assurance. Everything she still had difficulty believing she too had become.

"I don't suppose it matters now," Marielle said.

"If it concerns you, it matters very much to *me,*" Barry countered deeply, his rich eyes still holding her. Still so calm, she thought, and full of that lovely confidence.

She felt a shining little spark of hope flicker between them. In spite of the woman. When the words began to tumble out, she turned away, unable to bear the sincerity so rich on his face.

"I'm sorry I went away with Calum. I would like to

say that I did it for Jennie. That she was the only reason. But you know that wouldn't be the truth. And you mean too much to me for there to be a lie that grand between us."

"And what *did* you find when you went to Glasgow with him?"

She turned back around and made herself face him. "I found the truth. The ugliness in it. About Colleen. About him. About myself. And about what I feel for you."

"What *do* ye *feel* for me, Marielle?"

"Oh, Barry. I am just so very sorry about all of that." She wrapped her arms around herself again, chilled from the sudden breeze that had come up off of the Seine. "I've been such an unbelievable fool. Because of so many things about my father, I mistook physical strength for—"

He lifted a hand. "Ye need no' be explainin' that part of it to me."

"Oh, but I do need to."

"Might I ask why?"

"Because I am in love with you, damn it! No matter what you say next, no matter where life has taken you since we parted, the simple truth is that I love you, Barry Buchanan, and I always will. For the part of myself you showed me. For the generous gift of your heart that you offered me."

He was quiet for what seemed an eternity, standing there, gazing down at her, his eyes shimmering beneath that tousle of maple-colored hair.

Marielle felt her mouth trembling along with the rest of her.

Barry touched her face then, softly, until her jaw

came to rest in the palm of his hand. For the first time with him, Marielle felt the passion rise very quickly inside of her as their eyes met again. "The woman you're with tonight is very beautiful," she could not help herself from saying.

"Aye. Sheila is that. She's from my publicist's office in London. She used to be a fashion model. They send her out every time I have one of these things. 'Tis so I look a bit more worldly, I expect. Beautiful women keep up the mystique of an artist, ye know."

His smile was like sunshine just then, full of promise and forgiveness. Marielle flung her arms around his neck and clung to him. And in that same impulsive moment, he kissed her. Deeply. More fully than ever, his mouth open and seeking. Marielle was enveloped by the solid, woody aroma of him. *Still so silently strong*, she thought, *still so full of quiet power.* And Marielle wanted more than anything to be kissed this way. Held this way. By this man alone. For the first time in her life, she felt completely whole, free of the torment from the past. As if suddenly now she was at the end of a very long journey that had brought her through the fires of indecision, conflict, and mystery.

Then finally, back to Barry. *He* was her home.